THE
OTHER
HALF
OF YOU

ALSO BY MICHAEL MOHAMMED AHMAD

The Tribe
The Lebs

MICHAEL
MOHAMMED
AHMAD

THE OTHER HALF OF YOU

AUSTRALIA

hachette
AUSTRALIA

Published in Australia and New Zealand in 2021
by Hachette Australia
(an imprint of Hachette Australia Pty Limited)
Level 17, 207 Kent Street, Sydney NSW 2000
www.hachette.com.au

 A catalogue record for this
book is available from the
National Library of Australia

ISBN: 978 0 7336 3903 6 (paperback)

Cover design by Christabella Designs
Cover images courtesy of Shutterstock
Author photograph courtesy of Anna Kučera
Typeset in Adobe Garamond Pro by Kirby Jones
Printed and bound in Great Britain by Clays Ltd, Elcograf S.p.A.

Your children are not your children.
They are the sons and daughters of Life's longing for itself.
They come through you but not from you,
And though they are with you yet they belong not to you.

Gibran Kahlil Gibran

ALL THAT WAS

ONE

RUST IS MY BLOOD. Stardust is my soul. And you are the blood of my soul. Kah-lil: the back of the tongue taking a trip to the front of the palate to ululate, at one, on the teeth. You come tearing through your mother and into this universe like zamzam water, which sprung from the desert of your ancestors. Kah. Lil. You are thrown into your mother's frail and freckled and fair arms. Aajin against aajin – dough against dough. Kahlil. I have seen you emerge from her with my face on your face, and in this way, we three are connected for eternity. But do you know, my aajin, my zamzam, my blood soul, my rust and stardust, that you may have never been sent forth as a living arrow, at least not through the bow of your mother and me, looking like the little White Wog that you are, were it not for the Brown girl who wore a cross. You brought me here. Now let me take you back.

——

Back when the internet was foreign to our third-world parents, I met her on a dial-up chat site. This was the only way that Lebs like me, who grew up in the western suburbs of Sydney and went to Punchbowl Boys High School, knew how to find girls. My online name was Leb-Prince. Hers was Desert-Girl. She sent me a message that said, *Can I be your princess?* I gave her my mobile number and for three months she called me every morning as soon as she woke up. She told me her real name was Sahara and that she had spent her childhood at a women's refuge in Glebe and that she used to suck on old chicken bones. She had a bubbly voice that bounced like argileh every time she giggled. I told her I had a big broken nose. She said she didn't care about looks, so I asked her to meet me in person. 'I'm not pretty either,' she warned. That was the first time I wanted to hold her. I did not expect a woman to be thin and fair and blonde and blue-eyed and button-nosed.

She agreed to have a coffee with me in Newtown on 1 February, my nineteenth birthday, even though neither of us drank coffee. 'I can meet you at that cafe near the cinema, Sin-Key,' I told her. Sahara chuckled and said it was pronounced, 'Chin-Kway'. She was wiser than any Leb girl I had ever met in Bankstown, those girls who said 'Macdanas' instead of 'McDonald's'.

Sahara was sitting at a table in the cafe, dressed in a wife-beater and reading *A Woman of No Importance* when I arrived. I knew I loved her the moment she raised her tomato-shaped head and looked at me. Her eyes were big and brown and bright and sad. I could see her entire childhood at the centre of her pupils – her father beating her mother in front of her, and the chicken bones she hid under her bed. Maybe love comes in pieces; and I loved the pieces I'd gathered from her over the phone, and now

4

I loved the sight of her. Or maybe love is just one piece; and I was already in love with all of her, and she was going to be beautiful to me no matter what.

Sahara smiled like a child and said in the bubbling voice I had come to know so well, 'Heya Bani.' She was broad-shouldered and solid for a Leb chick, who were often busty but thin everywhere else, and she was dark-skinned for a Lebanese Christian, the tanned complexion of a sand-girl, a copper coating that glowed golden in the daylight. Her hair was dark brown and bushy and her eyebrows were thick, her nose pudgy and cheeks puffy. Sahara's gaze on me was like the sun, too powerful for my eyes to bear. As though it were against my will, I found my glare dropping down past our table and at her feet. Her legs, much like her shoulders and arms, were thick, and she'd shaved them only to the point where you could still see the black dots of her stubble. She wore black flip-flops and her second toes were longer than her big toes. They reminded me of Uma Thurman's toes in *Kill Bill*, when The Bride stares at them inside the yellow car and tries to make them twitch. Fine black hairs covered Sahara's big toes and ran all the way up her legs towards her denim shorts. Again, I thought about the chicks I'd grown up with in Bankstown. Those girls straightened and dyed their hair blonde and wore skimpy singlets and skinny jeans; they were always drenched in make-up like clowns and waxed every part of their bodies – legs, arms, armpits, eyebrows and whiskers. Sahara was something else: too much Glebe in her to be a Leb, too much Lebanon in her to be a hippie.

Staring back into her eyes, my heart roared inside my chest as though it were trying to break free from my rib cage. You see, Kahlil, I already knew that I was not allowed to be with a girl who was not an Arab Muslim Alawite. It did not matter that Sahara was Lebanese, that our parents and grandparents had come from the same village and had the same complexions. She was Christian. And it wouldn't have mattered if she converted to Muslim, because she could never convert to Alawite, a branch of Shi'ism that could only be passed on through our bloodline. I heard my father's voice inside my head. Ten Ramadans ago, while breaking our fast on halal cheeseburgers at Lakemba McDonald's, he said to me, 'You can drink, you can gamble, you don't need to pray, I will throw you the biggest wedding, I will buy you the biggest house, on one condition: you don't ever marry an outsider.' That's what we called a person who wasn't Arab Muslim Alawite – *outsider*. My father had told me stories of Alawites foolish enough to take one, that they had been disowned and banished and then struck down by a thunderbolt from Allah for having contaminated our divine origin. In contrast, he reassured me how much easier it would be with a girl from our tribe: 'You will be free, rich, protected, safe, included, *loved*.'

For the next twenty-four months Sahara and I dated in secret, spending most of our time at her housing commission unit. On her bed, which was just a mattress on the floor, she shared her story with me. Her mother, Lola, was a triplet who had twenty-one siblings. She came to Australia alone and against her father's blessing to be with the man she loved, a taxi driver from Jabal Mohsen named Antoun, who whipped her with his belt for nine years. Sahara's earliest memory was fleeing to the refuge with her mother late one night while her father was out doing his taxi route. By the time she and Lola had been offered a home by the housing commission, her parents were divorced and she never saw her father again. Nor did she ever meet any of her father's relatives, who called her mother a whore for leaving him, or her mother's relatives, who blamed Lola and disowned her for choosing the wrong man against their wishes. Over the years, Sahara's mother met a handful of other migrant women in those housing commission units in a similar situation to her own, and they all got jobs at the only kebab shop on Glebe Point Road, where they worked and gossiped during the daytime. Meanwhile, Sahara attended Glebe High School, failing all her subjects until she dropped out in Year 9 and got an evening job at Ultimo McDonald's. This set-up meant that I almost never saw my girlfriend's mother – while she was out during the day, Sahara would be at home, and just as her mother was returning, Sahara would leave for work and I left with her. All except for this one time when I had fallen asleep on the couch and Sahara left for work without waking me up. Her mother covered me in a blanket and watched television on mute until I stirred. I shook the sleep from my face as the petite olive-skinned woman took in a deep sigh, her hand to her chest, and said in Arabic, 'This home belongs to children whose fathers do not want them. If your father doesn't want you, you can stay here with us.'

'Ba'ed al-shar,' I mumbled, half-asleep. 'May such a fate be prolonged.' Her daughter had not finished school, but she was a girl who understood the importance of being earnest – so I spent the next morning on Sahara's mattress explaining why the comma needed to be put in, and the next afternoon in her kitchen explaining why the comma needed to be taken out. Sahara made spaghetti bolognaise for me, which she couldn't eat herself because she was a vegetarian; and I used the sheet of Lebanese bread in her freezer and whatever vegetables she had in the fridge to bake her a homemade pizza, which I cooked for too long and burned to charcoal. Sahara cracked up at me and said, 'Next time leave the comma in and take the pizza out.'

Being the first in my family to go to university, I could exaggerate to my parents about how much time a student was required to spend on campus, and when I wasn't at lectures and tutorials, which absorbed only two days of my week, I was hiding out in Glebe with Sahara. She rubbed my back with her bare masculine hands while I wrote uni essays about Madam Bovary and Anna Karenina and Romeo and Juliet and Layla and Majnun. We too were doomed like these tragic figures of literature; one day my people would tear us from one another. Already the rumours were spreading like scabies. Aunt Yasmine spotted me at Broadway Shopping Centre holding hands with a girl who wore a cross around her neck. Aunt Yasmine told Aunt Amina and Aunt Amina told Aunt Mariam and Aunt Mariam told Uncle Ibrahim and Uncle Ibrahim told Uncle Osama and Uncle Osama told my godfather and my godfather told his daughter to pass a message onto me via my sister Yocheved, who attended the same hair salon as her. Yocheved came home with blonde streaks through her black hair and a sunken frown through her teeth, delivering my godfather's memo on trembling lips: *We will never allow you to disgrace us with that whore.* Hearing those words was like having a fork jammed into my neck. Yocheved, who was only a year younger than me and had the same big crooked nose, took my hand gently in hers. At only five foot four, which was average for a Leb girl, she looked up at me and said, 'I'd rather be a whore than a slave.' I knew then that I could turn to my siblings for support: my gym-junkie older brother, Bilal, who said to me, 'Sahara's a top chick, bro,' and my sixteen-year-old emo sister, Lulu, who said, 'I heard she doesn't shave her legs – that's so cool,' and my twelve-year-old introverted sister, Abira, who said, 'Sahara sounds like the name of a restaurant,' and my chubby three-year-old sister, Amani, who said, 'Do you have some salt and vinegar chips?'

On my twenty-first birthday, Sahara bought me a toothbrush. It was light purple with hard bristles. I waited until I arrived at her place every morning to brush my teeth and I would brush them again every evening before I went back home, back to my parents and my five siblings in Lakemba, who thought I had spent my day on campus. I loved that toothbrush. I loved knowing that inside Sahara's bathroom was a toothbrush that belonged to me sitting beside the one that belonged to her. I loved that toothbrush and the bathroom where that toothbrush slept, the bathroom that was tight and tiled blue and lined with candles on the windowsill. We spent a lot of time together in that bathroom. I kept a lighter in the back pocket of my bumbag so I could always light the wicks for Sahara. She would undress me down to my boxer shorts, and I would undress her down to her underpants and bra – you see, we had promised to keep our bodies from one another until we were married. I would stand half-naked in her shower, warm water running through my thick black curly hair and down my slender arms and flat chest, and Sahara would wash me with her hands, soapy brown hands like the clay of Mecca. Then she would step under the water and I would stand behind her and wash her hair, her dark-brown hair – dark brown until the setting sun peered through the bathroom window and illuminated the flames of the candles before the light hit us, and then her hair was like honey. I remember the smell of her conditioner. Butter and sugar and milk. Her smell.

Sahara's cheeks were high and round and shiny when she smiled. I pressed mine against them until they warped and flattened into one another. And when our cheeks were apart, I called her every two hours. I needed to know she was safe.

'Hey Sahara.'

'Hey Bani.'

'Bye Sahara.'

'Bye Bani.'

If she didn't answer I'd panic. My heart would thud. My hands would sweat. My thoughts would spiral into madness – something's happened to her, she's been hit by a car, she's been mugged, she's been raped, she's hurt, she's dead, she's gone. I would crawl into bed and keep calling her while my parents and siblings clattered in the living room. I knew how many times Sahara's phone would ring before it went to voicemail. Twelve. Each time I counted and listened to her notification: 'Calm down, Bani. Everyone else, leave a message.' I would hang up and call again. When she finally answered, my agony vanished and my sanity returned, my heart rate eased and my thoughts became clear. She was safe. She had twenty-six missed calls because she was at the movies and there was no reception in the cinema, but she was safe. I sat up on my bed and held my phone tightly to my ear.

'Hey Sahara.'

'Hey Bani.'

'Bye Sahara.'

'Bye Bani.'

Then we would hang up at the same time and everything would be still and quiet in my room; every time we hung up except this one time. As I stared at my reflection in the wardrobe mirror, wondering how Sahara could ever love a boy whose nose looked like a boomerang, my bedroom door exploded open. My father stood in the doorway, his face like a shard of brick, the veins in his neck palpitating, his shredded arms seething. 'People are talking!' he screamed.

I sprung to my feet; they spasmed as soon as I hit the floor. From the moment I had set my eyes on Sahara I knew this day was coming and no amount of toothbrushes could have prepared me for it. My father had taught me long ago that he was the source of all my strength and all my weakness – I was only six and playing with my marbles outside our first house in Alexandria, which we shared with my grandmother; my uncle Osama; his wife and their three daughters; my uncle Ibrahim, a divorced drug addict who lived in the backyard garage; his two daughters, who were with us three nights a week; and my youngest uncle, Ali. From the alleyway that joined our street, a large drunken man with an M-shaped moustache approached me, grunting, 'Get ye dad's fucking ute out me driveway!' But my dad didn't own a ute and there were no driveways on our street. Just as the man leaned in to touch my face, Dad swept out of the house and threw an over-the-top jab, knocking him onto the kerb. Picking me up with one hand, as if I were a piece of bread, my father carried me inside and said, 'If that man touched you, I'd have killed him.' From then on I feared my dad, not like I feared barking dogs and child molesters, but like I feared the sun, which gave me life, and could just as easily incinerate me.

Back in my bedroom, my mother and five siblings piled up in the corridor behind Dad, their faces white, as though they were the Brady Bunch. Maybe they were sad that I would be forced to give up the woman I loved, or maybe they were terrified to see what Dad would do if I refused to give her up – banish me, disown me, stand aside and watch as God struck me down. Mum held Dad by the arm, trying to ease him out of the room, as he pummelled his open palm into the doorframe. She would not have wanted me to marry an outsider either, but if my father accepted Sahara, she would follow his will. When my dad asked for her hand twenty-two years ago she looked at his biceps, which were like potatoes, and responded, 'Mashallah, if you slap me, you'll send me flying, I will be your wife.' This was how my mother measured the strength of a man: against her own. They were married three weeks later. Bilal was born nine months after that. I was born twelve months after him. And Yocheved was born twelve months after me.

'What? What's going on?' I said to my father, teeth clattering. I had to play dumb to find out how much he knew – maybe he had just found the lighter in my bumbag and thought I was smoking cigarettes. 'I do not accept this girl,' he said firmly, his voice as precise and certain as the Wahhabis of Lakemba Mosque.

I fell to my bedroom tiles, which were large and white like all the tiles in all the houses that belonged to all the Lebs of the west. My knees clapped against the porcelain as I wailed, 'Please let me go, let me go to her, let me go.'

'You will bring shame to the House of Adam,' my father said. This was the only truth our people feared, not Allah or the Prophet Muhammad, nothing except the Arab tongue. Dad's frown withered and a look of despair fell upon his sandstone face, his eyes a swirl of black and his nose protruding like a spear. 'I only ever asked you for one thing,' he said, a quiver in his voice.

12

'Just this one thing.' It was as though I had smashed the Ten Commandments.

'Oh father,' I cried, grovelling at his ankles while my mother and siblings looked on. 'The one thing you asked of me – is everything.'

TWO

KAHLIL, MY HEART MEANDERING outside my body, know this, *you* are everything. And know that I called Sahara the next morning and told her I would run away to live with her and her mother. She whimpered, 'My family is broken, Bani Adam, please don't ask me to break yours.' I knew then, as certain as I knew I was going to die, that this girl, who grew up with nothing, was worth more than anything I could ever offer her. As she said goodbye I thought of her eyelashes – when I took a siesta on her living room floor and drifted to sleep. Feeling a faint brush against my cheek, I woke to find her crouching beside me, blinking her eyes on me, kissing me with her lashes. By the time she hung up the phone, I was standing on the rooftop of a carpark in Bankstown, watching the sun paint the sky pink as it rose. My heart was imploding and my throat was clenching and there was no air. I could not go an hour without hearing her voice. *Oh Allah, Most Gracious, Most Merciful, have mercy upon me – how could I go into a day and into a week and into a month and into a year and into eternity without Sahara?*

Two hours later I called her. The phone rang twelve times and went to voicemail. 'Calm down, Bani. Everyone else, leave a message.' Two days later I called again. It rang twelve times and told me to calm down. Two weeks later, there were eighteen rings and then it beeped three times and automatically disconnected. Two months later it did not ring at all.

I tried to disappear into the streets of Lakemba, where I walked for hours amid the hijabs and the beards, searching for a tomato-faced girl who wore a cross. All I found was the gay Wog whom I met at the community arts centre in Bankstown five years earlier. Back then I had been trying to distinguish myself from the other Lebs at Punchbowl Boys High School by reading Dostoevsky and Faulkner and Hemingway. Then one day, while Bucky and I stood on the platform of Bankstown train station, he took me in his arms and told me I was beautiful exactly as I was, as a Leb. He was the first person to ever really love me that way, and it was gay, so fucken gay. But this time Bucky couldn't help me – he was broken too. His boyfriend of three and a half years, an Anglo colonoscopist from Kings Cross, had left him for a Swedish cosmetic surgeon from North Sydney.

Like me, Bucky had been wandering around Lakemba like a stonehead, his dark eyes sunken and his fat lips flopped and his stubble-ridden cheeks sagging. That point on, I began picking him up from his parents' home in Belmore once a week and taking him for a walk while his medication for manic depression kicked in. I had to lock his arm in mine to ensure he didn't wander off in front of a car. During our strolls, I would talk, and he would listen, or at least this was how I interpreted his unresponsiveness. I asked, 'Is Sahara putting in the comma right now?' and he gave no answer. I asked, 'Is Sahara taking out the comma right now?' and he gave no answer.

Unable to feel her in my hood, I tried to feel Sahara among the cohort of working-class ethnic kids who were completing their arts degrees at the Bankstown campus of Western Sydney University. Like me, they were the first in their families to continue their education after high school – a blessing and a curse. On the one hand, my father and mother took great pride in my academic achievements, drifting around the Alawite mosque on Eid informing all their brothers and sisters and cousins and second cousins and our sheikhs and elders that I was destined to lead The Tribe; and on the other hand, they were confused and disappointed and ashamed that all I did with my arts degree was use it to contest their most fundamental beliefs:

Mum said, 'Pooftas is yuck.'

I said, 'Homophobia.'

Dad said, 'No education for the woman.'

I said, 'Patriarchy.'

Mum said, 'I wish my children had fair skin and blue eyes.'

I said, 'White supremacy.'

Dad said, 'Alawites only.'

I said, '*Sahara*.'

Sahara in the House of Adam. Sahara in the lecture theatre. Professor Roland, who was from Ireland and looked like a blimp, sounded like Liam Neeson and had sweat patches under the armpits of his shirt, spoke about *Romeo and Juliet* while I wrote over and over on my notepad, *Sahara, Sahara, wherefore art thou Sahara?* Sahara in her bed. Sahara upon my rib. Sahara in my head. Sahara in my words. The desert-girl was wondering, 'What did you wanna be when you were a boy, Bani?' And I said, 'A verse-maker.' And she asked, 'Will you write a story for me?' And I answered, 'You are the story.' And she said, 'But I'm nothing special.' And I replied, 'A pen is nothing special.' And she said, 'Write that.' And I said, 'I already have.'

I roamed the university campus as a lost case, staring at the young Brown women and young Brown men around me, who all looked so bright with their unit readers held against their chests, and so beautiful with their dark hair cut and gelled and moussed and waxed and clipped and groomed. Yet I kept telling myself, *No one will ever do.* I stopped like a wilted flower in a long line at the student centre, waiting to submit my Graduate in Absentia forms. I was one month away from becoming the first university graduate in my family's history, and I could imagine a version of reality where my parents and siblings and aunts and uncles and cousins were applauding and ululating and taking photographs inside the auditorium as I walked up to the stage to receive my degree. But every time I played out this fantasy, my heart twisted and my eyes twitched and my fingers shook and my stomach ached. *Why should I give them the satisfaction?* I thought. *They show off about my education and at the same time they prevent me from using that education to actually improve my life!*

I had been in line at the student centre for almost ten minutes before I noticed the head of long black curls in front of me. 'I know these locks.' The words just fell out of my mouth as she turned; sharp nose striking me like a defibrillator. Laila Haimi – Mrs Laila Haimi – returned to me. I had not seen her since Year 10, when she was my teacher in high school and introduced me to her favourite writers: James Joyce, who swooned among all the living and the dead; Gabriel García Márquez, who flew beside a very old man with enormous wings; and Vladimir Nabokov, who was stuck between aurochs and angels, the secret of durable pigments, prophetic sonnets, the refuge of art. Day by day I sighed with passion; fantasising about Mrs Laila Haimi driving me down an endless desert road, away from Lebs and laws; every day until the day she left me to take on a head teacher position at another high school.

'Subhaan-allah,' she said to me in her squeaky voice; six years had not changed it even a bit, nor had it changed her skin, which was smooth and tight and fair. 'Bani, you made it!'

As the line slowly moved forward, Mrs Laila Haimi told me about her life, details she could never tell me when I was her student – she had been beaten by her father and forced into an arranged marriage with her cousin when she was fresh out of high school. By the age of twenty, she'd had enough, disowning her parents and divorcing her cousin and enrolling at university, where she would begin her journey to becoming my English teacher and meeting her second husband, an engineer originally from Nigeria named Muhammad. After that she became a head teacher at a high school in The Hills Shire, and now she was a doctoral candidate in literary studies at the university. I stared silently at her as she spoke, my whole life undone. You see, I'd always wondered what happened when a past love came back into your world. Did your heart swell for them once again? No. Not when you had eyes. And not when they were on Sahara. There was so much I wanted to tell Mrs Laila Haimi about: my high school graduation, which involved me skolling an entire bottle of vodka and throwing up all over my bedroom tiles; my debut amateur boxing match, which ended with me breaking a Skip's nose; my creative development with the White performance artists from the inner west, who called the Prophet Muhammad a camel f—; the F my professor gave me in Psychology 101 for submitting an essay titled 'Freud Fucked My Mum', and the High Distinction my professor gave me in Philosophy 101 for submitting an essay titled 'Freud Fucked My Mum'; and the day Sahara finished reading *A Woman of No Importance* and said to me, 'So Oscar was just into dick, right?'

But time was running out as Mrs Laila Haimi and I neared the reception desk, where a wrinkly old White lady spoke condescendingly to all the students before us. I summarised my journey in three words for her: 'You weren't here.'

Laila Haimi began fidgeting with a gold evil eye pendant around her neck. She smiled and said, 'Sure wasn't, you got this far without me.'

The wrinkled lady at the counter shouted, 'Come on, come on, next!' and Laila's enormous head of curls faced me once more as she squeaked a few words at her and collected some papers. Stepping past me – out of the student centre and out of my life – Mrs Laila Haimi schooled me all over again: 'See you in another few years, Bani Adam, imagine where you'll be by then …' I tried not to turn back and look for her, but I couldn't resist, and I found myself doing a full one-eighty of the campus, searching for where she might have gone. All I saw was an obese Lebo standing in line behind me, grinning with his eyebrows up like he had been watching me this whole time, thinking, *You're a fucken gronk, bro.*

———

In the late afternoons, I would go to the boxing gym where I had been training as an amateur fighter for the past three years, but instead of throwing punches, I walked into them, allowing the Fobs, Wogs, Nips and Lebos to pound into me until they broke open my guard and flattened my nose, filling it with blood. My eyes watered, and my nostrils throbbed and stung, releasing the tightness in my chest, derailing the memory of Sahara eating directly from a box of Nutri-Grain while watching *Sex and the City*.

I would arrive home and go straight to my bedroom and weep into the night, my heart clenched inside a fist as the blood up my nose dried out. My parents and my brother and my four sisters were sleeping in silent breath when Sahara came to me. Sometimes I wonder if it happened. But I knew her. I knew her voice when she whispered, 'Bani Adam, Child of Adam, formed from the dust of the ground and the breath of life.' I knew her touch – which was warm. I knew her smile – which was miserable. And I knew her eyes – which were full and black; I knew them when they looked at me and told me they were mine and I knew them when they loved me. They loved me then. She blinked slowly because they were so large, like full moons, round and glowing. And when they opened again, they squinted as she looked into me, little rings forming below her eyelashes.

Her hands were solid and strong, but she placed them upon me gently. Her hands took their time. Long golden fingers working their way along my back like trickling sand, every nail an extension of my own bones, as though they could fade into my skin and through me. But before she could show me that she was a ghost, her fingers pulled away. My entire body burned and throbbed and screamed to intertwine with hers as she gave me her next smile – the short curl of a smart-arse. Looking down at me, she murmured, 'Big busted nose – all this fuss just for some houso?'

The next night she returned without her lips. Sahara stepped forward and gave me her body instead. Holding her around the waist and pressing my head against her womb, my face against her skin; I heard a powerful heartbeat burst into sawdust. I pressed harder, my cheeks and jaw and ear meshing into her flesh, searching for the sound once more, and suddenly I fell forward, straight through her, and she was gone. I didn't know where she was or who she was with or what she'd been doing. Maybe she was alone and scared, maybe she had been raped or murdered. Maybe she was hurting; I hoped, pathetically, that she had been hurting; hurting for me. Then again, maybe she was fine, maybe she had already found another man, who was free to love her, and she had forgotten about me, placing me in the back of her mind where thoughts were left to decay and disappear into nothingness.

I carried this vision home with me from university on a Thursday afternoon. My father and mother were sitting in the living room with my godfather, Abu Hassan, a short, stocky man who looked like Danny DeVito. He was the spiritual adviser assigned to me at age fourteen, his job to teach me the ways of our people. On the day he became my godfather, Abu Hassan handed me a ribbed condom and said, 'Fuck as many sluts as you want, if you can get 'em, but remember it's a sin to marry a White girl.' Atticus Finch was rolling in his grave as this man sat on his chair, which was shaped like a throne, in the living room of his three-storey house, his pot belly sitting on his lap. His wife entered and served him Turkish coffee and cigarettes on a silver tray and then

21

disappeared back into the kitchen. My godfather blew smoke into the air and said to me, 'The Prophet Muhammad hated show-offs. Don't think you are smarter than me just because you go to the universities.'

That was how he always spoke to me, always except for this one Thursday that he visited my house: while my parents looked on, my godfather sat me down at our dining room table, flicking prayer beads and smiling at me with ease as he said in Arabic, 'Bani, no one will ever love you as much as your mum and dad – please let us find you a pretty girl in this fruitful tribe of ours, and you'll forget about that cross-worshipper in less than a week.'

Kahlil, I can give you many reasons why I said 'yes' and none of them deserve your respect. Maybe in my despair I was simply not thinking clearly; or maybe 21-year-olds do not think clearly at any point in their twenty-one years on this earth. Maybe in spite of the fact that I was mad at my parents, I also wanted to make them happy, for I could see us all together on my wedding day, hips tussling and arms swinging in the air, along with our hundreds of relatives like all those ancient Arabs who had come before us. Maybe I was angry at the tomato-faced girl for letting me go, and I wanted to punish her. Or maybe, probably, it was exactly the reason my godfather had offered: I believed a pretty girl from our tribe would help me forget about the outsider who wore a cross, who had hairy legs and hairy armpits and broad shoulders and dressed in wife-beaters and grew up in a housing commission unit. What was her name again?

THREE

MY HALF-CASTE, HALF-INSIDER, HALF-OUTSIDER, you are the descendant of Alawites. Your grandparents taught me from a young age that we were only allowed to marry other Alawites, not because the Qur'an said so, but because marrying an outsider would pollute our pure bloodline, which could be traced back to the Prophet Muhammad. Next second I was at Lakemba Public School, surrounded by hundreds of Sunni kids. They observed my mother and my aunties dropping my sisters and my brother and my girl cousins and my boy cousins and me off at the school gates in the mornings. Eventually those Sunni kids all came to the same conclusion: 'You're not real Muslims – none of the girls in your family wear hijab!' I went home and told my father what the Sunni kids were saying, and he replied, 'Sunnis are shit.'

By and by, I discovered that your grandfather's mother was Sunni before she married my grandfather. 'Why was Jidoo allowed to marry an outsider?' I asked my dad.

'Because he was worthy,' Dad answered assertively. 'And who are you to question him?'

He proceeded to tell me about my grandfather, the man I was named after. Bani Adam was so wise he could recite the Sunni and Shi'ite scriptures as well as any imam in any mosque anywhere in the Middle East, and he was so strong he could carry two one-hundred-kilo bags of flour on his shoulders. He left Lebanon and came to Australia in 1969. My grandfather worked as a baker in Redfern for the next two years, saving money so he could bring his family here, his wife and eight of his eleven children – the other three had died of measles many years earlier and were buried at Al-Ghuraba, a cemetery in Tripoli. Then one night, while Bani Adam sat on the living room couch, smoking cigarettes and watching his children play with a deck of cards on the floor in front of him, he had a heart attack and dropped to his death.

'I was so scared growing up without my father,' Dad said to me as he drove down the Hume Highway towards Bass Hill. My mum was in the passenger seat using the mirror in the sun visor to fill her eyes with mascara. It was impossible for me to imagine my father being scared of anything. He was the most powerful human being I had ever known, with a goatee and a moustache he'd kept for longer than I had lived and a large strong nose which he must have inherited from a pharaoh. Dad always seemed to be frowning, his sharp eyebrows caving in even when he smiled, and I was often afraid to look him straight in the eye. Staring at him was like staring into the earth's core: if I held my gaze for too long, I would be cremated. The source of his strength was his arms, which were shredded with muscle lines like they had been chiselled by Michelangelo. My father was the reason I never feared anything, other than him. But my child, you never have to be afraid of anything including me, especially me.

A full moon had risen and the night air was hot and sticky when we pulled into the driveway of a man named Abu Kareem. In Arabic, 'Abu' means 'Father Of' and is followed by the name of a man's eldest son. That's why my father is called Abu Bilal, because my older brother is named Bilal, and why I am called Abu Kahlil, because I am your father. In Abu Kareem's case, however, he had three daughters and no sons, and instead of taking his eldest daughter's name, he took the name he would have given his son if he were to have one.

My mother had heard from her sister that Abu Kareem's three daughters were all thin and studying at university. The eldest, Nada, was twenty-one and already married. The second-eldest, Hanna, was twenty and just over six foot tall, which was five inches above me and therefore five inches too tall for me. My mum's sister informed us that the youngest of the girls, Dima, was probably the best suited for me – she was nineteen, about my height and studying nursing at Western Sydney University. My father phoned Abu Kareem the following night and said in Arabic, 'We would like to visit you with our son Bani, if you please.' There were about thirty thousand Arab Muslim Alawites living in Australia in the year 2008 and all of them knew that this request was code for: *We want to fix our son up with your daughter.*

Abu Kareem lived in a double-storey orange-brick house with a Tarago minibus parked in the driveway. My father told me that Abu Kareem used this bus to drive children with disabilities to and from school – one of the more dignified jobs you could have in our mostly uneducated community. 'See, this is a very noble man, a man of God,' Dad explained, nudging his strong chin towards the bus. 'You would be so blessed to become his son-in-law.' He was carrying a kilo of Lebanese sweets with him called znoud el-sit, which translates to 'ladies' fingers' because they look like the golden rolls of an old Arab woman's arms. Back in the village we probably would have come with a few lambs and a goat to offer Abu Kareem, but even ladies' fingers felt too 'ethnic' out here in the ghetto, where the Leb chicks preferred hair straighteners and make-up kits and McDonald's vouchers and rides in my 2000 Toyota Celica.

Dad led the way into the house, up a short set of stairs and past two concrete lions sitting upright, guarding the front door. Pretty much every Arab house in Western Sydney had stone lions somewhere in the front yard, including our own. This was because lions represented bravery and power in Muslim culture, but they boasted an added symbolism for The Tribe: the Alawite president of Syria and his father before him had the last name 'al-Assad', which meant 'The Lion'. My mother walked beside my father in a purple diamanté-studded dress and high heels that set her two inches off the ground, and still she was no taller than five-three.

I walked slowly behind them, dressed in brand-new white Nike Air Maxes and dark-blue jeans that flared over them. I also wore a brand-new skin-tight black T-shirt that cost twelve dollars from Lowes. This was the one advantage I had over boys my age: I was thin and cut like all lightweight boxers from the waist up, and could parade my upper body like a gangbanger. There was nothing I could do to hide my nose, which was so large I could see it when I crossed my eyes, and so crooked that I could see it better with my left eye than my right, but I could at least have a clean shave and pluck the hairs growing between my eyebrows so that I didn't look like Bert from *Sesame Street*. I had also got a haircut that day in Bankstown, a typical

Bankstown Lebo look copied from *The Fresh Prince of Bel-Air* and *Boyz n the Hood* – sides of the head shaved with a razor and the top left to grow out in a curly afro, which I had gelled back so that it gleamed like glass.

Climbing the stairs, I felt a mixture of excitement, in my loins, and anxiety, in my bowels: on the one hand, I might be meeting my wife, who at the sight of her hips and her breasts and her lips, I would fall madly in love with; and on the other hand, I felt like a total loser, allowing my parents to hook me up in this old-fashioned third-world way like some desperate ugly cunt who couldn't find his own woman. Truth be told I *was* desperate, but not to find a woman; I wanted to forget about Sahara and never feel the dull agony of a broken heart ever again. The only way that seemed possible was to control my gaze, focusing *only* on women who my parents and godfather would tolerate.

Dad knocked on the front door and within seconds Abu Kareem and his wife, Em Kareem, appeared in the corridor. 'Em' was the equivalent of 'Abu' for a woman, and meant 'Mother Of', but we never call your mum 'Em Kahlil' because it makes her blush. Em Kareem was at least a foot taller than her husband and looked ridiculous next to this man, like Nicole Kidman next to Tom Cruise, only without the fame, wholesome skin and the fertile smile. I realised where her second daughter had earned her tremendous height, and why The Tribe was recommending I hook up with the younger daughter, who I would at least be able to stare straight in the eyes. If I married the tall one, I'd have found myself in line with her cleavage, and everywhere we went, Lebs would point at us and call me a walking titty-sucker.

Abu Kareem and Em Kareem were both dressed casually, husband in a white short-sleeve shirt and bland grey pants, and wife in a long green dress like the one Marge wore in *The Simpsons*, only it went all the way up to her neck.

'Salaam alaikum,' my father said to Abu Kareem. He handed him the sweets and stepped in so they could kiss one another on each cheek, then they tipped their heads forward so they could kiss each other's shoulder at the same time, which was customary among Alawite men. Meanwhile, my mother and Em Kareem embraced, their heads moving back and forth as they kissed each other on the cheeks three times.

Now it was my turn to step forward and greet my potential in-laws. 'Salaam alaikum,' I said, reaching out to shake Abu Kareem's hand while he balanced the sweets on the palm of his other hand as if he were holding a pizza. One long dark hair hung from his nose, which I badly wanted to pluck. 'Ahla, ahla,' he said as we shook. 'Welcome, welcome.'

Next I turned to his wife, who was smiling at me wildly between thick red lipstick and thick white teeth, and greeted her by placing my hand by my heart, Islam's cultural equivalent of waving hello.

I followed my potential in-laws and my parents down the corridor, which, of course, had large white tiles. Every Leb in the hood had designed their floor like this, and they were now an official Wog hazard with the number of us slipping across wet ceramic. All along the white walls were pictures and paintings of Alawite sheikhs, which were the same portraits in my parents' home. Alawites are obsessed with hanging up images of these frowning and balding men, with their white beards and bright olive skin. I think it's our way of compensating for the fact that we have so few religious leaders compared with Sunnis and Shi'ites.

Once we reached the living room, Abu Kareem and Em Kareem stepped to the left and my mother and father stepped to the right, so that two young women stood before me. One was tall and thin – just as my auntie had informed us – and she seemed to be self-conscious about it because she was slouching forward. It's particularly hard being a tall Arab girl because Arab men are caught, both in terms of our geographical origins and our height, between Black men and Asian men. The girl, Hanna, was wearing a loose black dress that stretched all the way down her arms and her legs. She had a long neck and a dry pale face, long black eyelashes and long black hair. I admired her modesty and her obsession with the colour black. I liked her lips too, which were bright pink and fixed in a half-smile. This seemed to be her mouth's default position, and it gave me the impression that she was a little emo in nature – perhaps because she was embarrassed about her awkward stature, which intimidated and repelled the men in our tribe; or perhaps because she was trying to live up to some standard of the 'Good Lebanese Daughter', when all she really wanted was to date her high school sweetheart, some tall Enrique Iglesias wannabe who promised to be her hero.

Standing next to Hanna was a girl about the same height as me, whom her parents simultaneously introduced with a paralleling level of enthusiasm and an overemphasis on each of their syllables: 'This. Is. Our. Di. Ma!' The girl was dressed in skinny jeans and a tight bright-pink shirt with a deep V-neck collar. She was even fairer than her sister, the frail complexion of an Aussie, only without the freckles and blemishes, and a set of olive-green eyes. Dima had a more serious expression than her sister, her auburn fringe covering part of her face and her bright red lips pursed in the direction of a grimace. She reminded me of a supermodel who spent so much of her time concentrating on her appearance that all the joy had been sucked from her cheeks. It was only Dima's nose that gave her Arabness away, thin and long and a millimetre left of centre. I could see my life unfolding with this girl: *Make way for Abu Big Nose and Em Big Nose.*

None of the girls spoke to me during our introduction, nor did I speak to them. We ogled one another; me thinking, *Yeah, sure, whatever, she's as good as any other chick*; and Hanna probably thinking, *Thank god they're fixing this short-arse up with my sister and not me*; and Dima probably thinking, *Nice shoes but look at those freakin' jeans!* Son, I know this all sounds outdated and cringe-worthy for a child of your era, but let me assure you, it was chill, we had fifteen hundred years of tradition guiding us; we all knew what we were doing there, we had all seen it before when our young uncles and aunts and older siblings and cousins and second cousins went knocking and came out the other end in suits and wedding dresses and The Tribe ululating, 'Li-li-leeeee!' There were steps to follow, designed specifically to reduce the clumsiness of manufacturing love. First, we would see each other, keeping our words to a minimum. Second, we would tell our parents in private what we thought of each other, if there was some 'love at first sight' moment. Last is multiple choice: if both of us say we felt a connection, we would get talking the next time we meet; or if one of us says nope, nothing, not interested, we would both go our separate ways, only ever running into each other again at the next Alawite wedding. If this were to happen, we could both play dumb and feel fine in each other's presence because neither one directly rejected the other …

Once we had all been announced, and Dima and I got a few moments to eye one another, Em Kareem instructed her daughters to go to the kitchen, and I was invited to sit with my father and Abu Kareem on one of the living room couches. Em Kareem and my mother sat across from us, talking loudly about a woman named Em Haroun, who had recently left her husband and taken his kids and house. 'Sharmouta,' Em Kareem scoffed.

Meanwhile, my father and Abu Kareem exchanged criticisms on the Muslim Alawite community:

'The girls are all half-naked,' said Abu Kareem.

'The boys drink too much,' said my father.

'The children say fucken-fuck.'

'The elders all own three-storey houses.'

This carried on for another twenty minutes, the two of them clapping and laughing as they nodded along. I listened quietly while they spoke, my head down and my arms tucked between my legs, taking my cues from the import suitors who regularly came to our house with their parents to request my sister Yocheved's hand. It was already understood between my parents and Dima's parents that we were 'good children' from 'good families' so my only job that night was to demonstrate that I could sit still long enough not to curse in the name of thy lord or shit in my pants.

Eventually, Dima walked back into the living room carrying a tray containing a Lebanese coffee pot that looked like a genie's lamp and five small Lebanese coffee cups decorated in gold Arabic script. She bent over gently before her father and my father and declared, 'Itfadalouh,' a formal way of saying, 'Here you go,' and proceeded to lay the pot and cups and some pumpkin seeds out on the small coffee table between us. Meanwhile, Hanna, the giraffe, stepped into the living room with a tray of coffee, which she laid out for our mothers.

After Dima finished pouring a cup of coffee for my father and her father, she turned to me with a soft smile and asked in Arabic, 'Do you drink Lebanese coffee?' She was born in Australia so I knew she spoke fluent English, but in front of our parents we only spoke Arabic to each other – perhaps because it seemed fancier than English and we were trying to impress our parents with what they believed to be the superior language of our ancestors. I stared deep into Dima's green eyes and responded delicately, 'Eh, shukraan – Yeah, thank you.' I kept my focus on her and she kept her focus on me as she remained half-bent over and poured me a cup of thick black coffee.

The truth was that I had never drunk Lebanese coffee before that moment. I even hated White-people coffee, but I didn't want to give this poor girl any more work to do. If I said no, she would have had to go back into the kitchen and get me something else, some tea or juice or soft drink, in order to present herself in front of me, my parents and her own parents as a well-raised, obedient, respectable young woman who would make a good housewife. When she finished pouring my cup, she turned around and walked back towards the doorway with the empty tray in her hands, her hips swaying from side to side like a belly dancer. I had to resist the urge to stare at her back and butt in front of her parents. I didn't want them to think I was a sleaze-bucket who only wanted to marry their daughter for a root and yet I was utterly fascinated by her body, which might one day have to bear my children. This was a complicated space to negotiate: Dima and I were not allowed to interact with each other alone at this stage in our fix-up, but we had to learn as much as possible about one another through these subtle interactions to decide if we were interested in getting married.

Once Dima disappeared through the door, I did not see her again. I sat quietly, watching the coffee grow cold as my father told a story about the Imam Ali – a great philosopher and warrior who was the son-in-law and cousin of the Prophet Muhammad. The Muslim Alawite sect was named after the Imam Ali, who, my people believed, was the rightful caliph of Islam following the death of the Prophet Muhammad in 632 AD. Many Alawites wore the Imam Ali's sword around their neck as a symbol of their devotion to him. We believed that the sword, called Zulfiqar, was given to Ali by Muhammad, and was brought to Muhammad by the Angel Jibreel as an order from Allah. My father said, 'Imam Ali was so upset one time that he swung Zulfiqar towards the ground, and had Jibreel not been there to catch it in his palm before the blade hit the surface, the sword would have split the world in two.' Such stories about the Imam Ali were a staple in every conversation between the older men of The Tribe. Even if we'd all heard the exact same stories a hundred times before, whenever one was shared, all the other men present went still and listened as though they were hearing it for the first time, excited that the Imam's memory and spirit had been invoked. As the storyteller, my dad was demonstrating his devotion to Ali by finding whatever opportunity he could to recount the events and teachings of his life; and as the listener, Abu Kareem was demonstrating his devotion to Ali by sitting in silent awe, smiling and nodding like he was listening to his favourite childhood song.

Finishing off his story, my father stood up, cueing to my mum and me that it was time for us to leave. As my parents and I made our way down the corridor and back to the front door of the house, I felt a stubby hand land on the back of my shoulder. Abu Kareem leaned in from behind me and said, 'Inshallah I will be at your wedding one day.'

On the way home, Mum began to prod: 'She was pretty, wasn't she? Admit it, she was pretty.'

'She was pretty,' I parroted bluntly, attempting to express my indifference to Mum's standards of beauty. It wasn't that I did not find Dima physically attractive, it's that I did not find her *more* attractive than any tomato-faced girl who did not shave her legs, which I knew my mum would never understand.

'You didn't like her?' my father asked, deliberately driving down the Hume as slowly as possible so we could debrief – even the fact we were in the right lane and the cars behind were tailgating and hastily overtaking us did not seem to bother him.

'I didn't talk to her.'

'She definitely liked you, she was looking at your new shoes,' my mother said. 'So do you want to get your nose fixed before you get married?'

'Wha-at?' I bellowed, like I'd been sucker-punched. I was aware that people could tell I had a big broken nose, but I never expected anyone to come right out and suggest I get a nose job, especially not my mother. Wasn't your mother supposed to be the one to tell you that you were beautiful when everyone else made you feel ugly?

'When there's a problem, and you can afford to fix it, you should fix it,' Dad added casually, staring straight ahead. He had a lot of nerve telling me to fix my nose, when clearly I had inherited it from him. Why hadn't *he* fixed his nose? Of course it was disrespectful even to ask such a question. In Islam, it is said that the nose is the most sinful part of the body for one to mock.

'We'll do Arit Fatiha and then a khitby in two months,' Dad said to Mum, as though I were not even there anymore. 'Arit Fatiha' is a Qur'anic reading ceremony that would provide Dima and me with a blessing from God to date one another, and 'khitby' is an engagement party – your grandparents were already planning my wedding. Part of me took no offence. Growing up in a household where I regularly overheard my mum and dad discussing all six of their children's future marriages, I knew that this was typical Wog behaviour – even on the day my youngest sister, Amani, was born, I remember my mum in her hospital bed debating with my aunties about which one of their sons this thirteen-hour-old girl was going to marry when she turned sixteen. But another part of me felt like this time the conversation was different; that my parents were desperate to marry me off as quickly as possible, sealing the deal before I had the chance to fall in love with another outsider.

While my family members slept peacefully in their rooms, I lay awake all night trying to work out what Abu Kareem had meant when he said, 'Inshallah I will be at your wedding one day.' Was that his way of saying, 'Congratulations, you are going to be my son-in-law,' or was it, 'Sorry, best of luck with some other girl'? Maybe Dima had taken one look at my small frame and my enormous nose and my flared jeans, went into the kitchen and had a huge cry in front of her sister, and then casually came back into the living room with the Lebanese coffee, only to give her parents secret facial signals which meant *No, no way, no freakin' way, not in a million years, I'd rather die, just kill me now.*

Mum called Em Kareem early the next morning to find out. As I stood there watching her dial the numbers, I thought about the times that Sahara and I used to wrestle on her bedroom mattress. She was the hardest Leb chick I'd ever met, her prickly brown legs and thighs like wooden logs. Sahara screamed and cackled and tried to push me off with her feet as I attempted to pin her to the bed, until we gave up and I was lying on top of her, both of us panting and expanding and contracting as we caught our breath. I had been so preoccupied with what Dima thought of me that I had not even considered what I thought of *her*: a soft, skinny, fair-skinned girl who, compared to the woman I was still in love with, looked breakable as a china doll.

My mum began speaking into the phone as soon as someone on the other end answered, and all the while I argued with myself: *She's not Sahara! But Sahara's not Sahara! Sahara's gone! You're never gonna find a girl like Sahara again! You're never gonna love anyone like you loved Sahara again! Dima's here! She's as good as any other chick! Any other chick that isn't Sahara! Just marry her! If she says yes, just marry her! At least you'll have a woman to hold every night! At least your parents will be happy! At least your godfather will be happy! At least your god will be happy!*

Finally, I focused on my mum, who had the cordless telephone wedged between her left ear and her left shoulder while she twiddled her thumbs like a gossipmonger. I listened carefully as she 'mmmd' and 'mmmd' over the phone. At last she said, 'Salmo,' which means 'Give everyone our regards,' and hung up. She bit her lip and smiled sympathetically at me. 'Meh – that girl wasn't pretty anyway.'

FOUR

Your grandfather owned an army disposal business called Cave of Wonders. It was located on Canterbury Road in Lakemba. During my university years, I ran the shop on weekends, but after I submitted my graduation forms, I started working there full-time to save money so I could get married. Dad paid me one hundred and fifty dollars cash a day for this work, which was plenty for a boy who lived at home with parents who covered all the bills and cooked all his meals, and who did nothing in his evenings except train at the PCYC and read books. The last time I had wasted my money on anything seriously dumb was straight after high school, when I went out drinking with the Lebs of Punchbowl Boys and found myself back at home, spewing my guts as Dad swept up my vomit and hissed, 'Shame on you.' From that point on, I steeped myself in my boxing and my studies and my job at the shop. Dad was as proud as any Wog could ever be: a rough Brown man who had turned to boxing in his own youth, he knew the ring would keep me healthy and off the streets; an illiterate Brown man who had been deprived of schooling in his own youth, he knew the classroom would elevate me above the self-professed scholars of The Tribe; and a poor Brown man who had come to Australia with nothing but the dirt under his fingernails, he could thank Allah every night for the small business that provided enough to support his wife and four daughters and employment for his two sons.

By May 2008, I had saved enough money from the family business to pay off my first car, cover my uni fees, and eventually fund a wedding, a honeymoon, and a deposit for a home – all the things that my father said made me a *real* man.

But Dad was more than a real man. He was a *real* Arab. He ran Cave of Wonders like a fifth-century desert merchant – no cash register, no computer, no price tags on any of the products. Once a fortnight, a customer named Shady came in and bought a new pocketknife for thirty dollars. Shady handed my father a fifty-dollar note. Dad took the fifty, opened his wallet, pulled out a twenty and handed it to Shady, then he put the fifty in his wallet and slipped it back into his pocket. No receipts. No plastic bags. No refunds.

The shop was a total mess – mounds of second-hand backpacks and sleeping bags piled up in corners; army shirts, army singlets, army pants and army jackets stacked on rustic trestle tables; hundreds of hunting knives and machetes and binoculars and compasses pushed up into a flaking wooden showcase; gas stoves and tents and billy cans and cast-iron pots and mess kits scattered across the concrete floor, which my father had painted brown; and camping accessories including knife-fork-and-spoon sets, air-bed repair kits, dog whistles and waterproof matches hanging in front of each other off screws on the brick walls. Customers constantly tripped over as they rummaged through the stock looking for a product. I used to try and tidy up the shop, but every time I'd make some space, Dad would come in straight after me and fill it with a new item, such as balaclavas, which in Lakemba sold like beef kebabs. That's how Dad liked it – as crazy as the shop became, he always knew where everything was, and in this way he was always in control. The cadets from Trinity Grammar would come in one after the other. 'I need some hoochie cord,' they would say, and my father knew it was hanging on that screw behind the compass, the disposable poncho and the army face paint.

I watched over Cave of Wonders throughout the day while my father and brother met with suppliers and ran market stalls all over Sydney. Most of our customers were shifty Lakemba Arabs who bargained like my dad's shop was a souk, and we also got a lot of tight-arse Nips and Curries and Fobs who came in, but none of the customers upset me like the Aussies did.

First thing Wednesday morning, exactly one week after Dima rejected me, a freckle-faced redhead named Luke, who bought a new colour of army pants every month, came in and purchased a tiger knife, which had a three-inch stainless-steel serrated blade and a black metal handle. Just before he left, Luke pierced me with his light-brown eyes. 'You got a missus or two?' he asked.

'I'm looking to get married,' I responded. Right then I realised that if Dima had said she was interested in me, I would have answered such a question with, 'I'm engaged.' Thing is, I wasn't hurt that Dima turned me down. I wanted to get married, but I genuinely believed that any girl would do so long as she was from The Tribe, and so my parents just needed to keep making the calls until someone said yes.

'You're looking?' Luke scoffed. 'Why would a healthy young bloke like you be looking? When I was your age, all I did was fuck sluts.'

Luke's words made my dick shrivel – the reverse effect to what I think he intended – but still he raised an important question: *Why did I want to get married?* In some ways, I understood it was a direct response to Sahara – I was so heartbroken that I was desperately seeking to replace her – but, then again, if The Tribe had accepted Sahara, I'd have been engaged to her by now, and Luke would have been confused as to why someone my age wanted to get married all the same. Back at Punchbowl Boys, every Leb in my school carried on exactly like him until they were eighteen, fucking as many 'sluts' as they could find, however, by the time they reached their twenties, all of them were married. I said to Luke, 'I guess that's just how we do it in my culture, mate.'

'Well, I took my girlfriend's virginity last night,' he responded, smiling on a series of jagged buckteeth. 'You know what really bothers me though? While we were fucking she moaned in pleasure and I thought, you're supposed to be a good girl but you've literally got my shlong inside ya and you love it, you skank.' Confused, Kahlil? Me too. I knew the Lebs who hated women for keeping them out, but never the White boys who hated women for letting them in.

That same day, just before I closed the shop, another White man, this one short with leathery red skin, came in and asked for a wide-brim camouflage hat. 'Gonna need some cover. Them bushfires in Vic are shockers, aye matey.'

I immediately labelled him your typical bush-kangaroo Skip, nasal as a dingbat. Whenever I encountered this kind of Aussie, I always replied in my most ocker accent. 'Yeah, we lucky Oz don't get them really big disasters, aye mate?'

'We only been 'ere two 'undred years, bud,' he pushed back, as though this were a serious intellectual discussion as opposed to casual banter until he gave up his money. 'We dunno what this cunt of a country can do to us yet.'

'Yeah but da Aboriginals been here *thousands* of years but, aye?' I responded. As soon as the words came out of my mouth, I realised I had taken a wrong turn. Since I was six years old, I had watched my father engage in these kinds of discussions as a way of entertaining himself throughout the day, but unlike me, Dad had the ability to agree with whatever bullshit came out of the customer's mouth.

The White man's glare went sharp and dark, like a demon had swept over him. 'Abos been 'ere all dat fucken time an' didn't do jack fucken shit!'

Kahlil, humble guest of the Darug people, the traditional custodians of the land on which you were born, your father was a coward. I should have said to the White man, 'Blackfellas were cultivating this place while your mob was swinging on trees', but all I did was stare back into his icy blue eyes, nod like a House Arab and say, 'Fair fucken dinkum, aye.' You see, this business was our settler migrant family's bread and butter, this was our customer, and the customer is always right ...

The White man gave me a sly wink before wandering to the back of the shop. He went through a pile of hats until he uncovered a navy green one. 'How much is this fella, mate?' he asked as he wedged it onto his large square head.

I wanted to tell him I wasn't his mate, but instead I said, 'Twenty.' Straightaway he pulled out his wallet and handed me two ten-dollar bills, which I put into my pocket. Just then, five honey-brown men in black Muslim garb walked in, stopped at the doorway and began investigating the cast-iron gas stoves lined up across the left-hand wall. They spoke among themselves in their mother tongue, which was fast and choppy. It reminded me of my Indo friend from high school, Osama, whom we called a 'chipmunk' because of the sound of his language. In response, he called us all 'Sand Monkeys', which didn't really make sense because he looked like a Sand Monkey too.

'What's this, a fucken prayer meeting?' the White man said out loud, his new camouflage hat casting a shadow across half his face. He pushed through as the Indonesians continued talking among themselves, completely indifferent to his presence. Finally one of them turned to me, pointed at the double ring burner and said with an Asian-ish accent, 'How muh this one?'

'Fifty-five,' I answered, and immediately the five men, who all had round hairless faces, began screaming at me at the same time, 'Ah, come on, cheaper! Make cheaper! Discount, give discount!'

'Fifty,' I said.

'Forty-five,' one of them responded. 'Come on, forty-five.'

They left the shop feeling like they had got one over me because they had talked me into giving them ten dollars off. What they did not realise, however, is that I had been working at my father's shop since I was six years old, and I could always tell the difference between a Cracker who would pay full price without complaint and a bunch of Wogs and Nips who were going to bargain with me down to the very last cent. With these customers,

I always pre-empted their bargaining and jacked up the unmarked price of any product in the shop by twenty per cent. Sometimes twenty-five. Sometimes thirty. It depended on the thickness of their accent.

———

That night, like every night between Monday and Friday, I closed the shop, jogged down Canterbury Road past the Lakemba McDonald's towards Belmore, and turned left onto Burwood Road. I sprinted past the heritage houses, and past the surgery of Dr Yucub Assad, who had been appearing on the news trying to ease tensions between Arabs and Aussies ever since five thousand Bogans had rioted in Cronulla chanting, 'Fuck off Lebs!' I ran along a string of shops that included a sushi bar, three Korean barbecue restaurants, a Lebanese charcoal-chicken shop, two cafes run by Belmore's old-school Greeks, and the Canterbury Bulldogs merchandise store – Belmore was the original home ground of the Doggies, a football team that included the highest-ever point scorer in premiership history by 2009, a Lebo named Hazem El Masri. Beyond the Doggies store I slowed down and jogged past Belmore train station and then finally I started to walk and catch my breath as I entered the Belmore PCYC.

I had been training here with a former prize-fighter named Leo since I finished high school, preparing myself for monthly boxing bouts at South Sydney Juniors in Maroubra. Over that time, I'd entered fifteen amateur fights and won fourteen of them. I was robbed of my second amateur fight three-and-a-half years earlier to a Nip named Christopher who had a tattoo of Jesus on his right arm – I don't care how many points the judges awarded him; he was bleeding far more profusely than me by the end of that bout! Leo was under the impression that my victories were due to 'raw talent', unaware that my father had been teaching me to box since I was five years old. Back then Dad could not afford to buy any boxing equipment so he taught me to block by slapping repetitively at my head and he taught me to punch by covering up his face and ribs and allowing me to take bare-knuckled shots at him. By the time I began training and sparring and competing in headgear and twelve-ounce gloves, boxing felt like a pillow fight to me. Eventually Leo instructed me to turn pro, but unlike all the dumb cunts who trained at the Belmore PCYC, I was a university student and believed I had greater options than getting my head punched in for a living.

The only reason I kept training now was because I believed that being a husband and father meant that you needed to be a man who could physically hold his own against other men. I learned this lesson very early on in life: first, when I saw my father punch out the drunk guy with the M-shaped moustache; and second, just a few weeks later when a fair-skinned junkie with dreadlocks stuck his teeth in my mother's face while she walked alongside my father, my siblings and me down a street in Newtown. In one motion, Dad grabbed him by the shirt, spun him around and threw him into a parked car. The junkie scampered to his feet like a cockroach and sprinted across the street. I remember thinking, *Please Allah, when I'm all grown up, make me my dad.*

The front yard of the Belmore PCYC was a basketball court surrounded by a ten-foot chain-link fence. There was always a group of four or five Fobs in there playing basketball with

Mr Hitchens, the Christian man I used to call Santa because he was fat and kind and devout and vanilla.

After the basketball courts was the entry to the building, a long corridor that led to a reception desk, and a conjoining corridor that took you to a weights room and down into the boxing gym. The enormous Samoan woman named Tausa'afia, who had arms like plastic bags filled with warm water, was sitting behind the reception desk staring at the computer screen. 'Hi Tusafa,' I said as I flashed her my membership card and skipped past. She quickly stuck her head over the desk and called out, 'Stop trying to pronounce my name, you hippie. I told you to call me Queen Latifah.'

Down in the gym, my trainer, Leo, was standing in the boxing ring holding focus pads for one of his other fighters – a gangly Lebo named Ziad Tabeek. Leo had his chin down and was calling out basic combinations: 'one-two' signalled a left jab and a right cross; 'one-two-duck-right' signalled a left jab, a right cross, a scoop under the focus pad, and another right cross that would scream out through the gym like a gunshot when it landed. 'One-two,' Leo screeched, his teeth clenched. Ziad fired two solid punches which crackled onto the pads, but he was slow returning his right arm back towards his face. Leo quickly swung a left hook that landed flat against Ziad's right jaw – nothing too hard, just a quick nick as a reminder to always keep your guard up.

I met Leo straight after I graduated from Punchbowl Boys and wanted to defend myself against all the Lebs who called me a 'dog' for cutting them out of my life post high school. The first time I walked into that boxing gym, Leo had been standing in the centre of the ring with one of his prize-fighters. He looked down at me from over the ropes, the glare of a bull slapped on his Woggy mug – concave eyebrows, flattened nose, flaring nostrils. 'What?' he asked, and immediately I felt his fearlessness – a man carved from a sharp blade.

'I wanna ... wanna fight,' I had stuttered, staring up at him.

'Well, shut the fuck up and get in the ring.'

He taught me how to stand with my left foot out in front and my right foot back so I wouldn't fall over when I took a blow, how to jab with my body tipping forward with each punch so all my weight transferred into my knuckles, how to duck and slip and pivot. 'Come close, come close, come close,' he told me, indicating that I needed to get right up in his face in order to land a clean uppercut, but instead of calling 'uppercut' and holding down the focus pads for me, he threw a firm right hook into my temple, which rattled the insides of my head. 'Block bitch,' he taunted. After one round I was heaving for air and my chest was closing in on me. 'Always understand ...' Leo explained as he placed his unyielding arm over my shoulders and pulled me in toward him, 'a Tarago with a full tank will beat a Rexy with an empty tank every time!'

As soon as Leo saw me walk through the gym doorway, he yelled from inside the ring, 'Warm up, you little fag!' Then he called out for another 'one-two' back in the direction of Ziad, who snapped out a clean left jab followed by a clumsy right cross.

The boxing gym at Belmore PCYC was old, with cracked brick walls and the damp scent of blood and sweat and tired leather gloves drenching the air. There was a row of rusted mirrors mounted on the back wall of the gym for shadow-boxing, a floor-to-ceiling ball and a speedball in the far-left corner, and a set of withered punching bags hanging from metal beams across the ceiling.

I stood between the punching bags and the bench press and skipped for the next twenty minutes – bouncing from left foot to right foot, the rope flicking rapidly under my feet and over my head. This was my warm-up every day, falling into a rhythm as I analysed and scrutinised the fighters around me.

Mr Obeid, an amateur lightweight champion in his younger days, was shadow-sparring in front of the mirrors with his seventeen-year-old son, Jim The Knife Obeid. Both were small men at only five foot five, and both were shredded with veins and muscles, their brown skin carved out like a world atlas. Jim was training for the 2012 London Olympics, obsessed with becoming the first wood-worshipper – that's what Lebo Muslims called Lebo Christians in Belmore – to win gold.

Also working out in front of the mirrors was Giovanna, a pallid Italian woman who was the only female to turn up at the gym once every few weeks. She was lying on the concrete floor doing crunches like a true Wog chick – no yoga mat. I sped up the pace of my skipping, my feet springing no more than an inch off the ground with each swing as the abdominal muscles beneath Giovanna's tight skin-coloured singlet compressed. Her presence created a dimwitted tension within the gym, not only because she was a woman, but also because she was thin and blonde and had the most enormous breasts imaginable, pumped like a cow on steroids. You could see all the men watching her, especially when she bobbled around in the boxing ring doing pad work with Leo. I too was drawn to her chest, often wondering what it would feel like to plant my face into her breastplate, but unlike all the other fighters in sight, I was always far too shy and ashamed to reveal that she had my attention – six months earlier, during Giovanna's first night at the gym, she had asked me to teach her how to wrap bandages. I taped her dry hands into two white fists, staring at the ground the whole time.

As I began to crisscross, my eyes diverted to the three Nips working on the punching bags under the tutelage of martial artist Mr Tan Li. The rope went whip-whop whip-whop, and it felt like I was cutting through each of his fighters with my hands and a strip of leather as their thin arms, attached to bloated sixteen-ounce gloves, snapped at the bags. Mr Li was originally a taekwondo master, and all his fighters were Vietnamese – at least that's how I summed them up. It might have been broader than that, it's possible he trained all kinds of Asians, but I could never tell the difference between Vietnamese, Chinese, Japanese and every other kind of 'nese' aside from Lebanese. Sure, that was racist, but in my defence, Mr Li's fighters couldn't tell the difference between Lebanese, Syrian, Jordanian, Iraqi, Saudi and Palestinian, and they referred to all of us as 'Lebanon'. They even referred to Leo as 'Lebanon', and he was Greek, bro.

I skipped while running on the spot, building my speed up to a sprint. From behind me I sensed the heavy-footed Fobs dribbling on the speedball one at a time, so hard and fast that it felt like an army was charging the gym – I could *hear* the Fob lose control, ball fumbling from his fists, and the next Fob stepping in to start the rumble over again. As the collision of gloves against pads and bags reverberated throughout the gym, my heart shuddered inside my chest, wrists rotating, elbows straining, my neck pulling from my shoulders and the sweat on my forehead flickering like specks of dust. I was now skipping fast enough to double-under, the rope going whoa-whoa-whoa-whoa as it swirled over my head twice before my feet thudded against the ground. Ten seconds of this and my twenty-minute warm-up would be over. I halted, my feet hitting the floor hard one last time, the rope dropping dead by my sides. Gasping for air – my mouth sucking in my face – I caught one of the Viets staring at me. 'Very fast, Lebanon,' he said, and then he hammered a series of rips into the lower half of his punching bag.

Back inside the boxing ring, Ziad had finished his focus-mitt session with Leo and was resting his long muscular arms up over the ropes. Buckteeth poking through his lips, he said to me, 'Oi yeh gronk, you wanna go a few rounds?'

The first time Ziad and I 'went a few rounds' was three years earlier, and he had towered above me like a rottweiler over a pit bull. For those two minutes and fifty seconds, he threw wild hooks towards my head and ribs, and I dropped each of them with my right hand and countered with an over-the-top left hand that landed on his chin. I learned this technique from Muhammad Ali, having watched his fight with George Foreman over a hundred times. For eight rounds Ali had taken to the ropes and counterpunched body shot after body shot from Big George, who had done away with each of his previous opponents in less than three rounds. Finally, in Foreman's exhaustion, Ali stung him with a series of jabs that sent him towards the canvas. Then his shoulder twitched as he considered throwing a final punch, but he chose not to, aware that it would ruin the perfect image of an unstoppable force falling to his knees in front of the entire world. But I was no Muhammad Ali, and in the last ten seconds of the round I was so exhausted, having contaminated my body with a lifelong diet of KFC and McDonald's, that I had twisted my hips away from Ziad and hung my head between the ropes. I took in a deep breath, and right in that moment (it only ever takes a moment), Ziad threw a feral body shot as though he were trying to tackle a tree and his sixteen-ounce glove clapped upon my rib. I went down like a sandbag, the air completely sucked from my lungs. I tried to take in another breath, but instead I threw up all over the boxing ring – two pieces of original recipe chicken and hot chips and potato and gravy and coleslaw bursting from my mouth like diarrhoea. As I continued spewing, Leo called out to everyone in the gym to come watch. 'See, that's what happens when you treat your body like arse shit!'

That had been the one and only time I ever went down in the boxing ring.

'Yeah, let's go,' I told Ziad. And for the next three rounds, three minutes each followed by thirty seconds of rest, I countered right jabs to the head with left jabs to the chin, heart drumming, sweat reeling, but never once letting my guard down. Ziad threw a fast left jab and I slipped right, and then he followed through with a firm right cross that pushed my left glove into my cheek. I blinked and landed in Sahara's bed. I was trying to pin her arms against the headboard and she was laughing and squirming and foisting her pillows into my face, shrieking, 'Dog, bro, dog,' until we fumbled onto one another and kissed. By the time my eyes reopened, my guard was down and Ziad had punched me at least four times square in the head. My nose was puffing up with blood but I was completely numb to the pain. I could no longer feel anything except the dull sense that something was missing, like that moment after your baby tooth is plucked from its socket.

'No arse shit!' Leo screamed at me as I locked my arms between Ziad's and mounted my chin up on his shoulder in an attempt to hold him off. 'Stop calling it arse shit!' I grunted back at my trainer, blood splattering through my mouthguard. 'There's no other kind of shit, it's all arse shit, it's all shit.'

———

In the pitch of night, I ran through my front yard, which had been completely concreted; between our two stone lions; which guarded the entrance to the house; up the steps, with 'Lebz Rule' written on each of them in liquid paper; and straight through the front door, which had been left wide open. The corridor was decorated with a canvas of the Ninety-Nine Names of Allah on the left-hand side and a clock that was shaped like a mosque on the right-hand side. The air around me smelled like mincemeat and fried garlic and onion. At the head of the corridor were the two main bedrooms: I had the one on the right-hand side and my parents' room overlooked the verandah. Further down was the bathroom and Yocheved's bedroom, which she had shared with our grandmother before she died. I could hear my parents and my siblings and the football commentators on the television all cheering for Hazem El Masri from the living room, which was joined to the end of the corridor. At the other side of the house was an extension my father built ten years ago, which included a laundry and an old sunroom that had been converted into a large bedroom for my three youngest sisters, Lulu, Abira and Amani. Connected to the extension was also my brother Bilal's room, which had nothing inside it except a bed, a wardrobe and a bench press.

As soon as I entered the house, I took a sharp turn into my room, and immediately I spotted an A4 envelope on my glass desk. Inside was my degree, a thick piece of paper that featured a shiny silver print of the Western Sydney University logo, which was supposed to represent a phoenix, and in large bold letters the words 'Bani Adam' and 'Bachelor of Arts'. The document was signed by the Chancellor, the Vice-Chancellor and someone or something called the Academic Register. It was dated 25 April 2008. My first instinct was to take the paper into the living room to share with my family, to celebrate the first degree in the House of Adam, but as soon as I creaked my bedroom door back open, I heard the roar of ten thousand spectators and the commentators screaming over them: 'He's reaching between his legs,' and 'No one grips those slippery balls like he does,' and 'He's inside of him, he's all the way inside.' I thought of Professor Roland reading excerpts from D. H. Lawrence's *Women in Love* to my class in a subject called Sexuality and Textuality: a totally straight naked man wrestling another totally straight naked man, penetrating him, interfusing his body through the body of the other, as if to bring it subtly into subjection, always seizing with some rapid necromantic foreknowledge every motion of his flesh, converting it and counteracting it, playing with his limbs and his trunk like some hard wind. The entire cohort laughed with Professor Roland at the suggestion that the book should have been called *Men in Love*. But I knew there was no way I would ever laugh with my family about the fact that rugby league was as gay as Sodom and Gomorrah. I could already hear my mum and dad going mental, accusing me of corrupting my baby sisters: *'Why do you bring these filthy ideas into our sacred home?'*

Sealing my bedroom door, I decided to mark this occasion by notifying the only person in my life who could understand: a mentally unwell gay Wog named Bucky. I sent him a text message which said: *Just got my BA bro.* Ten seconds later, he texted back: *Welcome to the club. We can use our arts degrees to wipe our a-holes.* I opened my underwear drawer and slipped my certificate beneath ten pairs of black trunks. Arse shit. Nothing but arse shit.

FIVE

EVERY DAY AMID THE tents, the sleeping bags, the portable toilets and the snake bite kits, the drum of the speedball would roll in my head; every day until I was standing in front of the concrete walls of the gym and the speedball was drumming on my fists. On Thursday evening, my brother arrived at 5:30pm to take over my shift for late-night shopping. He looked like a cloud, bulky chest and shoulders bulging from his tight white singlet. For the next three and a half hours, he would do bicep curls and shoulder presses between serving customers. I slipped my gym bag over my back and headed straight for the door, Bilal asking, 'Where you goin', bro?' even though I was going to the same place I had been every night for the past four years. He even joined me sometimes, turning every head in the gym whenever Leo held the pads for him because he had the loudest and hardest punch anyone had ever heard. 'Belmore,' I said, stepping out onto Canterbury Road, a squad of motorcycles hammering past. My brother belched after me, 'Whatever bro, I still knock ya out.'

A ten-minute jog later, I was at the entrance to the Belmore PCYC. Fumbling through my gym bag as I approached the reception desk, I realised that a White girl was sitting in Queen Latifah's seat, typing firmly on the computer.

'I'm training,' I told her, pulling out my ID. She slowly drew her hand to take it from me while we eyed one another. I noticed she had a small bump on the left side of her nose. She begun to examine the ID. 'Where's the huge woman that works here?' I asked.

'Um, she's gone back to Samoa,' the girl said. I liked the way she 'ummed' before answering the question, as though she were ashamed to tell me she had stolen a Brown woman's job.

'I'm Bani Adam,' I said to her. 'I like talking, so I'll probably talk at you from now on.' The girl nodded without saying anything else, just handed back my membership card and returned to her computer.

I entered the empty boxing gym and breathed it in; the ring fuming from last night's sweat and blood and buckskin, the punching bags hanging like cow carcasses. It was ten to six; ten minutes till the Brown trainers and Brown professional fighters and Brown amateur fighters would arrive. Tonight was unique because members of the general public, mainly older White male promoters fishing for the next champion, or victim for the next champion, were joining to watch a series of sparring matches.

The first fight was between two Fobs – one was Samoan, short and built like a bull, and the other was Tongan, tall and lean like a goanna on its hind legs. The two men threw wild king hits at each other for three rounds, as the full sausage fest of fighters and trainers and promoters below screamed out useless advice, coming together in a single voice: 'Knock-fuck-hit-cunt-jab-duck-double-left-slip-shit-now-now-I-told-ya!' The fight ended in favour of the short Fob with a unanimous decision from the judges, three pale-faces I'd never seen before who were sitting ringside in front of a trestle table.

Next there was a bout between a skinny Vietnamese fighter named Duc, who was trained by Mr Li, and an equally skinny but far more shredded and veiny kid from the Sudan named Edus, who'd already had an incredible one hundred and twenty-seven amateur fights throughout his career and would be turning pro later that year. I'd met Edus at South Sydney Juniors nine months earlier, at my twelfth amateur bout, where he told me that back in Africa his father had made him and his older brother fight each other for their dinner every night – the winner ate and the loser starved. I told Edus that this story perpetuated racist stereotypes about Black people, to which he replied, 'Boxing racist. White man watch Black man eat each other.'

Edus was a pressure fighter, moving in quickly on Mr Li's boy and pinning him up against the ropes, giving him no room to move; hitting him hard and precisely with jabs and uppercuts for two whole minutes before Mr Li screamed something in his mother tongue, which sounded like a swearword, and threw in the towel.

While the third fight of the evening unfolded, Leo and I sat on one of the wooden benches at the back of the gym. Leo was wrapping my hands in bandages as the moist air roared with the smacks and smudges of twelve-ounce gloves and the grunts of the two fighters inside the ring and the relentless screams of the men and the boys watching from ringside – 'Fucken rip his heart out!' Amid all the bruises and fractures and cuts and welts I had ever drawn for Leo, these were my favourite moments with him: when he was sitting quietly in front of me, his breath steady, his eyes focused on my knuckles, which had dark-brown calluses between each of them, as he wrapped the bandages over my hands. White cloth around my left palm three times, I could hear nothing but Sahara humming the tune to the song 'My Girl'. White cloth around my left wrist three times, I could feel nothing but the winter sun on my face as Sahara and I slept on the grass that overlooked the Glebe Island Bridge. White cloth sliding between my index finger and between my middle finger and between my pinky, I could smell Sahara's soapy wet hair when she stepped out of the shower and sat beside me in her living room to watch *Everybody Loves Raymond*. Leo moved on to wrapping my right hand, and once the bandages had run their course, he secured both of my fists with white sticky tape. Then he slid on my red boxing gloves and tied their laces. Finally, he used masking tape to bind the entire wrists of the gloves so that my hands could no longer do anything except pummel another human being.

Two fighters, one who looked Lebo and the other who looked like a skinhead romper stomper, were leaving the ring with their mouths full of blood. Leo and I stood up and walked towards the blue corner. 'You sure you don't want any Vaseline?' Leo asked.

'Not tonight.'

'It's *your* head,' he responded, wedging my mouthguard over my teeth. He held the ropes open, hissing at me, 'I know you uni boys are into all that gay shit, but don't be a poof in here.' I'd been Leo's fighter for the past forty-eight months, and all the advice he'd ever given me before each boxing match was built on this combination of homophobia and anti-intellectualism. But he never offended me.

Following three years of university, filled with wealthy Caucasian academics who said things like 'race is a construct', I craved the vernacular of my days at Punchbowl Boys High School, where every guy was 'this faggot' and every chick was 'this bitch'.

Once inside the ring, I approached my opponent, a local Wog named Pani, which I noted as being freakishly similar to my own name. Pani looked exactly like me too: olive skin, curly black hair, staunch black eyes, thick conjoined eyebrows, big busted nose, slender frame, five foot seven.

Standing between Pani and me was our referee, Mr Obeid. He quickly announced the rules for the bout. 'Okay boys, I want a clean fight, no low blows ...' blah blah blah. I had heard these words so many times that I'd stopped listening, in the same way I'd stopped listening to flight attendants giving the safety procedure before take-off. I'd only ever flown to Melbourne by that point in my life, regularly visiting my mum's side of the family – her parents and brothers and sisters and dozens of nieces and nephews; so many Arabs that I didn't understand the difference between 'Melbourne' and 'Lebanon' until I was a teenager. But even a short flight from Sydney to Melbourne was more nerve-racking to me than a boxing match during this time. I remember walking back to my corner like I was on autopilot, mechanical and soulless.

'Go in with a jab, hook, uppercut, waste that pussy-arse-cunt-poof,' Leo seethed into my ear with a tremendous amount of hot breath. It was the kind of remark that he whispered loudly enough for everyone else in the gym to hear as well, designed to intimidate my competition.

The bell for the first round resounded through the gym and immediately the voices from below screamed, 'Crack him,

Bani!' Or maybe they were saying, 'Crack him, Pani!' Raising
my fists to cover my chin, I tumbled at full speed towards the
young Wog, throwing a succession of left jabs, each landing
flush upon his nose. 'Dog!' he garbled at me through his
mouthguard and it was like my loins had sunk into the ground.
I found myself stunned by the sound of Sahara's laughter as she
ploughed her pillows into my head. I dropped my hands and
looked beyond Pani's blue leather gloves, straight into his small
black eyes, where I hoped to find Sahara waiting for me to fall
on top of her. Pani's monobrow twitched and he shot off two
solid punches, a left hook which struck the left side of my face,
shattering my vision, followed by a right cross which arrived
flat against my left eye. My legs buckled and I was down on the
canvas like a block of lard. Mr Obeid flicked his fingers above
my head and Sahara laughed hysterically. I had been knocked
out in less than twenty seconds. And still I felt no pain. Still
I was numb. Still.

———

I stood under the cold gym shower waiting for the crowd of men
and boys to disperse and for the swelling in my eye to ease before
I turned off the taps.

By the time I dressed and made my way towards the exit,
everyone had left the building except for the White girl at
reception. She remained seated at the counter, her eyes locked
on the computer screen, fingers tapping loudly on the keyboard.
Suddenly she stopped and looked up. Catching sight of me, she
went completely static, like death had dawned upon her.

My left eye twitched as I tried to keep it open, but I could feel it swelling all over again. I was staring at the White girl half blind and half dumb, asking, 'Wh-at?' like I had a mouth full of Big Mac.

She remained motionless, staring until finally she blinked a few times and said, 'Does it hurt, that black eye?'

Oh Allah, Most Merciful – how I wish it would hurt, wish I could feel the things you have given me, rather than the things you have taken away! 'No,' I answered, then pointing my finger at her, I added, 'What's it to you?'

I did not mean to come off so aggressively, but I was always suspicious of the White woman's gaze – what she saw when she set her glare upon me. In all her meekness, the White woman had shown me many times that I could not trust her; that her words were loaded with judgement; that she would not hesitate to throw me under the RX-7. During my first year at university, I had been walking to the cafeteria when I spotted a hundred copies of a book called *Young, Ethnic and Evil* on a display rack at the entrance to the co-op bookshop. The cover of the book featured mugshots of two boys with olive complexions, thick black eyebrows, thick black hair and big crooked noses, and the subtitle: *The Brutal Gang Rapes that Shocked Australia.* Immediately I grabbed a copy and took it straight to the counter, anxious to read the only Australian novel I had ever seen with people who looked like me on the cover. A middle-aged woman, with bright blue eyes, dehydrated skin and straight silver hair took the book from me. 'I cried so much when I read what *yous* did to those girls,' she said, scanning the barcode. You see, Kahlil, if that White woman saw a rapist in one of us, she saw a rapist in *all* of us. But as for the White girl back at the

PCYC, I was not sure what she saw just yet. 'Tell me …' I pressed her, 'why are you interested in my black eye?'

She shrugged her brittle-looking shoulders at me and bit her lip, which was a salty shade of pink. 'Look, I'm really sorry,' she replied. 'I shouldn't have been so nosey.'

The thing is, I didn't think she was being nosey at all, just curious. And I was just curious too. We simply didn't speak the same language. She spoke like a hipster and I spoke like a Sand Monkey – did this mean we were incapable of ever having a coherent conversation?

The White girl's chin dropped and her fingers wandered back to her keyboard. It occurred to me that I might have made her feel unsafe – if I'd learned anything from my interaction with the woman at the university bookstore, it was that it didn't take much for men like me to trigger a Pale-face. I quickly began searching for a question that would restore the White girl's comfort: watching her closely, I noticed that she was typing a much longer and much more thoughtful sentence than anyone whose job it was to simply update gym memberships should have been. 'What are you writing?' I asked.

She bit her lip and winced. 'Um-um-um, they said I could work on my master's thesis when it's quiet.'

Why so many 'ums'? I thought. *Is she embarrassed that she's been caught not doing her 'real' job?*

'I write, I like to write!' I replied swiftly, to show her that unlike the other meatheads at the Belmore PCYC, she and I could probably relate. But as soon as I heard my own words come out of my mouth I realised how pathetic and insecure I must have sounded – this White girl seemed much further along in her education than me and probably grew up in a middle-class Anglo-Australian household where being literate was no big deal. She gave me a little smile at the corner of her lips, as though she found me endearing, and said in her honeycomb voice, 'What do you write?'

Only then did I realise that I was lying – I didn't write, not anymore, not since Sahara had taken the comma out and there was no longer any reason to put it back in. 'Nothing special,' I said to her, 'but I did go to uni.'

'Oh okay,' she responded acceptingly, head nodding, smile unbroken. 'Well, what did you study?'

'White nonsense,' I answered with a straight face. See – while I was frustrated at my family's inability to embrace my education, I was equally critical of the fact that my education had been Whitewashed. For our core unit readings, the course coordinator, Professor West, had started us off with Socrates and Plato and Aristotle, completely glossed over the Arab and Muslim philosophers who set the foundations for the European Renaissance, and went straight to Dante and Machiavelli and Kant and Hegel and Rousseau and Voltaire and Foucault and Nietzsche and Spinoza and Freud and Marx. Not long after, his colleague, also named Professor West, noticed the gender disparity, and she revised the unit readers to include works by Laura Bassi and Simone de Beauvoir and Mary Wollstonecraft and Hannah Arendt and Mary Ann Evans.

The White girl's small smile waned, her blue eyes drinking me in as though nothing in her education had ever prepared her for some Lebo who was caught between Arab ignorance and White arrogance. 'What's your name?' I asked, taking backward steps towards the doorway.

'Oli,' she answered.

'Oli,' I repeated. 'That's kinda weird, cuz – it's a nickname, right?'

She gave me a distant deadpan expression. 'Something like that ...'

Shooting off a smirk, I said, 'Well see ya, Something-Like-Oli.' I turned and skipped down the corridor, out into the sticky night air of Belmore. All of a sudden, my eye started to ache – a sharp stinging pain like the bones in my face had been pounded in with a mallet. At last, I had felt something. Praise be to Allah.

SIX

THREE WEEKS AFTER I was introduced to Dima, a story begun making headlines throughout Sydney about her father, Abu Kareem. He had been driving children with disabilities home from school as part of the bus service he worked for, and on nineteen separate occasions he had sexually assaulted a deaf Shi'ite girl, who was always the last one to be dropped off. The news reports said that the bus service had video footage of him biting her ear, pinching her breasts and forcing his hand down her crotch. My father laughed as he drove me to Abu Ali's house. 'See how much God loves you,' he said. 'Abu Kareem could have been your father-in-law.'

We were on our way to Abu Ali's to meet his daughter, Zena Kanaan. As my father drove, I sat silently and thought about Dima, who by now would have been my fiancée if she'd agreed to see me again. With her father's reputation and future completely destroyed, The Tribe would be quick to alienate him and his family, and very few men were likely to come asking for her hand again. Perhaps if she knew such a fate was coming, she would have agreed to be with me – her last chance to escape. I was sad that she had fallen into this situation, but at the same time I couldn't help feeling like it was her own fault for thinking she was too good for me. In spite of her father's crimes, I was one of the few young men in The Tribe who would have married her all the same and never expected her to pour another cup of Lebanese coffee for any man ever again. But it was too late: Dima couldn't just take back her decision; and even if she could, my father would never answer a call from her father; and even if he would, my mother had already fixed up this other girl for me to meet, and I was now on her doorstep ...

The front door to Abu Ali's was painted gold as though it were the entrance to an ancient Egyptian tomb. It swung open and Zena was standing before my dad and me, chunky sunburned thighs teeming out of her short denim shorts, enormous breasts bursting from her black singlet, russet shiny hair bobby-pinned into the air. Straightaway her small eyes shot open as they sealed onto mine in a mixture of shock and embarrassment. I had met this girl before – she was the 'ganga' from Punchbowl who called herself Sandy and had blown at least eight of my Lebo mates in high school. The boys would pick her up at Punchbowl station, take her to Hoyts Cinema Bankstown, get a head job from her and then pass on her number. On three separate occasions, I had sat alongside a friend at the movies while she sucked him off, though I tried my best to concentrate on the silver screen. One time, my friend Shaky, who had a White mum and a Leb dad – *but was nothing like you* – felt generous because I shouted him KFC. As we walked from the food court to the cinema to meet Sandy, he said, 'Want a head job from her after me?'

Please don't hate me for the company I kept, Kahlil. When you're a Punchbowl Boy, who is there to hang with but Punchbowl Boys? My options were three hundred Lebos with the same plan: *During high school, get as many head jobs as possible from sluts; after high school, travel to Lebanon and marry a virgin.* But I wasn't interested in head jobs; I was interested in Mrs Laila Haimi, reciting lines to her from *Lolita* as she walked down the English corridor: 'It was love at first sight, at last sight, at ever and ever sight.'

For the entire visit Zena Kanaan sat beside her father quiet and completely still, her beady brown eyes unblinking as she stared down past a long line of cleavage at the green carpet in her parents' living room. I think she was terrified I was going to tell her father that his daughter was a total skank. Instead I sat frozen and listened to him talking in Arabic about the sin of gossip. 'Allah tells us that backbiting is like eating the flesh of your dead brother,' he said in a taut, angry voice. He looked like Jack Nicholson, with a hexagonal head and a sinister grin and hair shaped like devil's horns. 'Ameen!' my father said out loud – he was always a sucker for Muslim scripture. Maybe Abu Ali was preaching to us about gossip because he had heard about his daughter's sexual activities and was trying to convince me that the rumours were untrue. I wished I could have told him that he and his daughter had nothing to worry about, I was not going to expose Zena Kanaan; it was as shameful for me to have known her as it was for her to have known me. What exactly would I say to her father: *I once sat beside your girl while she licked my mate's knob*? I kept nodding as Abu Ali continued to speak – something about how all your sins are cleared when you do the hajj – and focused my eyes onto a tapestry above his head that had the Arabic words for 'Imam Ali' woven in gold thread. I wondered if Imam Ali would have wanted me to marry Zena Kanaan, a believer who wore the caliph's sword between her boobs while she gave head jobs to the boys. Or if he would have preferred a nonbeliever for me, who was too self-conscious to share his blades with prying eyes …

By that point I had seen the White girl at the PCYC another eight times. First, before each of my workouts. I'd place my gym membership on the counter and she would examine it and say, 'Bani Adam.' And I'd take it back from her, our fingers touching momentarily, and reply, 'Something-Like-Oli.' And then again at the end of my workout while I was skipping up the corridor. I'd stop in front of the reception desk and say, 'Bye Something-Like-Oli; Oli Something Something.' She'd stop typing and stare silently at me like she was considering telling me her real name, but in the end, all she did was sigh through her nose. And I would stare back, leaning over the counter to admire the way she dressed: plain long skirts which flowed above a pair of canvas sneakers and old long-sleeved cardigans which rested just beneath her neckline. I admired the way she did her hair – *the way she didn't do her hair at all* – letting it hang messily and tangled and uneven in front of her forehead and below her shoulders, like she had more important things to worry about when she woke up in the morning.

During the drive home, my father asked if I was interested in seeing Zena Kanaan again. 'Nah, she wouldn't even look at me,' I said.

'So you want a girl who likes to stare at you?' Dad asked, dead serious.

I wound down the window and took in a gush of cold air. 'Something like that,' I breathed out. 'Something.'

———

Next I drove my mother to the house of her cousin's cousin, Em Abdullah. This woman was the widow of Abu Abdullah, an Alawite sheikh who died ten years earlier due to a blood clot in his brain. The house he left behind for his wife and children was an old cottage in Guildford, which sat between two double-storey brick duplexes. Em Abdullah had only two children, having lost the opportunity to produce half a dozen offspring like a typical Arab once her husband died. I knew she had a son named Abdullah because of her name, and she also had a daughter named Zainab, who had agreed to meet me when my mother called Em Abdullah to request a visit. Seeing as there was no father present, Dad decided to sit this appointment out and allow Mum to facilitate the match-up.

As soon as Em Abdullah answered her front door, which was flanked by two stone lionesses, she said to me, 'Zainab is in the backyard, go out and say hello.' This was certainly different from the last two houses I had visited; a testament to the way Muslim women conducted their business when there were no men in charge.

I walked through the old house, which was carpeted and had peeling purple wallpaper and a picture rail that displayed several photographs of a yellow-toned man with a short beard. I was certain this was Abu Abdullah. In most of the photos, he was alone in front of over-crowded roads and granular buildings which looked like the streets of Beirut, but in one particular image, he was standing between the lionesses on his front stairs with two fuzzy-haired babies in his arms.

The furniture was old too, weathered lounges boasting floral patterns in the fabric and floral etchings in the wood of the armrests, and a bulky black television shaped like a cardboard box. This often happened to older Muslim women who lost their husbands: they would become financially frozen on the last day of his life. I immediately began to care for the daughter of Abu and Em Abdullah, wanting to provide her with a decent house to live in and a diamond ring to show off to all her cousins.

I stepped through the back door of the house and was immediately drawn to the girl sitting on a swing that hung from a huge gum tree in the centre of the yard. She was staring down over a phone that rested in her hand on her lap; skinny thighs covered in black stockings beneath a short black skirt. Her hair was black too, except for her fringe, which had been dyed pink and covered her entire face. She kept her head low as I walked towards her. I was about to say salaam when suddenly she stared up at me and smiled on bright-pink lipstick. She had the biggest eyeballs I'd ever seen, like an octopus, and long eyelashes drenched in thick black mascara. Her piglet nose had a silver stud jutting from her right nostril, which was unheard of for a Muslim girl back in 2008. 'Can you do me a favour?' Her voice was high and husky.

Part of me thought it was pathetic that a Leb chick would try to act like a punk, but another part of me found it charming that she wanted to be so different from the rest of us. 'Shu?' I said. 'What up?'

'I need you to tell everyone you rejected me, okay? I've got an Aussie boyfriend.'

As soon as the words came out of her mouth, I realised her plan: she had agreed to meet me in order to get her mum off her back. One moment I was asking myself if I could marry a yippie, the next I was having a vision of a girl from our tribe crawling all over a scrawny Skip with freckles and straight blond hair and an uncircumcised penis. I wanted to puke in Zainab Abdullah's face, not for dishonouring the memory of her father, who was a respected sheikh in our small and sacred sect, but for using me. Instead I said, 'Inshallah.' I was such a loser, going from door to door like some fifth-century Meccan while every habiba in Australia was doing kegel exercises to restore her virginity. But if only Zainab Abdullah understood that I had been in her situation only a few months earlier, hopelessly committed to marrying a girl who wore a cross. And where did that get me except in Zainab's backyard, terrified to ever challenge The Tribe again. I knew that Zainab's fate was going to be even worse than mine; being a girl, when her brother and her male cousins and her father's brothers and her mother's brothers and her grandfathers discovered her plans, they would threaten to tear off her White boy's nuts the minute they found him. She'd be wishing she just fell in love with a boy from The Tribe, and if that was the case, who better than me? I wasn't the man she wanted, but at least I was the man who understood!

On the way home, we drove towards Greenacre Coles, the only major supermarket in Sydney we would go to because it had a halal meat section. 'She's not interested,' I told Mum, who was staring intently at herself in the sun visor mirror as she applied maroon lipstick. 'Zainab Abdullah has a boyfriend.'

My mother turned to me, her hands and the lipstick falling into her crotch. 'Well, that's what happens when there isn't a father in the house.' Then Mum clamped her lips together several times before she went on: 'Wait till the men in her family find out. They're gonna kill her.' She did not mean this literally, Kahlil, but it was true all the same.

SEVEN

'DON'T EAT SHIT.' DAD'S words. 'There's plenty of food at home.' Mum's words. She had made kefta and rice, and beans and rice, and zucchini stuffed with rice. There was also manoush, shanglish, haloumi, hummus, labni and olives. And Leb bread, which we just called 'bread', in contrast to bread, which we called 'Aussie bread'. 'The fruit rots beneath you,' Dad said. He was trying to get rid of a box of mandarins that had been sitting on our kitchen benchtop for over a week. Yocheved, Bilal and I nodded in unison as Dad jiggled his keys like a pimp, instructing my mum and three youngest sisters to get into the car. They were going to my cousin's cousin's second wedding, not because they liked him – they were still angry that he seated them in the back row at his first wedding – but because my parents were hunting for a husband for Yocheved, and a wife for Bilal, and a wife for me.

The three of us debated what to have for dinner as soon as Dad's four-wheel drive rattled out of the driveway. We all agreed it was going to be KFC, Hungry Jack's or Macca's. The three fast-food giants were lined up just beyond the main drag in Lakemba, along Canterbury Road. Bilal would go pick up the meals. He received his Ps first shot when he was seventeen in Dad's manual column-shift van – typical Lakemba Wog, could drive a car before he could read the words in the learner's handbook. I, on the other hand, read the handbook for fun, even though I had no particular fascination with cars. It was during that interim between finishing high school and starting university. Romeo and Juliet were dead, Hamlet was dead, Desdemona was dead, King Lear was dead, and there was nothing else to read.

Bilal returned fifteen minutes later. His exhaust was so huge, Yocheved and I could hear his Skyline as soon as he entered our street. Ice rattled in paper cups as he made his way from the front door to the living room, his boots tramping loudly along the hard floor. My dad had renovated the place year after year and then suddenly we were stuck with six kinds of tiles, each a different shade of white.

The living room was where we spent most of our time as children, spread out on the floral-print fabric sofas – the Woggiest lounge set my Wog mother could find at the Wog-run furniture store in Wog-ville. We had watched Van Damme, Stallone and Schwarzenegger movies on a small CRT television right up until we were teenagers and the screen evolved into a fifty-inch plasma. Above the TV hung a picture of Baby Jesus sleeping in a crib with a halo over his head. Jesus was a gift my mum had received from Em George, the Lebanese Maronite Christian woman who lived down the street, next door to my aunt Yasmine. My parents were caught between the Dome of the Rock and a hard place: they kept the picture hung out of respect – because the Qur'an teaches us to love thy neighbour – but as Muslims, they knew it was a sin to display images of God, Jesus, Muhammad, Moses or any other divine figures. First, Kahlil, because we believe that such images result in the worship of false gods and idols, and second, Kahlil, because even if it was okay to have pictures of God and the prophets, these particular images of Jesus always misrepresented the 2000-year-old Middle Eastern Hebrew as a white-skinned man with blond hair and blue eyes, which is evidence of the first reason.

'Yulla, come eat!' Bilal announced as he entered the room, Macca's bags in his veiny hands, Coke cups mounted on his juiced-up arms. The smell of fats and oils and sauces and plastics moistened my tongue – Bilal was into McChickens and my sister was into McNuggets and I was into McCheeseburgers and we were all into McChips.

Yocheved and I slid up the coffee tables and the three of us sat together before the television. We began sucking on our Cokes as we watched MTV, an episode of *Daria* screaming into our faces. *Daria* was an obnoxious animated show about a middle-class suburban White girl who was intentionally depressed, emo, liberal and cynical – everything a self-aware, self-hating Leb like me aspired to be. While the opening credits rolled, and the theme song squawked – *standing on my neck, standing on my neeck, standing on my neeeck* – I slowly unwrapped my cheeseburger. I lifted the top bun and laid my chips over the cheese and pickles. Then I covered it back up and while the theme song went, 'nah-nah-nah-nah-nah', I picked up the burger in both hands and took my first bite. The bun and the tomato sauce were sweet, and the mustard and the pickles and the chips and the onions were salty. 'This is the shit, bro!'

My love affair with McDonald's started when I was five years old. Dad had been running two camping stalls at Paddy's Markets, and he kept all his stock in a vast warehouse in Redfern: three mountains of factory-second sleeping bags and second-hand backpacks and second-hand shoes and brand-new cast-iron stoves. On Friday afternoons Dad would take Bilal and me to the warehouse to load his van for the market. And every Friday Bilal and I asked what we would get if we did the work. 'I'll buy you Macca's,' my dad would say, 'but only if you sweat.' The problem was, no matter how hard and fast I worked, I remained totally dry. And it made matters worse that Bilal looked like he'd been wandering the sand dunes. As soon as Dad disappeared to the bathroom, Bilal would come over and swipe his fingers across my forehead to see if I was sweating. 'Amid a-uu-nak,' he'd whisper, 'Close your eyes.' He would step back a metre, hock up a wad of phlegm and spit in my face. 'Quick, wipe it across your forehead.' When Dad returned, he would smear his hand across my forehead too, and say to me with a smile, 'Mabrouk – congrats!' Trust me, Kahlil, you haven't tasted McDonald's until you've taken a booger for it.

Bilal, Yocheved and I ate fast and watched quietly. In this episode, an art competition was running at the school and Daria had been encouraged to enter. 'What's this called?' asked Bilal. '*Diarrhoea?*' His comment lingered in the air and accepting that Yocheved and I were not going to laugh, he added, 'This show is fucked.' I cocked my head at him. He was sitting with his legs apart, elbows on his knees, McChicken clenched in both hands. As his arms moved to and from his mouth his biceps flexed, like he was doing curls at Fitness First.

'Just watch it, bro,' Yocheved said to him, her long black hair tied up in a bun, accentuating her taut face. She called Bilal 'bro' not because he was her brother, but because she was a classic Bankstown chick who called every guy 'bro'. Yocheved was sipping from her Macca's straw, and each time she sucked her neck muscles spasmed, which reminded me to feel sorry for her. My parents had been pushing her to get married since she had turned fifteen. The only guys who had come along were imports from Lebanon and Syria desperate for a visa. Yocheved rejected them one after the other: 'Can I at least have someone who speaks English. And no, cousins don't count.'

'But seriously, what's wrong with the people in this show?' Bilal continued. 'It's like they're all retarded.'

My sister and I maintained our focus on the television. Daria was giving a class presentation on her artwork. She'd painted a picture of a thin, fair-skinned blonde girl frowning at herself in the mirror. At the bottom of the painting was a caption that Daria read out to her class: *She's so much prettier, she's so much thinner, she goes to the bathroom to spew up her dinner.* Bilal stared at Yocheved and I cracking up, and then at the television, and then back at us. 'What's so funny?' he asked. We kept laughing, ignoring him. 'What?' he repeated, his jaw hanging open like a troll. 'Isn't what she said supposed to be, like, bad?'

Finally Yocheved caught her breath and mumbled, 'You're so dumb, bro.'

Bilal's lips tightened. He slammed down his burger and it fell to pieces across the floor. 'What'd you fucken say to me?' Yocheved went to pick up the burger – in what looked like a combination of feeling guilty because she'd insulted her older brother and a cleaning reflex that is the trademark of every domesticated Lebo in Western Sydney. 'Sorry,' Yocheved shot back swiftly.

'Disrespectful little shit,' Bilal bellowed, chunks of McChicken slingshotting from his mouth. 'Yulla, get the fuck out of my face.'

Yocheved quickly placed the scraps of burger back on the coffee table, stood up from her knees and scurried out of the living room. I stayed quiet and went to grab the bin from beneath the kitchen sink, rounding up the Macca's cups and bags and wrappers and leftover chips. Bilal had returned to the TV screen by the time I had returned to the kitchen, where akal al-beit – the food of the house – was waiting patiently for us on the breakfast bar, covered in cling wrap and alfoil. Also on the benchtop was the box of mandarins that had been there all week. From the sink, I caught Bilal releasing his frown, thick black eyebrows spreading apart, TV remote in his hand. He flicked through the channels and stopped on an episode of *Two and a Half Men*, a show predicated on the idea that women will fuck you if you treat them like shit – everything an ignorant, self-loving Leb would embrace. I thought, *Are you serious, bro? You picked a fight with your little sister just so you could change the channel?*

Unable to stand the sound of Charlie Sheen's voice beyond the words, 'dirty filthy girl,' I took to my room. The iMac G4 on my glass desk belonged to the whole family but stayed with me because I was the only one in the house who was at university when we had made the purchase. Back then, I told myself I wasn't a normal Leb. I wasn't going to end up a gym-junkie rev-head like my brother and I wasn't going to end up married to a domesticated bride-in-waiting such as my sister. I was going to be a writer and my desktop was filled with the unfinished short stories I had written throughout my undergraduate degree. They all began the same way: I was on the ground staring up at the spine of the moon, and plummeting towards the earth and into my arms was a heavy tomato-faced girl, giggling on her way down. As I stared at these words on my monitor, I heard Bilal's heavy footsteps trudge towards my sister's room. The computer screen flickered and Bilal's voice reverberated into the corridor. 'Dis-res-pect,' he started at Yocheved. 'You'll see when your father's home. I'm gonna get him to slap ya.'

Maybe it was the Lebo in me – I'm full of contradictions that way – but straight up, Bilal was being a gronk. 'All right, bro!' I shouted. 'Leave her alone.'

'Fuck up, you little poof.'

As soon as the words popped from his mouth, I sprung out of my room and tumbled into the corridor. 'What'd you call me, ya fucken dumb-bell!'

Bilal was flanking our sister's doorway. 'Poofta,' he said. 'You and all your university mates.' This was a popular theory among Lebs, if you're into reading, you're into cock. But what business did a Leb have between the legs of Jane Austen, where passion was stronger than virtue.

I pounced forward, Bilal's broad chest expanding into my palms as I shoved him. 'Come on,' he screeched, 'ya kalb!' I threw a fast left jab that hit him in the temple with a brassy thud. Of all the people I had fought, going back to my first punch-up at Alexandria Public School with a Chinese kid named Frank who called me 'Afro Fucken', I always found it easiest to fight Bilal. I knew I would not suffer serious consequences for attacking him – unlike Frank, he wasn't going to tell the principal I had headbutted him, and more importantly, I secretly respected that my older brother was so physically powerful that he could easily absorb a punch from me. I could rely on him if I ever got into a fight with the Skips at Cronulla, who hated us for being us.

'That's all you got, little bitch?' Bilal spewed at me as his jaw snapped back. I dug my arms and head around his torso, heaving him into the living room, screaming, 'Hit me!'

'Stop!' cried Yocheved. She was tugging on the back of my singlet, trying to pull me away. Bilal's body began to pulsate, his arms, shoulders and chest throbbing, his veins popping, and I knew, I knew I knew I knew, that he was restraining every urge to punch me out. 'Eaaahh!' Bilal screeched. I dug my head into him again and backed him towards the kitchen. He grabbed onto me, locking us together, Yocheved pulling at my neck, shouting, 'Yaaa Allah, let go!' Bilal wrenched me towards him and threw me off in one huge swing. Yocheved and I smacked onto the floor as Bilal bashed his arms against his chest. In his rage, he grabbed the box of mandarins on the kitchen bench and hurled it into the air. The mandarins splattered around me and Yocheved, flattening and unpeeling, juice covering three different kinds of tile.

'I said sorry,' Yocheved shrieked from the ground, her voice splitting my ear. She still thought it was her fault – Jane Austen would have been so proud.

Bilal stepped back into the corridor and punched the toilet door so hard it blew open, leaving a gaping hole in its centre. Tap turning. Water running. Hands scrubbing. 'B-ismi-llāhi r-rahmāni r-rahīmi. In the name of Allah, Most Gracious, Most Merciful.'

Kahlil, observe carefully as the House of Adam attempts to rewind: your uncle fled to his bedroom while your aunt and I collected as many half-decent mandarins as possible and put them back into the box. Each was soft and squishy, its skin loose. The mandarins brought to mind a story Leo once told me. A fighter named Frankie Campbell was struck so hard by Max Baer that his brain had detached from his skull. Yocheved mopped the floor and I vacuumed the debris from the toilet door. Like a true Arab, I had withdrawn into a state of pure denial: *Inshallah, the wood will grow back all on its own before Maama and Baaba get home. Al-humdulilaah.* Yocheved and I turned off all the lights in the house and, without a word, we both went to bed.

For the next two hours I lay silently in the darkness, asking myself how McDonald's had turned to arse shit. I should have stayed calm instead of going all Othello on my family. *What's the point of a university education if I'm just gonna act like another Desert Coon?* I must have fallen asleep after that thought, because the next thing I remember is my dad shouting out in the late hours of the night. Bilal, Yocheved and I all sprung from our bedrooms and stumbled into the living room at the same time. My father was standing in front of the kitchen bench, his jet-black suit gleaming in Hugo Boss perfume. 'Tell me what happened to the toilet door!' he yelled.

Mum stood quietly behind him, draped in a purple dress covered in diamantés. Lulu and Abira stood next to her, their eyelids red and sunken, and fast asleep on the couch was Amani, who, I figured, had been carried in from the car by my father.

Yocheved and I locked eyes. I could feel her making a pact with me to cover for our brother. I was about to say something like,

'We were playing cricket in the house,' when Bilal began crying and croaked, 'It was my fault, I punched it.'

Immediately our father's lips tightened, the hairs on his goatee twisted; his hands clenched and his veins started to bubble just below his cufflinks. 'Where do you all learn this fucken shit?' he screamed. His head shot sideways, looking for something to destroy. Seeing the box of mandarins on the kitchen bench, he grabbed it with both hands and threw it into the air. The mandarins were in pieces before they hit the tiles. And our father could not understand why.

EIGHT

SABR. PATIENCE. NOT YOUR grandfather's virtue. The morning after the mandarin incident, Dad ordered my mum, my siblings and me to gather in the living room and said, 'The time has come for marriage.'

'We've been trying,' I replied instinctively. God knows *I'd* been trying. It wasn't my fault none of the girls I had met were interested in me, and it seemed even less my fault that the girl who *was* interested in me wasn't good enough for this family. Maybe it was us who weren't good enough for Sahara. Maybe Christ loved her so much, he spared her the misery of joining The Tribe.

Dad considered my point, tapping his right index finger to his chin, and then he nodded swiftly and walked over to the picture of Baby Jesus above the television. He snatched it off the wall and said, 'No more blasphemy in this house.' At that exact moment, I received a text message from the gay Wog who once bragged that he had sucked over three hundred cocks during the time he worked at an inner-west porno bookshop. *I'm gonna kill myself,* Bucky had written. As soon as these words registered in my mind, I sprinted through the house and tumbled into my car, leaving my family and Baby Jesus behind me. I broke down the seconds as I sped towards Bucky's place. My street: ten seconds. Left down The Boulevarde, past three roundabouts and the intersection between Wiley Park and Lakemba: twenty-three seconds. Continuing down The Boulevarde, overtaking a Fob Tarago, past two more roundabouts and two more intersections, crossing over into Belmore: nineteen seconds. Right on Peel Street, up a Nissan's arse until it did a U-turn at the next roundabout: four seconds. Left on Leylands Parade, red light in front of me, zero traffic, turning green as I approached, accelerating across Burwood Road: eleven seconds. Past Acacia Lane, past Acacia Street, Belmore Sports Ground looming in front of me, left on Myall Street: seven seconds.

One and a quarter minutes had passed when I pulled up on the kerb in front of Bucky's red-brick house, which was engulfed by lemon trees and apple trees and orange trees – his parents had brought the village from the old country with them. And lying on his back across the nature strip with a five o'clock shadow in a pair of Adidas trackies and a tight Lonsdale singlet and a pair of Nike slides was Bucky. 'Bro!' I screamed out, squatting beside him. 'Seriously!' He sat up, eyes and cheeks drooping as a smile formed on his face – one of those narrow sad-looking smiles.

'You need to know,' Bucky grumbled at me, his hands clawing at my arms and neck, 'that Kim was a good man; White, but still a good man.'

I told Bucky 'I know' but the truth is their relationship always baffled me. I'd only ever met Kim one time. Just before he dumped Bucky, I ran into the two of them while they were subtly locking their fingers together and moseying down Burwood Road at the same moment that I was entering the PCYC. Bucky was completely clean-shaven and dressed in a fitted white shirt with a red bow tie and brown skinny jeans and maroon leather shoes, and his partner was dressed virtually the same, except he wore a regular necktie and his shoes were blue. The ex was a whole head taller than Bucky and a lot skinnier, but by far the most striking contrast between the two was their age. This man looked at least thirty years Bucky's senior, his hair completely silver, his pasty white skin wrinkled and loose, red sagging bags around his eyes, dry sun spots around his snub nose. Crossing paths, Bucky looked almost embarrassed to see me, puffing up his cheeks and shaking his head at the sight of my Everlast singlet and Everlast tracksuit pants and Air Max sneakers. Speaking extremely quick, he introduced his partner to me and me to his partner: 'Kim, Bani; Bani, Kim.'

'Salaam bro,' I said to Kim, but the man didn't reply, just looked me up and down like I was an exotic chimp. Then straightaway, Bucky tugged him past me without even saying goodbye.

Two hours later, while I was heading out of the gym, Bucky was back at the front gate, only this time he was alone. 'What the fuck was that, bro?' I said, absolutely not giving him the chance to jump on me first. 'You embarrassed by your dumb Lebo friend or something?'

'Screw you!' Bucky spat at me, and he suddenly began to swing a bunch of slow, clumsy hooks towards my head, all of which I saw coming a mile away and dodged effortlessly. After a few seconds Bucky gave up, crouching over with his hands on his knees and his neck up at the moon. 'Did it occur to you that maybe I was embarrassed by my sugar daddy?' he said, panting.

'Well then why you dating him?' I asked.

'Don't try to understand complicated gay shit,' Bucky replied. 'I only returned to shout you a kebab.'

Back on the kerb in front of Bucky's house, his medication was starting to take hold, his hands easing off my arms and neck and his face relaxing. I grabbed him by the shoulders and lifted him up, tugging that drama queen down the street. Bucky maintained his silence as I dragged him through the park in front of Belmore Stadium, the home ground of the Canterbury Bulldogs. 'If you kill yourself, you're gonna miss the party,' I told him. 'My dad's about to marry us all off ...'

———

Two months later, Bilal was wedded to a girl named Mandy. They met at the engagement of our cousin's cousin's step-sister, who was marrying her cousin. See, Kahlil, everyone in our tribe is connected through a cousin; consider yourself lucky that's only half your problem.

Mandy was the youngest of seven sisters, a girl who was chubby around the thighs and belly and butt and had a big head like a bulldog and skin dark like copper. Her hair was curly and dyed red. My brother said he liked his girls this way – 'Love the chunk, bro.' He spoke to her on the phone for four weeks, got engaged on the sixth week, and was married on the eighth week. They had an average-sized Lebanese Muslim wedding, which meant five hundred guests bouncing their hips from left to right at the Grand Paradiso in Fairfield.

It was customary that I would be my brother's best man at the wedding, simply by virtue of the fact that we were brothers.

He hand-picked my groomsman's suit, asserting that it was his wedding and I had to do it his way. All night, while The Tribe danced and drank and flung kisses and envelopes filled with hundred-dollar bills at my brother and his new wife, I stared down at my de-flared legs; those black trousers closing in on my ankles and those black leather shoes bulging around my feet. I was no longer the black sheep of The Tribe. I was a duck. A duck like every other man stomping his narrow feet to the beat of the dabke.

When Bilal and Mandy returned from their honeymoon on the Gold Coast – same place every Leb took his new bride – they moved straight into their home, a double-storey brick-veneer house my father had built across the road from our own house in Lakemba.

I was sitting next to Bilal on a red leather sofa in their living room. 'That couch cost us eight thousand dollars,' Mandy squeaked from the kitchen with a grin. She was wearing thin black high heels, to compensate for her short stature, and they clapped against the frosty white square-metre tiles throughout the house like a drumbaki. With each step, her enormous boobs bounced in her fluoro-orange singlet as if she were juggling two-litre Coke bottles. 'I had to marry a chick with big tits, bro. I can't be with a woman who has a smaller chest than me,' my brother gloated in my ear.

Bilal turned on the brand-new fifty-inch plasma television. Raymond Barone, the Wop to our Wog from *Everybody Loves Raymond*, glared back at me. His nose protruded from his face like a flamingo, and his whiny voice scraped through the air towards his parents, 'You psychopaths!'

All the Arabs in Lakemba loved *Everybody Loves Raymond*, and it seemed to go unnoticed that it was because the show mirrored our own dysfunctional experiences of choosing to live on the same street as our parents.

'That TV cost six thousand dollars – six thousand three hundred ninety-nine to be exact,' Mandy told me from the kitchen. 'But university people are against telly, aye?' Her voice was stretched-out and shrill. Whenever I heard it, I twitched. I usually had a lot to say about any topic, but my brother's wife left me feeling like a jarhead. If she asked me a question, I just reassured myself that it was rhetorical and did not require an answer – just because Mandy didn't know what 'rhetorical' meant, didn't mean she couldn't speak rhetorically.

'You want some water, bro?' Bilal asked with a snort, as though his nose was full of mucus.

'Nah, I'm good.'

'I'll fill ya a cup,' Mandy responded, ignoring me. 'The fridge has a built-in filter and ice-maker. It makes the sexiest water.'

I was about to ask how the hell can water be sexy, but Bilal pre-emptively nudged the side of my thigh with his knee, and said out loud, 'Yeah baby, bring us a cup.' Bilal always wanted me to knot my tongue around Mandy. 'She doesn't understand your humour,' he explained. 'She's from the sticks.' By that he meant Penrith.

There was a loud knock at the front door and before anyone could go to answer it, the handle turned and Dad appeared. In his arms was a brown wooden box with gold Arabic transcript on top. He strolled down the long white corridor towards us – the walk *through* Bilal's house further than the walk *to* Bilal's house.

'Salaam alaikum,' Dad announced with a big goofy smile as he approached. For all my father's rage, nothing had mellowed him like my brother's marriage to a girl from The Tribe. During the two years and three months I had been with Sahara, I convinced myself that Dad's beliefs were fuelled entirely by hatred, but in all fairness I understood that he was trying to 'protect' us. Alawites had been persecuted for centuries because we were the wrong kind of Muslim. Even some of the most celebrated figures in Muslim history, such as Salahuddin, were believed to have slaughtered Alawites in the thousands. I remember my father recounting stories from his own early childhood memories, of Sunni Muslims beating some random man in the streets of Tripoli because they discovered he was Alawite. My father saw the union of two Alawites, and the prospect of a dozen Alawite grandchildren, as key to our survival.

'Wa-alaikum asalaam, Baaba,' Bilal and I replied at the same time – Arab communication is scripted.

In the kitchen, our father kissed Mandy hello three times, cheek to cheek to cheek, his moustache making her face recoil. But it was tough luck for Mandy – even if Dad wanted to shave it off, my mum wouldn't let him. 'I swear on Allah, I'll divorce you,' was her recurring threat.

'This is for my daughter-in-law,' my dad said loudly, holding out the wooden box for all of us to see. 'You can leave it open on the coffee table.'

'What is it?' Mandy inquired, eyes flaring.

'This?' my father replied, with resounding pride in his voice. 'This is a Qur'an from Iraq. It will bring you good fortune.'

A gush of jealousy swept over me. I immediately realised the value of this gift, not only because it was a Qur'an and in a box that looked heavy and ancient and sacred, but also because it was from our father, who above all else saw himself as a man of God, and wanted nothing more than to see his sons as men of God too. 'Hey, waan taba'iey?' I asked. 'Where's mine?'

'When you get married,' my dad answered. And for the first time since Sahara left me, I saw myself living a pleasant life with a girl from The Tribe. I would own a McMansion on the same street as my parents and my siblings, and Dad would randomly rock up whenever he wanted with that big grin beneath his eternal moustache bearing elaborate gifts for me from the lands of our people.

My eyes wandered off my father's mouth towards Mandy's face, which had clenched as soon as she realised she was expected to be some kind of Muslim. 'Ah yeah, Bilal, just stick it in the bedroom, aye.'

Dad's lips flung open, revealing a vacant black hole between his off-white teeth. 'No, sweetheart, you have to leave it here in the living room.'

'We'll put it out later,' Mandy replied, sharply. I knew this was coming: there was no way Mandy would appreciate what she had just received – 1500-year-old revelations from Allah to Jibreel to Muhammad over twenty-three years were about to end up in a gold-plated wardrobe filled with fluoro dresses from Supré.

'Yeah, all right, I'll put it out later,' Mandy repeated. She flicked her bobblehead at Bilal, cueing for him to collect the Qur'an from our father and make it disappear quickly.

'There needs to be a Qur'an in your living room,' Dad said, only slightly more assertively this time. He was doing his best to restrain his frustration, proving himself to be far more patient with his child-in-law, who was still too much of a stranger for him to start abusing, than his children.

The bones in Mandy's shoulder contracted, transforming her into a skeleton dipped in skin. 'I'll have one in my living room, but can it at least match my furniture!'

NINE

HERE'S WHAT YOUR GRANDMOTHER said to me one morning: 'If you want to get married, you need to fix your nose first.' She had no filter. Earlier that week, we had been buying fruit in Lakemba and walked past a very dark-skinned man of African descent. 'Yul'amah, shu aswad,' my mum gasped at me, which meant 'My god, look how black he is.' Upon hearing her, the man quickly snapped his head towards Mum, gave her a sarcastic grin on a set of porcelain white teeth, and said, 'Shukraan!' which meant 'Thank you!' Next thing we were walking back home, each carrying a box of mandarins, as Mum sulked about the incident, blaming me for not warning her that Black people spoke Arabic. I told her this was not the part of the story that she needed to reflect on.

So, yes, your grandmother told me I needed to get a nose job. It was straight after I had asked her if there were any other girls she knew from The Tribe who might be interested in marrying me. Since puberty, people had commented on my big broken nose: the Punchbowl Boys nicknamed me 'Crooked', and my dad's brothers called me 'Pinocchio', and when I was sixteen the first girl I ever hit on at an under-eighteens dance party in Parramatta said to me, 'So, is your dick bent too?' It hurt every time, but in the end it was my mum who convinced me that I needed to have it professionally corrected. I already knew I wasn't a sexy cunt, but how could a mother struggle to see the beauty in the child that sprung from her womb? I must have been a real mutt.

The plastic surgeon, a North Shore Pakistani Muslim named Dr Muhammad Jabbar, didn't even examine my nose; as soon as I walked into his practice, he took one look at me and said, 'That's very broken.' I told him I was a boxer, and he replied, 'Well, I can fix it for you, but first you need to hang up those gloves.'

I headed straight for the Belmore PCYC after my meeting with Dr Jabbar. There was a yellow 'wet floor' sign at the front of the corridor and Oli was at her desk down the other end, staring intently at her computer. The PCYC was usually empty in the daytime and it was so quiet that I could hear her tapping on the keyboard from the entrance. 'Training early today?' she said gently, still staring at the screen. Her senses were finely-tuned – somehow, she could tell it was me from the moment I materialised in the doorway; and her voice was like a harp – soft and blue.

'Actually, I'm here to cancel my gym membership,' I replied, tiptoeing towards her. The greatest irony in the impulsiveness of this decision was that I had learned it from boxing – if I thought too hard about stepping into the ring, I would have realised the insanity of what I was about to do and pulled out, knowing full well that whether I won or lost, the impact was going to be the same: torn knuckles, reopened calluses, busted nose, black eyes, fractured ribs, shattered jaw, sliced cheeks. For the next three weeks, I would be pissing blood and hanging over the toilet bowl spewing up my guts; I would be struggling to hold a cup of water without it trembling in my hands and I would be unable to read the first page of *As I Lay Dying* without wondering what the fuck William Faulkner was going on about. From the day Sahara broke up with me, I entered into every decision as though it were my next bout: finish studying, save money, quit fighting, get a nose job, find a fiancée, buy a house, get married, make babies, and then, only then, would I assess if it had been worth it. I could imagine myself standing in the centre of the canvas at the end of this journey, Allah's sunrays blazing down on me from the skylight in the ceiling, my godfather raising my arms and declaring me victorious, five hundred members of The Tribe clapping and cheering for me.

'I'm getting a nose job,' I said to the White girl.

Oli immediately stopped typing and threw her chin towards the ceiling. I'd never seen a girl stare at me the way she did, blue eyes expanding into despair and dry pink lips folding in on themselves as though I had torn pages from the Qur'an. 'But …' she murmured, and then nothing.

It was only a 'but', a restrained and unexplained 'but', but I was surprised. She always came off as indifferent to the hyper-masculinity of the boys and men who dominated the building, and they were equally indifferent to her. Each night, the fighters, who varied from shades of yellow to brown to black, flashed their membership cards at the White girl without making eye contact, their dull expressions preoccupied with the thought of a right cross flat against their nose; and they would leave the gym two hours later, hot and sweaty and thrumming, once again ignoring Oli's subtle presence behind the counter, tapping lightly at her keyboard. She had no one's attention but mine, like a pen had the attention of a poet; but she was a White girl and I was an Arab man, and history had already decided that this would go nowhere. I didn't even know her real name. And she didn't know how messy it would be to know anything more than my real name.

'Is there something on your mind, Oli Something Something?' I asked.

Straightaway she shook her head, sucking in her cheeks.

'You just said "but".'

'No, I didn't,' she replied quietly, her eyes darting from my Adam's apple to my curls. Then, in a firmer, more confident voice, she said, 'PCYC will need your membership card.'

I handed it over and she stared at the picture of me with my Arab afro and my busted nose, which was on the other side of my face because I stared dead straight into the lens when the camera flashed. Oli punched a hole through the centre of the card and stood up to hand it back to me. Her eyes clamped on mine again, and this time it was as though I were being sucked into her pupils, which were black and surrounded by tinges of yellow like an exploding star. As I took back my card, my trembling hands met hers – in what I believed would be the last time. Her fingers were frail and warm, and just as I turned away from her, she mumbled, 'But I like your nose.'

I pretended not to hear it, walking slowly down the slippery corridor, out past the basketball court, across the road to the railway station and onto the train to Lakemba. My thoughts jutted with the wheels on the tracks: *Freaken hippie, bullshit she likes my nose, nobody likes my nose, even if she did, surgery scheduled, gonna be a sexy cunt, first time in my life, gonna be a sexy cunt.*

———

The anaesthetist, who was some kind of Islander with a shamelessly fat nose, placed a gasmask over my face as Dr Jabbar frowned intently at me, 'Just say, "Bismiallah al-rahmaan al-raheem".' The fact he was a Muslim gave me contradictory feelings: I was comforted by the familiar language and faith in Allah that rested on the tip of his tongue; but I didn't trust Muslim doctors, even though *I* was a Muslim, because I had internalised all the Fox News stereotypes about Muslims being barbaric and savage and primitive and backwards ... Then, I was with Sahara. She was looking down at me from her windowsill as I stood at the entry to her apartment block. Her enormous brown eyes were open like two full moons and her cheeks swelled as she smiled, baring all her teeth. 'Bani, Bani, wherefore art thou Bani?' she called loudly, and before I could say, 'I'm right here, Sahara,' her entire body jolted and she pegged a large ripe tomato three storeys down at me. It landed flat on my forehead and splattered all over my head and face, red juice dripping from the top of my nose. Sahara laughed so loudly that the noise filled the entire block of housing commission units, consuming the entire suburb of Glebe. 'But why, Sahara?' I screamed.

'Because I wanted to see you just as you are, one last time, Bani Adam.' And she waved at me, her hand moving back and forth slowly as the sky tore open above us and sucked me up into the vast darkness of space. I watched the entire universe expand, silver stars bursting in yellow flames until Dr Jabbar's thick grey eyebrows appeared before me. I tried to take in a deep breath through my nose, and realising it was completely blocked, I brought my hands up to feel my face. Dr Jabbar quickly grabbed both my arms and said, 'No, don't touch it.' Then he smiled gently at me. 'That was harder than I thought it would be – I had to break three bones.'

Dr Jabbar placed his hands over my heavily bandaged nose, which felt like it weighed a hundred kilos, and adjusted it, as though my entire face were made of jelly. I began to take conscious breaths through my mouth as he handed me a small mirror so I could look at myself. It was exactly like the Jack Nicholson Joker moment; and also like the Jack Nicholson Joker moment, I began laughing hysterically. My nose was plastered over and there was a loose bandage taped under my nostrils, presumably to stop any blood dripping from my brain. Both my eyes had swelled and blackened with tinges of red and pink dipping into my cheeks. I had copped a few black eyes from my years in the boxing ring, but this was extreme even for a boxer, as though I'd gone sixteen rounds with Rocky Marciano. My lips had whitened and my chin had turned pale blue. And the strangest feeling of all was that in spite of the fact that I looked like I had been hit by a bus, I couldn't feel anything. I was completely numb.

———

I tipped my seat all the way back and closed my eyes as my father drove me home, from Chatswood towards Lakemba. By the time we reached Marrickville, Dad had begun reciting verses from the Qur'an, starting with one of the shortest revelations that the Prophet Muhammad, Peace Be Upon Him, had received from Allah, the Most Glorified, the Most High: 'Koul huwa Allahu ahad. Allah hu samad. Lam yalid wa lam yulad, wa lam yakun lahu kufuwan ahad.' I had been memorising the Qur'an in Arabic since I was a small boy, and understood these words to mean in English: 'Say: He is Allah, the One and Only! Allah, the Eternal, Absolute; He begetteth not, nor is He begotten. And there is none like unto Him.' I recited this verse before I went to bed every night, comforted by the thought that I was at the mercy of an all-powerful and all-loving being. But this time, it wasn't the words that brought me comfort, it was the *sound* of the words, rolling and stretching and snapping off my father's tongue. The fact that my father could even recite these words with such eloquence was to me a miracle in and of itself. Dad was born in Lebanon and only went through two years of school before he came to Australia with my grandmother and his seven living siblings. He was nine years old when Jidoo died of a heart attack shortly after they arrived. He dropped out of school and became a paperboy to help my grandmother pay for food and rent. It wasn't until he was forty years old, around the time of my seventeenth birthday, that he decided he wanted to learn to read and write and become a qāri – a reciter of the Holy Qur'an. He studied with a soft-spoken sheikh named Emad from Lakemba Mosque, who would visit Dad at our camping store for three hours a day and practise with him between serving customers. Hearing my father recite the Qur'an while driving me home from my nose job reminded me that so long as I was breathing, there was always time to start over ...

I started over with Arabs, a shitload of Arabs. They were waiting at my parents' home – aunties and uncles and cousins eager to see my transformation. As my father walked me slowly past the stone lions upon our stairs, through the doorway and into the corridor, my mum's middle sister, Manel, who looked like Toula from *Fat Pizza*, said, 'Mabrouk, mabrouk,' and my dad's youngest brother, Uncle Ali, who looked like Elvis Presley, said, 'Now we'll have two good-looking men in our family.' I turned right into my bedroom, avoiding the other relatives who were waiting for me in the living room, and walked a one-centimetre step at a time towards my bed. Reaching my mattress, I leaned forward a few inches to untuck my Spider-Man blanket and felt the weight of my entire head gushing like a litre of blood and mucus into my bandaged nose. As though I were a hundred years old, I crept back-first into my bed, pulled the web-slinger up to my chin and eyeballed the ceiling, my entire face pumping and pounding. All I could do from that point on was shiver and listen to the screeching voice of my cousin Houda, who said, 'I've been thinking of getting a nose job too,' and of my cousin Nader, who said, 'I like having a big nose – big nose, big dick,' and my dad's oldest brother, Uncle Ehud, who said, 'Show some respect, your mum is standing right there.'

I slept for a day and a night, and after I woke the next morning, my mouth was parched like a piece of white coal. I slid my tongue from side to side, moistening the inside of my cheeks, and up against my hard palate and my soft palate until my mouth was slippery once again. It was at this point that I felt the assault that my nose, and by extension my entire head, had gone through. A tingling sensation beneath the plaster, like a thousand ants warring inside my nostrils, and a headache that started at the back of my skull and caved in on my eyes. Every four hours for the next week I took Panadeine Forte, which numbed me entirely, and I watched DVDs of *Seinfeld* in bed while my mum spoon-fed me lentil soup. Little sips at a time as I grumbled with a tight nasal voice, 'So, what's the deal with Semites and noses ...?' The spoon in Mum's hand froze in mid-air as she waited for the punchline. I took in a deep breath and all that came back up was a dried clot of blood.

TEN

BREATHING CLEARLY AND QUIETLY through my nose
for the first time in a month, I was in the living room watching
an episode of *Seinfeld* called 'The Hamptons'. George Costanza's
dick had just shrunk because he swam in cold water and my mum
walked into the living room with a massive grin on her face.
'I've got a girl for you!' She explained to me that the daughter
of Najwa Hamad was eighteen, skinny and blonde and that her
parents were keen to marry her off. 'Bet-janaan,' she said, which
in English meant something like, 'Her beauty turns people into
mental cases.' There was a time when such a comment would
have intimidated me, but seven days after my surgery, when
the swelling around my eyes had eased and Dr Jabbar removed the
plaster from the top of my nose and the stents from the inside of
my nose, I found myself arrogantly thinking, *Chicks be lining up
for this shit right here right now.* My nose was smooth and shiny
at first, and I wondered if Dr Jabbar had chopped off my old
schnoz and installed a plastic one in its place, justifying the term
'plastic surgery'. But, ultimately, it was small and it was straight,

the perfect kind of nose, so ordinary that no one would notice it anymore – one minute I was Gonzo, next I was Kermit. 'Yulla,' I said to my mum. 'Pimp me out!'

Over the decades your Arab grandparents and great-grandparents and great-great-grandparents had developed many strategies to introduce their sons and daughters to each other for the purpose of marriage, including casual visits to each other's homes for 'coffee' (your dad was disgracefully already too familiar with this tactic), and forcing us to attend cousins-of-cousins' weddings in the hope that we would fall in love with each other at first sight while on the dance floor (which worked out 'successfully' for your uncle Bilal and aunt Mandy). The strategy your grandmother deployed for me this time was the Service Call Hook-Up, in which a suitor would be invited to a girl's home to do some professional work for the family – that way the children would get a chance to see each other without it looking like a marriage proposal. Carpenters would be invited to Abu Noah's house to give a kitchen quote, even though Abu Noah had renovated his kitchen six months ago; mechanics would be invited to Em Hasan's house to replace her car battery, which went flat because she deliberately left the headlights on the night before; and plumbers would be invited to unclog Em Yusuf's toilet, which got blocked that morning because she intentionally flushed too much toilet paper down the bowl. In my case, I would go to Abu Mahmoud's house after closing my dad's shop on Sunday afternoon to teach him how to set up a tent he had purchased from us last year – even though the entire tribe had seen him competently assembling it at the annual Alawite picnic in Marrickville on 2 January.

In the time it was going to take me to set up Abu Mahmoud's tent, I would have fifteen minutes to impress his daughter, Fatima. With my new, smaller, straighter nose drawing less attention to itself and greater attention to my curly black hair, I was confident that she would like what she saw and agree to see more of me in the coming weeks. And yet, for all my newfound cockiness, I did not see myself as a chooser; only a beggar, who was still willing to marry the first girl from The Tribe that would have me, that would shed me of Sahara. I convinced myself that all Fatima needed to do was be present and willing, and from there, I would make it work like Tolstoy made his pen work – war would turn to peace; we are asleep until we fall in love.

First thing Sunday morning, I took one of my brother's dumbbells with me to my father's shop and worked on my biceps in between serving customers. You see, now that I had the nose, all I needed to do was concentrate on my body. I knew it didn't matter if I could knock out men twice my size as a boxer; what girls liked, based on the way I'd seen women stare at muscles in the street, was the illusion of a strong man, and weights were the perfect way to promote this illusion. At 9am I spent forty-five minutes doing six sets of twenty curls on each arm while staring at the shop entry. My forearms were bulging like Popeye's and my biceps were protruding like red desert rocks as soon as two short-arse Lebos with prickly beards walked in.

'You got machetes?' one said to me with a chuckle. I pulled a thirty-inch machete with a wooden handle out from beneath the shop counter and handed it to him. He swung it in the air while making 'wat-ah' Bruce Lee sounds for the next five minutes.

Finally, he put it down on the counter. 'We'll buy seven of them.' As I packed the machetes into a nylon duffle bag for him, the other Lebo said, 'Hectic, cuz,' and then went on to ask me, 'You got any balaclavas, brother?'

By lunchtime I had completed another six sets of curls when a Vietnamese woman came in wanting to return a +5 degrees sleeping bag because it had a jammed zipper. I told her I only had −0 degrees sleeping bags left, which was a lie, and that I would happily exchange it for her if she paid the sixty-dollar difference. It was my father who had taught me how to squeeze every cent out of a customer. In the case of a return, the customer had already parted with their money, so the goal was to hang onto it and get them to spend even more. The Vietnamese woman fell for my Arab shiftiness, but only in exchange for her Asian thriftiness – haggling with me until I dropped the extra sixty dollars down to forty dollars.

At 3.45pm, fifteen minutes to closing time, my biceps had got such a pump that I could no longer stretch my arms out all the way. Abruptly, two coppers walked in, both Aussies and six feet tall, black batons dangling down their thighs like enormous cocks. Straightaway one of the officers said, 'We arrested two fellas earlier today who were planning an armed robbery. Did they buy some machetes from you?'

'Yeah,' I responded calmly. 'They told me they were going hunting.' This was another trick I had learned from my father – no matter how dodgy a customer seemed, we were always to assume they were buying our products for camping and recreation.

'I knew it was this place!' the second officer said, his voice deep and proud, writing on a small notepad. I almost laughed in his face; what a try-hard sad-case, acting as though he'd just done some amazing detective work, like he was Sherlock Holmes.

The officers left at 3.57pm. I did one more set of curls on each arm, the final pump exposing a series of blue veins that ran down my biceps. I sprayed myself with half a can of Lynx deodorant and closed the shop, stinking so sexy.

———

I arrived in Berala at 4:25pm and strolled down Abu Mahmoud's driveway, my legs going weak and my heart hammering as I entered his backyard. I crossed my eyes to stare at my nose, reminding myself that it was straight and no longer more visible to my right eye than my left eye. *You got this, bro,* I told myself as though I was some sick cunt, striding on. Abu Mahmoud stood in the centre of a small square space that was entirely concreted, the shadow of his double-storey McMansion looming over his bronzed complexion, collared green shirt and baggy beige trousers. This setting was common among Arabs in the western suburbs, who would knock down their old terrace, sacrifice their long backyard for an enormous house, and then cover what little yard they had left in concrete so they wouldn't need to mow grass ever again.

In front of Abu Mahmoud was the tent he had bought from my father, lying flat across the concrete, ready for me to set up. I walked like a stiffy towards him, the sleeves of my black shirt sliding up and pressing into my biceps.

'Salaam alaikum, Amu,' I said. Kahlil, 'amu' means 'uncle', but you'll basically use this term to address every older Arab man who is not your father, grandfather, brother or cousin. 'Amu' would also be the formal term I'd use to address Abu Mahmoud if he were to become my father-in-law. For a moment, I thought maybe his daughter would look like him, and that my mum's description of her was a lie to get me there, but as quickly as the thought came, it was vanquished by the direction of Abu Mahmoud's pudgy index finger, which pointed towards the bench at the back patio of the house. 'That's my Fatima.'

I twisted.

The first detail I noticed was her nose, which was long and sharp and thin at the tip. How ironic that I'd got a nose job simply so I could marry a girl with a schnoz! Next, I took in her bright blonde hair, hanging straight just below her shoulders. I knew it was not her natural colour – I don't think I'd ever met an Arab woman who was naturally blonde. But who were these girls trying to impress? The Arab boys I had grown up around saw straight blonde hair and dry fair skin and stark blue eyes as a random head job; it was the olive-skinned girl with the black eyes and the long black eyelashes and the black curly hair who they saw as the mother of their children. In the year 2000, the school captain at Punchbowl Boys was a Syrian kid named Jamal. He had been asked to prepare a few remarks for assembly on International Women's Day. 'Wog chicks rule, Aussie chicks drool!' he screamed, and three hundred monobrows below applauded and drummed their feet on the varnished floorboards of the school hall, hollering 'yaaaaaaaaaaaaa' and 'woh, woh, woh.' The principal, Mr Whitechurch, quickly snatched the microphone from Jamal and blurted out, 'Stop disrespecting your mothers!' and Jamal immediately spat back, 'We ain't disrespecting our mothers, bro, we're disrespecting *yours!*'

My gaze eased from Fatima's hair onto her chest, which was enormous compared to her slender shoulders and arms, another uniquely Arab woman trait that Arab boys revered, even though our sisters hated it. I regularly heard Yocheved wishing she could get breast reductions because her bust gave her backaches. Fatima's chest was bursting against a tight long-sleeve blue cardigan. It was at least thirty degrees that day, so this was the first bit of evidence I had that Fatima was a 'good Muslim girl', dressed far too modestly for such heat. I quickly turned back to Abu Mahmoud and mumbled, 'Ammmm-hmmmmm.' What else was I supposed to do, tell him, *Your daughter's hot, bro*? This is what I hated about our customs: hook-ups were so coded and subtle that they became intentionally awkward. Our Arab parents couldn't openly admit their formula: Random Alawite Boy + Random Alawite Girl × Six Months = Wedding.

I proceeded to set up the tent for Abu Mahmoud, speaking loudly and confidently about how it pieced together, in a pathetic attempt to show Fatima that I was a man. I could feel her watching me closely while she sat casually on the backyard bench, pretending to be on her phone. I connected the first set of fibreglass tent poles, bent them over into an arch and instructed Abu Mahmoud to pin them at one corner of the tent while I clipped them to the lining. Once this was done, I instructed Abu Mahmoud to hold the poles up in place as I connected the second set of poles together, bent and clipped them to the lining as well. Now there was a freestanding six-person nylon structure wobbling on the concrete yard, no grass to secure its base with the tent pegs.

Abu Mahmoud grinned at me when the dome was complete, eyebrows cocked with pride as though I had built the Harbour

Bridge with my bare hands. His eyes veered towards his daughter, to check if she was as impressed by my ability to erect tents as he was. Meanwhile, my phone silently vibrated in my pocket. 'I have to answer this,' I said to Abu Mahmoud, holding the phone to my ear in a way that obtruded my bicep. I turned towards Fatima, who had now stretched out her daddy-long-legged legs in skinny jeans while she quietly stared at me.

On the phone was Bucky, who I had not taken for a walk since my nose job. 'Hey what's up, bro?' I said, my bicep squeezing against the short sleeves of my shirt.

'Bani, I'm at The Gap,' Bucky told me, his voice loose and limp, like he had half a tongue. 'I'm going to jump, I've developed self-destructive tendencies.' That was Bucky: even in his darkest moments, he was self-aware and self-reflective.

'Don't do it, bro,' I grumbled at him, 'only gronks kill themselves.' I probably should have said something more thoughtful, but Bucky had threatened to kill himself like this many times before. I no longer believed him by that point and I was more interested in using his phone call as an opportunity to strut in front of Fatima. She was still on her phone, pressing digits like she was texting a friend, but every now and again, her drawn-out eyelashes would spring up at me, like she was intrigued. 'Yulla, mad cuz,' I said to Bucky in typical Leb fashion, loud enough for Fatima to hear. 'I'm entering into the eye of the camel.' I hung up the phone and gave Fatima a little smile, which I hoped she would read as charming rather than arrogant. Her eyelashes flared up at me one more time, dark pupils ablaze.

After dogging Bucky, I farewelled Abu Mahmoud with a soft, sweaty handshake. Already, I was imagining this man as my father-in-law. His Mr Potato Head appearance gave the impression that he would be a sweet and gentle 'amu', nothing like the 'amu' that came before him, a man who called himself Abu Kareem, but was really Abu Humbert Humbert.

On my way out of the yard, down the driveway where I'd parked my Celica, I gave Fatima one last look. She was no tomato face. And she wore no cross. She coiled her bright red lips at me and I experienced her smile. It stretched from one side of her face to the other like that of a five-year-old girl, revealing a row of perfectly straight white teeth. She reminded me of a rose that grew from a crack in the concrete. *Fatima, Fatima, Fatima.* I kept repeating her name in my head as I drove home, speakers rumbling, Tupac swearing he'd never call his bitch a bitch again. *Fatima. Fatima. Fatima. Fatima. Fatima.* Tomorrow my mum would ask her mum if she wanted to marry me. If Fatima said yes, I would say yes.

ELEVEN

YOU + WHOEVER × WHENEVER = WHATEVER. But for me, it was this: 'We've waited all day, are you going to marry Fatima, yes or no?' Mum stared at me like a suburban vampire.

'Just kill me, bro,' I scoffed. We were sitting on the front porch of our house at sunset, air hot and sticky, mosquitos quietly sucking my blood.

'God only loves people who marry their own kind,' my mum stressed, pushing the air through the gaps in her teeth.

'What about your second cousin, Shakira, or is she your third cousin?' I protested. 'She's happy with that Christian. God doesn't love her?' I felt a pinch on my index finger. The largest mosquito I'd ever seen, around the size of a fly, had pricked me. I gave it a hard smack with my other hand and it squished against my flesh, my blood bursting out of it. Wiping mosquito bile across my jeans, I looked back at my mother.

'Not second, not third, she's my nothing cousin!' Mum snapped. 'Of course God doesn't love her – her sons aren't even circumcised.'

Impulsively, I retorted, 'Well, then I guess God's gonna hate me too, because I'm not gonna circumcise my sons either!' But, Kahlil, you already know I said this purely to spite her. As your grandmother's make-up-ridden face imploded at the sound of my blasphemy, I remembered the night Sahara and I had taken an evening walk across the beach at Cronulla. It had been over two years since five thousand Crackers 'took back' their shire, chanting 'Fuck off Lebs' and physically assaulting anyone who looked like us. The seaweed was chafing between my toes and the waves were shattering upon the shore and the pink seashells were gleaming before the horizon when four topless waxheads, all twice my size, barged through Sahara and me. 'Freaken Sand N—' one of them bellowed, his drunken breath in my face. Then, as all four of them shoved past, the largest and fattest among them, who had an elephant's forehead, turned back and scowled, 'No more cut cocks on our beach.' My heart drummed so loud I could hear it inside my ears as I prepared to charge at them with all my strength, to swing as fast and as wild as a baboon until they smothered and kicked the shit out of me, but Sahara grabbed me tightly by the arm and pushed us forward. 'Just keep walking, Bani Adam, I like your cut cock.' From then on, I carried my dick around like a badge of honour. In a country that took no shame in making me feel unwelcome, circumcision had become a declaration of my right to call myself Australian – and a declaration of yours.

———

At 7.01pm I locked my bedroom door and dialled Fatima's home number. As the phone rang, I thought about that tomato-faced girl who kept me moving forward, back in that other life where I had a big crooked nose. I bet myself she'd have been incredibly jealous if she knew I had found someone so quickly; I bet she'd have been heartbroken too, but honestly, I wasn't doing this out of revenge. I was doing this because I was lonely, because I missed Sahara's hands in mine, and the scent of milk and honey in her hair when she stepped out of the shower. I missed the feeling of being connected to her, of wondering where she was when she wasn't with me. I missed the pain in my chest and in my head that came from being helplessly in love – Sahara and I on her mattress, my hand creeping up her leg, her thick black hairs prickling my fingers. She was like, 'I'll shave them for you,' and I was like, 'Don't you ever.' I wanted that all over again. This time, however, I would fall in love the *right* way, with the support of my family and my godfather and my tribe – no shame, no secrets, complete freedom.

'Aloo,' answered a man's voice, which I recognised as Abu Mahmoud's. He sounded goofy and serious at the same time, like Genie from *Aladdin*.

'Salaam alaikum,' I replied. 'Is Fatima available?'

'Eh,' he said. In English 'eh' means 'whatever', but in Arabic it means a casual 'yes', which was a good sign. 'Who is this?' he asked. I cringed at how ignorant we all pretended to be. I had met this man yesterday with the specific intention of getting a look at his daughter, and he knew full well that I would be calling at seven o'clock that night to speak to her as a first step towards us getting married.

I took in a deep breath and said as clearly and firmly as possible, 'This is Bani Adam, Son of Jibreel Adam.' The other end of the phone went silent and next a high voice with a slight American twang said, 'Helloooo?'

'So, listen,' I announced straightaway, 'has anyone forced you into this?' Based on my own history with The Tribe meddling in my relationships, and dictating who I was allowed to love, it did not go over my head that Fatima might have been pressured into marrying me. To be with a woman against her will was my greatest fear – naked and on top of her on our wedding night, unaware that she was disgusted by my body, asking herself as though she were Madame Bovary: *Oh, why, dear god, did I marry him?*

'Nooooooo,' she replied, again with that American twang, squeaky and drawn out. She sounded like one of the chicks from *The Hills* or *Keeping Up with the Kardashians*.

'Are you sure?'

'Nooo, I mean, yeeeeah.'

There was a pause, which dragged on until I realised she had nothing else to contribute to this matter. 'So, do you want to know anything about me?' I asked.

'Sure,' she responded.

I waited patiently for her to ask me whatever she wanted, but there was nothing except another long pause, and I counted ten seconds before I gave up waiting. 'Well, I used to be a boxer, and I have an arts degree, but now I'm working at my father's shop to save money so I can get married.'

'Oh,' she said. 'That's really cute.'

Once again there was a pause, during which I asked myself what exactly she found cute. Getting punched in the head? Reading French literature? Setting up tents? I'd convinced myself that any girl from The Tribe would do, but I couldn't help feeling disappointed by her indifference towards me. She'd said 'yes' to getting to know me, so there must have been something about me that she liked, but I couldn't understand why she wasn't interested in finding out as much as possible about me – about the habib she would be marrying, the habib she would be waking up beside every morning, the habib whose little habibs and habibas she would birth. 'Is there *nothing* else you'd like to know?' I asked her.

One last pause followed by a series of 'ers' and 'ums' before she finally said excitedly, 'Oh, I have a thing! If I marry you, will you let me wear G-strings?'

I knew then that Fatima would wed the first guy who promised her some Aussie version of freedom. Tell me, Madame Bovary, how oft the warmth of the sun above, makes a pretty young girl dream of love?

'You can wear whatever you like,' I promised Fatima.

We were engaged three weeks later.

ALL THAT IS

TWELVE

CHILD OF ADAM IS a clinging clot. I am the dust of the ground. And you are the breath of life. Salaam alaikum, Kahlil. Come and breathe in your mother. You emerge from her womb in the year two thousand and fifteen with an ancient frown. She has powered through her contractions at home and is eight centimetres dilated by the time we reach the hospital. 'You're a miracle worker,' the midwife tells her. But your mother does not believe in miracles before you are born ... She takes in the deepest breath and pushes and screams as you make your way through her body. I am right here by her side, my hands beneath her hair and around her neck, and my forehead firmly against her brow, which is burning in sweat. I say these words – words I have only ever meant for this woman, 'Love beckoned us, and we followed her, though her ways were hard and steep. And when her wings enfolded us, we yielded to her, though the sword hidden among her pinions wounded us. And when she spoke to us, we believed in her, though her voice had shattered our dreams as the north wind laid waste the garden. Even as love crowned us, she crucified us. Even as she was for our growth, so was she for our pruning. Like sheaves of corn she gathered us unto herself. She threshed us to make us naked. She sifted us to free us from our husks. She grinded us to whiteness.' Your mother pants and thrusts and the yellow at the centre of the blue in her irises explodes into stardust. She screams out your name for the very first time – *Kahlil* – as your face erupts from between her legs: you have her soft lips, and your tayta's desert eyelashes, and your jidoo's angry wrinkles, and your grandfather's chubby earlobes, and your grandmother's fragile skin, and your father's enormous nose – the nose I had before my nose job, which I miss so much at the sight of you. The midwife tosses you straight into your mother's arms, and I hear your mother cry to no one but herself, 'Thank you, God.' And as you lie there against her chest, against that heartbeat that you have come to know so well, covered in her blood and your own shit, I weep uncontrollably, as though my soul is pouring out through my eyes. Any mistakes that brought me to this moment, I would not hesitate to make again.

THIRTEEN

THE SYRIAN PRESIDENT HAFEZ al-Assad watched me with a tired smile from inside a gold-plated picture frame. I was surrounded by sixty men, sweat patches forming around the armpits of my black shirt and droplets of sweat running down the inside of my grey flared trousers, which I had paid a Turkish tailor from Auburn two hundred dollars to stitch for me. Among the men were my brother, my father and my father's four brothers: his oldest brother, Uncle Ehud; his ex-drug-addict brother, Uncle Ibrahim; his manic-depressive brother, Uncle Osama; and his youngest brother, Uncle Ali. Also among the men were Fatima's father, her brother, Mahmoud, and her father's brothers, Usuf who had a big nose and Mustafa who had a bigger nose and Yucub who had the biggest nose – like a toucan in a suit. My male cousins and Fatima's male cousins stood in jeans and long-sleeve shirts and at the centre of them all stood my short and pudgy godfather, Abu Hassan, an emperor penguin wearing a thobe. Outside in the backyard where less than a month ago I had set up a tent, I could hear the women – Fatima and her mum and her sister and her aunties and her girl cousins and my mum and my sisters and my aunties and my girl cousins – talking and dancing to Arabic music.

I zeroed in on my godfather, my father and my future father-in-law, all of whom were grinning widely at me with what I could only interpret as 'tribe pride' – the joy that comes from knowing I will reproduce with one of our *own* and prolong our existence; prolong ours at the expense of yours. Kahlil, my sabr; so much more patient than your father, bearing with me, in no rush to inhale the breath of life …

Abu Hassan began the ceremony with a prayer, in which he recited the opening verse of the Qur'an, Al-Fatiha: 'All praise is for Allah – lord of all worlds, the most compassionate, most merciful.' His voice deepened and quivered as he went on. 'Master of the Day of Judgement. Thee do we worship, and thine aid we seek. Guide us along the straight path, the path of those on whom thou hast bestowed thy grace, those whose portion is not wrath, and who go not astray.'

Once the verse was complete, the men called for Fatima, and her mother brought her in. This was the first time I'd seen my new fiancée that night. She looked exceptionally thin, like a stick insect; told me on the phone that morning that she got this way by consuming just one can of Coke a day and nothing else. 'You're gonna disappear,' I said to her, knowing she was already a naturally thin girl who had the metabolism of a five-year-old. 'Just until the wedding,' she replied. 'After that it'll be ice cream and cheeseburgers and pizza and pasta every day.' Even though I knew this was dangerous for her health, I must admit that seeing Fatima so thin made me wonder if maybe she was better suited to me, at least physically, than Sahara. I never had a problem with the fact that Sahara was ten kilos heavier than me, and even fifteen kilos heavier than me by the end of our twenty-seven months together, but it bothered Sahara, who constantly complained that I was below sixty kilos, which was unusual for an ordinary man my height, but totally normal for a lightweight boxer like myself. Once when I was sitting in Sahara's living room eating a Big Mac, she said to me, 'You need to gain weight, you make me feel like a fat bitch.' I got so upset that I threw the Big Mac across the room and watched it splatter against her bright-blue wall, secret sauce leaching down like mucus. I told her that harassing me to get heavier while I ate McDonald's was like harassing a boxer to fight just as he was about to knock out Ivan Drago.

At the behest of her mother, Fatima's hair had been dyed back to her natural black colour. 'Blonde is the bait,' my mother-in-law-to-be said to us both earlier that week, 'and black is the fish in the frypan.' Fatima also had her hair flattened to look 'Chinese straight', and her make-up was caked all over her face. She was wearing a sleeveless bright red dress, thin brown arms flailing from her shoulders like twigs and her enormous breasts bulging before the male gaze of our tribe. She had wanted to wear a pink dress but my mother-in-law-to-be demanded that I buy her daughter a red one. 'If blonde is for bait, then pink is for whores,' Em Mahmoud said to me.

'Red it shall be,' I replied. And I meant it. I fully understood how important it was to keep my future in-laws happy, having heard many stories in the past of engagements being called off because the bride's mother or father did not get their way. My plan was to follow their orders one hundred per cent until their daughter was my wife and no longer under their jurisdiction. Then Fatima would be free to do whatever she wanted – wear a pink dress, wear a G-string, and no one could interfere. I explained it exactly like that to Fatima as we sat in my car, each drinking a can of Coke. She took my hand, kissed it and said, 'That's why I agreed to marry you – because I knew you had come to save me.'

Absorbing the sight of Em Mahmoud in the doorway with Fatima made me want to throw up. My mother-in-law-to-be was wearing a pink dress! That sad old woman making her daughter wear a red dress on her own engagement day because she wanted to wear pink. And as though this wasn't shameless enough, she gave me an enormous smile, parading her bloated gums as she entered, like our conversation about the colour pink never happened.

If I was the fish, then Em Mahmoud was the frypan. I was disgusted, but I also understood the reason why she acted this way: unlike her import husband, who was shaped like a baked potato, my mother-in-law-to-be was conventionally attractive, with bright brown skin, flowing brown hair, straight white teeth and a small straight nose. Having been born and raised in Australia, she also spoke fluent English and had finished high school. I knew she could have done better than the life she had been forced into, that she could have gone to university and pursued a career, that she could have married an Australian-born Arab who could offer her stimulating conversations and expect more from her than just birthing his children. This wasn't her engagement, but she wished it were.

Fatima stood nervously among the men, her freshly waxed calves twitching, as my godfather said gently in Arabic, 'Fatima, in front of your father and Bani's father, do you want to be married to Bani and do you accept his proposal?' I wanted Fatima to look at me when she answered this question, I wanted her to be so in love with me that everyone around her faded away and I was all she saw, but instead she stared at the floor and replied, 'Yep.' Em Mahmoud wrapped her arm around Fatima's waist and tugged her out through the men, smirking and jerking her right eyebrow at me as she turned; turned in a way that overtly showed off her coat hanger hips and large butt. And in that moment, I knew we were both thinking the same thing: *Pink is for whores.*

Next my godfather focused his energy on me, and said sternly, 'Bani, you will be engaged to Fatima, yes ...' I couldn't tell if it was a question or an order. What you need to understand, Kahlil, is that for at least one half of your ancestry, an engagement is not a commitment to marry because you love each other; it is permission to fall in love before a marriage. The purpose of my engagement to Fatima, so far as I understood it, was so we could get to know one another, so I could take her on dates without The Tribe whispering behind her back, 'What a skank.' I guzzled a deep breath, closed my eyes, and answered out loud, 'Yes, inshallah.' My father and father-in-law-to-be nodded in approval as one of the older women in the kitchen, eavesdropping like a harem girl, began ululating, 'Li-li-li-li-li-li-li-leeeeeee,' and then I heard Fatima in the backyard screaming, 'I'm engaged! Sucked in, I'm engaged!'

As my brother and cousins and uncles gathered around me, patting me on the back and squeezing my neck and shaking my hands, Abu Hassan tugged my arm towards his bulbous head, cocked his lips up into my ear, and spluttered in Arabic, 'You have earned my respect – Allah will definitely make life easier for you now.' He let go of my arm and straightaway Fatima's father grabbed me by the shoulders and said, 'Ahla, ahla, ahla, ahla, ahla.' He kissed my left cheek and as he moved across my face to kiss my right cheek, his long sharp nose wisped against mine, which was still highly sensitive from my nose job. I accepted the kisses with a forced smile while fantasising about knocking him out cold – at such close range I could give him a hard right uppercut, followed by a right hook, then a left hook straight to the ground.

You see, over the past three weeks, Fatima had whispered many secrets to me about her father: he beat her with his shoe because she forgot to turn off the stove, he whipped her with his belt because she showered for forty-five minutes, and he punched her with his bare hands because she tried to go out to the movies in a miniskirt. Look, Kahlil, at how these fathers raised their children with the stick, a cycle which was broken with you – unless we include that incident shortly after your third birthday: you screamed out 'bum-shit,' and I punished you by pouring a cup of lukewarm water over your head. I saw it as my duty to save Fatima from her father, and be the kind of man every girl deserves. I told myself that this would be the only purposeful life worth living if I had to spend the rest of it without Sahara.

I walked outside with the five dozen men behind me. Fatima was in the centre of the concrete backyard, which had been decorated with glittering pink and white streamers hanging from the porch pergola and metal fencing, and hundreds of plastic chairs and tables that had been hired from the local Alawite masjid. As I wobbled towards her, nerves prickling the soles of my feet, I found myself being kissed and hugged by a hundred different women, all of whom were covered in diamantés. The music blasted through the bass speaker, which had also been hired from the masjid, and 'Allah Alayk Ya Seedi', the only Arabic song any Lebo talked about that decade, deafened the April night air.

Fatima and I danced as Lebos, arms waving and hips tussling while our families made a ring around us, sealed hands and began to bounce. Once again I waited for my fiancée to look into my eyes, to see me and only me, but all I got were snippets of her titanic smile as she shot winks from Arab to Arab. I was hurt but I wasn't surprised – most teenage Wog chicks from our end of the suburbs only got married to be the centre of attention.

I reassured myself that Fatima could grow out of this with age, that I could teach her the meaning of love, as taught to me by your namesake, Kahlil: I would make spaces in our togetherness, and let the winds of the heavens dance between us. I would love her but make not a bond of love, rather letting it be a moving sea between the shores of our souls. Fatima and I would fill each other's cup but drink not from one cup, give one another our bread but eat not from the same loaf, sing and dance together and be joyous but let each one of us be alone, just as the strings of a lute are alone though they quiver with the same music.

I led by example, my sight set only on her. Until, from the corner of my right eye, I caught a glimpse of Fatima's cousin Amir. He was a few inches taller than me, with thick brown skin and black spikey hair. I'd never met him before but I'd seen a picture of him in Fatima's purse a few days back. He was sitting on a couch staring at the camera with a smug grin slapped on his cabbage-shaped head and Fatima was standing behind him with her arms wrapped around his neck and her lips on his cheek. Beware the cousin, Kahlil – he is tricky in our culture, closer than a friend but not close enough that he won't fuck his dad's brother's daughter. When I saw the photo, I asked Fatima, 'Who's that gronk?' and she replied with excitement, 'My cousin Amir. He said he can knock you out.' I knew then that this little shit had established himself as the alpha male in Fatima's life and would be in my way so long as I was in bed with his cousin.

While Fatima and I danced, sluggishly bobbing our heads and flapping our hands in front of each other, I felt Amir inching closer. All of a sudden he was between my fiancée and me, eyes glued on her and her eyes glued on him. The drums inside the bass speaker intensified as Amir thrust his pelvis and Fatima shook her entire body at her cousin, flinging her arms wildly in the air and twerking her shoulders and butt like a belly dancer.

I was not a confident dancer, too clumsy with my feet and slow with my hips to intervene in the coup, and more importantly, I did not have Fatima's affection as her cousin did, so I just stood there watching as our families sprung up and down, in orchestrated denial.

I was imagining taking Amir up on his challenge – giving him a little jab on the chin right there in front of his mum and dad – when I felt a warm stubby hand take mine and twist me away from my new fiancée and her cousin. It was Fatima's older sister, Rima. She tipped her head towards me and said, 'I'll dance with you.' And just like me, she could hardly dance. She just stood there facing me at eye level, as though her feet were rooted into the ground, and casually waved her arms between my ears. Her dress was baggy and grey, concealing her rolls of fat. She stepped in close to me and chimed into my ear, 'You're better than this.' I was too scared to turn back now, but I knew exactly what

Rima meant: she meant I could have, and probably *should* have, got engaged to her. She was older than Fatima, so was meant to be first in line to get married, and she was much smarter than Fatima, having completed a Bachelor of Science at Sydney Uni at the same time that I had completed my degree. She was a far more suitable partner than her sister for someone like me, and if I'd been introduced to her instead of Fatima, I probably would have married her and we might even have had some kind of functional life together. But because Rima was the fatter, 'uglier' sister, it had never occurred to any of the matchmakers in our tribe that a young man like me would be interested in her.

'Allah Alayk Ya Seedi' faded out and over it rose the slow harmonic tune of a piano, K-Ci and JoJo praying for a lover close like their mother, close like their father, close like their sister, close like their brother – the perfect ballad for a community built on incest. My mother and mother-in-law-to-be stepped in to move Amir and Rima out of the way, pulling Fatima and me into each other, as our hundreds of relatives quickly dispersed to the sides of the yard and began to yowl, 'Wheeeew.' Pressing my body against Fatima's perfect hourglass frame as we danced aroused me like a donkey on heat. I'd never been with a conventionally attractive woman before – the kind of woman men ogled in the street and then went home and masturbated over. I wrapped my arms around her waist and swayed with her from side to side, staring up at the girl who was an inch taller than me in nature, and an inch again in high heels, so two inches taller than me overall. I recognised our height difference the day after our first phone call. Fatima's father had granted me permission to visit her at home; and I found myself at her front door in my burnished

127

white Air Maxes and a pair of dirty denim flares and a tight black Bonds shirt. The stick-thin girl appeared between her parents as though she were a Barbie doll on strings. Standing face to face, I immediately calculated that the only reason we were at eye level was because she was wearing flats and my Nikes gave me several extra centimetres of stature.

While we waltzed, Aunt Amina and Aunt Yasmine stood beside each other like gypsies, pointing their sharp noses and sharp fingers in my direction as they laughed at the sight of Fatima lurching over me. I couldn't give a khara. A few months earlier, my insecurities about my height might have turned this into a deal-breaker, but now that I had a smaller, straighter nose, vanity had found its equilibrium – I was no longer a short ugly cunt with a tall sexy bitch; I was just another habib, and Fatima was just another habiba, and together we were just Bankstown, bro.

FOURTEEN

DOWN INSIDE MY PANTS, my phone vibrated against my crotch, and my ringtone screamed out the words of Tupac, 'Westside motherfucker'. I pulled out the mobile and put it to my ear.

'You always answer so quickly,' said Fatima.

I walked down the verandah of my house – fiancée upon my lobe and 'Lebz Rule' liquid papered on each of the steps beneath my sneakers. Dad was standing across the street talking to our neighbour, Abu Khaled, who had lived in Lakemba since 1970. Just like my family, Abu Khaled originally came from a small town in Lebanon, but we were not the same. He was a Wahhabi Sunni who once said to me, 'Your hand will burn in hell for seventy years for every second you masturbate.' In contrast, my family were from a branch of Shi'ites who pretended that women were supposed to wear their hijabs on the inside and that alcohol was Pepsi. Dad's four-wheel drive was parked halfway up our driveway. I squeezed between it and our giant brick fence. My father turned and waved, his arm muscles and veins and biceps tightening as he flexed.

On the phone, Fatima told me about how her dad had whipped her with his belt the night before because she'd gone out in white see-through pants that revealed her panties. Every time she told me her dad beat her, which was at least once a week, I wanted to drive over to his place and snap his neck, but I also knew that we would be married soon, and that this was certainly the easiest and safest way to get her out of her situation.

'That's like why like I chose you,' she reminded me, putting on that American drawl she'd learned from all the Hollywood TV shows she watched. 'Because you'll let me wear a thong when we're married and there's nothing my dad can do about it!'

Fatima thought of marriage as an expression of freedom, rather than love, which did not bother me. See, following Sahara, I no longer thought of marriage in terms of love either – I thought of it as a form of compassion: the morning after our engagement, I bought Fatima a 1990 Nissan Pulsar, a three-thousand-dollar car with a faded black paint job and twelve-month's rego she could drive around while on her red Ps. 'I fucken love you so much,' she squealed as I pulled up in her parents' driveway.

Walking down my street, my fingers tightened around the phone, forming a fist. 'If you ever die on me, I'm gonna kill you,' Fatima said, all whiney like a little girl.

There was a sudden chill in the air, but soon enough the wind would scatter the old leaves across the south-western suburbs, the living timber would burst with new buds and spring would come round again. 'No one can hurry me down to hell before my time,' I explained to my fiancée, 'but if a man's hour is come, be he brave or be he coward, there is no escape for him when he has once been born.'

'What's that?' she asked.

'Hector.'

'Eric Bana?'

'Homer.'

'*The Simpsons?*'

'*The Iliad.*'

I didn't hold Fatima's lack of intellectualism against her. Unlike me, she hadn't had the privilege of a tertiary education. She dropped out of high school in Year 9 with the expectation of becoming a housewife by the time she was nineteen – and she was right on track, having turned eighteen shortly before we met.

Hanging up on Fatima, I continued strolling down Caitlin Street like an old man, my hands meeting each other around my back. The sun was setting and the light was thickening down the road as a pink line in the sky divided the day and the night. This was no ordinary street, Kahlil; it led to the gates of Hades, where men hid one thing in their hearts and spoke another.

I walked past Abu Jafar's house, the second from our house. This was home to our closest Alawite neighbours. All the other Muslim families on that end of Caitlin Street were Sunni. Abu Jafar's youngest son, Saaf, was sitting on the low brick fence of the McMansion talking on an original iPhone, which was still new at the time. Saaf was in his late twenties now and his hair was starting to thin, but I remember him when I was twelve and he was eighteen, doing wheelies on his motorcycle up and down the street – no wonder the local Arabs gave him the name 'Shaytaan', which means 'Satan'. Across the street from where Saaf lived, he and his oldest brother, Jafar, were building a duplex that they would move into with their wives after they got married.

Next door to Abu Jafar's house was the red-brick double-storey home of Abu Mohammed Jamal, whom we called Abu MJ for short. Abu MJ's picket fence was covered in chicken wire and he always had chickens in his front yard. Once I even saw a lamb tied to a rope in the carport. Abu MJ raised animals until Eid al-Adha, the Festival of Sacrifice, and then he beheaded them. This practice traced its roots back to the Prophet Ibrahim, who had been commanded by Allah to sacrifice his son. But before Ibrahim slit his son's throat, Allah offered him a lamb to sacrifice in his place. It's a good thing too, otherwise MJ would have lost his head by now. I'm not kidding either – these Lakemba Wahhabis took the scripture literally!

I walked past the alleyway that joined my street to Alice Street, a shortcut to my old primary school. There were three hundred students at the school back then and two hundred and ninety-four of us had parents from Lebanon, which is why we called it 'Leb-kemba Public'.

Beyond the first house beside the alleyway was Em George's house. You might remember that she was the Maronite woman who gifted your grandmother with the picture of Baby Jesus. Em George was kind enough to tolerate, but I always wondered if her family secretly hated us, along with all the other Muslims in our neighbourhood. One time, her youngest son, Kenny, said to me, 'Why are they blaming Lebs for the gang rapes? Bilal Skaf and the others are Muslims, so why don't they blame Muslims?' I told him, 'Because there's no difference between us to Aussies, ya dumb cunt.' He fixed his black eyes on me and did the Sign of the Cross, touching his hand to his forehead, lower chest and both shoulders. 'In the name of the Father, and of the Son, and of the Holy Spirit.'

Em George was standing on her verandah. She was dumpy and wide and had short black curly hair like a Porch Monkey. Hunched down beside her was Abu George, her husband. He was short too, but skinny and completely bald; his skin looking like it had been drenched in olive oil. Abu and Em George had been my aunt Yasmine's next-door neighbours for almost thirty years.

'Salaam alaikum,' I said. Growing up in Lakemba, the other Lebanese Muslim kids instructed me never to greet Lebanese Christians this way – 'Salaam alaikum' should be exclusively reserved for Muslims. But don't listen to these Taliban wannabes, my son; the love you give is the love you get.

Immediately Abu George popped up and peered over his verandah. 'Ah, Bani Adam! Wa-alaikum asalaam!'

You see what I mean, Kahlil?

'When's the big day?' Em George asked with a dry Arabic accent.

'Six months.'

'I'll dance with you at your wedding,' she said, 'because you drink like us and don't wear hijab.' Unlike Sunni and Shia Muslims, Alawites were known to get drunk and dress as immodestly as Westerners in public. While Em George may have considered her words a compliment, I found them offensive – a subtle way of saying that the only good Muslim was a non-practising one.

Finally, I reached the house of my father's second-oldest sister. She had twin sons, Zack and Zane, and a daughter, Mouna, who was the closest to my age and usually the reason I visited. Aunt

Yasmine's status in our family had no value until my grandmother passed away twelve years ago, then all of a sudden she became obsessed with feeding us. She cooked all my grandmother's old recipes – malfouf, which was rice and meat wrapped in cabbage; and warak enab, which was rice and meat wrapped in vine leaves; and kousa, which was rice and meat stuffed in zucchinis – and distributed the food to the homes of Baat Adam, which were all just a few streets from each other.

Aunt Yasmine's house was a single-storey, old and orange. The concrete fence that guarded it was also orange. My cousin Zane's ute was parked in the driveway and I could hear him clattering inside the front garage. I caught snatches of his small head and overgrown arms as I walked past and up round the back of the house. I couldn't be bothered saying hey. Zane had been using steroids for the past ten years, and his arms and his ego were always bloated like a stomach-ache. But bulking up didn't mean you could fight. Before my nose job, Zane would occasionally come over to my house and we'd throw hands in the backyard using my two pairs of fourteen-ounce gloves. I was sixty kilos of skin and vein and bone and he was a hundred kilos of muscle, yet he could never land a punch on me. Then again, what would happen if he took a shot at me now? Following weeks out of the ring, I could feel each of the muscles I had perfected for lightning fast and precise jabs, hooks and uppercuts dissipating; I could feel the stiffness in each of the bones attached to my spine slowing down my reflexes, to a point where I could no longer block and slip and duck a punch before it came at me; and most frighteningly of all, I could feel the newfound sensitivity in my nose, which had become so fragile

134

you could snap it off with a light jab. Suddenly longing for that time when my big crooked nose was impervious to any man's punch, I heard the awkward White girl's final plea before I had said goodbye: *But ...*

'Something, something, something,' I mumbled to myself, remembering Oli's harp-like voice. I entered the back patio, which contained an old-school coal barbecue and a bunch of plastic chairs, and banged on the back shutter. 'Shu, cuz!' I said with a grin as Mouna appeared. I put my hand in hers, shaking hard. Mouna was a total tomboy, with big bones and sharp cheekbones and a short haircut. She always wore board shorts and singlets, which pressed hard against her flat chest and beefy stomach. As a child, I had been grossed out by Mouna's masculinity, as were the rest of our family members who whispered that she had a penis, but in recent months I had warmed to her. The way she spoke and dressed and carried herself reminded me of the tomato-faced girl who wore a cross, and so I visited her as often as I could as compensation for Sahara's absence.

Mouna let me in and I sat down in the living room. It was no different from every other Wog's living room: white tiles and box-shaped white leather couches and a fifty-inch LCD TV and white walls filled with framed portraits of dead relatives. They all looked like us – the sheikhs in the pictures. They were our ancestors; grandfathers and great-grandfathers, frowning bearded old men, watching over our family.

My cousin Noor was nestled deep into the couch in front of me. He was the tallest member of our family – almost six foot, and he was also the heaviest, weighing about one hundred and sixty kilos. Noor's father was Uncle Ehud, my father's oldest brother.

Usually when Noor was in Lakemba he came straight to my place; we were supposed to be, like, 'best cousins' or something. He slept over at my house and on the same mattress as me every weekend and during the school holidays – first when we were both children in Alexandria, and second when I was still a child and he had become a teenager in Lakemba. Then one night I felt the bed vibrating. 'What's going on?' I whispered, and Noor hissed back at me, 'Shush, you're just cold.' In the evenings that followed, his sexual curiosity drew closer and closer to my body, and eventually he was on his side, pressing his dick against my boxer shorts and tugging at it until the fabric on my skin became hot and wet. I pretended to be asleep, or maybe I was half-asleep, or maybe I was completely asleep. The next morning I told my father about it. 'That's normal for a boy your cousin's age,' Dad said, but it was the last time he allowed Noor to sleep over. And while I often doubted that it even happened – that I hadn't just dreamed it – I never once allowed you, Kahlil, to sleep in a bed with your cousins. And from the day you were born to the day you were old enough to bathe yourself, I washed you, and washed *with* you in our bathtub, but always in shorts and a singlet, unwilling to ever be naked around you.

Eyeing-out Noor, I asked, 'What ya doing here, brah?'

'What are you talking about?' Noor said, his face shrinking as though he was genuinely confused. 'I'm always *here.*'

What the fuck was this about? Noor was never there. Hang on, hang on … I knew what was going on: *Street Fighter*! I beat that fat shit three times in a row last week and he couldn't hack it, so now he was visiting Mouna instead of me as payback.

'You're stuffed, bro!' I said to him, and he gave me a huge sinister grin – baring his fangs, each tooth divided by black gaps.

'More stuffed than you'll ever know,' Mouna added, plopping herself on the couch beside Noor. Sleeping in the La-Z-Boy recliner next to them was Mouna's dad, Abu Zack, whose bald head glimmered under the fluorescent lights of the white ceiling. The La-Z-Boy was Abu Zack's throne, and no one was allowed to park their arse there except him. The only time Abu Zack let me sit on it was the day after my engagement. 'You're a man now,' he told me. Abu Zack was an import: he came to Australia in his twenties, which was far too late to shake his accent. Like his father before him, and his grandfather before that, he was a heavy smoker and drinker and a misogynist who casually beat his wife. Then one day he stopped doing all three of those things and became a half-decent husband, and all that was left from the old village was his thick Arab tongue.

Aunt Yasmine was standing over the stove in her open-plan kitchen, which faced the living room. 'How are you?' she asked, stirring a large aluminium pot. I didn't know what she was cooking, but the entire house smelled like fried garlic and onion.

'Humdulilaah,' I told her.

'What'd your mum make today?'

'Kousa.'

She nodded and smiled mischievously into her broth. She knew I didn't like kousa. Aunt Yasmine was supposed to be the best cook in our family and of course she competed with my mother.

'I'm not hungry,' I said before she could offer me anything.

'How's your fiancée?' Mouna asked. She always spoke with a coarse grumble, like Vin Diesel in *The Fast and the Furious*.

'How's *yours*?' I replied. That's Arabs for you, Kahlil – we were all engaged by twenty-two. In my case it was to get over Sahara;

in Mouna's case it was to conceal the fact that she was totally into girls. Her fiancé's name was Ali, a skinny panel beater from Syria whom she'd only ever seen in photographs and spoken to on the phone. He would be flying to Australia in six weeks with the intention of marrying Mouna immediately to secure his visa.

I turned to Noor with a smirk. 'How's the Nips?' Mouna tried to hold back a laugh and coughed to cover it. Noor was a manager at the Marrickville KFC and only ever dated the Viet chicks who worked for him. All of Noor's friends were Viets too – he claimed to have Asian connections in Cabramatta. My obese cousin didn't respond to my question; just stared at me with machetes in his eyes. Here we go, *Street Fighter* all over again.

The back shutter-door clapped open and my cousin Zane walked through the living room and down the corridor that led to the bedrooms. Three seconds later he reappeared with his phone in his hand. 'How ya doin', aye, cuz?' he mumbled, walking by without looking at me.

'Hectic,' I replied, staring at Zane's upper-half as he left the way he came in. He was a five-foot-five short-arse with the head of a wrestler, disproportionately smaller than his body, and biceps that bulged out of his tight black T-shirt like rockmelons.

I turned back to Mouna and Noor. 'Yous wanna go to the movies tonight?'

'How bout we watch that new Schwarzeneg—' Mouna began, when suddenly, there was a high-pitched scream from outside. I thought nothing of it at first but Mouna's face instantly transformed before me. Her harsh cheeks compressed and her brown eyes closed in on themselves, her mouth retracted, and her ears sprung to life, shooting up and opening and taking over her entire body, like giant

138

sonars sweeping through the walls to the kerb. I was about to ask her what was wrong but she popped to her feet and shot straight out the back door. And I was right behind her, sprinting down the side path of the house, no idea why ...

Mouna tumbled onto the kerb screaming, 'Get off him! Get off him!' She collided into two figures ripping each other apart on the nature strip like a pair of pit bulls. I should have jumped right on top too, but instead I froze and watched: you see, no man was going to hurl me to jahanam unless it was fated. 'Get off him!' Mouna screamed out again. Then, past me and into the pile was Abu Zack, who had been fast asleep on his La-Z-Boy just a second ago, and Aunt Yasmine, who just had her head in a pot, and my cousin Noor, staggering like a stunted rhino behind them. Em George was standing in front of her house moaning, 'Aam yet telou baa'doun! – They're killing each other!' as her son Kenny sprinted out from the side gate of his house into the scrum like a rugby player. There was pulling and tugging and the sharp sound of a cloth tearing and then the collective scream, 'Get off him!'

Suddenly my cousin Zane stumbled back towards me, shirt ripped wide open, wobbling, groaning, 'Ooaagh.' Everybody in the huddle broke free and spread across the street like skittles, and from the centre of the brawl emerged Koda, his tree-trunk-thick arms swinging and his bald head scraping the moonlight, screaming, 'You're dead, dog cunt, you're fucken dead!' Koda looked like he was made of rock, his face stretched out as though someone had pulled his skin tight and pinned it to the back of his head. His teeth were transparent and jagged like pieces of glass and his traps had completely engulfed his neck. Koda's mother was the younger sister of Abu Zack, making him Zane's first cousin.

They were supposed to be bum-chums; they went to Fitness First together every weeknight, went clubbing together every Saturday night, and went to brothels together every Sunday night. On one occasion I had even caught them outside the toilet at Greenacre Park injecting roids into each other's arse cheeks.

Koda looked around the street and caught sight of me, still frozen, as though I was in the presence of a demon. 'Go tha fuck home!' Mouna shouted at him, stepping in between us. Koda could have knocked Mouna out cold with a single blow, but instead he turned away from her and tromped across the street. Abu Zack limped up beside his daughter and onto the road. He was wearing a white bandage around his right leg, having recently fallen from a roof after taking a new job cleaning gutters. 'You attack my son in front of me, yaa sharmout!' he shouted. 'Sharmout' was the Arabic word for 'male slut' – unlike in English, both women and men could be labelled hoes in our language. Suddenly, Abu Zack raised his arm and threw an over-the-top jab to the back of his nephew's head. In one motion Koda ducked before the shot landed on him and turned to face his uncle. Just like everyone else on the street, my auntie's husband was no match for Koda; he must have been deeply insulted to risk getting into a fistfight with him. This man was an old-school Arab from Syria, where dishonour was worse than death. 'My son! My house!' Abu Zack bellowed.

'I'm gonna snap him in half!' Koda spat back, pounding his hands upon his Herculean chest.

'I said fuck home!' Mouna screamed over the two of them, re-emerging alongside her father.

At last, Koda found himself up against his old Camry, parked across the street from my aunt's house. You'd imagine a psycho

Lebo such as Koda driving a sports car, like an RX-7 or a Rexy, but cops pull over Lebs who stand out. Koda opened his car door and got in backwards – facing all of us on the street – but as he was about to close it, Abu Zack slammed the door shut, shoving its weight against Koda's right shoulder. 'Rooh, yaa kalb!' he shouted. 'Be gone, you dog!'

Koda's face was seething, like a snake in the hills, guarding its hole, bloated with poison. He revved the engine and reversed, colliding with the parked car behind him. Then he tipped the wheel and accelerated towards us. A collective gasp shot through Lakemba: 'Whoa-shit-wait-jeez-god-ghuh.' I ran to the left and Mouna ran to the right. Abu Zack ran towards his house as the Camry dipped into the road, front bumper clipping his heel. He fell and rolled like a sack, like a man wrapped in a body bag.

'Fucken cunt!' Mouna screamed. She kicked Koda's door as the Camry passed her and disappeared into the darkness of Caitlin Street. Moonshine is blinding. And only Allah sees all ...

FIFTEEN

EVEN FOR A BUNCH of Sand Coons, Koda was savage. Did he not fear God, from whom he could not hide? I watched as Mouna rushed onto the asphalt to help up her father. I should have been helping too, but once again I was stagnant; longing for the fist on the punching bag and the rumble of the speedball slamming against the dashboard and the swinging of the leather skipping rope scraping the concrete and the blue-eyed puncture of the something something|reverberating through the soft cartilage in the centre of my face. I forced myself onto the footpath like a jahash, legs shuddering from my kneecaps to my heels. I couldn't believe that freak tried to run us over.

'Oi Bani,' a smooth voice hooted at me from between Aunt Yasmine and Em George. My neighbour Saaf stepped up into my face, so close that I could smell the VB on his breath. He must have heard the shouting from down the street. 'Shu fee?' he asked. 'What's up?'

I looked around, disorientated. Was he talking to me? Where was Zane? Noor? Kenny? 'Ah, the boys, fight,' I shrugged.

'Who?' Saaf asked.

I kept scanning, trying to pinpoint everyone on the street, when suddenly Noor's white Holden Commodore swept down the road. Screams of muffled English could be heard from inside.

'Who fought?' Saaf asked again.

'Koda and one of the twins,' I mumbled, finally bolting my line of sight onto Zane. He was standing with Kenny, who was a short-arse just like him, in front of his ute, head cocked up at the first star to appear that evening, groaning like a wounded cow.

'Aren't they cousins?' Saaf pressed.

I didn't answer, continuing to probe the street, trying to identify where everyone had ended up. Abu Zack was limping against Mouna on the nature strip, his arm over her neck. A stabbing pain engulfed my loins. I saw on my butch cousin's traps the wide masculine shoulders of my ex-girlfriend, who used to wander the alleyways of Glebe in her wife-beater on muggy evenings. Kahlil – we are but Arabs.

Noor's car rushed past again from the other end of the street, and this time, as he swept by, I heard him scream out, 'Come now!' before the vehicle swished away. Zane stumbled up the back of his house behind his father and his sister, Aunt Yasmine and Em George behind him, and Saaf and Kenny behind them. I was left standing on the street alone as Noor's Commodore roared past for the third time. 'Fucken come down, now!' Noor screamed. I wasn't sure who he was addressing, but if I had to guess, he was pretending to be on his mobile phone ordering his imaginary Asian gangsta connections to mobilise and draw their machetes.

Once the street was empty, I sprinted down the road towards Bilal's brand-new house, where he had been living comfortably with his new wife for almost six months now. I was grateful in that moment that my dad intended to do the same for me one day: build me a brick house on the other side of Caitlin Street, which I would move into after Fatima and I were married. It was nice to know we'd all be so close in an emergency. I ran through my brother's front gate and banged on his double glass door. 'Bilal!' I hollered. 'Bilal!'

I pulled out my phone and called him. It rang for a full minute with no answer. The lights were on, so he must have been home with his wife – newlyweds of The Tribe rarely strayed far from each other in that first year of marriage. I called again. This time he answered before it even rang. 'What, bro? I'm in da shower.'

'Koda and Zane punched on!' I shouted. Then my phone dropped out. I was about to dial his number again but before I could Bilal burst out of the front door dripping wet in a pair of shorts and a singlet. He was wearing one shoe and sliding the other on as he dashed past me.

'Come on, let's go!' he yelled.

'Wait,' I called. 'Wait …' It was too late, Bilal was already halfway down the street and I raced after him.

My brother ran in through the back door to our aunt's house. 'Where is he? Where is he?' he growled. Bilal was not as big as Koda or Zane, but he was just as strong, having recently reached a bench press of one hundred and thirty kilos – not bad for a seventy-five-kilo boy who wasn't on roids.

The family was dotted across the living room and the kitchen, Aunt Yasmine and Abu Zack and Mouna and our neighbours Em George and Kenny and Saaf. My cousin Zane was at the centre of their attention, standing in front of the LCD TV like he'd been

144

arse-fucked. I couldn't see it when he was outside in the dark, but in the living room, under the fluorescent downlights that bounced off the white Woggy tiles, it looked as though Zane was just mauled by a gorilla. His freshly waxed chest, gleaming from his torn shirt, was covered in bright ruddy scars. There were lumps and bruises throbbing on his forehead. The entire left side of his face was orange and flattened. His nose was swollen and bleeding and there was a sharp gash across its tip. And Jesus – his right eye! It was gouged and had turned completely red from the inside, like Koda had pushed his whole thumb into the socket. My brother expressed his concern in slow motion: 'Maaaaan, faaark, oouufff, are youuuu okaaaay, cuz?' I could hear Aunt Yasmine inside the kitchen, saying, 'Look, look, look, his eyes,' and Em George moaning back, 'They screaming "fucken dog" and then they killing each other.'

My cousin walked in circles like he was on speed, groaning as everyone's gaze followed him. Abruptly a phone went off, and Zane pulled his Nokia from his pocket before the ringtone could echo through the living room. 'What!' he screamed into the phone. 'Dogs die?'

'Koda, ya shaytaan!' Mouna shouted, her voice chafing like sandpaper. 'Eat shit.'

Zane ended the call and looked around the room, from one Arab nose to the other. 'He told me dogs die ...'

Just then my phone rang from inside my pocket too, Tupac calling out 'Westside' and 'Motherfucker' and 'Right here'. Everyone snapped towards me. It was like we'd all become rodents, senses super alert.

Kenny stared up at me from the white leather couch, his dark-olive face squeezing. 'Is it Koda?' he asked. What a donkey question. As if I'd give a piece of shit like Koda my number. We were not related! Wahyaat Allah, Koda and I were not related! I shook my head and walked outside, taking the phone out of my pocket and answering on the back porch. 'Lek shu?'

'Aye, brah.' It was my cousin Noor. He sounded furious, but I knew his schtick too well to believe him. 'I called my connections from Cabramatta,' he told me. 'They're coming down to Koda's house with hockey sticks.'

He was full of crap but I played along anyway. 'It's all right, cuz, just relax your ball sacks.' I stared at one of the plastic chairs on my aunt's porch; it had a dick drawn on it in liquid paper. Hundred-dollar bet my cousin Mouna drew it – ever since we were kids she'd been obsessed with dicks, having kneed mine several times.

'Nutt,' continued Noor. 'I was gonna let it go but when that snake tried to run us over – they're coming down, watch, they're waiting for him!'

The phone went silent and not even a second after Noor had hung up, it rang again, this time my fiancée's name flashing on the screen. At first, I just stared at the phone while it vibrated in my hand. I didn't know what to say to Fatima. She was going to do what she always did: call with a list of complaints about her father and beg me to marry her tomorrow so she could be free to get a belly ring. With each groan I'd have to find the right words to make everything better – 'Just hang in there, baby,' and 'We'll be married soon, baby,' and 'Want me to knock your dad out for ya, baby?' The phone kept ringing and I imagined Fatima on the other end, innocently unaware that the one person in her life she could depend on was deliberately ignoring her call. At last I put the phone to my ear. 'Hey, what's wrong, what's happened, what do you need?'

There was a drawn-out delay, and I could hear Fatima breathing gently on the other end as she absorbed the frenetic energy of my voice. 'Why have you answered me, dear heart, with all these questions? I promise you I will do everything just as you ask. But come closer. Let us give in to grief, however briefly, in each other's arms.' Then she giggled, and hung up. Hearing *The Iliad* slip through her lips, I could have cried. All at once and for the first time and finally, I had met the woman I was going to marry. I wished I could disappear with Fatima right then; hidden in an oasis within the deserts of our ancestors, I would rest in her arms and listen to her breathing and her heart beating inside her chest, and together we would both be free from our families. Spare me your pity, oh child of iliads and odysseys – this was the best I could imagine for myself; the best I could imagine before hearing the sound of your breath.

I walked back into my aunt's house, where Saaf was telling Zane, 'We can call some of the brothers down if you want.' Saaf and Zane were not really friends, but they were around the same age and had gone to Punchbowl Boys, so maybe they were connected to the same crew. Zane's phone rang again, and Mouna snatched it from his hand and pegged it across the room. It hit the laundry door and smacked onto the tiles. Aunt Yasmine looked to my brother. 'Please, can you take him to the doctor?' The phone stopped ringing and Abu Zack said in Arabic, 'Yalla Zaan, a'l mastashfa,' which meant 'Come on, Zane, off to the hospital.' Abu Zack was in his La-Z-Boy again, reclined with his bandaged right leg up.

'No, I'm all right, no!' Zane said as he paced up and down the living room. Em George wobbled up to him, held him by the shoulders and said calmly, 'Zaan, have some pity for your mother.'

Right then, my brother's wife, Mandy, bounced in through the back shutter like a walking bobblehead – her ginormous chest and gushing red hair flailing before us. 'What happened?' she shrilled with a smirk, like she was excited.

Mouna grabbed Zane's arm and tugged him towards the back door. 'You're goin' to da hospital,' she said.

Bilal looked to his wife. 'I'm gonna go with 'em,' he told her, running out after our cousins.

From the floor near the laundry, Zane's phone rang again, *da-ren, da-ren, da-ren, da re-re-re-re da-ren* ... 'Mexican Hat Dance' on repeat. Everyone in the house turned to look at it, the phone vibrating as though it were possessed by the djinn – a demon of smokeless fire. It stopped and three seconds later it started over. *Da-ren, da-ren, da-ren, da re-re-re-re da-ren* ... Finally I picked it up, a Nokia 8850 with a titanium cover and a blue screen like the one I had in high school. The name King Koda flashed blue in my face, taunting me, tormenting me, *hectoring* me. 'Argh,' I blurted, rejecting the call and shoving the phone into my pocket.

'Hal taleephaan, taleephaan,' whined Em George. 'That telephone, telephone.' She stumbled into the kitchen to join Aunt Yasmine, who was back at her stove, stirring her pot. Mandy made for the kitchen as well, a cocky smile still slapped on her face. Since she got married she'd become a true Lakemba woman, domesticated and bored out of her brain; nothing to do except linger in front of the pots and gossip.

That night, the gossip was about Dalia Yusuf – my cousin Zane's new woman, the sixth daughter of Sheikh Abu Taj from Guildford. I'd never met her but everyone in The Tribe said she looked like J-Lo. The women talked about her glowing skin and shining hair and big green eyes, and the boys talked about her bubble-shaped arse and dome-shaped titties. Aunt Yasmine said that Koda was jealous because Dalia chose her son over him. *Is she serious? This is all about a girl? How insipidly predictable!* I couldn't believe a chick would come between Zane and Koda.

Having heard enough talk, Abu Zack erupted from his La-Z-Boy and limped over to the landline. He dialled some numbers and straightaway shouted into the phone, 'Layki Sanaat, you tell son not come my house anymore, you understan!' Kenny and Saaf huddled around Abu Zack like a wolf pack as he waited for the person on the other end, who I presumed was his younger sister, Sanaat, to respond. She was so loud I could hear her muffled voice screaming back at him from my position at the other end of the living room: 'On his way … shoot yous … because of that sharmouta!'

'What? What? Coming back? Gonna shoot us?' Abu Zack repeated. I remembered one time when Mouna and I were hanging outside her front porch, and Koda pulled into the driveway. While waiting for Zane to come out of the house, he wound down his window, tilted a pair of freshly plucked eyebrows at me and said, 'I sleep with an uzi under my pillow, cuz.' I took him seriously, but it was hard to believe that he'd actually cap his cousin over some chick. For god's sake, who was this princess supposed to be, the Face that Launched a Thousand WRXs? *Well, fuck it then*, I thought. *Let us die – but not without struggle, not without glory, in a clash of fists that even Lebs coming will hear of down the years!*

Abu Zack hung up the phone. 'Call the police,' he garbled into the air. 'Call the police!'

It's hard to know why everyone seemed to mutually agree that I would be the one to call the cops (maybe because my family thought this required some level of university education), but either way, I was careful not to make the call on my own phone, and instead decided to use my cousin's 8850, which was still in my pocket. Running back outside onto the nature strip, I punched in triple zero and contemplated whether I should push the dial key. Was I being a hard cunt right now or a pussy cunt? Why did I freeze in the fight? Why didn't I throw any punches? Was it because I was a wuss? Because I was afraid of Koda? Because I knew I couldn't beat him, just like Hector knew he could not beat Achilles, and Paris knew he could not beat Menelaus? What if Koda had been on top of *my brother*? What if he had been on top of *my fiancée*?

I was nineteen the first time I met Koda; he'd been loitering in the carpark at the back of Zane's unit in Yagoona. I was watching him from the top of the stairwell when out of nowhere, he hoisted himself up onto a sharp dusty beam and started doing chin-ups.

'What's the point of that, bro?' I asked, looking down at him.

Koda slowly lowered himself from the beam and stared up at me. 'What do you mean?' he scoffed; teeth clenched.

'I *mean*, what's the point of jumping up on a beam and randomly doing chin-ups?'

He grimaced and said, 'Look at me, look at you ...'

Back on the nature strip, my thumb still hovering over the dial key, I decided to take Koda up on his offer – to see him and to see myself. The phone rumbled inside my ear, and I counted each ring, *one ... two ... three ... four ...* until there was an answer.

'I need the police to come,' I told the operator.

'Why?' she asked.

'We need the police,' I said.

'What happened?' She spoke slowly, like it was just another Tuesday night.

'I need the police. There was a brawl. I need the police. Seventy-four Caitlin Street. They're gonna shoot my cousin.'

'Who?'

'His cousin, my cousin's cousin, he's gonna shoot my cousin!'

'Is he there?'

'No, no, he's coming, with an uzi. He just bashed him.'

'What's your name?' she asked.

'Why?'

'I need a name.'

Great, I was gonna tell her my name was Bani Adam, and then she was gonna think, *Typical Muslims!* 'Benny,' I said.

'And is this your phone, is that your number?'

'Yes,' I lied.

'I'll dispatch a unit now,' the operator told me. Then she proceeded to give me more information, which I didn't hear because I was staring into the darkness where a figure was materialising from the direction of my parents' house. I ended the call as my father's moustache appeared before me.

'Shu suar?' Dad asked calmly.

'Koda and Zane ...' I began to explain, and he nodded as though he already knew, and strode up his sister's driveway. He looked around and found an old shovel up against the garage door. It was short and covered in dried cement, with a thick metal head and a solid wooden handle. My father walked back past me with the shovel in his hands and headed for the front door of his sister's house. I grabbed his arm, which was dense as concrete, and tugged him towards me. When Dad was my age, he would have gone the distance against Koda, having grown up on the streets of Redfern, rumbling with junkies and roid-munchers every night. Now I wasn't so sure. 'What are you doing?' I hissed at him. 'Go home and look after *our* family.'

My father's pitch-black eyes closed in on me. 'This *is* our family,' he said. 'You think I'm gonna let that poofta hurt my nephew?' Then he disappeared through the front door of the house, the light from inside engulfing him.

A phone rang again. At first I thought it was Zane's, which was still in my hand, but then I realised it was mine, Tupac cussing from my pocket. I pulled it out and read the flashing screen: *Incoming call, Noor.* For fuck's sake, as if we had time for his ADHD right now. 'Yeah, cuz?'

'Aye cuz, I'm outside Koda's house.'

'What are you doing there?' I asked, casually. He was probably parked around the corner in front of Lakemba Public School.

'I'm waiting for the boys. They're coming with hockey sticks. They're coming from Cabra.'

'It's okay, cuz, just drive back. It's okay.'

'Aye, is my dad there?' Noor asked.

'No. Why? Did you call him?'

Noor didn't respond, hanging up on me instead. And just as he did, a grey station wagon pulled up in front of Em

George's house. It was Noor's father, Uncle Ehud. I couldn't believe Noor went squealing to him. Uncle Ehud had recently been diagnosed with kidney disease and was on dialysis four days a week; like he needed this bullshit right now. My uncle slowly got out of his car and drifted towards me. He was a cross between Santa Claus and Zeus, with a teddy-bear face and a large stomach and broad shoulders; a godlike figure in our family. To understand how he had acquired this position, I need to take you back, Kahlil, before Lakemba, to Lebanon. Your great-grandparents lived in a building in Al-Jabal, The Mountain, where they were raising eleven children. We liked to pretend they fled to Australia because of the Civil War, which erupted in 1975, but they actually fled from a war within our own family seven years earlier. One of my aunts, Mariam, who was a child at the time, had informed my grandfather that his oldest brother, Taahir, had been sexually abusing her. My father told me that Jidoo was devastated to have heard this, but rather than take any action, he began plans to relocate his kids and my grandmother to Australia.

'Dad, why can't we just take back the words in *Lolita*,' I cried, 'make them safe for our children?'

Your grandfather looked at me like a simple, noble-winged seraph caught in a tangle of thorns. 'Huh? What the hell are you talking about?'

'The police,' I said. 'Why didn't Jidoo just report his brother to the police?'

'Are you a majnun?' Dad spat back. 'You don't ever, ever, ever dob your own family in to the police, do you understand, never, never, never!'

Two and a half years after my grandfather arrived in Australia, and six months after the rest of the family arrived in Sydney, Jidoo had a heart attack in the living room and dropped dead in front of my grandmother and all his children. He was the first Muslim Alawite to die in Australia, and at age nineteen, Uncle Ehud became the head of the family. He said to me that it was his responsibility to financially provide for my grandmother and raise his siblings.

'Is Noor all good?' I asked as Uncle Ehud approached.

'He is okay,' my uncle said soothingly, nodding. 'He's just upset for his cousin.' Uncle Ehud began to make his way up his sister's driveway.

'Amu,' I called to him. 'Hallat, they're saying Koda's coming back.'

Uncle Ehud turned to face me, wide-eyed. 'Look, Bani, don't get involved, all right.' I considered Uncle Ehud to be my grandfather – his words were the law. 'They're cousins, relatives,' he said. 'They'll fight but they'll forgive each other. You're not related to Koda. He won't pardon you ...'

Then my uncle's eyes veered to the left. Another car pulled up and out leaped Zane's twin brother, Zack. Zane and Zack looked exactly alike, same height and same oval-shaped head, but Zack had stopped using steroids after he got married a few years ago, so he was now thinner and softer than his six-minute-younger brother.

Gina also slipped out of the car and waddled around to the kerb. She was Zack's wife and first cousin, a curly-haired mail-order bride from Syria. 'Go inside,' Zack instructed her, and she did as she was told without comment. The power dynamic between the two was no coincidence; three years earlier, Zack had shown me a picture of his bride-to-be standing in front of her family home in Damascus and said, 'The girls in Australia are skanks, cuz. You see this girl here, when she arrives, I'm gonna have her under my thumb!' Gina half-smiled at me as she passed. I always felt sorry for our sisters in Syria and Lebanon, who were so desperate to migrate to Australia that they would happily marry the rejects in our tribe, whom no one else wanted. In one particular case, my dimwitted second cousin Usuf, from Penrith, was married off to a girl named Ferdous from the mountains in Lebanon. Three months after they were married and she moved to Australia, Usuf spread a rumour that she wasn't a virgin and sent her on a cheap flight back to the Middle East. Shortly after, I heard from my sister, who heard from my mum, who heard from her mum, who heard from her sister, who heard from her daughter, who heard from her second cousin, that Ferdous had been killed when a bomb hit her building while she was showering, loose ceiling cables falling into the basin and electrocuting her to death.

'Where's Zane?' Zack asked.

'They took him to the hospital.'

Zack pulled out his phone and made a call while Uncle Ehud and I watched on. 'Listen ...' he began, but he was immediately interrupted at the other end. 'Can I just talk to you? Listen, just listen, Ramsey, just listen.'

I snapped towards my uncle. 'Who's he talking to?'

'I think this is Koda's younger brother,' Uncle Ehud told me, keeping his eyes on Zack.

'All right – would you just relax?' Zack continued. 'He's not a dog, it's *her* choice, cuz ...'

A moment later Mouna pulled her brother's ute back into the driveway, Zane sitting in the passenger seat with his head slanted upwards. Zack ended his call and rushed over, opening the passenger door and peering at his brother. They didn't look like twins anymore, not after the thrashing Zane had copped.

Mouna emerged from the driver's seat, quickly followed by Bilal, who was sitting in the middle seat. 'Koda just called me, he's on his way back!' my brother shouted. 'We're gonna drop him. Hallat, we're gonna drop him.' He hadn't been this hyped up since he'd thrown that box of mandarins in the air.

'Ramsey's bringing soldiers down,' Zack said.

'Soldiers?' I blurted, unable to hold my tongue any longer. 'Tell him to fucken go back to the fucken Crusades, the sad fuck!' I felt my uncle Ehud's hand ease gently onto my back. 'Stay calm,' he whispered into my ear.

'Good,' Bilal said. 'Better to clash in battle, now, at once – *see* which fighter Allah rewards the glory.' I may have romanticised *The Iliad*, but my brother had romanticised *Troy* and Achilles and Brad Pitt. He started bouncing around on the street like a hound-dog. 'Y'know what, bro,' he said out loud. 'Me and one bloke had a big fight over a skank once, but my hands will never do battle for a bitch again.' Then Bilal turned to face my aunt's house. 'Maaaan-daay!' he bellowed.

I remembered the cops, still on their way. Shit, shit, shit. Maybe I shouldn't have called them. Maybe we should have just sorted this out within the family. Shit. Shit. 'Why are yous back?' I asked Mouna, but it came out anxiously, like I was scared. She was standing against the edge of the bonnet, her sharp jaw and cheekbones penetrating the hazy street lights. 'I thought you were going to the hospital.'

'These gronks couldn't be bothered waiting,' Mouna replied bluntly.

Zane stepped out of the car carefully with his brother's assistance and stumbled over towards me. His eye was still red and the lumps on his forehead were still bulging, but at least his nose had stopped bleeding. 'Aye cuz, do you know where my phone is?'

'Here-ya,' I said, giving it to him. I wondered what he'd think when he checked his call log. The last dialled number was 000. The rest were missed calls from King Koda.

Zane looked around – his twin brother to his cousins to his uncle. 'Oi listen, I think I'm gonna go spend the night at Dalia's,' he mumbled with a strained voice. 'They won't do anything if I'm gone.' He eased his gaze onto Mouna. 'Sis, move my ute. Park it in the next street. I'm gonna get Amu Ehud to give me a lift.' Then Zane turned back to me. 'Thanks for everything, cuz,' he said. I was so ashamed of myself. Why was he thanking me? I dogged him. Froze. Pussied out. Just stood there and watched him cop a belting. I spent so much time trying to rid myself of the rage that came with being an Arab man, that I had also lost the strength that came with being one. Perhaps that is what the awkward White girl back at the PCYC meant when she had said, 'But – but I like your nose.' I could hear her calling to me, asking me was the nose job worth it. And all I wanted to do was sprint back into the gym chanting, 'Something Something,' as I tumbled towards the punching bags, swinging until the breath left my bones ...

'Maaaandy!' Bilal called again, his wife finally darting her watermelon-shaped head out of the house. 'Seriously, you gotta go home.'

'Hey,' she said, ignoring him. She walked down to the nature strip and picked up a small brown object. 'It's a wallet,' she grinned, ecstatic.

'It belongs to Koda,' Zane explained. I think that was the first time he'd ever spoken to her. It's like that with Wogs – there are so many cousins and second cousins and third cousins, and everyone is freshly married and having kids, so you end up with relatives living in your own street who you never get round to knowing.

Mandy opened the wallet and looked inside, tilting it towards the streetlight. 'No, no, it's not his. It's, it's, En-riq-uue Gon-zaaa-les?'

'That's *him*,' Zane said. And then I remembered the time Koda bragged in front of my brother, our cousins and me that he'd had his licence revoked for a hundred and fifty years. He must have changed his name after that.

'There's a lot of money in it,' Mandy said.

My brother frowned at her, snatching the wallet from her pudgy fingers and putting it in his pocket.

Zane staggered back up the driveway with his twin brother beside him. At the same time, Mouna started up the ute and reversed it into the street, taking off around the corner. Bilal followed Zane. Mandy followed Bilal. Seconds later my father stepped out of the front door to greet Uncle Ehud, but without the shovel he collected on his way into the house. I watched my relatives move on and off Caitlin Street as if it were an episode of *Neighbours* – if *Neighbours* weren't so lame and shit and White.

Quietly, I began to stroll down the street, wanting to be the first to see the cops. Maybe I could tell them it was all sorted and they would leave.

I walked through the darkness, blinked and *he* emerged – Koda standing right there in my face. 'Oi, get my wallet,' he said firmly.

'Ah ... ah,' I stuttered. He stared at me while I fumbled for words like a weasel. 'Yeah, yeah, no worries.' I turned and ran back, my heart alliterating: *Coppers coming. Coppers coming. Coppers coming.* Koda was going to go nuts if he knew I had called them – I'd be a dog, and dogs die, that's what he said. My dad and uncle were whispering to each other on the nature strip when I zipped past. I rushed up into my aunt's house, onto the patio, where Zack's wife, Gina, was resting on one of the plastic chairs with her head back and belly out, like she might have been pregnant. Her father was a commando for Hafez al-Assad, the first Alawite president of Syria, and he had been shot in the head, right between his eyes, by a Salafi one morning while he was walking Gina and her three sisters to school. I gave her no acknowledgement as I ran through the back shutter, knowing full well that the problems on Caitlin Street were as insignificant to her as two ants fighting between a crack in some concrete.

'Bilal, give me Koda's wallet!' I shouted.

Bilal twisted. 'Why?'

'Koda's outside. He wants it.'

Nine noses snapped at me. 'Where is he?' Zack asked.

I ignored the question, barking, 'Give it!'

My brother pulled Koda's wallet out from his pocket and slapped it into my palm like he was giving me a high-five.

I turned and ran back outside. Koda was standing in front of my father and Uncle Ehud now. 'It's okay, nephew,' Uncle Ehud was telling him in Arabic. 'You're family, he's your blood.'

'You don't know Zane,' Koda seethed as I rushed up to him. 'He's a dog. He told her I was in a porno, sucking cocks!'

Holy fuck! The comment jarred me like a punch in the face, reverting me to the kind of teenage Sand Coon you only ever heard along the train lines between Belmore and Bankstown: *Yeah, that's dog, bro, that's so fucken dog.*

Shaking my head, I stepped up and handed Koda the wallet. 'Here, cuz.' I needed to get him out of there as quickly as possible. He took it from me without making eye contact and walked across the street, towards his Camry. But then Zane and Zack and Bilal and Abu Zack and Kenny and Saaf and Aunt Yasmine and Em George and Mandy and Gina all came pouring out of the house as though it were bush week.

Koda swivelled and honed in on Zane. 'I'm not finished with you, dog-cunt-bitch,' he spluttered, pointing his finger at Zane like it was an arrow.

Out of the darkness, Mouna, who had returned from parking the ute, hurtled towards Koda. 'Pussy cunt!' she screamed. Straightaway my brother and I jumped on Mouna, grasping her by the shoulders and dragging her back with all our strength. Our cousin was muscular and grounded for a chick, as forceful as any man I had ever tussled with. 'Easy, sis, easy!' my brother screeched.

'You think I won't slap a bitch?' said Koda, throwing his arms into the air and leaping towards Mouna.

My father and Saaf and Kenny and Zack charged, colliding with Koda and pushing him back towards his car, where they pinned him against the door. 'Aaaarggh!' Koda screamed, throwing them off him one by one as though they were pieces of bread. The men dispersed across the street while Koda went crazy, swinging his arms like a 21-year-old Mike Tyson into the driver's side window of his car. Phack! Phack! Phack! The glass shattered and the sound ricocheted through all of Caitlin Street and all of Lakemba. Finally, Koda stopped, arms throbbing out in front of him as he took fast breaths in and out, looking around from one man to another, ready to take us all.

Slowly, very slowly, Uncle Ehud approached him. He reached his hands out and placed them over Koda's arms. 'It's okay, nephew,' Amu Ehud said in Arabic. 'Please come inside with me now and make a binding oath with your cousin to put this behind you.'

'A binding oath?' Koda replied, pulling Uncle Ehud's hands away from him. 'There are no binding oaths between men and dogs!'

Head and chest cocked, Koda got into his car, unfazed by the pieces of window all over his seat, and ignited the engine. He reversed a few metres and twisted the vehicle towards Uncle Ehud, shards of glass, spread all over the road, crackling beneath the tyres as they rolled and spun.

'Run!' Mouna shouted to everyone.

'Amu, Amu …' I grabbed Uncle Ehud's arm and tugged him towards me, but he didn't move, standing his ground like Tank Man, the Tiananmen Square protestor. Inside the shitbox, Koda's blackened gaze fixed on Uncle Ehud as he accelerated towards him. I blinked in dread, unable to watch. The engine let out a resounding roar, the voice of a thousand stone lions guarding the houses of the south-west springing to life. I opened my eyes a second later and the Camry had stopped an inch from Uncle Ehud's knees. Koda withdrew down the road, straightened his tyres and took off on a burnout.

The shitbox vanished beneath the smoke and smell of burning rubber from one end of the street as red and blue lights flashed from the other end. A police car slowed down and double-parked alongside Uncle Ehud's station wagon. We huddled together on the nature strip as three police officers stepped out; two male officers from the front and a large female officer from the back, who had a smug wince across her face and a thick Magnum torch in her hand. Her hips bounced with each step towards us; giant belt holstered at her waist, flaunting a gun, cuffs, capsicum spray, and a thick black baton. She stopped before Zane and stared down at him. One of the male cops, who was scrawny and bald, stood to the left of her and the other male cop, who was pudgy and wrinkled, stood to the right. *Why are they always Crackers? Why aren't there ever any ethnics on the force?* The red and blue lights of the police car flickered silently into the night, amplified against the shadows of Caitlin Street.

The cops waited while our entire mob lined up on the nature strip and then the female officer flicked on her torch and zoomed it around from Arab to Arab before stopping on Zane. Behind her, a Camry with a broken driver's side window slid towards Aunt Yasmine's house and, at the sight of the cop car, continued moving down the street. Zane slipped his phone into his pocket and looked up at the officer. She stared down at his short-arse with the torch poised on his face, moving it slightly from Zane's eye to his forehead, to his nose and then back to his eye. She squinted and said, 'So, what 'appened?' He didn't say anything. She looked around at the rest of us again, pointing the torch at my cousin and cousin and cousin, and then at me and my brother and my father, and then at my aunt and my aunt's husband, and at my uncle and my sister-in-law and cousin-in-law, and at my neighbour and neighbour and neighbour. Nobody said anything. She looked back at Zane. 'How did this happen?' she asked. Zane didn't reply. 'Do you know the person who did it?' No reply. She stared at him for a few more seconds, examining his wounds. I knew what she was thinking: *Ya bunch of Bin Ladens.* And I knew what we were all thinking: *Just keep our mouths shut and the police will piss off* ... But then the phone in Zane's pocket rang, and the Mexicans began their hat dance: *Da-ren, da-ren, da-ren, da re-re-re-re da-ren.*

The officer glared at Zane. 'Are you gonna answer that?' Zane stared at her as if he had stitches woven through his mouth. Finally, the ringing stopped, and it was like, *Fuck that was awkward!* Then the hat dance started again, jabbing out each note like we were being punched back to Lebanon, and it was like, *Dumb-cunt-cuz-stop-cunt-stop!* Nobody flinched as the officer raised her eyebrows and said, 'What, can't you hear it? I can hear it, you can't hear it?' But Zane's expression didn't change. No, he couldn't hear it. And neither could the rest of us, not me or Mouna or Zack or Abu Zack or Dad or Bilal or Mandy or Gina or Aunt Yasmine or Em George or Kenny or Uncle Ehud or Saaf. We did not hear the phone ringing. We never heard a thing. Never, never, never.

SIXTEEN

7AM. SOMEWHERE BETWEEN BEING asleep and being on my feet, on the morning of my wedding day, the girl with the cross refused to leave me in peace. Her bubbly accent, whispering with a giggle, 'If you did this to forget me, then you'll never forget me.' Fatima, concentrate on Fatima. I slid the wedding ring onto her finger. White gold. One-carat diamond. Eight thousand dollars. She said, 'My dream came true. Has yours?' As was custom, I also had to buy my own wedding ring. White gold. Four hundred dollars. I said, 'Yes it did.'

8am. Sahara.

9am. Black pants, tailor-made to flare at the bottom, seventies style. White shirt, skin-tight, thin black tie. Black jacket, one button. A huge lump of gel through my hair, coagulating and thickening into black rings. My shoes, black platforms like Prince, so that today Fatima and I would be the same height.

10am. My parents' house was chocked with relatives, three of my dad's sisters from the neighbouring streets and seven of my mum's sisters from Melbourne lined up in shiny dresses covered in diamantés, Medusa hairstyles held together with nine-hundred-and-ninety-nine bobby pins. Four of my dad's brothers in black suits, and four of my mum's brothers in black suits. And cousins, hundreds of cousins, adorned in Tarocash shirts and cleavage-ridden dresses, reeking of perfume and hairspray. The click-clack of leather shoes and high heels against the floor tiles. Voices screaming over each other in an orgy of Arabic and English, 'Alf mabrouk al zawaj,' which means 'A thousand congratulations for the bride and groom,' and 'Biza taula'a,' which means 'Her tits are falling out,' and 'Give me the eyeliner,' and 'Guess who's getting a divorce?' My face covered in lipstick from all the kisses. My hands covered in scabies from all the handshakes. My dad screaming into the phone, 'He's not welcome, tell that son of a bitch, he's not welcome.'

11am. First Leb-for-Hire: the wedding photographer waited on our verandah to be paid. I stuck four thousand dollars cash into his right jeans pocket. His camera began flashing. Second Leb-for-Hire: the video photographer waited on our front porch. I slid four thousand dollars cash into his right jacket pocket. His camera began rolling. All this money, and all the money I had spent on the rest of the wedding, from the invitations to the bridesmaids' dresses to the wedding dress to the groomsmen's suits to the reception flowers to the reception dinner to the reception alcohol that none of us were even supposed to be drinking, I would get back in envelopes filled with cash as wedding gifts from The Tribe. And all the money that was returned to me would go back into my savings account in order to give birth to the next generation of Alawites.

The stretch Hummer arrived out the front of my parents' house with a resounding, 'Beeeeeeeeeeeee!' I paid the Indian driver another two thousand three hundred in cash so he could drive us around for the next six hours like a bunch of sad cunts. My three groomsmen were my brother, who was the best man, Fatima's nineteen-year-old brother, Mahmoud, who was a Lebo on stilts, and my obese cousin Noor, who was already sweating profusely in his two-sizes-too-small black suit. The four of us tumbled into the Hummer, which revealed itself to be a wandering nightclub – full of flashing lights and leather seats and tinted glass and lots of speakers. I would've liked Bucky to be one of my groomsmen, but my family would never have accepted a Greek in the bridal party, who would have to dance with one of my bridesmaid sisters later on, let alone a homosexual. Two dozen cars packed with my parents and aunts and uncles and cousins took off behind us towards Fatima's house, honking nonstop as they drove, filling the western suburbs with the chaos of Lebanon.

12pm. I stood at the centre of the House of Adam as we waited before Fatima's McMansion. Her family, rows of big noses and big breasts and glimmering dresses and gloomy suits, spilled out of the front door, followed by my sister Yocheved in a red bridesmaid's dress, and my sister Lulu in a red bridesmaid's dress, and my sister-in-law-to-be Rima in a red bridesmaid's dress, and a Lebanese drummer with a tubble in his hands, bom-bom-boming into the street. I watched the doorway, nervously counting the seconds until my fiancée, the woman with whom I would spend the rest of my life, appeared. Her stiff glistening hair was pinned proudly into the air, exposing her rose-gold complexion and long elegant neck. Her lips were dipped in bright red lipstick, and her smile, when her mouth spread open, revealed a set of teeth that shone like opals in contrast to her enormous dark eyes and endless eyelashes, which were drenched in thick black mascara. Down past her neck, she wore a pearl necklace, which was nestled between the bones of her décolletage. Fatima's shining white dress was pressed tightly against her balloon breasts and flat stomach, exploding open like the wings of an angel from her hips to her feet, elevated by a pair of white high heels. Perhaps it was her sheer beauty, or perhaps it was the power of The Tribe, which had been holding us in place for the past fifteen hundred years, but in that moment I felt a deep and rich connection to Fatima, a combination of pride and joy and arrogance that came together in the most stubborn love I had ever known, as though the hands of Allah had forced themselves around us.

Swept up in all the emotion, and all the attention, Fatima began to cry. And her mum began to cry. And my mum began to cry. And my father began to cry. Not even the wedding of his first-born son had brought him to tears, but then again, there was never any doubt that Bilal would marry inside The Tribe, never any concern that Bilal would be struck down by our creator.

1pm. Out on the front porch, the godfather was standing before us with his hands behind his back and The Tribe was scattered behind us like a scene from *The Sopranos*. Abu Hassan instructed Fatima to repeat after him in Arabic: 'I offer you myself in marriage and in accordance with the instructions of the Holy Qur'an and the Holy Prophet, peace and blessing be upon him. I pledge, in honesty and with sincerity, to be for you a respectful and faithful wife.' Fatima spoke confidently and pronounced each word fluently, her bright red lips pouting and punctuating each syllable, as though she'd been rehearsing this moment since she hit puberty. Her smile cut back and forth from mine to her parents to her siblings to her aunts to her uncles to her cousins to her second cousins as she rolled with the language of our ancestors. Alhamdulillah. Alhamdulillah. Alhamdulillah. Alhamdulillah.

Abu Hassan turned to me – his hands still behind his back and his gut panning the entire street with him as he moved – and instructed that I also repeat after him in Arabic: 'I pledge, in honesty and sincerity, to be for you a faithful and helpful husband.' I spoke with my voice raised high, fully aware that this was more than a promise to Fatima; this was a promise to every Alawite who had come before us and was to come after us. Allahu Akbar. Allahu Akbar. Allahu Akbar. Allahu Akbar.

Only then did my godfather reveal his hands from behind his back, which this whole time had been holding some papers and an inky black pen attached to a clipboard. He handed the pen to Fatima, held up the clipboard and said, 'Daughter, write your name here.' After she was done, Fatima passed the pen to me, and my godfather held up the clipboard again and said, 'Son, write your name here.' I autographed the document like I was a third-world celebrity on tour – the kind that no one recognises or values except for his own mob – and as my name formed along the dotted line, I felt my brother's muscular hand clench my shoulder. He stuck his mouth against my ear and hissed, 'Sign your life away, bro.' The men called out, 'Mabrouk, mabrouk, mabrouk,' and the women ululated, 'Li-li-li-li-li-li-li-leeeeeee.' Had I been given even a moment to reflect on the gravity of my brother's joke, I might have taken a great deep breath and bolted for my life down the street, but already I was being pushed by my groomsmen into the stretch Hummer, into the next stage of the celebration, while Fatima's bridesmaids shoved her in beside me.

2pm. It had begun to sprinkle, which meant there would be no photos in front of the Harbour Bridge. Instead, our photographer took us to the entrance of a five-star hotel on George Street, where there was an old grand piano in the corner of a granite and marble lobby. 'Girl, sit on piano, and boy, look at her and pretend to play,' the photographer said with a huge crooked grin, incredibly pleased with himself.

'But I'm not into piano,' I said to him.

'No matter,' he replied bluntly, already snapping photos of Fatima, who had side-saddled herself up onto the piano lid. 'I make you look classy.'

I sat on the stool and placed my fingers across the white keys, staring up at my new wife with a contrived smile. The flash of the camera flickered in my eyes as Fatima posed like a supermodel for *Cosmopolitan* – cutesy over the shoulder; serious towards the ceiling. 'Listen, Bani,' Fatima finally said, staring down at me from the shiny lid. 'After we're married, I'm gonna change my name.'

'You wanna take my last name?' I asked, surprised. Though this had become a normal custom among Muslims in the West, one that all women in our tribe had adopted; it was not part of our actual history and culture. None of the Prophet Muhammad's wives had taken his last name, nor did any of his daughters take their husband's last name. 'I think it's better you keep your own surname,' I responded. You see I was certain: *A progressive Muslim man supports his wife to love herself.*

'No, I mean I'm going to change my *first* name,' Fatima stressed. 'It's disgusting.'

My fingers spasmed and pressed down hard on the piano keys, hum reverberating through the lobby and twisting all the old White heads at reception in our direction. *Disgusting? Disgusting!* 'Fatima' is one of the most sacred names in our religion, Kahlil, the name of the Prophet Muhammad's most beloved daughter, whom we affectionately remember as al-Zahra, which means 'the Flower'.

'What do you want to change it to?' I asked my wife, camera flash piercing my retinas.

'Something sexy,' she replied, her grin on the photographer's coiled monobrow. 'Like Chanel.'

Look at how much the West has taught us to hate ourselves that we prefer the name of a handbag to the name of our ancestors. Always take pride in your name, after my mother's father, a hard man who came from an old world; and after the great Lebanese poet Gibran Kahlil Gibran.

'O! Be some other name: what's in a name?' I grunted at Fatima. 'That which we call the Flower by any other name would smell as sweet.' You see I was uncertain: *a progressive Muslim man supports his wife to hate herself.*

Fatima and I stepped out of the hotel lobby and followed the photographer across George Street, back to where our bridal party was waiting beside the Hummer. Behind us, a thin Bogan woman standing at the traffic lights was screeching in ocker at two hotel security guards, 'I just wanted a ciggy, ya cocksuckers, I ain't hookin' ya guests.' Then the Bogan spotted Fatima holding up the front of her massive white dress as she tiptoed across the street with me, and her entire mood and tone shifted, 'Oh my, oh my, you look so fucking gorgeous, darling.'

3pm. Eight milk crates in the Lakemba McDonald's carpark. Fatima, Rima, Yocheved and Lulu sitting with their mouths tipped away from their bodies; and Bilal, Mahmoud, Noor and me sitting with our legs spread open and our mouths inside that space between our knees, shovelling in Big Macs and Quarter Pounders and McChickens.

4pm. Inside the Hummer, heading towards the Grand Royale in Granville. Disco lights flashing as Noor groaned, 'I'm still hungry. Big Mac, need another Big Mac.' Fatima stuck her head out of the sunroof and hollered repeatedly across Canterbury Road, 'I'm so cute!' My sisters staring at me in silence, their sharp frowns screaming, *Your new wife is an idiot!* And they were right, she was an idiot, but here's the thing, Fatima was right too, she was cute; not because she said she was cute, but because she was so dumb not to realise how not cute it was to call herself cute. My brother holding Fatima's brother in a headlock, his biceps bursting through his long-sleeve shirt as he cackled, 'Yulla, give up, cuz.' Rima holding the karaoke microphone, trying to follow the beat

171

of the music blasting through the bass speakers, butchering the words that appeared on the LCD screen – 'A whole new giiiiiiiirl.' I thought she was supposed to be the smart one in the family. It's 'a whole new world', you waste of space. Even if she hadn't seen *Aladdin* a thousand and one times like the rest of us, the words were right there on the fucken screen, right there: A. Whole. New. World. Fuck my life, Kahlil. Fuck my life and pardon the language – this is just how one half of you thinks.

5pm. Waiting anxiously in the green room out the front of the reception. Already tired, and the wedding hadn't even started yet. My gaze on a poster pinned to the wall. It was Pamela Anderson in a red swimsuit during her *Baywatch* days, frighteningly thin waist and flat crotch and humongous chest, bright blonde hair draped across her shoulders. I recognised this poster as part of my childhood. Had bought it from the local newsagent. Walked it home and headed straight for the bathroom. Stared at Pamela's famous fake tits until my dick throbbed in agony. Rubbed fast and hard for a total of seven seconds. A thick white liquid squirting all over my hands. I was so horrified and ashamed that after washing myself up, I went straight to my dad and gave him all my savings, thirteen dollars, and said, 'Please give this to charity.' Pamela was my first. And now that I was married, she would be my last. Why would I need to jerk off ever again? I had a wife now. Sex every night for the rest of my life. Silence among the bridal party, and silence in the reception hall, except for the rising hum of that song they always played behind the Olympic runner, something about chariots and fires and whatever.

6pm. Still waiting. But the air was filling quickly with the murmurs and clinks of family and friends as they arrived at the reception. The grumbling voice of my aunt's husband vibrating through the walls. 'Sharmouta. Sharmouta. Sharmouta.'

7pm. I had seen it many times before, lingering among my relatives, waiting for the doors to blast open amid a sea of drums, the bride and groom emerging and taking their walk down the aisle. But never had I seen it from this angle, lingering anxiously behind the doors with Fatima's bony hand in mine. The bridal party and our parents had already been announced and taken their walk, and now, my heart thumped as the thick ethnic voice of the MC hailed, 'Put your hands together for the new Mr and Mrs Bani Adam.' The white doors flung open and the Arabic drums rumbled and the MC sang, 'Jeena o'jeena o'jeena, jebna'l aroos o'jeena!' – 'We've come, we've come, we've come, we've brought the bride and come!' My veins began twitching, stepped into the hall with my wife – *Holy shit, this is my wedding!* I held her palm tight with my left hand, and waved my right hand in the air as we took our walk towards the dance floor, family member after family member popping up from all round us with the largest smiles I had ever seen, their heels springing and hips tossing and arms waving. Fag among breeders, sheep among wolves, my best man in the closet, Bucky, skipped onto the walkway in a dark-blue suit and pulled my head forward, his lips to my ear. 'Don't you know you're beautiful, Bani.' Then his large head disappeared into an ocean of Arabs, his olive skin and dark eyes and dark hair camouflaged amidst The Tribe. It reminded me of the last time this Greek and this Leb were walking through Haldon Street in

173

Lakemba, the suburb where we both grew up. Bucky had been pointing out all the Wogs and Fobs and Curry-munchers buying fruit and prayer beads, and he said, 'It's not that we're not different, it's just that people look alike.'

Uncle Ehud to my left, nodding gently, a soft smile on closed lips; Uncle Osama right up in front of me, laughing like a hyena as he breathed cigarette smoke in my face; Uncle Ibrahim twitching a cup of whisky in the air, eyes bloodshot before the party had even begun. My cousin Mouna, next to her father, inelegantly standing in a loose brown dress. She wanted to wear jeans but her father had said, 'No dick, no pants.' And standing next to her were the twin brothers, one compact and pudgy, the other compact and muscly. Zane's face had almost healed entirely but I could still see the remnants of a black eye above his right cheekbone and the dent of snapped cartilage at the bridge of his nose. Seven of my mum's sisters were standing in a straight line to my right, like a band of babushka dolls. They wailed, 'Le-le-leeeeeeeeeeeee,' the sound shuddering through my entire body until all at once I had become the beating heart of our tribe. I grabbed Fatima around the waist, lifted her like she was a Disney princess, and twirled her in the air.

8pm. The drumbaki battered like an electrocution and the MC sang, 'Allah-alaq ya seedi,' which meant 'Well done, my master,' and 'Alab dat fi edey,' which meant 'Your heart melted in my hand,' and my dad's youngest sister, Mariam, grabbed my wrist this way, and my mum grabbed my wrist that way, and my father and my new father-in-law popped and trembled their hands in front of me, and my younger smart-alec-dozens-of-cousins from Melbourne kept pinching my arse and slipping into the crowd before I could catch them, and my new wife threw her arms and shoulders from side to side as she tipped herself backwards like she was doing the limbo while her cousin Amir thrusted his hips towards her, and my father's youngest brother, Ali, screamed, 'Yaa Allahu,' and cracked open a can of Tooheys, and my new mother-in-law was lifted into the air, nestling onto her youngest brother's shoulders, hailed from below as though this were *her* wedding, and my mum's oldest sister's husband, Bashar, was flinging a cigar between his fingers, screaming into the crowd, 'Yulla ya kalbi; come on you bitch,' and Bucky was smiling through the gaps in his teeth and dancing with my younger sisters, and Bilal held his wife around the hip with one arm and had my new brother-in-law's neck in a headlock with the other.

9pm. I'd already written my wedding speech for her, my future wife, a decade ago, back when I imagined she would look like a girl from *Baywatch* and speak like a poet from the desert. In front of five hundred sweaty Alawites, I declared my fate. *'Oh Fatima: Love threshes us to make us naked. Love sifts us to free us from our husks. Love grinds us to whiteness.'* Forgive me. These words came from your namesake. They were never meant for the one who was chosen for me. They were meant for the one I chose for myself. They were meant for your mother.

10pm. Fatima and I standing in the middle of the dance floor all alone. 'Endless Love' rising up through the speakers. I placed my hands around my wife's ribs and began to sway. The Tribe roared 'whoooo' and 'wheeew' like a bunch of Aussies. The ground exhumed in a blanket of smoke. We danced on a cloud. We sang our vows. I'll be a fool for youuuuuuuuuuuuuuuuuuuu.

11pm. Dresses so short you could spot the bottoms of my female cousins' butt cheeks as they went off on a round of hip-hop and R'n'B – 'sexy bitch' this and 'suck my lollipop' that. So much alcohol throughout the night that my male cousins sweltered and panted and stank like swine, but heaven forbid we would ever eat the beast. Some ran outside to throw up. All under the eyes of Allah. One month earlier, my godfather had sacrificed a flock of chickens in his backyard, boiling and carving them up into pieces before distributing them to all the families in The Tribe from Marrickville to Campbelltown. A few hours later, every Alawite, including my entire family and me, was shitting violently, the salmonella poisoning so severe that our infants and our elderly were rushed to hospital. And we wondered; we wondered why God had forsaken us.

12am. Outside on the streets of Granville, amid the thick stench of charcoal chicken and lemon and garlic, after the herd had thinned, the remaining two hundred Arabs, including my parents, siblings and new in-laws, wept and said repeatedly, 'Allah-y haneekon,' which meant 'God bring both of you good fortune.' A Mercedes convertible, driven by a bald Egyptian who wore black sunglasses in the pitch of night, arrived to take us to our hotel. The entire family kissed Fatima and me three times each on our cheeks, so that by the end of it, I was drenched in a hurricane of spit and lipstick and perspiration and whisky breath. Just before I got into the car, my father grabbed me and gave me a tight hug, his arms of concrete wrapping around my rib cage. Into my ear he said, 'Allah knows, I could never let you go.' Fatima was on the kerb, crying so much that her mascara was running down her cheeks like a black plague, but it was not her father or her mother consoling her, it was her cousin Amir. Her head rested on his shoulder, and he had his hairy brown hands around her neck, and he was whispering words down her eardrum, many words, too many words.

1am. Fatima was the first woman I'd ever been alone with in a hotel room, the first woman I would ever share a bed with for a full night's sleep, and as her new husband, that night Fatima could also have been the first woman I ever made love with. But just because we were in a hotel room, and just because it was now halal, did not mean that we needed to fuck. The very idea that our entire tribe was expecting us to consummate our marriage made my skin crawl. The day before the wedding, after Bucky and I walked five laps around Belmore Sports Ground, he finally broke his silence and introduced me to a radical idea: 'Don't fuck because you're married, fuck because you're ready.' His words penetrated an old tear in my flesh: Sahara. Lying on her mattress, my loins scorching as we tongued and dry-humped until she stopped and groaned, 'Can we wait?' And I did wait. I waited as the pizza in her oven turned to charcoal. I waited as the chicken bones under her mattress went hollow. I waited still ...

Now I had decided that it was okay to wait with Fatima as well, to familiarise myself with her mind and body, and for Fatima to familiarise herself with mine, before we attempted to make love. I showered alone, and then got dressed into my black tracksuit pants and black singlet and slipped into the hotel bed, facing a large window that overlooked the Harbour Bridge. Fatima wobbled into the bathroom in her enormous white dress, and when she returned, she was in lingerie, a one-piece red satin outfit with black trim that exposed her long brown legs and accentuated her tight crotch and thin waist and cropped her breasts. She stood in front of the bed with her hands on her hips like Wonder Woman and said, 'Are you turned on?' As far as my body was concerned, I had only two vices: cheeseburgers and fried chicken. But I was twenty-three years old. And I did not smoke. And I did not drink. And I did not choof or sniff or inject. And I was lean and well-knit and fit enough for the boxing ring, which continually called to me, 'something like that'. And yet, in spite of every law in a young man's nature, I *wasn't* turned on. From the moment the women in our tribe had seen Fatima, they had said, 'Bet-janaan', that she's so beautiful she makes you insane. But I was sane. And I was scared. And I didn't know her. 'Come,' I whispered, flipping off the lights. Fatima slipped into the sheets like a cat. I felt sorry for her, the way everything she seemed to know about romance and sex and hotel rooms came from some Hollywood movie, like *American Pie* and *American Pie 2* and *American Pie 3*. I held her firm warm body against mine, and I looked into her eyes, which glowed in the darkness. I told her, 'I'm still falling in love with you.'

2am. So black it was bright, so bright it was blinding, so blind it was black.

3am. Fatima breathing peacefully in my arms, her small frame intertwined with mine, like Eve from the breast of Adam. See how we fit so perfectly together. Sahara and I did not fit. She called us Kit Kat and Kit Kat Chunky; lying in her bed, making out for half an hour until she told me to show her my dick. I said, 'I thought you wanted to wait,' but she insisted, 'I'm not suggesting we lose our virginity, I'm just so curious about what one looks like ...' I pulled my pants down and lifted the sheets, and there was my hard circumcised knob staring up at her. She laughed out loud like a masochist, not specifically at *my* penis, rather at the sight of a penis in general, but I shrivelled in shame all the same. Later that night Sahara called me while I was driving home and told me she felt like a slut, and I spent an hour apologising to her: 'It's not your fault. I shouldn't have shown you.'

4am. Ouff! In a few hours I would be on a plane to Italy. How did I go, in a matter of weeks, from a virgin who'd never left the country to a married man travelling back to the Renaissance with a teenage girl I hardly knew? What if Fatima was kidnapped by a European sex-slave syndicate and sold off as a virgin to some oily Arab prince, like in *Taken*? If only Fatima hadn't watched *Gladiator*, then maybe we'd have been going to the Gold Coast for our honeymoon like the normal dumb-arse newlyweds of Bankstown. 'Where would you like me to take you?' I had asked her the night of our engagement. 'I've always wanted to go to Rome,' Fatima replied, her voice squeaking like a parrot. 'Wow, you wanna see the Sistine Chapel?' I asked, impressed by her classy request. She stared at me with her eyebrows slumping and her eyes jerking. 'What's the Sixteen Chapel?'

5am. Fatima's warm breath wheezing across my face. Her firm thigh stretched over my hip. Her tight crotch pressed hard against my groin. Thoughts in my loins: *There is no one but your wife. No one but your wife.*

6am. Sahara.

7am. As the sun rose into our hotel room and lit up the Harbour Bridge, my mum called me. 'Did you get married?' she asked hastily – before I could even say hello. Fatima was still asleep, her bright red lingerie shimmering as she rolled over, turning away from me and the sunlight. 'Of course I got married, you were at the wedding,' I said, peering out the window of my hotel room, staring down at a pink stretch Hummer on its way to pick up the next round of Wogs. 'You know what I mean,' Mum responded, frustrated. 'Did you get *married* in the hotel?' I could hear her breathing loudly through the speaker as she waited for me to process her question. And when it finally hit me, like an uppercut to the chin, I screamed into the phone, 'That's none of your fucken business!'

SEVENTEEN

LAKEMBA TO ROME; LEB-KEMBA to the cradle of the Wog. First time I had to wear an Adidas bumbag on the inside of my flares, hiding my euros from the gypsy with one eye. First time I saw four women riding on a single scooter, all in summer dresses and high heels. First time I knew only two words to share with a cab driver, 'buongiorno' and 'grazie', both of which I had learned from *Everybody Loves Raymond*. First time I only had one person to comfort me after I screamed out, 'Fuck, I miss Punchbowl.' Fatima grunted as we approached the entrance to our hotel, 'That homeless guy with no legs on the street corner was staring up my skirt.' The Hotel White was so European that she cried when we stepped inside our room and realised it ended as soon as you entered. A bed with a television in front of it and a small bathroom to the left, which included the only bidet I had ever seen. Then it was dark, and the bed felt like it was in front of an open field. Fatima began kissing me, quickly, jaggedly, our teeth cracking on each other. She slid off her undies and pulled down my boxer shorts; rubbed her crotch hard against my dick until

I was halfway up inside her. My heartbeat pounded alongside her pounding heartbeat as we brushed across one another, and she moaned and cried and told me to keep going. Eh eh eh for the next two minutes. I tried to concentrate on Fatima's dilated pupils, flickering wildly in the shadows. 'I couldn't wait!' she groaned, and suddenly I was back on Sahara's mattress, my entire body throbbing out of control as I grinded against her nylon tracksuit pants. The girl who wore a cross said to me, 'I'll wait forever.'

My dick went completely limp inside my wife's body and her thighs contracted, pushing me out of her. 'I'm really sorry ...' I said, voice squirming. Fatima had become a black outline of herself, which I kissed repeatedly and remorsefully and repentantly, my lips landing on the edge of her forehead and the plate between her breasts and the bottom of her chin. 'We have plenty of time, Fatima.' I stood up, naked and vulnerable, and walked to the bathroom. I washed in the dark, too afraid to watch what I was rinsing off of me. You see, the Lebs of Punchbowl had told me that when you break in a virgin, she bleeds all over you. But the White women who taught gender studies at university said that was bullshit.

———

We woke up at the same time facing each other, jet-lagged and deflowered. She beamed at the sight of my proportionate, symmetrical nose, and said, 'Bahebak,' which meant 'I love you' to a man, and I replied, 'Bahebik,' which meant 'I love you' to a woman. Fatima asked me what smile of hers was my favourite – her lips springing into a cute pout; her lips narrowly curling into a smart-arse smirk; her teeth blaring as she mustered an enormous grin like the Cheshire Cat. Then she smiled because she thought her game was funny, a smile so natural it was neither here nor there, and I told her in Arabic, 'That one, that's my favourite.' She smiled when we spoke in the language of our bloodline. She smiled when she lifted the blanket and showed off the small blotches of blood that stained our white bedsheets. And she smiled inside L'Amore, a small cafe beyond an ancient fountain. I popped my video camera open and pointed it at her. 'Why are you so happy?' I narrated. 'I'm gonna have ice cream,' she announced like a child, bobbing her shoulders up and down with her hands closed over her chest. I turned our camera to the large doorway of the restaurant and zoomed in. Outside you could see and hear Manchester United fans chanting in Italian in front of the Trevi. The air was hot and dry and the water in the fountain was pristine. Fair-skinned tourists in American baseball caps washed their faces and fanned their foreheads with their maps. Tight streets hid the polished horses, which pounced on us when Fatima and I stepped into the light. This was a good place to celebrate historic events – I threw two coins at the sea god to celebrate the historic loss of our innocence.

———

Staring into the mirror, I spotted one hair peeking from the centre of my eyebrow in typical Wog fashion, and asked my wife to pluck it before we left the hotel room. She opened her handbag – a fake Chanel she had bought from an African street vendor – and pulled out a pair of tweezers. 'Beauty is more painful than sex,' she muttered.

All this agony for all that agony for nothing.

Fatima leaned into my face, close enough for me to kiss her, and without her heels, we were almost at eye level. The tweezers came up and pressed against my monobrow. Under the light of our tight hotel room, my wife's head rose before me as though it were the sky. I witnessed a dopey smile forming on her mouth, but she did not notice me staring at her because she was so focused on the small hair. I tried to hold in my pleasure but I couldn't, laughing so hard that little bits of spit from my tongue exposed the foundation on her cheeks. For it was here, when she was completely in the moment and unaware, that Fatima was most beautiful to me, her childlike emptiness dancing between all that she was and all that she could be.

'What?' she said, losing her focus.

'Nothing. Please, tweezer the hair.'

Half an hour after the pluck, we were outside the Colosseum, which rose before me like Fatima's face, its off-white concrete walls engulfing a sharp red sky. We peered like spectators over its arena and sat like Sand Coons inside its dungeons. I pocketed little white rocks as souvenirs while strolling up and down its staircases, as though I were some lame White kid from the gentrified sidewalks of Sydney's inner west.

'Holy shit, come see this,' I called to Fatima, popping my video camera open to film. Someone had carved 'kes emak' onto one of the Colosseum steps, which means 'your mum's cunt' in Arabic. Fatima didn't reply. I thought she'd get excited because our people, from Beirut to Bankstown, had let us know that they had been here. Instead my wife snorted at the ancient walls surrounding her. She was still angry at me for cracking up back at the hotel.

'You know, I'm probably gonna laugh at a lot of things you do over the next fifty years,' I told her, the camera still recording. Fatima's groomed eyebrows and droopy brown cheeks thickened. 'Then I'm probably gonna get shitty at you a lot over the next fifty years.' The screams of ten thousand gladiators reverberated through pillars of dirt and dust. 'Kes emak, kes emak, kes emak, kes emak, kes emak.'

———

The signs said no cameras but the huddled tourists flashed up at that ceiling as if Diana were dying all over again. And speaking of princesses, Fatima was whinging, 'It stinks in here.' I slid my camera under my shirt, my thumb on the record button. My initial attempt to absorb the Renaissance master in one go, he blurred my sight into a Rainbow Paddle Pop. Then the smell hit me; five hundred years of sweat, beginning with the drop that ran from Michelangelo's finger, down his arm, off his elbow, and to the ground beneath my Air Maxes. I blinked to refocus and cocked my head, staring back up at the ceiling, one image at a time. Jonah. He was the size of five men. I remember thinking, *Isn't Jonah's fish supposed to be the giant?* Adam. Reaching out to his maker. An inch from eternity. Bani. Reaching out to his wife. An eternity from inches. She was staring at the ground. 'These tiles are dirty.' Of all the eyes in this universe, why did Allah bind me to the only pair that gaped at the *floor* of the Sistine Chapel? 'I thought you liked history,' I said to her. 'Remember when we were discussing Homer?'

'*The Simpsons?*' she asked, history, both ancient and modern, repeating itself.

'*The Iliad!* Remember? You quoted it to me the night my cousins brawled.'

'Oh yup, nutt,' Fatima replied. 'My sister told me to tell you that.'

I pressed record and swung my camera towards the ceiling. Later that night, inside our sardine can, I played the video back to my wife. She blinked twice and said, 'I feel like a Rainbow Paddle Pop.'

———

The police officer in a dark-blue uniform with a red stripe down the side of his pants stood at the bottom of the Spanish Steps and stared at Fatima's breasts, which were bursting from her white V-neck singlet. The wrinkled old man who sat with his granddaughter halfway up the stairs caught the sound of Fatima's black high heels clacking upon the concrete and stared up at her long legs and through her chequered miniskirt, which was a millimetre from her butt. And the three young men at the top of the stairs, who should have been enjoying that space between an old orange building and an old white building, were each fixed on that space between Fatima's skirt and singlet, where a brand-new silver ring dangled off her belly button.

From her heels, to her long waxed legs, to her short skirts, to her naked stomach, to her sports bras, to her blazing cleavage, to her bony décolletage, she drew the male gaze upon us both like a plague. Part of me was angry at the men because they had eyes, but a greater part of me was angry at Fatima, not because she garnered the attention of other men, but because I knew

186

deep down she had only married me to be free to act like this, to mutilate herself in jewellery and G-strings and miniskirts and push-up bras – all the things her conservative father had restricted her from doing in order to find her a decent husband. The teenage boy inside me constantly screamed, *You don't get married so you can act like a hoe, you get married because you're ready to stop acting like a hoe!* Why couldn't Fatima just be like Sahara, who chose of her own free will to take no interest in make-up and shaving her underarms and legs and wearing skimpy outfits. At the head of the Spanish Steps, the earth sprawled before me. I saw the tomato-faced girl, trudging out of the water at Bondi Beach in her board shorts and Bonds singlet like the Swamp Lady, hairs on her arms and legs taped to her brown skin. I sat and watched her from the sand as the sun baked my back, whispering to myself, 'Beautiful things spoil nothing.'

———

Spaghetti al pomodoro in front of the Grand Canal, where stripped-down gondolas shot back and forth. Fatima slurped so hard that droplets of tomato sauce flicked onto my face. She said, 'Italians invented the best food.' And I said, 'Actually, I'm pretty sure pasta came from China.' And then she said, 'That's noodles, you idiot.'

———

Pieces of square woodfired margherita with deep charred crusts and oozing blotches of fresh bocconcini in the pizza shop window, catching her attention as we escaped from the gothic arches of Doge's Palace. Fatima held up two fingers, indicating to the merchant – a short bronze-skinned man who looked exactly like her father – that she wanted two pieces. We inhaled them in less than ten seconds, cheese melting our faces as we clambered along the golden tiles of a purple sunset. The prison walls of rotting stone and concrete, prison doors of wretched hardwood and corroded steel, the limbs and teeth of ancient torture devices, pulled at my shadow the further we inched from the palace. 'What's on your mind?' Fatima asked. She rarely showed an interest in my thoughts, but when she did, it aroused me – I fantasised about us having endless conversations, which connected the stones and tiles and breads all around us to the stories I had read throughout my teenage years. At last we would arrive back at our hotel and make passionate love, our arms and legs intertwined. *'Death in Venice,'* I answered. 'How about you?' She went silent for thirty seconds, contemplating till her eyebrows and mouth shot open. 'Gelato!'

———

We were strolling along St Mark's Square when Fatima singled out a pigeon, shuffling slowly across the concrete. 'Fat pigeon,' she gasped with a laugh. 'Film it. Film it.' Her innocence concealed her vanity, which sprung into action a moment later as she removed her pocket mirror and foundation and touched up her face, sweltering in the summer heat. Such was Venice, the wheedling, shady beauty, a city half fairytale, half tourist trap, in whose foul air the arts had once flourished luxuriantly, inspiring musicians with undulating, lullingly licentious harmonies. I felt

188

my eyes drinking in its voluptuousness, my ears being wooed by its melodies; I recognised, too, that the pigeons were diseased and the city was sinking.

Our room inside The Hotel Colombina, which oversaw one of four hundred canals and a 400-year-old church bell, looked like a princess's chamber from a Disney movie, the walls draped in gold-trimmed wallpaper. While brushing her teeth in a black bra and black G-string, Fatima waddled out of the bathroom and peered over the bedsheets at me. 'Have you ever used my toothbrush?' she yelled, as though she was sickened by the thought of my germs mixing with hers.

'No,' I replied, nestling my head into a down-feather pillow. 'Have you ever used mine?'

'Once!' she shouted back, not yet registering that she'd turned out to be the culprit and I'd turned out to be the casualty. Then she continued brushing like she'd said nothing at all. See how her accusation backfired, Kahlil? I found that so endearing. She was a child. And my fleeting moments of attraction to this child would be the death of me here in Venice. I was Aschenbach and she had become my Tadzio and we hovered in a limbo between creation and decay.

———

On the final sleep of our honeymoon, we lay amid doonas and pillows of feathers and kissed for three minutes, my wife's lips pressing on mine like two thin sheets of paper. Fatima's saliva was saturating my tongue, sliding down my throat, sinking between my lungs, churning in my stomach. I told her I didn't think we needed to keep trying to have sex just because we were married, that we could take our time getting to know each other's bodies, but she ignored me, springing naked from the sheets and drawing herself up on top of me. She rubbed fiercely until she was wet and I was hard. And once I was inside her, she thrusted vigorously and yowled. I held onto Fatima, my thighs aching, my groin rasping, my guts twisting, nausea as I breathed in her flowery perfume. Groaning, her neck and chin and eyes were directed towards the ceiling, as though I were just some piece of meat. There was no point in resisting this any longer; I was a naked young husband with his naked young wife on top of him – bound together for life, I accepted that this was the only intimacy we would ever know; and that it was better than no intimacy at all. I closed my eyes and tipped back my head and neck, and shoved up into Fatima as vehemently as she was shoving down into me, the pressure around my dick surging until I was on the verge of ejaculating. 'Fa-ti-maaa!' I moaned. All of a sudden she stopped moving, sinking as far down into my crotch as possible, throwing her hands upon my chest and tipping her sharp nose into my forehead. 'Call me Chanel,' she rasped.

At once, my dick went dead; the burning urge to orgasm easing back into my bones. 'I'm not doing that!' I grunted, a powerful contraction rising from my abdomen, Adam's apple retching. 'I like your real name.'

The weight of Fatima's narrow hips and slender frame and busty upper body deflated as she released her hands from my pecs and lifted her left leg right over my waist. 'Fine, I won't mention it again,' she said, turning her bare back to me as she curled into the sheets.

I stood up and limped to the bathroom. Crouching naked over the toilet bowl, my guts heaved up into my mouth yet again, thrusting once, twice, three times, till at last I was chucking up a ruddy coagulation of pizza and spaghetti and second-hand saliva. I was still nothing but a Punchbowl Boy: seventeen and celebrating my high school graduation; skolling a bottle of vodka at the park as the Lebs smoked marijuana and watched on. After I began to lose consciousness, Osama, Mahmoud and Isa had dragged me home and dumped me on my father's doorstep, where I mewled and gagged all over myself. Dad mopped up my vomit and said in Arabic, 'Shame on you, shame on you.' Now, on the other side of the earth, I was spewing up my guts once more as my wife lay in our hotel bed like a stunned mullet. Pulling my head out of the toilet and resting my chin on the seat, I cried out to my father: *Are you proud of me now? I was searching for poetry but I settled for ice cream. I was searching for the Prophet's daughter but all I got was a designer handbag. Yet this time, you won't need to pull out the bucket and mop. This time, I flush my shame into depths of the sewer. This time, I pull myself up from the shit bowl and stand on my own feet. Tell me you're not proud …*

While in the shower, I closed my eyes and thought about Pamela Anderson, rubbing my face on her plastic breasts. I pulled myself for seven seconds and was done, a thick white liquid squirting all over the shower glass. The running water rushed over me, so cold my loins withered. My entire body began to tremble, my skin turning blue. Not even in the city of romance could I convince myself that I was in love. I was a camel caught in the eye of an hourglass. The rust-coloured sand was running soundless and fine through the narrow glass neck, and when the upper bulb was nearly empty a small raging whirlpool formed amid the running water of the spattering showerhead.

I stepped out of the bath, dried myself, and lay coiled in the towel on the toilet floor, staring up at the bright orange lights for the next hour, my death looming like a traveller among the plague. Lying still and alone, I understood that solitude begets originality, bold and disconcerting beauty, poetry. But solitude can also beget perversity, disparity, the absurd and the forbidden. The hot air within the bathroom microwaved my quivering limbs, drifting me towards an endless desert.

The next morning, as the sunlight bounced off the canals and made its way through the narrow toilet window, I stood up and stepped back into the bedroom to get dressed. Fatima was asleep. Either she didn't notice that I had spent the night in the bathroom or she didn't care. I could feel myself slowly disintegrating as I pressed my forehead against the wall adjacent to my wife's wheezing breaths. Leaning back, arms sagging, spine shuddering, I whispered the standard formula of longing for something else – impossible, ridiculous and sacrilegious: 'I don't love you.'

EIGHTEEN

WHERE DO ARABS DUMP their kids once they've pushed them into marriage? In most cases, the children just return home to live with their mums and dads, but for Fatima, that defeated the purpose of why she married me in the first place – to escape the overbearing presence of her parents. And in my older brother's case, Cave of Wonders had generated enough business throughout the years that our dad could afford to build him a house across the street from the family home. Unfortunately, when I got married, we were in the middle of the Global Financial Crisis, interest rates were through the roof and shop sales were beneath the white tiles. 'I'm going bankrupt,' Dad confessed. 'We can't risk buying another property until business is better, but don't you complain, when I first came to Australia—' Of course, having heard this argument a dozen times already, I knew exactly where Dad was going with it and took the liberty of finishing the sentence for him. '—You went to school barefoot. Yeah, I know.'

As a compromise, I persuaded Fatima to live with me in the garage connected to the back of our shop – at least until the family business was making enough money for me to pay off another house on Caitlin Street.

'If you ever leave me, I'm gonna blow myself up,' Fatima said, holding tightly onto my arm as our aircraft bounced through a storm. 'Blow yourself up?' I mocked. 'Don't go saying shit like that when you're Muslim and flying!' I was only half-serious, finding her comment cute and unpretentious, but I still scanned the cabin to make sure no one had heard her, including the antique Italian woman fast asleep in the window seat beside us, and the young Islander-looking dude with dreadlocks and a flat nose across the aisle, who had headphones in his ears and was reading a comic book.

'I'm being real with you,' Fatima continued. 'If you ever leave me, I'll kill myself. Promise me, promise me it'll only ever be me and you.' I struggled to understand why Fatima wanted someone like me in her life – who could not satisfy her sexually and had no interest in miniskirts and make-up kits and fat pigeons. But sleeping peacefully on my shoulder as our plane roared into the Southern Hemisphere, she murmured, 'I'd rather live under the roof of a soft-cock than the roof of a hard cunt …' Lightning mellowed the darkness outside my window and Fatima's childlike dependence on me levelled the turbulence. *Soon*, I convinced myself, *the winds will settle and the clouds will dissolve and we will be floating through a clear moonlit sky.* 'Just you and me,' I said to Fatima. 'Wahyaat Allah …'

———

By the time we arrived in Sydney, jet-lagged as jihad, and caught a taxi to our garage, Dad had tiled its concrete floor and installed

194

a kitchenette and small bathroom. Later that night, he arrived at the door holding an overgrown watermelon in his hands. 'Salaam alaikum,' he said with a proud smile, his dark eyes squinting. He handed over the watermelon and kissed me on both cheeks. The second I felt the weight of that cold boulder of fruit weighing me down to the floor, I immediately remembered the day Dad had arrived at Bilal and Mandy's house with a Qur'an inside a wooden box from Iraq, which at that very moment, was tucked away in some sock drawer.

The watermelon wouldn't fit in our mini fridge, so I plopped it on the benchtop of the kitchenette as my father embraced Fatima in an affectionate hug, giving her three kisses on the forehead. Fatima and I sat on our double bed and Dad sat on the old floral couch that had previously been left on the verandah at home. 'So this is pretty nice, aye?' my dad said. 'Just pretend you're living somewhere in New York.'

I always struggled to understand my father's way of thinking. Was he in total denial about the crappiness of this new living situation? Was he aware but just trying to make us feel better? Perhaps make himself feel better for putting us here? Or was the quality of his own forty-six years on this planet so dismal that he honestly could not understand the difference between a garage in the back of a shop in Lakemba and some hipster studio apartment in New York City? Throughout my childhood, while sharing one bedroom with all of my siblings and two of my cousins in a house in Alexandria, Dad had repeatedly reminded me of how fortunate we were to be growing up in Australia, recollecting his childhood in Lebanon. 'My parents and ten siblings slept on mattresses wherever we could find space,' he said. 'Some of us slept in the kitchen, I slept in the toilet, but at least my children will never have to sleep in a shitter.'

I sat quietly as Dad and Fatima exchanged casual banter about Italy, mostly concerning all the designer dresses and handbags and sunglasses my wife had purchased, while she touched up her make-up with her small pocket mirror. This seemed to be an addiction for Fatima – compulsively reaching for that mirror and make-up and slathering it all over her face every few hours like a chain-smoker reaching for cigarettes. I was now experiencing the anti-climactic conclusion to the encouragement and commotion and celebration and energy and enthusiasm and joy of Arab weddings. You're all good getting into the white convertible that drives you to a hotel room so you can fuck. You're all good flying across the ocean so you can keep fucking in more hotel rooms and fly back again. But then life goes on. You're nothing but a man and a woman with a watermelon.

Not even fifteen minutes after he'd arrived, my father became visibly bored and began to yawn, as though *he* were jet-lagged. He stood up, flexed his pulsating arms, and headed straight for the garage exit. On his way out, he slammed the door hard behind him and I watched in slow motion as his wedding gift rolled off the kitchenette counter and splattered in pieces across our fresh white tiles. All good.

NINETEEN

OVER THE NEXT THIRTY-ONE days, I attempted to settle into my life as a married man. I woke up early in the morning as Fatima remained fast asleep, her mouth wide open; showered for fifteen minutes, randomly selecting one of the twenty different shampoos, conditioners and body washes that belonged to her; dressed in my flared jeans, black T-shirt and black sports cap; and walked from the garage door at the back of the shop to the double glass door at the front. I fought with customers about the prices of pocketknives and gas stoves and tents and sleeping bags between 8am and 5pm while Fatima stayed put in the garage, neither of us speaking to one another throughout the entire working day. I could not hear her between the wall that divided the shop and the garage as she washed our dishes and our clothes and mopped the floors, but I could always hear the faint sound of our television, which she watched nonstop. Fatima had bought the DVD box sets of *Friends*, *Will & Grace*, *Two and a Half Men*, *How I Met Your Mother* and *The Nanny*, and viewed them on repeat. During the rare occasions that I would need to duck back into the garage to grab a new book to read, I would see her sitting quietly on our bed in a bra and undies. Her silver belly ring would be twinkling at me, the stomach flesh around her piercing glowing bright red because it was starting to get infected. Ross and Rachel and Joey and Monica and Chandler and Phoebe were in her eyes; a fork and a cup of two-minute noodles were in her lap. 'I'm becoming Fatty-Fatima!' she'd blurt out with a chuckle, even though, miraculously, she'd hardly gained any weight at all since our wedding. I attributed her physiology – the Keira Knightly legs and Angelina Jolie arms and Jessica Alba stomach; the Kim Kardashian butt and Mariah Carey boobs and Beyonce thighs – to pure luck. Part of me – the fighting part that longed to return to the boxing ring – was revolted by her lack of motivation, but another part of me – the sympathetic part which fully understood that Fatima's paradise was nothing more than to be free from her mother's pink envy and her father's fist – was happy for her. How could I even judge her for such a thing? Marriage provided some distance from my parents too: Mum, who could no longer insult me with her views on Black people and uncircumcised penises and crooked noses. Now all she could do was send me the same text message once a week: *Where are my grandchildren?* I always gave her the same reply: *One day, Inshallah.* And then there was my dad, who still hadn't worked out that the mandarins in his house splatter in cycles. Having never discussed Sahara again since she broke up with me, there was always a tension between us – me because I resented him; he because I betrayed him. This meant that Dad and I could never drop our guard around each other and have a meaningless conversation. The only time I felt close to my father was Thursday nights, when I could hear his deep voice through the wall between us. I would leave the shop at 5pm and he and my brother would take over for the late-night shopping hours. Fatima would be in the bathroom, shaving her legs, clipping her nails, plucking her eyebrows, straightening her hair; and doing squats, which she'd never let me see, but claimed to have mastered, dropping her bum low enough to make contact with the tiles. Meanwhile I sat on the couch eavesdropping. Bilal's dry voice hollered through the timber, 'Do you have any idea how powerful Tyson's right uppercut was, he would have crippled Ali!' and Dad scoffed back, 'You really think Mike Tyson's right uppercut could have got within an inch of Muhammad Ali, you young fool!' Of course, I was on Dad's side. My brother was such a lost cunt. Ali would have run rings around Tyson! I listened in on them with a bittersweet smile, wishing I could join in their discussion without my father looking at me like: *We both know deep down you were gonna leave us for that wood-worshipper.*

The following Thursday night, unable to bear the sound of my father and brother's debates through the walls any longer, drowned out only by Fatima's sporadic groans as she did her squats in the bathroom, I found myself on the kerb along Canterbury Road. Focusing on nothing but the long strip of dirty concrete between the grass and a thousand exhaust pipes, I followed it all the way down into the next suburb, Belmore. Then I turned left onto Burwood Road, continuing to trail the concrete until I was standing outside the Belmore PCYC. I held on to the wires of the chain-link fence, sticking my brittle nose through one of the gaps and searching for the scent of sweat and leather and Vaseline. I could hear Leo in the wind, screaming, 'No arse shit,' and the rumble of the speedball and the swinging of the skipping rope and the explosion of the right cross upon the pads, but it was the faint sound of a girl's footsteps wandering the corridor that weakened my kneecaps: the memory of Oli hovering towards the bathroom, dressed in a pair of canvas Volleys and loose jeans and a green hoodie at the same time that I was heading towards the gym. Sensing me behind her, she turned and quickly I stuck my hands up and shook my head. 'I'm not following you,' I had said.

Oli giggled to herself, eyes crinkling, and replied, 'But it's something like that, isn't it?'

Pulling my nose out of the chain-link fence, a voice inside reassured me: *No. Nothing like that.* I eased back onto the concrete strip between the grass and the exhaust pipes, following it through the darkness back to my wife.

And so, I returned to that garage to fulfill the duties of a husband. My role in the relationship was as simple as paying for groceries, car expenses, clothes, Fatima's DVDs and my books – both of which she had lined up on the shelves of our wardrobe; saving for our house; and sharing the bed with her. I'd psyche myself up for sex by doing fifty push-ups in the bathroom before I came out naked and sweating. No more than six minutes later, we were panting and staring at the ceiling; my father's Frankenstein monster of gyprock panels nailed unevenly into the old garage beams. Fatima said, 'That's all, you're done already?' I might have felt humiliated and emasculated by such a question had I the slightest desire to impress her, but by now I was far too uninspired to maintain an erection for longer than a few moments. I remained silent, wondering how different it would have been to marry a woman who was a mystery to me – I would tell her I read so and so today and she would tell me she read something something today as our souls screamed to know one another and we would spend the rest of the night between so and something.

Staring up at the patchwork ceiling, which embodied all the gaps that came with being the child of illiterate immigrants, I craved the lecture theatre once more, where each week a professor would fill the spaces between the stanzas in a poem with annotations. This yearning led me straight back to Lakemba Library, where I rummaged through old poetry collections that lay hidden and untouched on a shelf that had a rotten used condom slipped between two of the books. I sat cross-legged on the library floor, reading poem after poem until I discovered a piece of writing called 'Bani Adam' by the thirteenth-century Persian poet, Sadi of Shiraz:

Human beings are members of a whole,
In creation of one essence and soul.

If one member is afflicted with pain,
Other members uneasy will remain.

If you've no sympathy for human pain,
The name of human you cannot retain!

I re-read the poem a hundred times while watching over Cave of Wonders, trapping Shiraz inside my head. Standing outside the shop with my mobile phone wedged between my beret and my ear, I recited the words to Bucky: 'Human beings are members of a whole'.

Semi-trailers and motorcycles roared across Canterbury Road as the manic depressive scoffed through his phone speaker. 'Wogs aren't human,' Bucky said, voice quaking. Before I could respond he hung up. Bucky had changed a lot since he first declared himself the 'one-dimensional gay subplot' to my 'hetero bullshit'. We became friends in 2001, when he was working as a project officer for Bankstown Multicultural Arts and I was freelancing as a wannabe actor for the organisation next door, the Bankstown Theatre Company. 'You an actor?' Bucky had jeered. 'Sure, if you wanna play some clit chopper.' This was his way of educating me on race without ever just saying, 'White people are only interested in casting Lebs as terrorists, gangsters, drug-dealers and rapists.' That part, he let me uncover for myself. Bucky was sharp and witty and as charming as hell back then, but this new incarnation was always dejected. And just like before, he left me to fend for myself: I would have to uncover the humanity in Wogs alone …

Back inside the garage, Fatima was sitting on the couch in front of the television. Ross was screaming, 'We were on a break!' and my wife chortled like she'd never heard him say those words fifty times already. As soon as she spotted me in the doorway, she paused the DVD player and squinted like she'd been caught watching a porno. She acted like a prisoner. My prisoner. I could already hear the Fox News headlines: *Genie in a bottle: Beautiful young bride found chained inside Aladdin's cave of wonders.* In reality, however, I wanted nothing more than for this girl to visit Bondi Beach with her siblings and cousins, or perhaps go and find a part-time job at a store in Bankstown, or enrol in a course and complete some kind of certificate at Bankstown TAFE. The only time she went out alone was when she walked to the

Centrelink in Lakemba to collect her unemployment cheques. The day after we returned from our honeymoon, while getting dressed to work at my father's shop, I asked Fatima what she intended to do with her newfound freedom. Coiled up in our bedsheets like a leopard, she gave me three intense blinks and answered, 'All I want from now on is to shower every day for a whole hour, wear whatever I want around the house, and watch whatever I want on the tele.' I originally considered this to be a joke – something she would do for a few days before she began thinking seriously about her future – but as the weeks went by, I realised she was serious, this was all she seemed to ever want from our marriage.

Now, while Ross's head remained frozen on the TV screen, Fatima rose from the couch and limped to the kitchenette, her bones stiff from having been on the sofa all day. She was in a pink G-string and tight white sports bra, a recurring outfit she began wearing straight after we moved into the garage. At first, I wondered if she was doing it for my arousal but eventually I noticed that she'd be in the garage all day on her own dressed the same way. One night I walked in and caught her sitting on the couch in nothing but a white T-string with her freshly shaven legs wide open. As soon as she spotted me, her thighs sprung shut and she covered her bare chest with her arms. 'Fuck, I thought you were Daddy,' she blurted. Only then did I understand what she was doing in that jail cell on her own all day: laughing in her father's face.

Yet as much as I sympathised with Fatima's circumstances, I could not bring myself to enjoy the fact that there was a skinny young woman with big jugs manoeuvring through my home in her underwear. I could hear all the Lebs from my high school years – who spent their afternoons at the Bankstown food court eating Big Macs and staring at women's arses, trying to make out the outlines of their undies – calling me a gay cunt. I even understood what they meant: Fatima looked like one of the models on the cover of a *Playboy* magazine, showing off her long hairless brown legs and perfectly rounded butt cheeks, only to discover a lifeless dick in my pants night after night.

I took my Nikes off and slipped into our bed, which was still warm from Fatima's body heat and smelled like her jasmine-infused shampoo. 'What you cooking?' I asked her.

She replied from the kitchen benchtop, her back and butt to me, 'I'm making a sandwich.'

Just to be clear, father to son, man to man, I never wanted a 'domesticated' partner. As a boy, I imagined being married to a woman with a full-time job. We would arrive home at the same hour, make fairy bread for dinner together, eat on the living room floor together, wash the dishes together, and then stay up all night discussing the Teenage Mutant Ninja Turtles. I told your grandfather about this just before I started high school: 'Dad, I'm gonna marry a working girl.' He laughed and replied, 'You want a prostitute?'

Of course, that's not what I meant, but what difference did it make in the end? My wife turned out to be Fatima; I had worked for nine hours straight while she watched sitcom after sitcom. As she cut up the vegetables, I found myself wondering if she was going to offer to make me a sandwich too, but no such offer came. Finally, I asked, 'Are there enough ingredients for both of us, babe?'

My wife murmured something to herself and thirty seconds later turned back to me with a sandwich on thin white bread that contained a slice of cheese, one sheet of lettuce, one slice of tomato and a shitload of mayonnaise. I sat up in our bed and ate, staring at the paused screen of *Friends*, Ross frozen in black leather pants, while Fatima continued clattering on the kitchen benchtop. The mayonnaise oozed over my fingers like pus and for a moment I felt sorry for Fatima, who did not even know how to make a decent sanga.

By the time I was halfway through my sandwich, Fatima turned from the benchtop with her own, and I felt like I had been punched in the face. Hers was at least four times thicker than the one she had made for me. I could see multiple slices of cheese and tomato and lettuce evenly spread out, but not only that, she had red onion and grated carrots and beetroot and sheets of corned beef. Despite the sandwich's height, it looked so perfectly and carefully assembled that it reminded me of those fake pictures of Big Macs on the McDonald's billboards.

Fatima sat next to me, un-paused her *Friends* episode and continued watching as she slowly devoured her masterpiece. She chewed and laughed and chewed and laughed and chewed and laughed, the name of human unretained.

———

Fixated on my wedding band – white gold reflecting my olive complexion in its contours. Most days, I forgot I was even wearing the damn thing, but on Friday morning, I became obsessed with its perfect circular shape. A ring has no beginning and no end.

Deep within the Cave of Wonders, it was transforming me into Gollum. Wicked, tricksy, false!

The GFC had hit Australia so hard by then that there were periods when the only person who popped in to the shop was my father to drop off stock. He always looked exhausted, his sharp eyebrows imploding and the dark circles beneath his eyes rippling across his entire face. Dad and my brother had returned to working at the markets from Minto to Bankstown to Flemington to Prestons in order to make ends meet.

'You and Fatima doing okay?' he asked, but before I could answer, he added, 'Your wife is a young girl in a grown woman's body. Instruct her to be more modest when she's walking to Centrelink.' He pointed out the shop door, down towards the street where the ummah wandered. 'The men here are people of *God*.' And once again he did not give me a chance to respond, tossing a wrapped-up eight-man tent onto his extenuated shoulder and thudding out of the shop. It was for the best – he wouldn't have understood. I was raised in a house where he sold billy cans all day while my mother patiently and meticulously wrapped hundreds of vine leaves at the kitchen benchtop. Then I had found myself at a university where I was educated by middle-class White women who told me that my father was a tyrant and my mother was a slave, dividing the world between Torvalds and Noras. Was it even possible that Fatima and I could love each other somewhere between the kitchen and the classroom? Or was my wife meant to turn from the chopping board one day and say, 'Our house has been nothing but a nursery. Here I have been your doll-wife, just as at home I used to be papa's doll-child.'

At 5pm I closed the shop and returned to the garage. As soon as I walked through the doorway, Fatima stood in front of me wearing a long white dress and a cartoonish frown, her lips tight and sullen.

'What's wrong?' I asked hastily.

She stuck out her index finger and placed it in front of my face. I observed it closely, spotting a thick dry translucent patch covering the top section. It reminded me of a game I used to play with my dad when I was a kid; he would place a little bit of superglue on his finger and then press it against mine, and after ten seconds, we would tug our fingers away from each other, our skin stinging and ripping as the glue came undone.

'Is that superglue?' I asked Fatima.

She gave me a puppy-dog nod.

Grabbing a paring knife from the kitchen draw, I eased my wife down onto our bed and carefully began scraping the adhesive from her skin. Sitting there quietly together, Fatima's warm hand in mine and all my focus on her finger, I finally felt like a man and a husband. Not even a second later, my heart sank into my bowels. I stopped grating, gawked into her dull open eyes and said firmly, 'Wait up, what were you doing with superglue, anyway?'

Fatima gave me another puppy-dog expression. 'Nothing,' she whispered. But I knew it was something – something serious, and worse, something moronic.

'Tell me!' I shouted, dropping the knife and springing to my feet, taking her by the shoulders and lifting her up with me.

Fatima looked scared, her jaw hanging wide open and her thin figure trembling, but she was nowhere near as frightened as I was in that moment. I finally understood that I was not a man,

I was only a boy, a boy who had been married off to a child, a child whose combination of vanity and naivety threatened her own safety. Slowly Fatima lifted her white dress, exposing her bare legs, her bright orange G-string and her flat stomach. I looked down and stared in utter despair at the flesh around her silver belly ring, which was swollen and covered in a translucent patch of dried superglue just like her finger. 'You stuck your dead meat back together to stop your ring from falling off?' I squealed.

Fatima's eyelids, lips and cheeks drooped at me as she nodded – her puppy-dog expression on its last leg.

We spent the night in the emergency room at Canterbury Hospital. Fixated on my wedding band, olive complexion in its contours, I found myself waiting for my wife in a space between the Noras and the Torvalds: an Arab boy, who wanted to be a husband; an Arab girl, who needed a father.

TWENTY

WHILE DRIVING TO GREENACRE Coles to pick up some
halal corned beef, my mobile began ringing. 'Salaam alaikum,'
I answered, phone to my ear in one hand, steering wheel in the
other. The chafed voice of my godfather instantaneously pricked
me. 'You will come to see me first thing in the morning.' Then
the phone went silent as I pulled swiftly into a loading zone and
clicked on my hazard lights, already in the process of texting my
brother: *Bilal, I need you to open the shop tomorrow bro. Abu Hassan
has ordered to see me.* By the time I parked in front of Coles, Bilal
had texted me back: *No worries. Hes gonna bust ur balls brah.
Remember to keep ya mouth shut.*

––––

He sat with his enormous pot belly over his legs, a tiny cup of
Turkish coffee and an ashtray with a dozen cigarette butts on the
coffee table in front of him. Right behind his swollen head was a
picture of his grandfather, who looked exactly like Joe Pesci; but

not the *Home Alone* Joe Pesci, the *Goodfellas* Joe Pesci, no funny guy, no shine box. A few years ago, my godfather claimed that this grandfather of his, Abu Ali Hamza, could perform miracles, such as having the power to bring down Israeli war aeroplanes with his eyes, and that he was so intelligent he invented a remote that could control the tanks of the US Army. 'Then why didn't he just destroy Israel?' I asked sincerely – sincerely because when I first heard these stories at the age of fifteen, I believed them.

'Hssssssssssss,' my godfather seethed at me. 'Our religion is not about asking questions, it's about faaaaaaaaith.' I learned then that whenever Abu Hassan spoke, I should just sit quietly and listen.

I had listened when he instructed me to get married and I listened now while he breathed smoke into the air and got high off his own voice. 'Don't ever think you're better than anyone just because you went to university,' he said in Arabic. 'I've sent three of my other students to the big library in the city,' – I think he meant the State Library of New South Wales – 'and they've all read about Socrates now and they're all smarter than you.' I nodded vigorously as Abu Hassan continued. 'And don't worry about praying, or fasting, or giving zakat, or even going to the hajj, so long as you call me once a week and receive my blessings.' At this point, Abu Hassan's wife, who was his first cousin, stepped into the living room with a gold pot of coffee, refilled his cup and left. Abu Hassan paused for a moment to take a sip and then went on, in English this time. 'And don't wear that hat anymore,' he said, pointing at my white Adidas baseball cap, which I'd bought from the Adidas outlet in Rome. 'I was watching the SBS and I saw a sex and the man was riding the girl and he was covering his face with that hat, maybe it was you.' After eight years of these lectures, in which my godfather regularly sneered at my education, regularly threatened that Allah would smite me if I ever went against The Tribe, and regularly affiliated my brief involvement in the arts with me engaging in pornographic sex scenes, his words were starting to take their toll. Bowing my head, I realised that nothing was ever going to change, nothing was ever going to get easier – this was the rest of my life. I would nod at my godfather whenever he accused me of being a closeted porn star; I would nod at my parents whenever they insisted that marrying a girl from The Tribe was better than anything I could ever have had with Sahara; and I would nod whenever Fatima asked me, 'Do you love me?' I knew then, as surely as I knew I was going to die, which I hoped would be soon, that this was not the life I wanted, this was no life at all …

I nodded for so long that my godfather realised I wasn't listening to him anymore, and he said, 'Your chin is moving too much, your mind elsewhere, see how smart I am, I catch you.'

'It's nothing,' I replied. The combination of cigarette smoke, the smell of dark Turkish coffee and his ego made me feel like vomiting all over his grandfather's photograph. 'Please, Godfather, continue.'

'I'm not just your godfather, I am your father, your brother and your best friend,' he said. 'Tell me what's wrong.'

'Well, it's just …' I began, because, you see, I really wanted to tell someone, even if it was him. For months I had held these thoughts inside like a rude secret. If I sucked it up any longer, my brain was going to explode from the inside out – head bloodied, hair torn out by the roots, lips blue and swollen, eyes bursting like pickled onions, forehead stove in, chin crushed to pink pulp, two dark holes instead of my nose – and worst of all, I wouldn't be crying, for I had given in to this fate. 'I'm not sure Fatima and I are right for each other,' I said to Abu Hassan. 'I feel like I'm her dad rather than her husband.' Saying those words out loud was chilling, like I had confessed to being a paedophile; I expected nothing less than my godfather to gag at the thought of me fucking my own daughter.

He bobbed his head with a gremlin-like smile, as though he understood exactly what I meant and had the perfect advice to solve my problem. 'Not just her dad,' he replied. 'You are her dad and her mum. See how smart I am?'

While kissing Abu Hassan's hand goodbye, I seamlessly slipped fifty dollars into his palm, the customary dowery for his services. Then I rose slowly and reluctantly as a ninety-year-old cock and stepped outside onto the street kerb. A gust of hot air ploughed into me, bringing on the first taste of spring. As I wandered along the fence of the Punchbowl train line like some tired philosopher, a calming voice of reason swept over me: *I am a smarter cunt than my godfather. It is likely that both of us are dumb cunts, but he thinks he knows shit when he does not, whereas I do not know shit, neither do I think I know shit; so I am likely to be less of a dumb cunt than he to this small extent, that I do not think I know shit that I do not know.*

TWENTY-ONE

IT HAD BEEN FOUR and a half months since we were married, two and a half months since we'd had sex, and one night while sitting up naked in bed eating McChickens with a large fan blowing hot wind in our faces, Fatima turned to me and said, 'Is there something wrong with you? I thought the guy was the one who was supposed to always want sex.' I knew she had come to this conclusion from the nonstop sitcoms she'd been watching, especially *Everybody Loves Raymond*. The lead character, Ray Barone, would beg his wife of nine years, Debra Barone, for sex in almost every episode, which she usually rejected. But even by Debra's standards, I knew that seventy-five days without sex for newlyweds was weird; and that it was only a matter of time before Fatima would start asking questions. I stuffed the last piece of the McChicken into my mouth and began kissing her fervently, running my hand through her hair and along the back of her neck, pressing my forehead against her brow as our tongues moistened one another's lips. Fatima threw the rest of her McChicken onto the tiles, as some kind of passionate gesture, and jumped on top of me, rubbing her waxed groin across my limp dick. 'Stop,' I said, throwing my hands around her waist and holding her down so it was clear I did not want her to keep thrusting on me. 'Listen, we can't just start fucking, okay? If you want to make love, you have to help me get hard.' I placed my head against Fatima's bare chest and listened to her heartbeat, which was pounding wildly. She looked down at me with her long eyelashes fluttering. 'What am I supposed to do?' she whispered, her voice sinking into a shudder.

Oh Kahlil, look away child, for what is your father but an animal? If my wife would … just use her hands on me … I knew I could get hard enough to have sex with her.

'Can you touch me down there?' I requested, my lungs throbbing, not because I was excited, but because I was ashamed to ask.

Fatima slid off my thighs and stared at me, all of me, her face recoiling. 'Well, can I at least put on a glove?'

Fuuuuuuuuuuuck!

It was fine, completely fine, that Fatima was disgusted by the thought of touching my dick, or any dick for that matter, but why, why, why, Allah why, did she marry me? She clearly was not ready for marriage or sex or the grotesque and foreign pieces of a man in her bed. How I wished she would stop waiting for a man to swoop in and save her; how I wished she were the kind of woman that would take control of her own life already – a woman like Mrs Laila Haimi. As a boy I had dreamed of being with this woman, which made me feel like Lolita, and now, as a man, I found myself in bed with a girl, which made me feel like Humbert. Kah-lil: I could not take the words back just yet and make them safe for you. My heart was limping towards eternity, and the last lap was the hardest. I had been dumped where the weeds decay, and the rest was lust and sawdust. I felt like a rapist, forcing an innocent young girl to pleasure me against her will, when in reality I did not want her to touch me just as much as she did not want to touch me. 'All right,' I said, 'cover your hands.'

Fatima walked to the kitchenette sink and slipped on the green rubber gloves, which were still damp from the dishes I'd washed half an hour earlier. She grunted on her knees in front of me, her hair blowing fiercely amid the gust of the fan, the moist rubber chafing at my circumcised flesh as she pulled, my dick blistering. Finally, I placed my hand over hers and said, 'I'm really really sorry.'

I slipped out of bed and hobbled to the toilet, my genitals stinging. Naked, I crouched over the toilet bowl and forced my hand down my throat, once, twice, three times. I heaved, throwing up my lunch and dinner, a green clotting of my mum's vine leaves and a can of lemonade and a semi-digested McChicken. Perhaps Fatima couldn't hear me groaning in misery, or perhaps she could and didn't want to deal with the reality of our situation, hoping that if she just stayed quiet our problems would piss off. I did not want this problem to piss off, I wanted the opposite: I wanted Fatima to appear, her hands ready to love me. I remembered Sahara's hands. Sitting at her dining table, she had been slicing strawberries, feeding them to me one piece at a time. And I was thinking, *This please – for the rest of my life.* Out of nowhere I was overcome by a swell of anxiety, and found myself sprinting to the bathroom to vomit, my guts splattering all over the porcelain. But I was alone for no more than three seconds before I felt Sahara's hands tenderly rubbing my back as I spewed and sobbed.

Now, not even a year later, I waited; waited for thirty minutes with my head inside a toilet bowl, waited for something; something in that swirling space; that swirling space between the tomato-faced girl who wore a cross and the stick insect girl who'd superglued her belly ring to her belly button. Finally, I accepted that no one was coming for me. I stood up and spread out a towel on the white tiles of the bathroom floor. I had returned to Rome, lying in front of a shitter, bright fluorescent lights hovering above me like a half-witted angel. One thought: *Why, dear Allah, did I marry her?* Madame Bovary whispering back into my ear: 'Such is the will of God!' The future was a dark corridor; at the far end the door was bolted, and trapped behind it was a fist the size of a child's heart. Your knuckle dimples knocking. Dadda. Dadda. Dadda.

TWENTY-TWO

THERE WERE ALWAYS GINGER cats having sex out the front of Bucky's house, where he lived with his seventy-year-old Greek immigrant parents. I picked him up on Saturday evening to take him on one of our classic mental health strolls. As usual, I spoke and he listened, clinging on to my arm in his zombie-like medicated state. I told him about Fatima's belly-ring incident, the glove incident, the nights I had spent on the bathroom floor and the relief I felt when I could be in the garage alone because Fatima had spent the day shopping at Parramatta Westfield with her cousin Amir – the man she kept a photo of herself kissing in her purse. We turned a corner onto Burwood Road, ambling past the Korean barbecue restaurant, the Lebanese charcoal-chicken shop and a brand-new chemist which had 'Instantly Whiter Teeth' painted on the front glass. The words reminded me of a desert-girl inside her bathroom every morning, gargling until the toothpaste was foaming out of her mouth. I tightened my grip around Bucky and said out loud, 'I wonder if Sahara threw out my toothbrush.'

Bucky took in a deep breath, and for a moment I thought he was going to say something, but instead he rested his head on my shoulder and wiped his weeping eyes against my sleeve. I tugged him past the high chain-link fence of the PCYC where a young woman was calmly emerging from the front gate. She was dressed in a light-pink cardigan, sleeves so long they covered her hands, her fingers fumbling with keys beneath the cotton as she locked the entrance to the building. 'Oli!' I called out. She stared straight at me, her bright blue eyes widening, cheeks swelling. 'You look so different,' she mumbled – softest ocker I'd ever heard; a mixture of shame, awkwardness and excitement.

'Yeah, I got that nose job,' I replied. 'Does it look good?'

She paused, her messy brown hair falling in front of her own asymmetrical nose as her gaze fixed on mine. 'I don't want to say yes,' she said hesitantly, 'because then it would mean I didn't think you were beautiful before.' The left side of Oli's lips curled towards the setting sun. She waved her keys at me, gave a little head-bob to the silent man attached to my arm, whispered 'Bye-bye Bani,' and then scuttled off in the direction we had just come. She was as subtle and repressed as a Jane Austen novel. Kahlil, dare not say that man forgets sooner than woman, that his love has an earlier death. Unjust I may have been, weak and resentful, but never inconstant.

Once Oli was completely out of our presence, I gave Bucky's rib a nudge with my elbow to indicate I was ready to keep walking, but he did not budge. I turned to him, to see what was up. His lower lip had protruded from his mouth like a caveman's and his eyes were glassy and still, eyelids sunken. 'There's something between you and that White girl,' he said. The only words he had spoken all day, piercing my soul. I was half agony, half hope.

TWENTY-THREE

Lying on the grass in front of the Belmore Sports Ground, the howls of the mighty Bulldogs brushed through the gum trees. Bucky was nestled beside me, inhaling heavily as his stomach swelled. 'So, your cousin Mouna won't eat pork but she'll eat pussy, yeah?' he said, exhaling. This was Bucky's way of telling me that my tomboy cousin, whom he met briefly at my wedding, was all kinds of gay and Muslim and fucked up. He usually claimed everyone was gay, or at least everyone was a little bit gay, which I only ever considered to be a rhetorical point, but in this specific case he was spot-on.

'She married an import with wonky eyes,' I told him. 'Because she looks too much like a bloke to get a guy from here ...'

'Perfect,' Bucky snorted. 'He'll get his visa, then they'll get divorced, and she'll move in with a suburban butch who solicits truckers in Mount Druitt.' This was Unmedicated Bucky, straddling that fine line between smart-arse and enlightened witness.

I took in a deep breath, catching sight of the stadium wall where someone had spray-painted: *skank's revenge – piss on a muzlim head.* I stared at it for several minutes, and so did Bucky, until he rolled over and said to me in a depressed tone of voice, 'Does that turn you on?' I told him that a Leb must have done something despicable to some poor girl for her to hate us so much. Any one of the chicks my friends dated back in high school might have ended up writing that message: Samantha, whom Shaky ran away from after he fucked her without a condom in the cinema; Nada, whom Osama dumped after she gave him a head job in a public toilet; Ashley, who gave hand jobs to Mahmoud and Omar and Osman and Isa at the Wentworthville Formula 1 Hotel in exchange for a stolen Nokia 3210.

I rolled back to face the sky and groaned out loud. 'My heart aches so much, bro.'

Bucky responded, 'That's gay.'

But I didn't mean it like a cliché, I meant it like my heart was literally aching inside me, pounding hard against my ribs and pushing blood up inside my throat, Adam's apple about to burst. I had spent the past three nights sitting on the edge of our bed, holding on to my pillow and watching the moon through our small garage window as my wife slept. It was Bucky's fault: for who was Oli to Bani and Bani to Oli but something in the background until he saw us together? Now all of a sudden, Oli was three letters that tormented me whenever I closed my eyes. You see, Kahlil, up until then I had been scarred by the White woman too many times to ever trust her. Back at Punchbowl Boys, the head teacher of English, Ms Lyon, was obsessed with keeping the Arab in his place. When Osama said, 'I wanna write about guns and Tupac,' she responded, 'Why don't you write about your fondness for packets of chips you bought from Aldi instead?' When Isa said, 'Palestine was stolen,' she responded, 'The Holocaust.' When Mahmoud said, 'Bilal Skaf got fifty-five years because he was Leb,' she responded, 'Men are shit.' And when Shaky said, 'White people are shit,' she responded, 'Reverse racism.' Six years later, while rummaging through the co-op bookshop at university, I stumbled upon a young adult novel that Ms Lyon had written during the years she taught us. The book, *Small Indiscretions of the Incredible Boat Boys*, boasted a Prime Minister's Literary Award sticker on the cover and a quote which declared the text: 'A Truly Authentic Western Sydney Voice'. I read the dedication – 'For my first-born son, Aladdin' – and the first page of the novel, which started with the line, 'Some people say Punchbowl like it's ice cream in the gutter, but me and my boys love it as much as we love kebabs and charcoal chicken.'

I wondered if Oli was the kind of White woman who wanted to wear my skin (like the high school teacher that stole our voice), or the kind of White woman who cried so much at the thought of my skin (like the cashier at the university bookshop that referred to every individual Leb as 'yous'), or the kind of White woman who wanted to scorch my skin (like the performance artist that called my prophet a camel f—). Then again, was there a chance that Oli was the kind of White woman, the kind of woman, the kind of person, that just wanted to know what was beneath my skin. I longed to be known in such a way, to be with a woman who saw me just as I was: Bani Adam.

'Do me a favour,' I pleaded. Bucky turned and stared at me, his monobrow concaving. 'Please punch me in the head.' Anything to distract me from the agony of thinking about the girl with the fair and freckled complexion: the something that had followed me from Belmore to Lakemba to North Sydney to Bass Hill to Granville to Rome to Venice to my pillowslip; the something between a cross and a belly ring; the something that gave me a reason to put the comma back in.

'No!' Bucky sulked. 'I'm not getting involved in your heterosexual nonsense.'

'You did this shit,' I told him. 'You're the one that put her in my head.'

As I turned my glare towards the sky again, I felt a thud upon my cheekbone, like I'd been smacked with a small bag of ice, snapping me back into the boxing ring – black gloves pummelling my big crooked nose; Leo screaming no arse shit; cold water trickling down my naked body as my face swelled; floating down the corridor; Oli caught in a trance; staring at my engorged eye – and then I was back on the grass of the Belmore Sports Ground, Bucky smiling at me with his hand in a fist. 'Feel better, princess?'

Remembering Oli's gaze upon me eased my pain, but at the same time, my heart felt like it was clenched in an eagle's talons. I wasn't supposed to end up in a garage at the back of a camping shop with a blistered dick and my head inside a toilet bowl; in the beginning I wanted to read, read until I knew how to teach, teach until I knew how to write, write until I knew how to bring you into existence …

'Look at the mess I've created, Bucky. I'm such a fucken gronk.'

'No, you're not,' he replied with a chubby smirk. 'You're just a Leb; a Leb who followed the same script that all Lebs follow.'

Staring back at the graffiti on the wall, I grumbled, 'Someone ought to just piss on my head already.' The air went still and we both watched patiently as the sun slid behind a lone cloud in the sky.

'Here's a better idea,' Bucky eventually responded. 'Just run off with that Aussie slut, bro. Your wife thinks you're a fag anyway.'

I ignored the gay point in Bucky's advice – that was just his usual rhetoric, remember – and asked myself what would happen to Fatima if I actually left. The Tribe wasn't known to be generous towards divorced women who were no longer virgins. My whole life I overheard what the grown-ups and the elders said about them: *She's spoiled meat. She's damaged goods. She's impure. She's loose. She's cursed. She's spastic. She's a sharmouta.* In most cases these girls ended up being shipped off to Lebanon or Syria to be remarried to a freshie who wanted a visa into Australia. I did not want that for Fatima, but similarly, I did not want to be with her anymore – I wanted to be with the three letters that had been gracing my sleep.

'Sorry bro, gotta dog ya right now,' I said to Bucky, springing to my feet and sprinting through the grounds, in the direction of Belmore train station and the Belmore PCYC.

I heard Bucky calling behind me, 'Ah, Bani, Bani, Bani …'

I stopped but did not turn around. I had my sights on a vision in front of me: a child with the eyelashes of a camel and the brown curly hair of the bush that had risen upon Moses. 'You can't trust a White girl, bro,' Bucky yelled. 'Did you learn nothing from Mayella Ewell?' His laughter filled the grounds like ten thousand Wogs cheering for a bunch of dogs. I took off again, running towards the girl who once told me she liked my nose just the way it was.

Shot through the gates of the PCYC, down the corridor and up to the front office. Oli was sitting behind the desk, her elongated fingers pressing down slowly onto a keyboard. 'Hello Something-Like-Oli,' I said. 'Oli Something Something.' She skewed her head towards me, cobalt eyes widening. 'Bani?' Quickly the White girl tucked her hands under the desk, as though she'd been caught with her thumb in the hummus. 'What's wrong?' she asked, raising her thin eyebrows at me like a smart-arse, like someone who *knew* – from the moment she'd locked eyes on me the day before – that she could lure me back to her desk as easily as a mockingbird could lure my ears to a tree.

'I just wanted to tell you what I read recently.'

'Hit me with it,' she said, hands still hidden.

'I don't know,' I replied. But I was lying. I did know: there's just one kind of folks. Folks.

She gave me a steady nod, even though my words made no sense, and stood up, withdrawing her hands and reaching for the handbag beside her computer monitor. It was a small yellow canvas shoulder bag, like the ones my father sold at Cave of Wonders.

'Wait, where ya goin'?'

'I have uni.'

'I'll come,' I said impulsively. 'I have to go in whatever direction that is anyway.'

Once again, Oli gave me a steady nod, only this time she chuckled as well – perhaps she saw a goofy dog in me, chasing an ambulance.

Our shoulders met at the exact same height as we walked side by side towards Belmore station. I asked Oli for the name of her favourite book, and she said, 'I'll let you know when I get a library card.' I asked Oli for the name of her favourite movie, and she said, 'I'll let you know when I get a television.' I asked Oli if she'd ever seen anything that changed her life, and she said, 'I'll let you know when I have eyes.'

Next we were sitting quietly opposite each other as the train staggered towards the inner west, me admiring the White girl's outfit. She was sporting the thin light-pink cardigan I'd see her wearing in the past – the one with the long sleeves. Apparently, she'd stolen it from a high school friend who was unusually tall. 'I like things that have already been loved,' Oli explained, tugging down on the ends of the cardigan's sleeves to cover her hands once again. But just for a moment, she let go of the sleeves and I finally caught a clear glimpse of her fingertips.

'Do you cut your nails?' I asked her.

'No, I bite them,' she told me with a gawky smile. 'How about you?'

'I cut them, but they come out crooked anyway.' I opened my right fist, consciously presenting the hand that did not display my wedding band, and spread my fingers for Oli to see. My knuckles were busted and in between each one were my old calluses from boxing. All five of my fingernails were jagged: a left-hander using right-handed scissors, I'd spent my childhood cutting all of them unevenly. By the time I was as an adult, the white point of each nail that I could cut and the pink point of each nail that covered my flesh had divided like a wave.

Oli stared at my fingers intently but said nothing. I interpreted her silence as a form of intelligence; she never seemed to speak before first considering her thoughts. Directly behind her was a Viet in a corkscrew hat who randomly began humming the theme song to *Titanic*, specifically that flute section that all the Wog chicks in Bankstown wouldn't shut the fuck up about back in 1998.

'Now you have to show me yours,' I told Oli.

She hesitated, but only for a second, and then slid her right hand out from the thin sleeve of her friend's cardigan. Each fingernail sat right on the tip of each finger. They were entirely pink, bitten straight to the edge; lacking the smooth lining of a nail that had been cut with a pair of clippers; serrated across each tip so imperfectly perfect that my loins caught fire – shameful, frightening and thrilling all at once. The humming rose above the clack of the tracks and I fantasised about Oli's hand flinging wildly against the steamed-up window of the train. I was drowning in her sweat. I was sinking into her breath.

Her hair, light brown, was somewhere between curly and straight; long and cracked at the tips, the same as her fingernails. And just like the way she hid her fingers beneath her sleeves, she hid the freckles on her plump right cheek with her fringe. 'Do you brush it?' I asked, pointing my finger right in her face.

'I like that you're not the kind of person who can tell,' she responded. I wondered what she meant. Did she think I was stupid or naive? Was she patronising me, or worse, taking advantage of me; plotting to turn me into a case study, a guinea pig, for her next anthropological assessment? Kahlil, I understand that these may have seemed like far-fetched assumptions to draw from some random White girl whom *I* chose to pursue, but it had happened to me before! Let me tell you more about that incident I keep bringing up; about the White performance artist who called the Prophet Muhammad a camel f—. I was nineteen and aspiring to be an actor when Jo came to Bankstown looking for a 'Leb' to be in a theatre show she was producing about violence. Throughout the week that I participated in her creative development, she and the other White women on her team invited themselves to scream out insults about the prophet. This, they explained, was *art*. Then they instructed me to shout out the word 'slut', only to attack me for saying it, White tears soaking the brown floorboards of the Bankstown Arts Service as they screamed in my face, 'Fuck me, Muslim.' This, they explained, was *feminism*.

A few weeks after the development, I sent the White performance artist a text message: *I need to talk to you about some things that happened to me in your show.* I always made sure my text messages were written in grammatically correct English – an attempt to compensate for being a dumb Lebo from Punchbowl Boys High. Three days later, Jo replied, *ur not white enough 4 me 2 care and ur not black enough 4 me 2 pretend 2 care ;)*

I wanted to believe that Oli was different from all the other White women I had known, and in the back of my mind, as each second played itself out, I tossed up which of us posed a greater threat to the other: *She probably thinks all Muslim men are Osama bin Laden, who hang televisions from their trees; I think all White women are Hillary Clinton, who bathe in oil wells. She probably thinks all Leb guys are Bilal Skaf, who got fifty-five years; I think all Caucasian chicks are Linda Fairstein, who prosecuted the Central Park Five. Her father will probably threaten to take her name off the will if she brings home a Sand Coon; my father will shove my head through a wall if I ever bring home an Aussie skank. Her mum probably wants her to get married in a church; I'm already married!*

The closer we got to Oli's stop, the less I spoke, in an attempt to purify our final moments together – your father is so dramatic, isn't he, Kahlil? Even Porphyria, whose lover strangled her with all her hair in one yellow string, was telling me to get on with it already.

Staring, I continued to admire Oli's hands, which seemed so sacred that she could not resist hiding them beneath tables and sleeves and her teeth. I hated the glaring irony that her modesty was more 'Muslim' than the 'Muslim' I had married – the White girl's dark-blue skirt hovering below her ankles and her pink cardigan concealing her arms, stomach and chest. It wasn't that I objected to the way Fatima dressed, I just couldn't stand anymore that I had sacrificed my happiness, and my life, for a tribe that was built on contradictions and hypocrisy.

With each second I knew that my time with Oli was fading. Her anxious eyes would pause on mine, smile, as eyes do, and then flick to the window, where outside the wide suburban houses of south-west Sydney grew older and narrower and browner as we approached the inner west. Once we arrived at Central station, I walked slowly alongside the White girl, finding providence in the fact that we were the same height. I could imagine us walking shoulder to shoulder like this for the rest of our lives, holding hands; her fingers stretched over each of my calluses. We pushed through White men in grey business suits and White women in bohemian trousers and Brown boys in Adidas tracksuits and only one Muslim girl I spotted, who wore a bright red hijab.

'People stare at you a lot,' Oli finally said to me. She had her eyes on the sad cunts, and the sad cunts had their eyes on me, and I had my eyes on her.

'It's because of the way I dress,' I explained.

'What about the way you dress?' she asked. And now I understood what she meant when she had said to me, *I like that you're not the kind of person who can tell.* Even Sahara, who was the least superficial person I had ever met, could tell. She regularly attempted to change my outfits. Once, at Broadway Shopping Centre, she put on a nonchalant voice, pointed at a Levi's outlet and said, 'Hey, just for fun, wanna go into that store and try on some men's pants?' I knew it was her passive-aggressive way of saying I dressed like a homo, and it was painfully sardonic to me that a girl who never shaved her legs, and only ever went out in board shorts and wife-beaters was embarrassed that her boyfriend did not conform to traditional gender norms.

'Um, I'm going this way,' Oli mumbled as we approached the exit. She casually pointed towards the tunnel that led to Sydney University, where hundreds of people scuttled along like crabs.

Standing in line behind her at the gates, I watched over Oli's shoulder as she opened a bright green purse to pull out a train ticket. Inside the purse I noticed several cards on the left-hand side, including a student ID and a bank card; several cards on the right-hand side, including a wallet-sized photograph of an older, plumier, red-headed version of herself; and in the middle of the purse was her driver's licence. She looked half a decade younger in the licence photo, a blend between Hannah Montana and Pippi Longstocking, and her nose was completely straight, which meant that she must have only busted it within the last few years. Then I noticed her name on the licence: *Olive.*

The White girl stuck her train ticket into the machine, and the triangular gate flaps flung open. She hovered through the narrow space and turned to face me, yellow tinges in her pulsing blue eyes expanding.

'Your name is Olive,' I said out loud, unable to withhold my Arab tongue. 'Why wouldn't you tell me?'

The gates snapped shut between us and the porcelain face of the White girl wilted like a daisy in a drought. 'Because Olive is so ordinary,' she said, clipping her gaze onto my wedding band. 'I suppose you'll be catching a train back to your wife now?' She turned quickly and scurried towards the tunnel, disappearing between an ocean of flesh and cloth and claws. Oh Ordinary Olive: subtle, passive, passive-aggressive, self-aware, so self-aware; rip my heart out, remind me that this could never be anything more than what it was.

TWENTY-FOUR

ONE THOUSAND AND ONE nights, one thousand and two nights, one thousand and three nights, one thousand and four nights. Trapped within the Cave of Wonders, staring through that opening all day, down Canterbury Road to the next suburb, Belmore, where the awkward girl with frail skin and brown freckles tormented me. What did she do while she sat at her desk all day – did she type, a thesis perhaps that offered yet another solution for the Palestinians? And who was she when she got off that train and crossed through those gates – was she the girlfriend of some hipster, who had dirty straight brown hair and large square glasses and a patchy beard and who stayed up all night with her to discuss the intertextual references in *Napoleon Dynamite*? Did she live far away from her parents – parents who I bet read to her when she was a kid – in a share house with all her quirky second-hand-clothes-wearing friends from Sydney Uni? My assumptions about her were built on every beatnik stereotype I had accumulated from my undergraduate degree and Triple J and Woody Allen and Wes Anderson films, but please know that

I was not passing judgement on her, I was jealous, wanting so desperately to be a part of her world.

The vibration of movie after movie resounded through the wall between my wife and me – Fatima's hysterical laughter when the boy who found himself home alone hurled bricks at the heads of the intruders, and her sudden gasps and screams when the man with a chainsaw dismembered a group of teenagers. My father came into the store at 4.30pm to take my shift. I sprung up immediately, ready to crawl into my bed, close my eyes and hope that Oli would appear before me. Dad frowned and said, 'Your aunt Yasmine saw you on a train the other day with a woman that wasn't your wife.'

My fists clenched and my teeth juddered. *That fucken big mouth fucken gossip fucken chinwag!* At the very least, I wanted to be Oli's friend, I wanted to be free to sit in front of her and admire her hair, but even this was too much.

'Never again, you understand,' my father said. He pointed his index finger at the toilet door behind me. 'Your face will be in that wood if you embarrass us.'

How I could have put my own face through that door right then. Do you remember, Kahlil, what my dad had said to me all those Ramandans ago at Macca's, listing the benefits of marrying a girl from The Tribe: 'You will be free, rich, protected, safe, included, *loved*.' And I believed him – my only consolation for this life I chose was his promise that it would be so much easier than being with an outsider, that somehow my choice would get him to back off and just feel pride that he had two good sons. But finally, I understood, the deeper inside The Tribe you go, the more they own you, the more they think they can control you and decide what you're allowed to do – after all, you've shown them they can get away with it.

'Whatta-ya want from me?' I screamed at my dad, pounding my fists into my chest. 'You want me to be like Yasmine's children – brawling with my cousin over some princess in the street; or marrying my import cousin so no woman ever talks back at me; or how about pretending to be straight my whole life because you're all a bunch of homophobes!' In my anger I threw a punch flat against the toilet door, so hard that my knuckles created four dimples in the wood. The sting shot through my flesh and bones, driving me back to a time when I was a fighter; when every punch I threw and every punch I took was a breath of air. My father stood unusually calm and silent, the wrinkles in his face relaxing, as though he was confused – concerned even. I suddenly saw him for what he was; just an Arab man passing on what Arab men passed on. His godfather had been assigned to him at age twelve, and he gave my father a very simple script to live by: 'Never marry an outsider, never have less than five children, never go against the family, never go against the village, and never question me.'

I was so tired of never, never, never; the phone was always ringing and none of us picked up. But when a forty-year-old widow was on the other end, the Prophet Muhammad answered the call. And when a Sunni woman was on the other end, my grandfather answered the call. Now it was Oli on the other end. I started running, harder than I'd ever run in my life. Dad was out the front of his shop screaming after me, 'Baaaaaani! Baaaaaani! Baaaaaani!' but I did not turn back, not this time. One thousand and five. One thousand and six.

TWENTY-FIVE

A PERFECTLY BROKEN NOSE — the White girl sitting behind her reception desk. But unlike every other time I'd ever seen her at the gym, she wasn't typing on her computer. She was still, staring innocently down the corridor like she was far off in thought, waiting. I appeared before her sweltering and panting uncontrollably, my arteries twitching. She gasped at the sight of me. 'You.'

My knuckles were stinging. It had been so long since I'd thrown a punch that my calluses had softened and I'd torn them open. It felt so good — the blood bursting through my veins once again. I planted my old membership card in front of the White girl and tumbled down the corridor towards the gym, the smell of sweat and vapour rub and leather rushing through my lungs, bringing back the sound of Leo's voice, which rumbled in my ears — 'waste that pussy-arse-cunt-poof!' Inside the empty gym, I locked onto the largest heavy-bag I could find and staggered at it with a wild left cross. The bag swung and flung back at me, and I smashed into it, jabbing and hooking and uppercutting and screeching and squealing in agony as my heart tried to keep up with my arms. Inevitably I collapsed to the ground, opening my trembling hands out in front of me as though I were holding a Qur'an and breathing what felt like my final breaths.

The swivel that held the heavy-bag squeaked as it rocked back and forth, and everything else was silent in the gym, everything else until a pair of canvas sneakers slinked through the doorway. 'All this fuss just for some Aussie skank?' Oli said with a smirk. She gently sank down beside me, her white skirt spreading over my knees and across the floor like a blanket. And reaching out ever so slowly, she took my hands in hers, holding them still. 'Shhhhhhhh-shhhhhhhh-shhhhhhhh.'

My breath eased, my heart settled, my knuckles retracted. My blood, my soul, converging, roaring towards you. You – who was so certain that you could be. You – who needed no invitation. You – who knew exactly how to get here. You – who winked at me and went back to sleep. Shhhhhhhh.

ALL THAT WILL BE

TWENTY-SIX

HOUSE OF ADAM IS my curse. Fatima is my fate. And your mother is my fate un-cursed. She comes tearing through my bloodline, like love threshing me to whiteness, and in this way, Kahlil, your bloodline is written. Eight centimetres dilated by the time we will reach the hospital. The midwife will say, 'You're a miracle worker.' I will call your mother's father and tell him you are born, that the midwife declared it a miracle. Your grandfather will reply, 'There's no such thing as miracles, but I am in tears all the same.' Next, I will call my father and tell him you are born, that the midwife declared it a miracle. Your jidoo will reply, 'Take my grandson in your arms, Bani, and whisper these words into his ear, Ash-hadu alla ilaha illallah, wa ash-hadu anna Muhammadar-Rasulullah.' Your ear will be dough and powder upon my trembling lips. And the hospital will be dark and restless and aching when we take you to our room. Your mum will hold you out in her arms, this little head wrapped firmly in a bright-pink blanket. She will cradle you from side to side and hum while you screech and groan eeh-eeh-eeh, the anguish of existence, attempting to stare back at her like a pebble falling into an abyss. You will be an ancient frown, your buttery face rippled and wrinkled and your tight eyelids warring with themselves to open. Your mother will breathe you in through her nose, freckles flickering, and dance with you in her brittle attempt to help you settle. I will watch as your tiny eyes of silver emerge upon her before you cannot hold them up any longer – Allah will find all kinds of ways to wink at us. Your mother will cry as she breastfeeds you for the sixth time, staring straight at me and shrieking, 'It's like sandpaper on my flesh.' I will take your weightless body from her grip and hold your head, which blazes like the birth of a brand-new star, across my arms. I will tell you about your great-grandfather's arms, which carried his eleven children through the streets of Tripoli and Beirut; and I will tell you about your grandfather's arms, which carried his six children through the streets of Alexandria and Newtown and Redfern; and perhaps one day you will tell your son about my arms, which will carry you through the streets of Lakemba and Punchbowl and Bankstown, where the Arabs will ask me, 'Your son?' and I will reply, 'No, my sun.' You lump, will you please explain to me how you earn my affection so effortlessly? Lying there like a wad of flour, deep ringed lines under each of your eyes and a deep groove above your Cupid's bow just like your mother's, arms and legs clenched to themselves, your voice like a broken flute, your blocked nose whistling, your face cringing as you puff through your nostrils like you're cracking rice bubbles. I will hold your blanket away from your airways so you can breathe. Every second that I will keep you asleep is another second that your mother will rest, and heal, until you begin to cry all over again for her blood and her bones and her skin. Our room will be still and silent and strewn in shadows, with nothing but your mother's wheeze to fill the void. Your brittle face will crumple into my elbow pit as she rolls over, half-opens her eyes, murmurs, 'Shhhhhhhh-shhhhhhhh-shhhhhhhh,' and slips back into sleep. I will be stricken by the flame of a burning bush, filling the midnight slumber of the hospital with a crackling echo. Your mouth will bring the purest smile to my face – the subtle kind we share with no one but God – as your lips spread open and reveal a petite tongue and tender blunt gums. You will start to suck at the air, searching for your mother's nipple. Just before you find your voice, which will shatter my organs and hold me at your complete mercy, your left eye will fling open and close shut. Allah finds all kinds of ways to wink at us.

TWENTY-SEVEN

12 AM. A FIGURE WAS sitting on a milk crate out the front of the family business, which in the blackness, with nothing but the glow of traffic lights, could have been anyone, were it not for the silhouette of my father's extravagant nose giving him away. He kept his glare on the random car here and there driving past as I approached. 'Your wife is asleep in case you were wondering ...' I said nothing, just stood before him, like a peasant before a king. 'Please don't hurt yourself like that again,' he said next, turning to face me, dark circles under his eyes sucking in his frown, making him look hollow. 'When you are wounded, I bleed too.'

I plopped myself down next to him, my back against the glass shopfront, and stared out onto the road, waiting for the next car or motorcycle or truck to drive by, waiting for the right words to come out of my mouth. *Oh Allah – how could we ever make my father understand that this was not to be or not to be: to love an outsider was not to hate him; to hate myself was not to love him. Oh Allah. Oh Allah. Oh Allah. What more could my father bear to hear?*

'Oh Allah.'

Neither of us said anything for a while after that, both just staring as the vehicles driving by became less frequent; watching the traffic lights on the intersection between Canterbury Road and Haldon Street snapping from green to orange to red and back again as though they were waiting too.

At last your grandfather spoke. 'I didn't love your mother when I married her,' he said, in the gentlest tone of voice he'd ever used on me. 'Your tayta said there was a nice girl in The Tribe from a good family that I should meet. She was chubby and had this innocent-until-proven-guilty kind of look so I said yes and twenty days later she was my wife. On Allah, I never once raised a hand upon your mother, but first week of our marriage, she asked me for new curtains and I was too embarrassed to admit I couldn't afford them, so I punched a hole in the wall and locked myself in the bathroom ...' Dad took in a deep breath, like he was ashamed, and then he went on. 'But you know, a year later she gives birth to your brother – he came out bum first; and a year after that she gives birth to you – jeez you had a big head; and a year after that she gives birth to your sister – we name her after my mum; and each time I held one of you in my arms, I remember thinking, *This woman, mashallah, this woman.*' Dad stopped talking at that point and waited for a huge semi-trailer to thunder past. The road went still once more and the lights snapped from orange to red to green. 'It gets easier, Bani,' he said. 'You just need to stop thinking so much.'

TWENTY-EIGHT

1AM. BACK IN THAT garage, I slipped off my Air Maxes and my white Adidas ankle socks and my black muscle shirt and my flared jeans and my black boxer shorts. I crawled between the bedsheets next to my wife; draped my arm over her bare stomach, eased my palm onto her belly ring scar, pressed my groin between the back of her thighs, pushed my head through her freshly straightened hair, rested my lips on her neck, kissed her as she crooned in her slumber, drifting towards the calamity of so long life. To die, to sleep – to sleep, perchance to dream.

TWENTY-NINE

2AM. OLI. OLI. OLI. Oli. Oli. Oli. Oli. Oli. Oli. Oli. Oli. Oli. Oli. Oli. Oli. Oli. Oli. Oli. Oli. Oli. Oli. Oli. Oli. Oli. Oli. Oli. Oli. Oli. Oli. Oli. Oli. Oli. Oli. Oli. Oli. Oli. Oli. Oli. Oli. Oli. Oli. Oli. Oli. Oli. Oli. Oli. Oli. Oli. Oli. Oli. Oli. Oli. Oli. Oli. Oli. Oli. Oli. Oli. Oli. Oli. Oli. Oli. Oli. Oli. Oli. Oli. Oli. Oli. Oli. Oli. Oli. Oli. Oli. Oli. Oli. Oli. Oli. Oli. Oli. Oli. Oli. Oli. Oli. Oli. Oli. Oli. Oli. Oli. Oli. Oli. Oli. Oli. Oli. Oli. Oli.

THIRTY

3 AM. 'WHAT?' I WOKE in heat and darkness, the air eating itself alive, my eyelids heavy and damp, limbs limp, loins throbbing. Fatima murmured in her breathy childlike voice, 'You said ordinary.' Allah, forgive me. I was dreaming of an olive in a sea of never never nevers while I was in bed with my wife. She was ordinary. So ordinary. How strange.

THIRTY-ONE

SIX MONTHS INTO OUR marriage, having finally run out
of DVDs to watch, Fatima began visiting her parents, where
she could hang out with her cousin Amir who lived in the same
street as them. The first time I went with her was the night after
my dream, only to find myself sitting with my father-in-law and
nodding along as he told me that faggots, sluts, gamblers and
alcoholics were all going to hell. I could hear Fatima in the next
room laughing hysterically as she and Amir had what sounded
like a pillow fight.

During the drive home, I told Fatima that maybe I should no
longer come to her parents' house. She was staring at herself in her
pocket mirror and touching up her lipstick as though we were on
our way to a wedding, and without hesitation, she replied, 'Yessss.'

She didn't want me there, bearing witness to the intense sexual
tension between her and her cousin, any more than I wanted
to be there. I wished so badly that during one of their tickling
contests they would start to kiss, and then have sex, and then
finally realise that they were, and always had been, in love with

each other, and run away together. Then again, Fatima was my wife, I was her husband; and we were still both meant to be living under the assumption that we would be faithful to one another forever. Hitting the breaks hard and skidding before the next red traffic light, I found myself fuming at my wife's enthusiasm. 'I said "maybe", okay, let me think about it.'

Fatima and Amir's relationship had me tossing in bed all night: *They wanna fuck, right, no girl shakes her body on the dance floor that hard for a man she doesn't wanna ride; actually no, no way, yuck, that's gross, they're just cousins, they grew up together, they grew up in Australia, Arabs in Australia don't like to fuck their own cousins, right, right.* As I began to fall asleep, I told myself to wake up. *She's never gonna leave you, not even for her cousin. You sad cunt. You pathetic cunt. You trapped cunt.*

The next day, I decided to accompany Fatima once more to visit her parents, watching on as she squeezed into the tightest white pants I had ever seen, which completely revealed the outline of her pink G-string. Although she looked disappointed with my choice, she was unable to think up a good reason for why I shouldn't attend and reluctantly said, 'Whatevs.' This time I sat in the living room with Fatima's mum as well as her dad, and Amir's two-year-old sister, Hiba, whom they were babysitting, while Fatima hung out in the backyard with Amir – that same backyard where less than a year ago she and I had decided to be with one another for the rest of our lives. The cousins were debating loudly about who had a nicer arse, Kim Kardashian or Jennifer Lopez. 'Kim Kardashian has a Bankstown girl's arse,' laughed Amir, and Fatima was chuckling back as she said, 'Ooh you like Bankstown girls' arses do you, you like Bankstown girls' arses?'

I could see my father-in-law doing the best he could to ignore them, left side of his face twitching. He was unable to police his daughter's dress code and language like he used to, but I think he was trying to communicate in code what he expected me to do with Fatima, saying in Arabic, 'Don't listen to what the hippie Muslims tell you, the Prophet said it *is* okay to beat your wife.' And then my mother-in-law added, 'With a toothbrush, beat her with the bristles of a toothbrush.'

Just then, the piercing sound of glass shattering on tiles shot through the house, and all at the same time, the three of us turned to see Baby Hiba screaming, having pulled a large cup off the kitchen benchtop. Perhaps it was the noise that frightened her, or perhaps it was the awareness that she was responsible for the noise, or perhaps it was both. I remained seated but my in-laws immediately sprung upwards and tumbled towards the brown-skinned child with the thick brown curly hair. I expected them to comfort the girl; calm her down and make sure she didn't get any pieces of glass on her, but instead they mutually crouched over her, my father-in-law ripping off one of his flip-flops and slapping her hand hard with its sole, and my mother-in-law smacking her bum, the nappy puffing on repeat. I was witnessing the violence that had trailed Fatima's childhood, and I knew it was not going to end with my wife, that it would be passed on to her children, to *my* children. If I had you with Fatima, in whatever version of you Allah may have given us, her family would have struck you, struck you while your mother was flirting with her cousin in the backyard and I was sitting right in front of you, repressing every ounce of dignity that I could imagine for you.

249

On the way home, while Fatima reapplied make-up to her face, I suggested that both of us stop visiting her parents, reminding her that she married me precisely to get away from them. 'I already said you can stop coming with me,' she retorted. 'But I like my family now.'

The traffic lights down the Hume turned orange as we approached an intersection, and I could have sped up to make it, but instead I hit the brakes hard just like the night before, the cars behind me beeping in frustration. 'Just because they stopped hitting you doesn't mean they're not arseholes anymore,' I shouted at Fatima. 'I saw your parents bashing your baby cousin!'

Fatima snapped shut her make-up kit and gave me a scowl. 'That's different,' she squealed. 'That girl deserves to be hit – she's a little shit!'

On the third night that Fatima visited her parents, I stood in front of the traffic lights on Canterbury Road and watched her Pulsar disappear. Then, while my father and brother looked after Cave of Wonders, I wandered the streets of Lakemba like a Rug Rider, confused and sleep deprived: *Little shit? Little shit? Little shit? Is this Fatima's criteria for beating our own children? Which child of mine will ever pass such a test?*

Walking down Haldon Street in the direction of the train station – manoeuvring through a hundred beards and a hundred hijabs, a dozen Muslim bookstores and a dozen Lebanese restaurants – I heard my name being screamed out from across the road. 'Oh my god, Bani!' My sister Yocheved scrambled towards me; slipping between the cars that moved slowly up and down the road. Her long black hair was tied in a bun like a pineapple, and she was wearing a baggy white T-shirt, black tights and white

Reeboks. Her face was pink and flustered in sweat, her dark eyes bright and wide open, her breathing fast and sporadic. She looked strong and healthy, having lost at least six kilos since the last time we spoke, which was just over a month ago when I briefly stopped by my parents' house to collect a plate of kefta and rice. Yocheved had been sitting on our front verandah with her new fiancé, a softly-spoken second-gen Syrian man who was dressed in his beige overalls, peeling an orange for her with his bare hands. My sister's eyes were glued on him with innocent joy, that pure kind of love that sends you jogging through the streets. I respected her for holding out, rejecting import after import, until a man who appreciated her taste in fruit finally arrived.

I was about to tell Yocheved that she looked great, when she said, 'You look like death!' Taken aback by the comment, I suddenly spun away from her and into the black glass shopfront of a Commonwealth Bank. 'Look at you,' she continued. 'Seriously, look at yourself.' And for the first time since I had come back from Italy, I did look at myself, absorbing my reflection in the window. Staring back at me was a being of smokeless fire. Its face had sunken into its own skull, and thick dark circles had engulfed its eyes like two supernovas. Its skin was withered and raw, its hair dry and rotten – the roots of a dead cedar tree creeping from its scalp. The djinn had no lips, no teeth, no ears, no eyebrows and a piece of melted plastic for its nose.

'Bani, let me help you,' Yocheved whispered, her bright reflection appearing in the glass as she stepped behind me. Her skin, in contrast to mine, glowed golden, and it reminded me of her namesake, our grandmother, Yocheved, who died when I was eleven years old and my sister was ten. Our tayta; who was born Sunni and disowned by her entire family for choosing to marry our grandfather, an Alawite. I remembered Tayta in the kitchen, where my sister helped her crush olives and garlic for six hours. In the bathroom, where my sister helped her get undressed from one muu-muu, wash between her legs, and then get into another muu-muu. In the laundry, where my sister helped her load the washing machine with socks and underwear from every one of our seventeen house members. On the front porch, where my sister sat with her on milk crates in the summer evenings and watched the birds until the sun went down. And sleeping on the living room couch, where my sister was nestled on her aching legs to ease her pain. Tayta would look out upon our family, her sons and daughters-in-law and grandchildren, and she would say, 'When I die, I leave my spirit with this little one for all of you ...' Three years later, my tayta was dead and all of my father's sisters began calling our house and pleading with him to allow Yocheved to spend nights at their places. 'Ree-hit emi fee-hah!' they cried. 'The smell of my mother is inside her!'

I did not understand back then but now, thirteen years on, I could smell my grandmother too – crushed garlic and crushed olives and fabric softener and the summer heat – radiating from the sweat upon my sister's brow. 'You already have helped me,' I said to Yocheved. 'Thank you for reminding me of who we are.' I turned and kissed her on the forehead before legging it towards the station. I caught the first train that arrived and got off at the next stop, where I waited, waited for the White girl named Olive, Olive who was ordinary, so ordinary that she was stranger to me than anyone I had ever met, ever met at least until I met you, you whose first word was 'tractor', seriously, why, why 'tractor', why?

Four trains came and went in the direction of the city. As the fifth train arrived, three Lebos in Nike caps staggered down the stairs to the platform, one of them screaming for the transit guard to hold the doors, 'Ociffer, Ociffer, please, wait, we got a disabled fat cunt with us.' And behind them, floating down each of the steps, were Oli's bare white feet in black flip-flops, and then her thin legs and her kneecaps and her thighs and her hips, all wrapped in blue denim, and then her brown leather belt, the bottom of her pink cardigan, her hands tugging down on her pink sleeves, and then her small chest and her freckled décolletage, her neck and her round little chin and her dry lips, her busted nose, and her eyes – the yellow between the blue and the black exploding before me. Oli's gaze locked on to mine and, nudging her chin at the three Lebos who just tumbled onto the train, she said, 'Are you here for your cousins?'

A great swirl of laughter erupted from my chest, that true kind of laughter you can't help, your throat aching as you reassemble your focus, the kind of laughter I had not experienced since I was a boy; sprinting in the rain, slipping on my arse. I asked myself: *Is it a sin for a married man to find another woman so funny?*

'Nah,' I replied. 'I'm here to pick up an Aussie slut ...' She laughed back at me, as though she too were remembering what it was like to be a child running in the pouring rain. I wasn't as subtle as she was, but we got each other.

On the train, I kept my eyes on Oli, thinking how beautifully her messy brown hair knotted at its ends. And once more I asked myself: *Is it a sin for a married man to admire another woman's hair?*

She smiled gently, left cheekbones veering towards the window, our train rattling from Belmore to Campsie to Erskineville to Redfern to Central. As the brakes squealed and the train came to a halt, Oli winced at me and said, 'Bani, when you were a boy, what did you want to be?'

I spoke without any pauses for the next ten minutes, Oli's unwavering attention caught on the base of my tongue. I told her that my earliest memory was that of thirst, not thirst for my mother's milk; thirst for the black ink you find on a cream-coloured page. But none of the adults on either side of my family, who had all migrated to Australia from Lebanon between 1968 and 1975, had finished school and learned to read and write. By the time I was six years of age, I began rummaging through the drawers and closets of my grandmother, parents, aunts, uncles, siblings and cousins searching for any document that contained words. During my explorations, I read my father's father's name, Bani Adam, etched into a gold ring; the thin instruction manual inside a box of condoms; a *Hustler* magazine article about a Russian man who had sexual intercourse with the empty eye socket of a blind lady; and a *Women's Weekly* feature about a two-hundred-kilo British woman who was so fat the doctors stitched up her lips. Then we moved to Lakemba and all it took was a ten-minute walk up my street and down The Boulevarde to reach the local library. This was where I obtained my first library card; and where I finally satisfied my thirst, drinking in the ink of a thousand verse-makers. I read Kahlil Gibran, who taught me that love can bleed willingly and joyfully. And I read Toni Morrison, who taught me that love can be deep-down, spooky. Ink was my first love. It had filled my veins. And ever

254

since I felt it surging inside me, desperate to explode all over the pages.

When I finished speaking, Oli frowned, her entire face wilting like a petal. She said, 'Is it wrong to be attracted to a married man?' I did not answer, but this time, when the train arrived at Central station, I followed her through the gates and down the station tunnel towards Glebe, past White women with green hair and White men in skin-tight jeans, all the way down Bay Street, which led to the old housing commission units where Sahara lived. It was the first time I had returned since the desert-girl broke up with me. I had been afraid, you see, but not anymore. Kahlil, my little shit, just be a little shit – not even the bristles of a toothbrush will ever harm your skin. Your soul was dwindling mischievously in the sunlight. And my soul had freckled. If I ran into the tomato-face who wore a cross in that moment, Ordinary Olive by my side, I know what I would have asked her: 'Is it a sin for a married man to have finally got over you, but not because of his wife?'

Neither Oli nor I spoke a single word as we strolled towards her home, a two-bedroom brick townhouse she had been renting in one of the backstreets of 2037. Approaching the White girl's doorstep, I asked her, 'Is it a sin that I've seen your room in my dreams?' And she replied, 'Only if you weren't invited.' I knew exactly what I wanted to be when I was a boy. I wanted to be a verse-maker. And I knew exactly what I wanted to be when I was welcomed into your mother's bedroom. The author of this book. Sth.

THIRTY-TWO

HER ROOM WAS ANTI-ARAB. The floor was covered in clothes – long multicoloured skirts and plain white and pink T-shirts and black work pants and purple polka-dot pyjama pants and white bras and light-blue cardigans and thick woollen jumpers and jackets. I also spotted old packets of potato chips, silver coins, a little wooden Buddha, a withered rose, a sealed bottle of coconut water, a pile of books – *The Female Eunuch* on top – and a yellow Spice Girls ring among the mound. In the centre of the tight room was Oli's bed, a queen-size mattress in a brown wooden frame. It wasn't made, her thin white blanket crumpled as if she had just woken up beneath it. Her pillows were spread out, a stack of two at the head of the mattress, another lying vertically in the middle and one hanging off the lower left corner.

The thought of Oli having no time to clean because she needed to stay up all night and complete her essays made me want to sit behind her and tenderly unknot her hair. At the same time, however, I found myself wondering if I could ever really be with a woman whose work and studies seemed to outweigh her need

to live in a clean and tidy space. No Arab woman would ever let
her room get to the state Oli's was in, or the rest of the house for
that matter. I had been raised in a home where the women were
conditioned to clean so efficiently that they would be watching
my plate while I ate kefta and rice, and not even a moment after
I was done licking the tomato sauce from the dish, I blinked
and it was in the sink, my mum having swept in to collect it.
And the same conditioning had taken place in the home of my
wife, who regularly showed me that she was far more interested
in tidiness and order than reading about the ways that women
had been historically castrated by men. Our wardrobe, which sat
between our bed and our television, featured three shelves that
were Fatima's, containing over one hundred pieces of make-up,
including lipsticks, foundations and mascaras, all sorted by size,
date, brand and shades from lightest to darkest.

The Arab woman's compulsion to clean had completely rubbed
off on me. Standing inside Oli's bedroom, my immediate instinct
was to fold all of her clothes, sort out her ornaments, throw out
the rubbish and vacuum her floor (which I still wasn't sure even
existed). But then, as Oli elegantly stepped between her heap and
dropped her green purse amid a pile of exercise books in the right-
hand corner, I found myself charmed by her indifference to the
mess. For in the clothing that had come off her body and been
thrown inside-out straight onto the floor, and in her unmade
bed, I saw her ghost from last night, sleeping peacefully and
free, a pillow for her freckled cheeks, a pillow between her frail
arms and a pillow between her shapely thighs. Feeling the blood
prickle my muscles, I wanted to become a part of this mess, a
lingering spirit in the traces of Oli's day. I used my right foot to

kick my left shoe off and my left foot to kick my right shoe off. Then, pulling my shirt off in one single thrust and throwing it on top of her mountain of clothing, I dived bare-chested onto Oli's mattress, slipping beneath her puffy sheets and sinking my head into her pillow. Engulfed in the scent of buttermilk and sweat and moisturising cream and tears and her warm breath, I had been thwarted by a malign star, sleep dwelling upon my eyes, peace in my breast, and if only I were sleep and peace, so sweet to rest.

'You're in my bed,' Oli gasped – highest pitch her voice could muster.

'I'm sorry,' I replied. 'I'll get out if you want me to.'

Oli sat at the edge of her mattress, her back facing me. 'Please don't,' she muttered. 'You're just the strangest person I've ever met.'

I found myself confused by her confusion – growing up in the streets of Punchbowl, the other Lebs called me 'strange' because I dressed and read and acted like a hippie, but Oli was a hippie, so what did she find strange about me? Right then it finally dawned upon me: I was no label; I was fortune's fool!

Sitting up close behind Oli, I could feel her breathing rapidly, her heartbeat reverberating through her cotton bedsheets. And my heart reverberated in unison – to undress her would be to break my vow to Fatima, my vow to The Tribe, my vow to Allah. I could go and live, or stay and die. I placed my hand at the bottom of her cardigan and her undershirt, and together, we slowly raised them over her head and threw them in with my black shirt. Eyes upon Oli's bare skin, my entire body began to shudder and throb, thin black hairs along my arms and legs and on the back of my neck prickling. You see, I did not fully appreciate white skin, truly white skin, in contrast to my own olive complexion, until Oli showed me who she was beneath that shy and awkward wardrobe of hers. White as milk, as snow, as paper, dotted with tight brown freckles. I brought my lips towards her back, and I mmmmmm'd across her flesh, moving up past the clip of her pink bra and towards her right shoulder blade, where a deep jagged scar frowned back at me. 'White skin is cursed,' Oli explained. I would never be more Arab than I had become in that moment. And thus, with a kiss I died.

'Am I just supposed to forget that you're married?' Oli asked, voice quivering, cheek turning over her shoulder.

'Am I just supposed to forget to think?' I replied, unclipping her bra and running my lips slowly along the small round bones in her spine, breathing her in. My blood hardened to rust. Her freckles withered to stardust. She said, 'Bani Adam, I'll never live up to your sins.' I said, 'Ordinary Olive, give me my sins again.' The White girl lay on her back and stared straight into my eyes, unblinking, unflinching, and I lay on top of her, wrapping my arms tightly around her ribs, holding my forehead upon her fringe. Kahlil, child of rust and stardust, by now I've told you more than you probably ever wanted to know, but forgive me for sharing with you this one last detail – before you were born, I was reborn.

THIRTY-THREE

WRAPPED IN HER BEDSHEET, and wrapped in one another, my head clamped between Oli's neck and shoulder; a plump woman with red hair inside a polaroid leered at me. The picture was in a small seashell frame on Oli's bedside table. I recognised this lady from a similar photo I spotted a few weeks earlier, back at the train station when I had peeked into Oli's purse. 'Is that your mum?' I queried, my lips caressing her ear. 'Yeah, she died,' Oli said in a depleted voice. 'But please don't feel sorry for me; just imagine me.' Her arms tightened around my ribcage as she spoke under the sheets about her tribe: her mother, a primary school teacher before she was diagnosed with stage four melanoma; her father, an ESL teacher for TAFE NSW; her sister, a dancer currently on an eight-month national tour playing a swan; her one uncle on her father's side, who voted for Pauline Hanson's One Nation Party; her one aunt on her mother's side, who majored in geography; and her three cousins, *three in total*, all of whom were stoners.

I placed my hand around Oli's neck and pulled back to stare at her – to see her as she asked me to see her – and nudged the tip of her busted nose with my new plastic one. 'How'd you break it?'

Oli flinched, as if she were reliving the memory. 'I hit it against the steering wheel when I rear-ended a car.'

I couldn't help but smile at the idea of this self-conscious White girl, so lost in her thoughts that she had become a public menace. I kissed the flat tip of her nose and found my bottom lip trembling. Was this girl the doorway between what I was, a big busted nose; and what I could be, the writer who had emerged from the barbed-wire fences and surveillance cameras that surrounded Punchbowl Boys High School? For the first time since I graduated from university, I imagined myself quitting my father's shop and continuing with my education, if only to finally free what was behind that bolted door at the far end of the dark corridor …

I released Oli from my grip and we both lay sideways across her bed, facing one another. 'Bani, promise me something,' she said, curling up into her bedsheet, 'if you're trapped in your marriage, you'll keep having these affairs.' I had never even thought about it that way but perhaps she was right – perhaps I was destined to live out the rest of my life as an adulterer. My godfather had taught me the 'Islamic' consequences for adultery in my mid-teens: if there were four witnesses, my infidelity should be punished by wrapping me up in white sheets and stoning me to death. I knew it would never happen to me but still I found myself reflecting on my train ride to Oli's house, and asking if anyone had seen me with her. I was certain there hadn't been, but how could I be sure, when I had my eyes on no one but this frail and freckled girl the whole time, thinking, *I defy you, stars!*

Oli's chin veered to her chest. 'Just promise me I never find out.'

Kahlil, as I lay in your mother's bed, with everything she owned out on display, I imagined her. What I saw was her entire life intertwined in mine forevermore, but at what cost? Abandoning a young woman who was so co-dependent she regularly said things like, 'If you leave me, I'll blow myself up.' What had Fatima ever done to gain my hand in marriage other than be herself? When had she ever lied to me about who she was and what she wanted from a husband? It was me who had lied, who had told her that it would only ever be me and her, even while the ghost of a tomato-faced wood-worshipper continued to haunt me.

The thought of breaking Fatima's heart was already too much to contemplate, but a divorce in The Tribe would also mean breaking up with her parents, who had not pushed her onto me so quickly only so they could take her back so easily; and also my parents, particularly my father, who had convinced himself that so long as he was happy, I was happy, as though he were the one who had to wake up next to my wife every morning. I also knew that ending my marriage would mean taking on my godfather, who I had been taught to believe had an affinity with God, and could instruct Allah to strike me down if I ever defied him. My entire body ached as I thought through the consequences of a divorce and all I could do was reply to the White girl, 'I promise.'

I slid out of Oli's bed, still covered in her, in everything that she was, and slipped back into my black briefs, my flared jeans, my black shirt, my Adidas socks and Nike Air Maxes. Once I was dressed, Oli stood up, her body completely wrapped up in her bedsheet, transformed into the armless white statue of Aphrodite.

I walked down the stairs towards her front door, which was beside the doorway to her kitchen, Oli hovering one step behind me, until I reached the bottom of the staircase. As I turned around to say goodbye, I was caught off guard by a to-do list pinned on her thin white refrigerator. In neat cursive handwriting at the very top it said: *Buy sponges.*

Looking back at Oli, who was staring innocently at me, I felt the blood gush out of my heart. I did not want her to be the electrifying memory of a deep dark sin. I wanted her to be the boring, ordinary mundanity of my life. I wanted to be wandering the aisles at Woolworths with her, filling up our trolley with sponges so that I could cook for her and eat with her and scrub her dishes until I was dead. I wanted to smash my head against a concrete wall asking myself why I was being deprived of such a basic pillar of humanity, and I heard a hundred voices screaming back at me: *Fuck all the sluts you want all the sluts you want but remember it's a sin a sin to marry a white girl you will bring shame to the house of adam shame to the house of adam I only ever asked you for one thing see how smart I am her sons aren't even circumcised can I at least buy a qur'an that matches my furniture will you let me wear g-strings wear g-strings don't think you're smarter than me just because you went to university piss on a muzlim head a muzlim head fuck up you little poof you look like death like death like death so do you want to get your nose fixed if you die on me I'm gonna kill you beat her with the bristles of a toothbrush a toothbrush you were riding a female dog on the sbs we will never allow you to disgrace us with that whore with that whore that whore our religion is not about asking questions it's about faaaaaaaaaaaaaaaith!* Allah, how I could not bear it anymore. Thank Allah for sponges. Sponges absorbed the madness that had been pumped into my veins. Sponges soaked my brain with clarity. I knew I had two options, this whole time I only ever had *two*: love or death. For a life without love, was death by default. Oli was standing in front of me like a mirage, an oasis glowing amid the empty desert that had become my future, rattling my bones. I ran into her, enveloping her sheet and her fragile body in my arms and kissing her lips and her cheeks and her busted nose and her forehead and her neck and this one little freckle in the centre of her chest. The White girl said, 'What?' And the Leb said, 'Everything.'

THIRTY-FOUR

'MAYBE BUCKY COULD TAKE me shopping.' This is what I heard upon entering the garage at 8:30pm. Now that it was too cold in the year for frolicking around in her underwear, Fatima was snaked up on our bed in a black robe, watching an episode of *Queer Eye for the Straight Guy*. Her face was brightly lit in the glow of the television screen, red lips curled into a dopey-looking smile.

'Bucky's not that kind of fag,' I spat back firmly. 'Does everything you know come from a damn television? I've got a hundred books in that wardrobe. *Read* something for a change!'

Straightaway my wife's neck snapped in my direction, breaking her concentration on the program. 'Huh?'

From the TV speakers, a campy White man was saying, 'Love this, it's a great colour for you, what a difference, what a difference a gay makes,' and from behind our thin garage walls was the loud and exhausted banter of my brother and father, who were finishing their final half-hour of the Thursday late-night shopping. If I thought about my next steps for too long, and all their consequences, I would panic and be unable to get the words out. I had to approach this like a boxing match; just clear my mind and get in that ring before it dawned upon me that I was about to get my face punched in.

'Fatima, talaq, talaq, talaq.' In Arabic, 'talaq' means 'repudiation' and 'divorce', and in Islamic law it refers to my right to end my marriage by simply saying it out loud three times. My heart thudded like a hundred-thousand uppercuts as I waited for Fatima to react in a succession of screams and sobs and running tears, but instead she remained coiled up on our bed, as illiterate in formal Arabic as she was in gibberish. She chuckled and replied, 'W-what does that mean?'

Feet so weak that my legs were caving in, hands clenched so tightly that my fingernails were cutting into my palms, I forced myself to go on. I had already started and if I just hung in there, it would all be over in less than a three-minute round. 'I am divorcing you,' I said. 'Do you understand? Divorcing you.'

Fatima sprung from the bed like a frightened mouse. 'No!' she screamed. 'I don't care, I don't care that you're a poofta!'

Jesus. I was so shocked that my entire body went stiff and my lips spontaneously clasped together. Bucky had been right! Fatima thought I was gay, from the very beginning that's what she thought, and still she wanted to stay with me. Her plea tore at my soul: how could I abandon someone so pathetic, and at the same time, how could I stay? A queer eye squealed, 'You're gonna start living better, you're gonna start living now,' and over it I squealed back at her, 'You watch too much of that shit!'

Fatima began to shudder, her head shaking wildly from left to right. 'No I don't, I don't even like TV.' She ran at the television and hauled it with both hands to the floor, the screen shattering as it hit the tiles. 'If you leave me, everyone will find out you're a gay,' she cried. 'Just let me help you, no other woman will put up with you!'

I wanted so badly to hold her right then, to hold her between her tiny stomach and wide hips, plant my forehead against her brow, and with my breath upon her mouth; beg her to forgive me. Forgive me for taking her virginity. Forgive me for breaking my promise that it would only ever be her and me. Forgive me for sending her back to her parents. Forgive me for making it so much harder now to find the Alawite that she was *meant* to spend her life with. Forgive me for not being the gay guy who simply could not desire the opposite sex. Forgive me for being the straight guy who simply didn't want her. Forgive me ... for choosing Oli. But when I tried to tell her about Oli, all that came out of my mouth was 'Ol' before Fatima squeaked, 'I'll kill myself. Wahyaat Allah, if you leave me, I'll kill myself.'

She clutched onto me, her screeching voice reverberating through the patchwork of the garage ceiling. 'I'll kill myself!' she bellowed one more time, shoving me towards the empty wall space between our bed and bathroom door. Her eyes were wide open and drenched in tears, her glare blurred into a ghostly smudge.

The back of my head collided with the wall, sending a dull pain down my spine, and in my frustration I spluttered at her, 'What do I owe ya, bro, what tha fuck do I owe ya?' I was so tired of these people constantly threatening me when I didn't do what they wanted; threatening to tell my tribe I had been in a porno, threatening to put my face through a toilet door because I'd been on a train with some girl, threatening to hold me ransom with their own life! There was no longer any threat that frightened me as much as the thought of a life without Oli; no longer any threat that could match the madness that had been swelling inside me, the madness of Majnun, who knew that however agonising the experience, if it is for love it is well; and the madness of Romeo, who warned us never to tempt a desperate man. I locked both my hands firmly around Fatima's wrists and pushed her off me, the collar of my Bonds shirt tearing as she stumbled back onto our bed. 'Happy dagger!' I screamed at her, and once again she stared at me in utter confusion, as though I was speaking gibberish. 'This is thy sheath; there rust, and let me die.' Closing my eyes, I thrusted towards the wall behind me, swinging my head with the greatest force I could muster into the wood. A piercing crackle reverberated through the building as Fatima shrieked in horror and a numbing sting flattened my forehead. I felt my legs buckle like I had taken a sledgehammer to the face, but rather than backing away I used the momentum to swing my head into the wall even harder, again and again, until I had left a hole in the timber the size of my own skull. On the final blow, my legs sank like they had been dunked in boiling oil, and I collapsed to the floor, my temple drubbing and twitching and burning and stinging and moistening as the first drops of blood oozed over my eyebrows. Lying there on the tiles I found myself drifting into my childhood. I was five years old and playing a game called 'lemons' with my uncles and male cousins, in which we would butt heads like two rams until one of us was concussed or gave up. The night I broke up with Fatima, I decided I would either die a lemon or become your father. 'Oh Oli,' I drooled along the tiles. 'You cannot imagine how much I am "Majnun". For you, I have lost myself.'

A second later, or at least in what felt like a second, I was raised up by my shoulders and eased onto the edge of my bed, where I fell into my father's arms like an infant. I remembered his arms, back when I was two-feet tall, lifting me up towards his chin as though I were Icarus. His golden hands were my wings, and his harsh face beaming down at me was the sun. Outside, I could hear Fatima sobbing out of control, and my brother's smooth voice on top of hers, asserting that it wasn't her fault, that his younger brother had always been a majnun – more majnun than a thousand majnuns. I dipped my face into my father's beating chest, soaking his grey shirt in the blood across my crown, crying into him, 'Please, teach me; teach me how I should forget to think.'

Your grandfather's grip tightened around me, his iron jaw sinking into my curly black hair and his breastplate expanding into a deep breath that sounded like he had swallowed the ocean. 'I should have let this one go,' he said. 'Allah knows, I should have let him go.'

THIRTY-FIVE

WHILE MY DAD WAS on the phone to my godfather, and my brother was on the phone to my mother, and my wife was on the phone to my mother-in-law, I sprinted from the garage door, running as fast as I could down Canterbury Road to the intersection between a bucket of fried chicken and two golden arches. *Pick me up from Macca's, bro?* I texted Bucky, pacing on the footpath, where a sharp crescent emerged from a withering fleet of clouds. I could feel the Prophet Muhammad staring down at me from the moon, reminding me of the time he stood up against the powerful tribes of Mecca. 'No god but God,' he declared, which, for the local merchants who had acquired their fortunes selling false idols made from clay, was bad for business. 'We'll give you wealth, land, women, whatever you desire,' they told Muhammad, to which he replied, 'If you put the sun in my right hand, and the moon in my left hand, I will not denounce my message, which is from God.' You see, Kahlil, how our prophet was so uncompromising. I was tired of compromising. I compromised with the Lebs of Punchbowl Boys, who divided the world into sluts and virgins; got as many head jobs as possible from the Aussie chicks of Campbelltown and then went to Lebanon to find an unspoiled bride. I compromised with the White women in the world of theatre, who taught me that if I wanted to be an artist, they would first have to pound the Arab man out of me; one of them striding up to me salaciously during an improvisation and threatening to shove a skipping rope handle up my arse. And I compromised with my tribe, who did not know the difference between chicken bones and belly rings and freckles.

The moon had slipped back into the clouds, taking Muhammad with it, by the time Bucky picked me up in his old white Corolla and drove me towards the inner west. His car floor was filled with Big Mac wrappers and McChicken wrappers and Quarter Pounder wrappers and Whopper wrappers, and the fabric of the ceiling had come loose and hung over our heads like bedsheets. 'Your poofta best friend driving you to your White whore,' Bucky cackled, his enormous lower lip flattening. 'I might as well be driving you straight to hell, bro.'

'It's better than driving myself to hell,' I exhaled, no longer able to stand the thought of being inside my own car.

I had my phone on silent, but I could feel it continually vibrating in my pocket, freezing only for a moment before the next attempt to contact me began. It was the Mexican Hat Dance all over again, only this time, it wasn't my cousin's head that had been pummelled, it was mine.

Bucky pulled up in front of Oli's townhouse and before I got out he said, 'Listen Bani, I'm going vegan for a little while, but

I'm still a Wog, okay, don't ever forget that.' I stared at him in gratitude, removing my wedding ring, sticking it in his hand and saying, 'For you.' I placed my fingers to my lips, kissed them, and pressed them against his own lips, the closest I had ever come to expressing my love for another man.

Somehow, only a few hours after I'd left Oli's bed, I was back on her mattress, trembling naked in her bedsheet. Oli held a warm towel across my forehead and wiped away the dry blood that had clotted over my wounds as tears ran silently down her cheeks, her eyes shimmering among the haze of candlelight. 'Have I cursed you?'

I answered her question with a story: fifteen hundred years ago, an illiterate merchant named Muhammad fell in love with Khadijah, a successful businesswoman who was a widow and fifteen years his senior. When Muhammad was twenty-five, he accepted a marriage proposal from Khadijah, and fifteen years after their wedding, while Muhammad meditated up on the mountain, he was waylaid by the Archangel Jibreel. The angel had come with a message: 'Read.' Muhammad replied, 'I am not of those who read,' and the angel repeated, 'Read, in the name of your lord who created, created humankind from a clinging clot, read.' Upon hearing these words – the very first words of the Qur'an – Muhammad returned to Khadijah in a state of terror. He pleaded for her to cover him with a blanket and recounted his experience to her. And she believed him – making her the first Muslim in history. 'If I'm cursed,' I said to the White girl, 'it's only the curse of my prophet's example.'

Oli held me close as the candle flickered and melted into the silent hours of the night. Our night, which was her uneven fingernail grazing the calluses between my knuckles; our night, which was my blood and sweat seeping into the fibres of her pillowslips; our night, which was your life longing for itself ...

THIRTY-SIX

A WHITE GAZE HOVERED over my days with Oli. We loitered in the bookstores on Glebe Point Road, where she ran into her ex-boyfriend – a short hippie in a chequered shirt and bow tie named Trent. He had a dry freckled face and a patchy orange beard, which he kept touching with the smallest fingers I'd ever seen on a man. He looked up at me and said, 'I heard you were Lebo – that's totally badass, bro.'

I gave him a fake smile and watched him like a pit bull on a rabbit as he kissed Oli goodbye and left the store without buying anything. 'Why would you date a loser like that?' I asked Oli, and she replied, 'He's a performance artist, just a little bit more interesting than the boys I grew up with in The Hills.'

Next, we loitered in the bookstores on King Street, Newtown, where Oli ran into her best friend from high school; a pimple-face named Liz who had bright green eyes and large square glasses and straight red hair. Oli hadn't seen her in six months because Liz had been in India with her English boyfriend, but she was back now and had moved from The Hills Shire to the inner west to complete a doctorate in literature at UNSW. Squaring off with my beret, she wobbled her head like a Curry-muncher and said in a husky voice, 'I heard you were Muslim – that's extreeeeme.'

I gave her a smile that matched the one I gave Trent and watched as she closed her eyes and took in a deep breath, pressing her chest tightly against Oli's and giving her a hug that lasted for several minutes. 'I'm so happy for you,' she hissed. 'Oh my god, I'm so jealous.'

Once Liz had exited the store, Oli cringed at me and said, 'She didn't mean "extreme" like a terrorist, just like, you know, like it's cool ...'

As though that was any less racist.

Afterwards, Oli took me to Marrickville to check out some of the second-hand clothing stores for seventies-style trousers – she knew the hipster shops of the inner west as well as I knew the kebab shops of Bankstown. We were in front of a Chinese mixed-business when she froze in front of a friend of a friend of her sister's walking towards us – a pale-faced actor I'd seen on television wearing brown make-up and an afro wig. 'Dick!' Oli yelped, 'I mean, Richard.' He ignored her and focused on me instead, looking down at my sneakers and then up to my flares and then up to my crotch like he was wondering how big my dick was before moving onto my veiny arms and my tight chest and my head of curls, as though I was a costume he wanted to wear. And I stared straight back like if this piece of shit didn't stop staring, I was gonna rip his fucken eyes out.

Finally, Oli and I were strolling on her empty street just as the sun was setting and the first evening star emerged. The steadiness of dusk was suddenly overcome with a squeak in my head: the silver-haired woman back at my university bookshop, saying, 'What yous did to those girls,' as though one Bilal Skaf meant we were all Bilal Skaf. I halted in the middle of the road. 'What is this, huh? You bored or some crap? I'm Othello now?' With all due respect, Kahlil, I know I was being harsh on her, but please don't be too harsh on me: I am the other, and you are half the other, and your mother is the other half of you.

Awkward as she was, the White girl did not hesitate this time, grabbing me with both hands tightly around the neck and taking in a deep breath. 'Bani, I can't apologise for being White – I am what I am, and I am not what I am not, but if you wanna know why I chose you, I'll tell you.' She was resisting the urge to cry, settling on a single tear that trickled down her left cheek and dissolved on the corner of her lip. 'It was that black eye,' she said, her cheekbones limping. 'You love things in the most miserable kind of way, and I'm so selfish, I wanted to be loved like that.'

I placed my hands around her neck, mirroring her own hands, and invited her into the gaps between my lashes. Kill us tomorrow; let us live tonight. For she had eyes and chose me.

THIRTY-SEVEN

EVERY TIME I TRIED to get out, my godfather was there to pull me back in. Thirty-two missed calls from him within the first week that I ran from that garage, from that wife, from that tribe. I ignored them at first, not because I was still afraid of him, but because I wasn't: the day he became my godfather, he told me, 'Nothing in your life will ever be more important to God than me. Whenever I call you, answer straightaway; whenever I summon you, arrive at my doorstep straightaway; and whenever I draw my hand unto you, kiss it and pay your dowry to me straightaway.'

Nothing is more important to God than love, I said to myself each time the phone rang and went to voicemail, but as the calls continued coming in, I became eager to discover if the legends I had been taught as a boy were true: Would Allah really strike me down if I rose up against my godfather? 'Salaam alaikum,' I answered calmly, standing barefoot on top of a mound of Oli's shirts and pants and skirts.

'Salaam alaikum? Salaam alaikum?' he scoffed, as though he was insulted that I wished him peace. Then he went silent, like he was waiting for me to respond, and when I didn't, he added, 'You are a shameless sinful impure coward.' Once again, he went silent, practically begging for some kind of reaction from me, but still I would not give him one, and so at last he said, 'I will tell our people you were riding a female dog on the SBS!'

My toes clenched into a pair of Oli's red underpants. 'Tell them!' I finally screamed out. 'I fear no one but God. And you're not God. There's no god but God.' I launched my phone into a wall across the room, my breath catching up to itself, my heartbeat paddling, my knuckles retracting, my toes releasing. And then I waited, ready to burst into flames or turn into a statue of salt. But nothing happened. I was as interesting to Allah as a speck of dust was to me.

Abu Hassan never dialled my phone number again after that, and we never saw each other again, except one time, three years later, when I caught his gaze upon Oli and me from the other end of the soap aisle in Bankstown Woolworths. He had gained at least another thirty kilos by then and now stood in his short stature like a dry slug, his thick eyebrows caving in on us.

'Who's that?' asked Oli. I did not answer; instead I grabbed her in the middle of the aisle and held my open mouth up against hers, shoving my tongue through her teeth and kissing her wildly until I felt him disappear from my peripheral vision. Sorry to have disrespected your mother like that, but after I stopped, she pulled me in for another round, her lips interlacing with mine – we were two porn stars on the supermarket floor with no one other than God to judge us. I screamed out, 'Allahu akbar!' Then I filled our trolley up with sponges. Hundreds of sponges.

THIRTY-EIGHT

FOUR THURSDAY EVENINGS AFTER that one fateful Thursday evening, I returned home. Cave of Wonders was closed up, and the back garage, which I remembered as being filled with the sound and the light of Fatima's DVD programs, was shrouded in shadows. I entered and turned on the garage light, which poured into every corner of the room, illuminating Fatima's final tracks. Our bed remained, but no bedsheets or pillows on the mattress. Our television, with its shattered screen, had been placed back onto the TV unit. There were no towels in the bathroom, no hair straightener or hairdryer in the vanity, no oils or creams or paracetamol tablets in the medicine cabinet, no jasmine shampoo or milk-and-honey body wash or lavender conditioner in the shower, and no cloths or sponges or soaps on the kitchen sink. When I opened our wardrobe, all my clothes remained on my side, but there were none of her clothes on the racks, and none of her G-strings in the drawers. There was no perfectly organised make-up, and no video camera on the shelf – but what point was there in taking both for someone like Fatima?

I had only ever switched the camera on once after returning from our honeymoon to show my brother a clip of us on a gondola. He observed carefully for a couple of minutes and responded, 'Nice boat, but why's your missus staring into her make-up mirror the whole time?' All the DVDs were gone from the shelves too, including mine, such as *Fight Club* and *Pulp Fiction* and *American Psycho* and *Raging Bull* and *Goodfellas* and *Spider-Man 2*. What remained, in perhaps Fatima's final reminder that we had been horribly mismatched, were my hundreds of books, none of which seemed worthy of the space in her baggage. I took my copy of *Lolita* from the shelf, which had bright red lips on the cover and foxed pages on the inside. Spreading the book open, I breathed in its scent of old wood and vanilla and sighed with relief. These words would not have been safe in the hands of my great-uncle, who had molested my baby aunt back in Tripoli, and these words would not have been safe in the hands of my cousin Noor, who had rubbed himself under the bedsheets until it was hot and wet on my boxer shorts, and these words would not have been safe in the hands of my father-in-law, who beat my wife with his bare fists back in Berala. But they were safe with me, Kahlil. Human life is but a series of footnotes to a vast obscure unfinished masterpiece. See how I made the words safe for you ...

I sat on the bed, alone, staring at the hole I had left in the wall. The wounds in my head had healed, but their ghosts lingered. I could hear Fatima's high voice outside, screaming, 'What's going on?' and 'What did I do?' and 'It wasn't meant to be like this.' I waited anxiously for her perfect face, drenched in bright red lipstick and black mascara, to appear in the doorway, but instead, my mother materialised before me, caked in make-up all the same.

'You're home,' she said gently. 'I came back every night with pillows and blankets and food for you.' I felt both shame and comfort in the unconditional parameters of an Arab mother's love. During my early teens, if she cooked falafel for dinner, which I hated, I would tell her I wasn't hungry and wait silently. In ten minutes, she would begin to panic and start cutting up potatoes to make me a fresh batch of deep-fried hot chips covered in chicken salt and barbecue sauce so that I wouldn't starve to death.

I tore through my mum's warak enab – vine leaves and rice and meat and oil and water and salt and lemon juice spasming on my tongue – like I had never seen food before.

Mum said, 'Mandy is pregnant.'

And I thought, *What a crappy uncle I will be.*

She said, 'Yocheved has set her wedding date.'

And I thought, *What a crappy brother-in-law I will be.*

She said, 'Fatima is back home with her parents.'

And I thought, *What a crappy husband I was.*

I looked up at Mum from my plate, jaw gnawing through rice that had been cooked for so long that it was as soft as butter, pressing her to elaborate with my eyes. 'Your father negotiated a divorce settlement of twenty-five thousand dollars with her father,' she said downheartedly, her cheeks and forehead crinkling. 'You'll have to pay it from the money you were saving for a home loan. But you don't care, do you?'

No, I didn't. There was no payment or punishment The Tribe could impose on me which would have alleviated the guilt I felt. For the first few days I had spent at Oli's, all I did was hide under her sheets and cry. I cried at the memory of Fatima's face, pallid and open and soaked in a mixture of fear and confusion – she was just a teenager who simply could not understand how our marriage, built on a bunch of wallahs, had come to such an abrupt end. I cried at the sound of her innocuous voice, shrieking outside the last words I heard from her, 'This wasn't supposed to happen!' Every story she had ever been told, be it from The Tribe that raised her or the American sitcoms that consumed her hours, assured her that if she just got skinny enough, eventually a man would come knocking, fall in love at the sight of her, marry her, take her on a honeymoon to a land where roads were rivers and cars were gondolas, buy her a home, have her children and that was that – that was life. I cried at the thought of her returning to her father, who would slap her if she was in the bathroom for too long, clipping her nails and shaving her legs and straightening her hair and doing her squats and all the other things that young women do in there. I cried because she would have to return to her mother, who had robbed Fatima of the chance to wear a pink dress at her own engagement, as though she wanted to be in her place. Did she want to be in her daughter's place now? And I cried hardest because I was the one who had sent Fatima back to them, breaking my one promise that it was always going to be just me and her. I had no excuses – for all of Fatima's shortcomings as a wife, she had been honest with me, she showed me exactly who she was the first time we spoke: 'Will you let me wear G-strings?' she asked. I did not deserve anyone's forgiveness for saying yes, Kahlil, anyone's except yours. Was it not you who orchestrated this? Was it not you who reminded me that I was only twenty-three, and that no mistake at twenty-three was worth your life ...?

Mum told me that Fatima's family was eager to receive the money as soon as possible. Apparently they had found her another husband, a cousin from Syria. They would send her to get engaged to him as soon as they had been compensated for my actions, and then they would send her again one year later, once the divorce was final, to officially marry him. 'I'll transfer it into Fatima's account tomorrow morning,' I said without hesitation, even though I was disgusted by what these people intended to do with my life savings. Why was marriage the only solution my tribe could think of for their children's problems? Not even a year after they had wedded their daughter to me, and not even a month after we had separated, they were already shipping her off to another man.

I just ate and nodded as my mum continued talking, not really listening to anything else she said, until she caught me with an unexpected question: 'Will you be staying or returning to live with the manuuk – the homosexual?' Only then did I realise that my family were under the impression that I had been living with Bucky this entire time. I wondered how she knew Bucky was gay; perhaps one of my sisters told her. I entrusted this kind of information to the girls in my family, who tended to be less homophobic than the boys, the men, and the women in the House of Adam; less homophobic than pretty much anyone who had some power and status within The Tribe. I chuckled and replied, 'You know I'm not gay, right?' And she said, 'Yes, of course I know, we all know. Why would anyone be a gay? Nobody said you're a gay. Even when you wore your funny jeans and funny hats, I never thought you were a gay.' Her face had swollen like a balloon and pinked like a piglet, relieved.

'Your dad will give you your old job back ...' she continued. I went stiff at the thought of working in that cave again. 'I'm not coming back to the shop, Mum, I wasn't born to sell tents, I was born to write stories.' Her face shrunk back to its normal size and her complexion went pale – as though, once again, she was wondering if maybe I was gay. But far more important than the question of whether I was into cocks was the issue of whether I wanted to stay here. I had certainly enjoyed my time hiding out in the inner west with Oli, sharing more food and memories and sweat with her in four weeks than I had with anyone else in my entire life. I was at such peace that I forgot to remember Sahara, till one night, when Oli asked me if the Alawites were going to reject her because she was an atheist. My heart heaved into my mouth – even a girl who believed in one god was not enough for The Tribe. I told Oli about Sahara, about her golden skin and her innocent brown eyes and her long black hair and her bubbly voice and the chicken bones she kept in her pockets.

'I'm sorry you never got to be with her,' Oli said gently, and I knew then that there was nothing to be sorry about; great love was no longer behind me, it was in front of me, sprawling down the inner-west train line, freckling in the summer, grinding itself to whiteness. I asked the White girl to thank Allah with me, and her voice cracked into a shard of salt. 'I was raised without God, Bani Adam, how can I thank someone I don't believe in?' Forgive her, Kahlil – it would be another five years before she held you in her frail arms.

Yes, I was grateful for the time I had spent in self-imposed exile with Oli, but I also missed the western suburbs. I missed the copper faces and thick beards and white hijabs down Haldon Street, the Call to Prayer out the front of Lakemba Mosque, the habibs on the train station stairs screaming out to each other, 'Luk

284

oh ma god, I can't talk,' the habibas ordering garlic and chicken from Abu Ahmad's and saying, 'I'm so excited my stomach is grumbliiiiiing,' and more than anything else I missed the sound of my father's and brother's voices between the walls of the shop and the garage, the reassurance that they were there, loudly disagreeing with one another about who would win in a fight between Muhammad Ali and Mike Tyson, but both agreeing that either one of them would have beaten Bruce Lee. Just as the White girl had shared her world with me, I longed to share this world with her, and I *would* return home so long as she was welcome to return with me. I had inhaled every vine leaf and was lapping up the remainder of the lemon juice with my spoon as I told Mum about Oli – who was Aussie and godless and two years older than me. Mum nodded for an unusually long time, and then she finally replied, 'See, of course you are not a gay.'

THIRTY-NINE

WIFE SCREAMING. *THIS WASN'T supposed to happen.* Me wailing. *Allah forgive me.* Waking up with tears around my eyelids. Moist and briny. An index finger in my mouth. Wrinkled and salty. Clasped my lips around Oli's fingernail. Reached for my phone, perched on top of a hardcover book with a thick spine: *A Vindication of the Rights of Woman.* One text message from Dad: *Come home.* One text back from me: *Not without Olive.*

'It's gonna break his heart,' I mumbled at the White girl, pushing out her finger with my tongue.

She blinked several times and took in a deep breath. 'We all have to break our dad's hearts in our own way,' she responded. *Far out,* I thought to myself, *maybe her dad is as afraid of me as my dad is afraid of her.* Throughout my teens, I was constantly reminded that White men did not want a Sand Coon anywhere near their daughters. One time, I strolled out of my philosophy tutorial with an Aussie chick named Claire, laughing about how our professor was a sweaty smelly fat shit. Suddenly, Claire stopped at the sight of a grey-bearded man in a white Camry, bit her lip and said to me, 'Hey, that's my dad picking me up, is it okay if you go the other way from here?' Being a Muslim with four younger sisters, I fully understood that many girls had to hide their male friends from their over-protective fathers, so I took no offence. But a few days later, I found myself trailing out of class behind Claire and a pimply Skip in flip-flops, and once again the grey-bearded man was in the carpark; only this time she walked the Skip all the way towards the white Camry and introduced them. Watching calmly through a pair of black sunglasses as the two men shook hands, I accepted that it wasn't the boy part she was hiding from her father; it was the Muslim part, the Arab part, the Leb part, the bin Laden part, the Bilal Skaf part.

'That's really shit,' Oli responded when I recounted this story to her. 'But no, my father doesn't care about the race part, it's the marriage part.' It suddenly dawned upon me that much like the way Oli always assumed that every conversation we had was going to be in English, I assumed that marriage was just a natural part of every young woman's life.

I asked Oli to teach me and tucked myself under our bedsheets, where it was warm and dark. I could absorb nothing but her morning voice, which creaked as she breathed in the air of daybreak. Oli told me she went to a high school in the Bogan bible belt of Western Sydney. In Year 9, after admitting to her class that she was born out of wedlock, they nicknamed her Edmund, a reference to the bastard son of the Earl of Gloucester in *King Lear*. A sidenote, Kahlil: Peckerwoods always try too hard – back at Punchbowl Boys we would have just called your mum a bastard. So, Oli went home and asked her dad why he never married her mum and he answered, 'Religion is stupid, weddings are stupid, rings are stupid, people are stupid.' But when Oli asked her mum the same question, she answered, 'It's what your dad wanted.' And this is where Oli found herself stuck: too much of a feminist to be married off and too much of a feminist to do what her father wanted. I saw myself squeezing so perfectly between this conundrum: a hopeless romantic who believed in the idea of an eternal union on one hand and a divorcé who saw through the charade of marriage and weddings on the other. Popping my head and arms out of the sheets, I gave Oli's broken nose a little squeeze, 'Just love me however you want.' At that exact moment, my phone vibrated. A final text message from my dad: *Inshallah.*

Before Fatima, there was the girl who wore a cross, to which my father said no. And after Fatima, there was the girl with the fair and freckled skin, to whom my father said yes. Fatima, the Flower. Fatima, the Chanel handbag. Fatima, my father's curse, who could not superglue his son to the belly of The Tribe. Fatima, my father's gift, who taught him that love could not be willed by men, love could only be willed by the stars. Every night that I slept in Oli's bed, I could hear Fatima pleading with me to take her back and wailing how this wasn't supposed to happen. And all I could do was pray for her. Allah yah-meeki, yaa Fatima. May Allah keep you safe, oh Fatima. I'm sorry, Fatima, but this *was* supposed to happen. Salaam, Fatima. Salaam.

FORTY

IN THE SECOND WEEK of December, I returned to the garage and mastered the art of living on my own – keeping the shattered television on from sunset to sunrise, filling the eeriness of night with the sound and vibrant colours of infomercials. Every other moment, I visited Oli's bedroom. One day, while she was working at the PCYC I even took the Arab liberty of spending the afternoon alone in her townhouse folding all her clothes. I especially enjoyed folding her white undershirts, of which she had at least a dozen, all smelling like a combination of sweat and deodorant and that musky scent of old garments when you enter a second-hand clothing store. As I sorted through Oli's mound, I also found over ninety dollars in change, which I stowed in an empty grey tea tin that had been hiding beneath a pile of odd socks, and a pair of seventies-style flared jeans which fit me perfectly. I was wearing them by the time Oli arrived home. She took one look at my Gumby-shaped legs, and said, 'See, mess leads to the discovery of many treasures ...'

Playfully, I asked, 'Is this the thanks I get for cleaning your room?'

'I am thankful,' Oli replied. 'But if you were gonna waste your hours while I'm at work, I'd prefer you wasted them closer to me.' This was how she persuaded me to return to the boxing gym. While I did not see any point in fighting again, my tired calluses had been aching for the sting of tired leather and my dehydrated skin had been longing for the moisture that ran from my shoulders to the canvas ever since I got my nose job. The sight of Oli at the reception desk tapping away at her computer as I walked down the PCYC corridor made me as hard as I had ever been at any point in my boxing years. I handed her my updated membership card with a grin and sprinted down towards the underground gym, where the smell of petroleum jelly and dried blood and hoary sweat poured through my wide-open nostrils. Leo was in the ring when I entered, screaming 'No arse shit!' at the boy he was instructing – a fresh generation of young Brown fighter. As soon as he saw me, he gave me his bull frown and sneered, 'That nose is hideous, but we'll fix it for ya!'

At the end of my workout, I stood in front of Oli at the reception desk, the vapour drying off my back as I recounted to her the time that I got hit so hard I vomited all over the canvas. Oli giggled straight on to 8pm, at which point it was time to close the building and I could escort her back to the bedroom where a mound of clothing and books and coins and trinkets had already begun to rematerialise across her carpet.

It was during this period that I re-enrolled in Western Sydney University to complete my honours degree – a result of feeling both deeply inspired and pathetically jealous of the White girl's education. In preparation for my post-graduate studies, I wrote several short stories and personal essays about my experiences as a Rug Rider and emailed them to newspaper editors and literary journal editors and magazine editors throughout the country. The first story I sent out detailed an incident from my childhood; the kind of incident that condemns a person like me to write. Up until I was nine years old, my favourite film was *Bloodsport*. Frank Dux, played by Jean-Claude Van Damme in the prime of his career, competes against the world's best fighters in the underground martial arts tournament called the Kumite.

On the opening day of the Kumite, Frank Dux's first fight is against a brown-skinned man in a traditional Saudi headdress named Hossein. As soon as the bell rings, Frank takes Hossein down with a few quick punches, breaking the world record for the fastest Kumite knockout in history. But shifty Hossein does not concede defeat and after Frank is declared victorious, the Arab pounces up and attempts to take a cheap shot at him from behind. Frank pre-empts the attack, and delivers a reverse elbow-punch combination that knocks Hossein out cold.

Whenever I had a fistfight at primary school, during my time in the working-class slums of the inner west, I always imagined myself as Frank Dux. I would throw three straight punches, one roundhouse kick and one helicopter fly-kick, concussing my opponent in a few seconds. One lunchtime, an eleven-year-old boy named Thomas Pearce, who had splitting blue eyes, called me a 'Lebanese shit'. As the other kids in his grade looked on, I threw a succession of punches and kicks, each of which missed him by a foot. Thomas stood back, watching me tire myself out, and then he stepped in towards me, gave me one hard push, and

I was down. Lying on the ground while Thomas and the other kids laughed at me and chanted 'Lebanese shit, Lebanese shit,' I finally realised I wasn't Frank Dux. I was Hossein.

A Leb boy and a White girl completing their humanities degrees from the same bed quickly turned into a culture war between the sheets and the pillows. I introduced Oli to James Baldwin: *The people who think of themselves as white have the choice of becoming human or irrelevant.* Oli introduced me to Germaine Greer: *Psychologists cannot fix the world so they fix women.* I introduced her to Edward Said: *If the Arab occupies space enough for attention, it is a negative value.* She introduced me to Judith Butler: *Let's face it. We're undone by each other.* We exchanged readings and argued all night until we found each other at the halfway point of Oli's mattress, where we agreed that both men and Whites sucked, and made rough love under her blanket, in pure darkness, no longer aware of where my dick ended and her skin began.

We woke up a few hours later, Oli's face blue and translucent as a jelly fish. Three months after we became a couple, the White girl informed me about an annual family get-together she had been dreading. It took place every Christmas Day at the house of her father's older brother, a retired food court cleaner named Barney. I had my head in Oli's lap, at the mercy of her fingernails, which were intertwined in my head of curls, as she asked, 'Who do you jerk off to when there's no one around?'

'Pamela Anderson,' I said, instantaneously.

'Well, my uncle jerks off to Pauline Hanson.'

A silver three-door 2000 Toyota Celica looked like the kind of car you'd find in a *Fast & Furious* sequel. I'd bought it from the Indian car dealer on Canterbury Road during the Christmas of 2007. Back then, even dropping a plate of my mum's food off at Aunt Yasmine's house, which was no more than a forty-second walk from our place, was a good enough excuse to start up the engine. Every Lebo on the street flung his hand up at the sight of me and screamed, 'Shu habib!' and I'd throw my hand out the wide driver's seat window and scream back, 'Yeah habib!' But by the morning of Christmas Day 2010, there was no one other than Oli who could get me back behind a steering wheel. Anxious about attending her uncle's annual get-together, she asked that I drive her to Granville – the suburb that hosted my wedding. Having slept in the driveway at the back of my father's shop undisturbed for several weeks, the Celica was restless, grunting and rumbling upon ignition. I let the engine run for several minutes before I took off down Haldon Street to collect Oli from Lakemba train station. As soon as she got in the car, she gave me a sly little smile, like she was trying to hold her tongue, before finally saying, 'This car is so Leb.'

'Hectic,' I replied. 'Your uncle's gonna love it, cuz.'

During the drive, Oli listed all the racist comments her father's brother had made about Muslims whenever she visited him – we hacked off clitorises, we funnelled drug money to Al-Qaida, we had four wives each and we had underground basements in Lakemba Mosque where we stockpiled weapons of mass destruction. Cruising along South Street, windows and sunroof down, while hundreds of Arabs and Muslims peacefully meandered between the grocery stores, charcoal-chicken shops and chemists, I found it hard to believe that an Aussie who lived among us could hate us so much. 'It's *because* he lives among you that he hates you,' Oli explained. 'It's easy to love multiculturalism when you're living in a gentrified community where people like you are not in our face all the time.' Having spent several years familiarising myself with Glebe, first through Sahara and now through Oli, I fully appreciated her point. Two weeks earlier we'd visited a thriving orientalist-themed Lebanese restaurant on Glebe Point Road called Al-Mustafa, which was dim and fitted with tapestries of camels and sand dunes and Bedouins along the walls, and cushions woven in Arabesque patterns along the carpeted floors. Oli and I were greeted at the entrance by the store owner, a Skip named Steve, who said to me in a nasal accent, 'Mar'haba.' Unlike the Lebanese restaurants in Lakemba filled with ayatollah frowns, Al-Mustafa was full of bleached smiles, and everything on the menu was four times the amount you'd pay for the exact same item anywhere in the western suburbs. 'Six falafels for twenty-fucken-two-dollars,' I had said to Oli as we read the menu. 'A Leb restaurant that's too expensive for a Leb!'

My tyres crackled over a pool of gumnuts as I pulled up to Oli's uncle's house, an old wooden terrace covered in cracked white paint. On the verandah, an Australian flag hung over the metal railing, only it had a red background instead of a blue one, immediately bringing to my mind the flags of the Confederate States of America. Oli slipped out of the car, walked across the nature strip and along the yellow grass of the front yard. She turned back, tugging down tightly on the waist of her long floral dress, which was already below her ankles and did not require any further modesty. I stuck my tongue out at her and she smiled, a nervous smile filled with love and guilt and twenty-two-dollar falafels.

After dropping Oli off, I drove to the Lebanese sweet shop next door to the Grand Royale, the reception Fatima chose for our wedding day. The building was empty, but as I stared at the glass doors that flanked the front stairs, I could feel the lililililililililili reverberating through my entire body and the hands of The Tribe all over mine and Fatima's arses, thrusting us into the air, bouncing us up and down, quivering under the whisky and vodka and piss.

Inside the sweet shop, I was served a cinnamon tea and a ladies' finger by a guy whose nametag said 'Hectic Muhammed'. He had a long thick beard and a freshly shaved head and wore a white T-shirt that featured a picture of George W. Bush above the words: *Wanted Terrorist*.

'You're a funny cunt,' I said.

He winked at me, long eyelashes flattening, and replied, 'Your mum's a funny cunt.'

Between sipping my tea and licking the syrup off my index finger, I thought about all the compromises my family had to make over the years in order to accommodate people like Oli's uncle. My parents had six children and four of us were born while we lived in Alexandria. Mum and Dad had been concerned that we might experience discrimination growing up in such an Anglo community so they gave us all Anglo names. I was named Bani in Arabic, but on my birth certificate it was written as Benny. My brother Bilal was named Bill. My sister Yocheved, whose name was hard to pronounce even for an Arab, became Cindy. When their fourth child was born, my parents didn't even bother giving her an Arabic name; they called her Lulu, after their half-Christian niece.

The four of us, along with my three younger cousins who lived upstairs, all went to Alexandria Public School – nine kids of migrant background in the whole school and we were seven of them. When I refused to eat a hot dog at the school sausage sizzle, the students forced me to say that I didn't eat pig meat because my god was a pig; when I denied stealing the rubber from Gary Smith's pencil case, the students forced me to cross-my-heart-and-hope-to-die; and whenever I accidentally spoke in Arabic instead of English, saying 'Inshallah' instead of 'Yes, sir,' and 'Humdulilaah' instead of 'Thank you, miss,' the students gathered around me at lunchtime and squealed, 'Speak English you Sand N—'

'Speak English,' I whispered to myself when my phone began to ring. Oli's face flashed on my pixelated Nokia screen. She was crying uncontrollably, forcing her words out between sobbing breaths. 'Hey ... can ... you ... come ... get ... me?'

Five minutes later, I was back on the front kerb of the Pauline Hanson Groupie's house, where Oli was standing on the nature strip, face in her hands, next to a tall older White man with a thick brown moustache and round glasses, the red Australian flag stinging my eyes directly behind them.

The man introduced himself as Oli's father, Cameron. *How ironic*, I thought, *this atheist looks exactly like Ned Flanders*. I would have laughed were it not for the fact that Oli was so visibly upset.

'I want to explain to you what happened,' Cameron said. 'My brother isn't particularly educated ... he thinks you'll force Oli to wear the headscarf.'

I gave your grandfather a little grin and said, 'Okilly dokilly.' Having grown up as an Alawite in Lakemba, I had spent my whole life being told by Sunnis and Shi'ites that I was not a *real* Muslim because my mother, my sisters, my aunts and cousins did not wear hijabs, only to end up on a street in the hood, no different from the Taliban.

Oli lifted her face from her hands. The flesh around her drenched eyes had turned to ink. 'My uncle said, "He's gonna put you in a hijab." I said, "He won't." He said, "He will." I said, "He won't." He said, "He will." I said, "*He won't.*" He said, "*He will.*" "He won't." "He will." "He won't." "He will." Over and over, over and over.'

I grabbed the White girl and held her tightly, my arms against the bones in her spine, my mouth against her ear. 'Listen, I gotta tell you something really important,' I hissed down her drum. 'Do you know your dad looks like Ned Flanders?'

Oli pulled free from my grip and stared straight into my eyes, completely bewildered, her sight parching. I think she was disappointed that I wasn't outraged by her uncle, that I didn't just explode like a suicide bomber right there on his lawn. You see, to your mother, racism was this whole new thing, and she was excited, but to me, racism was just a normal part of life, and I was bored.

Watching on, Cameron wiped his hands across his face and mumbled to himself, 'Only happy families are alike ...'

'... And each unhappy family is unhappy in its own way,' I replied.

Cameron's eyebrows shot up and he looked at me with a paternal kind of affection. 'Tolstoy,' he said. '*Exactly.*'

I knew then that whether this man believed in the institution of marriage or not, he was the father-in-law I'd always wanted. 'I'd be happy to become part of this unhappy family, sir,' I said to him, stepping back towards my car and opening the passenger door. Rusty joints screeched towards the verandah of the house as

I gestured for Oli to jump into the vehicle. Suddenly a large bald man with a stereotypically Aussie beer gut appeared from behind the red flag. He was wearing a baby-blue T-shirt that had a picture of Santa Claus on it, and the words: *Make Me A Sandwich, You Ho Ho Ho.*

As thick as he was, I saw right through him: his hatred of me revealed his fear in me and his fear in me made me as dangerous to him as all the drug dealers and gangsters and terrorists that he saw every night on the news. Embracing the Lebanese bravado that had overrun his suburb, I cocked my chin and chest towards him, and said out loud, 'I'm standing right here, bro, you got something you wanna say?'

Voice rumbling across the lawn, he blubbered, 'Your scumbag cousins called me a White cunt.'

My entire childhood rushed up inside me, every conversation I ever had, every conversation I ever heard: Aussie cunt, Leb cunt, Asian cunt, Fob cunt, Curry cunt, Black cunt, sick cunt, mad cunt, bad cunt, hard cunt, sad cunt, pussy cunt, cock cunt, dog cunt, sexy cunt, shit cunt, dumb cunt, fat cunt, bitch cunt, gay cunt, rich cunt, poor cunt, hectic cunt, dead cunt – that's just how we speak over here in the ghetto, Kahlil. Giving Oli and her father a quick wink, I pulled my phone from my pocket and held it out in front of me, shouting back over the lawn, 'How 'bout I call my scumbag cousins down right now so you can sort it out with 'em?' Oli's uncle began to quake, his jowls spasming as he spun and barged through his front door, slamming it shut behind his lard arse. 'Yeah run, ya racist cunt!'

FORTY-ONE

DUMB LEBS IN THEIR WRXs, slim Nips in their Honda Civics, uncircumcised Skips in their Holden Commodores, hefty Fobs in their Taragos. I was sitting out the front of Cave of Wonders while Dad sewed factory second sleeping bags inside, my skin sucking in the sting of the summer sun. Watching Canterbury Road gust by, I found myself overcome with the thought that any moment now, Fatima's Pulsar was going to mount the kerb in front of my father's shop. She'd step out in her short, chequered skirt and pink tank top and highest high heels, screaming, 'Marriage is forever, faggot!'

She could keep the twenty-five thousand dollars, keep the car, keep the wedding ring, keep all my DVDs and my video camera and my bedsheets and pillowcases and soaps. She could keep the dishwashing gloves too, which I hoped she had stuck in a bonfire along with all our engagement photos and wedding photos and honeymoon photos, scorching them to ashes. Nothing felt like it would be enough to clear my debt to her.

I held up my phone and stared at Bucky's name, texting him: *Am I an evil cunt bro? For ditching my wife?*

Instantaneously, Bucky replied: *Nah your aussie slut's the evil one. Fucken homewrecker ;)*

From the moment I met Bucky he had been a smart-arse, inhaling my beret and flared jeans in one breath and exhaling with 'Ohh-laa-di-daa Mr French Man'. I ignored the 'homewrecker' part of his response and focused on the 'nah' part: *But how do you know?*

This time Bucky made me wait fifteen minutes for a reply. Canterbury Road rumbled on – a bus, a semi-trailer, a fire engine. Finally he wrote back: *well ur the only one who didnt dog me when i was at the lowest point in my mental health.*

I began typing a response, something along the lines of *Love you bro* or *Thank you for looking after me too bro* or *I will always be there for you bro*, when he sent me one more message: *Now fuck off u evil cunt, this shit's gay.*

———

I found her at Bankstown train station just after 3pm – waiting for me at the front gates as hundreds of third-world-looking people moved on and off the platform. Oli was like a snowflake caught in a rainbow. I took her by the arm and strolled us into the community garden where ten years ago a friend of mine from high school named Omar had been shot by members of a Vietnamese gang. Omar was a random revenge kill in a turf war between Viets and Lebs, which had followed on from a similar shooting a few months earlier of a Korean boy named Edward by young men of 'Middle Eastern appearance'. I recounted this turbulent period to Oli as her white skin deteriorated under the blistering sky. She said, 'I'm so sorry about your friend,' and then she paused, thought for a moment and added, 'White people are terrified of the sun.'

'Not Arabs,' I replied. 'We're made of the sun.'

'We're terrified of you too.'

I walked Oli into the shade of Bankstown Shopping Centre, where the desert people congregated. Reaching the food court, she asked what I felt like for lunch. Over the past three months, in an attempt to align myself with her, I did not eat any fast food, restricting my stomach to pastas and stir fries we were cooking at home, as well as a handful of vegan and vegetarian restaurants in Glebe and Newtown, but now I felt ready to show her the other half of me. 'Kilou Fucken Cesseb,' I said straightaway.

'Kilou Fucken Cesseb?' she repeated, her pronunciation almost spot-on. 'What's that?'

In Arabic it meant 'All Fucken Lies', but this was just my nickname for Kentucky Fried Chicken.

'KFC,' I explained.

Oli chuckled as though I had told her a joke.

'Really, that's what I wanna eat,' I stressed, watching her anaemic jawlines compress as it dawned upon her that I wasn't bullshitting …

We lined up behind a Leb who had the sides of his head shaved to the skin and a long black mullet down between his shoulder blades. I stared wide-eyed at the menu and told Oli I was going to order a large plain gravy and skoll it down like a can of non-alcoholic beer. Oli nodded in silence, no longer able to tell if I was fucking around or being sincere, chin wandering nervously from one gronk to the other.

When the Leb in front of us reached the counter, he said, 'Can I please have three pieces of chicken and cholesterol?'

The KFC employee, a young Curry-muncher with pigtails, raised her tinted eyelashes at him. 'Cholesterol?'

The Leb hesitated, his mullet slinging from side to side as he shook his head. 'Oh fuck, I mean coleslaw, I always mix those two up!'

While I dunked my chicken strips into my gravy, Oli sat and stared at me quietly, still not speaking a word. Finally I asked, 'So what's your problem, aye?' I swallowed, my throat and my chest and my stomach clenching at the chicken as it went down, like I had ingested a lump of clay.

'I just don't understand how you can put that stuff in your body,' Oli said.

'Yeah, what should I put in my body, bro?' I slobbered back at her, my mouth now full of chips and chicken skin.

'Well there's, like, a hundred decent places around here,' she observed, and either by coincidence or ignorance, she cast her hand at the first stall in the food court that caught her attention. *Aladdin: Authentic Lebanese Cuisine.*

I gritted my teeth as my abdomen twisted into a knot. 'Tell me about your upbringing,' I said to her.

'What? I don't understand. Why?'

'Just please.'

Oli examined my expression, and realising that I was as serious about this as I was about a bucket of fried chicken, she described the five-bedroom house which was home to four people: her father,

her mother, her sister and herself. She told me about her own room, which was covered in *Beverly Hills 90210* and *South Park* posters and connected to the backyard balcony. She described a green yard with a salt-water swimming pool that she partied in every summer with her three stoner cousins and a wooden fence that separated her house from an endless creek where she fed tadpoles and kookaburras on the weekends. She told me about her university-educated parents who made her take a vitamin C tablet with her brown toast every morning and insisted they read over her homework every evening to make sure she spelled all her words and added up all her numbers correctly; the sprawling rows of books arranged in alphabetical order on the bookshelves in her living room, the boring trips her father made her take to the Maritime Museum and Powerhouse Museum and the boring trips her mother made her take to the Art Gallery of NSW and the Museum of Contemporary Art during her school holidays. Then she told me about the time she was grounded, which meant she was prohibited from watching television for a week, for saying the word 'cunt' – but she insisted it wasn't her fault because she had learned the C-word from her mother, who always used to grumble under her breath, 'Cunt of a life.' And lastly, Oli told me that her father never liked to cook and that her mum did, but wasn't very good at it, so they regularly took her and her sister out to the Indian restaurants and Lebanese restaurants and Italian restaurants and Chinese restaurants in Castle Hill.

When Oli was done, I told her about my upbringing, the aftermath of a family who came from war-torn Lebanon – broke and barefoot. I grew up in a house with five bedrooms too but it was home to over fifteen people, and I shared my bedroom with half a dozen other children until I was eleven years old. My bedroom wasn't connected to a balcony like hers, but the window in the corner did overlook our backyard, which was completely concrete and no more than eight steps from one end to the other. We had no swimming pool but in summer my grandmother sprayed my siblings, cousins and me with the garden hose while we ran around the yard in our underpants – and when I said cousins, I did not mean three cousins who were seen as recreational drug users, but thirty cousins, who were seen as criminal drug dealers. I told Oli that my breakfast always consisted of Coco Pops and Froot Loops, but we had a roach infestation and when I poured my cereal into a bowl, a cockroach would often come squirming out and I'd have to go without food until lunchtime or dinner. I told her that none of the adults in our house had finished high school; there was no one to check my spelling and arithmetic in the evenings and there were no books or bookshelves in our living room – the closest I came to owning a piece of literature as a boy was when my dad took me with him to the newsagency to buy a scratchie, and would purchase a magazine about bugs or dinosaurs for me. I explained to Oli that while she went to boring museums and art galleries, I was in my father's warehouse loading the van for the markets; and that I had got in trouble for swearing when I was a child too. I said to my brother, 'Kes emak' – 'Your mum's cunt,' which I had picked up from all the adults who casually used it in our house. In response, my mum and my aunties pinned me down, hitting me with their sandals and forcing a tablespoon of chilli powder into my mouth, a common Arab punishment for kids who say a filthy word. And I told Oli that while she was out eating at the local ethnic restaurants with her family, my family was rationing the homemade falafels my grandmother had prepared for dinner. But most importantly, I explained to the White girl that I did not resent my childhood, and I did not envy hers, because at the end of every week, my family would gather on the floor of our tight living room and share a bucket of KFC – my mother wrapping two pieces of chicken in sheets of Leb bread and distributing them to each of us. I would be sucking out the herbs and spices from under my fingernails as my dad was biting into a wing, which was his favourite piece. He would say, 'This chicken is too good to be real,' and my grandmother would spread her toothless lips into a grin and reply, 'Kilou Fucken Cesseb!'

Oli sat in complete silence, her hand over her mouth, and watched as I raised my container of gravy to my bottom lip, glugging down the remaining lumps of meat drippings and seasonings and stock and wheat and cornflower. 'Please just love me as I am,' I said to her. 'I am what I am.'

After I finished eating, the two of us wandered past Vibe, where Wog boys bought skin-tight shirts; and past Ice, where Wog girls bought skin-tight singlets; and past IGA, where Wog mums bought bundles of toilet paper and tubs of ice cream for their half-dozen children; and past Muzlims R Us, where Wog grandfathers bought prayer beads. Oli clasped her hand in mine when we stepped past the empty wholefoods store and tugged me the other way. In front of us was a young woman with bright red lips in a flower-patterned hijab, her eyes bolted entirely on me. Her perfume, which smelled like out-of-date mangoes, fumed as she swept by and quickly hissed into my ear, 'Dog.'

My stomach clawed into my mouth, gravy catching itself at the base of my throat. Oli released her warm grip from my hand and spun around, staring back at the hijabi and then at me in one twist. 'What did she say to you?'

'She called me a traitor because I'm with an Aussie,' I explained.

Oli's delicate fingers covered her mouth once again. 'Sorry,' she replied. But there was no need for Oli to apologise – everything the hijabi hated in me I already hated in myself. If Fatima's father ever raised his hands against her again, it was *my* fault. If Fatima's mother ever decided what Fatima was allowed to wear again, it was *my* fault. If Fatima's parents forced her to travel to Syria and marry her cousin against her will, it was *my* fault. And if one day, be it tomorrow or fifty years from now, Fatima looked back over her life and asked Allah where it all went wrong, she would hear a booming voice inside her head which said: 'The day you married the dog.'

Oli and I caught the train back to her townhouse, sitting face to face, neither of us saying a word to one another the whole trip. I wedged my temple between the headrest of the seat and the train window, closed my eyelids and found myself as the boy on my birth certificate: Benny Adam. Tomorrow he would wake up, paint his face white, insert blue contacts into his eyes, dye his hair blond and head for Cronulla, where he would march up and down the beach, topless and drunk, chanting, 'Fuck off Lebs!' Raising my eyelids, I found Oli in my face, staring at me as though I were an alien. *Shu hal binet bida min-ney?* I asked myself. *What does this girl want from me?* But I did not have the strength to ask her. My intestines had been squealing since the hijabi called me a dog; no, wait, maybe it was before that, since Oli had eyed me as I bit into my chicken strip.

As soon as Oli unlocked her front door, I sprinted past her up the stairs towards the bathroom and stuck my head over the toilet bowl. I spewed, clots of yellow stomach bile and brown gravy and undigested chunks of pure white chicken splattering all over the porcelain. The last time I threw up was just after Fatima had chafed the skin of my dick with a rubber glove, and all at once I was her husband again, alone and forgotten, my head retching down the shitter. My stomach continued to roil and my bowels forced themselves up into my throat. I braced myself for another heave, but this time when I convulsed, I felt a gentle hand ease itself onto my back, rubbing slowly in a circular motion, followed by Oli's voice, humming an endless line of *shhhhhhhhhhhhhh*.

My arms slid off the toilet seat and I landed face-flat on the blood orange tiles of the bathroom floor, a familiar place where I had spent many nights as a married man. Only now when I rolled over, I did not see the flickering light bulb that slung me into a long corridor bolted shut at the other end; I saw Oli – plump round cheeks and dotted brown freckles and dry fair lips materialising beside me. 'Next time we go to Kilou Fucken Cesseb,' she said with a simper, 'I'll order some cholesterol.' Her black pupils quivered at me while she reached out her hand to flush the toilet. As the water sucked away the descent of my last end, I heard the hollowed drain reverberating against the tiled walls of the bathroom: *Benny Adam. House Arab. Porch Monkey. Uncle Tom. Race Traitor. Backstabber. Dog.* My guts and my bones and my blood were rotting from the inside, and yet I did not break, I did not even blink, my gaze welded onto that White girl, unashamed, unafraid, undone. For when I looked at her pupils expanding into her irises, I saw a child of the sun and the desert. I saw you.

FORTY-TWO

FIRST. THE CLUB, DEEP within the shire of vanilla middle-class suburbia, was filled with Bogans and Yobbos and Skips and every other kind of Aussie you could imagine – from the drunk loudmouth with red skin and long white beard and black eyepatch to the overweight primary school teacher having a pizza with her three blonde teenage daughters. Beneath the dim lighting and lambent sports screens, I became acutely aware of my Arabness – 'Nobody wants me here, Olive.' Was it my Semitic nose, which even after a nose job was still bigger than the average Aussie's, my head of thick curly hair, my dark eyes and eyebrows, my olive complexion, that caught the attention of all these people? Maybe it was my Lebo walk, arms and legs swinging like we're looking for a brawl, or maybe it was the way I dressed, Air Maxes and baggy jeans and skin-tight shirts tucked in the front and hanging over my arse at the back. Or maybe it was something else entirely, my glare, my frown, my energy, that made it so obvious that I was different, that I did not belong.

'You all right?' Oli asked as we approached our table.

'If these Peckerwoods don't stop looking at me, I'm gonna knock one of 'em out,' I replied loudly, followed by a huge grin, an attempt to reassure her that I was kidding.

Oli quickly shot a look around the room, checking to see if anyone had heard me, but instead of her usual reaction – horror – I noticed what looked like a little smirk. This was new and confusing to me: whenever I used the word 'faggot' out loud on Glebe Point Road, she would look around like the ghost-face in *The Scream*, her hands to her ears and her eyes and mouth blowing wide open, as if she were expecting a posse of hippies to randomly appear and lead a protest against us, singing 'We shall overcome'.

Oli's father was already seated at our table, dressed in a dark-blue suit and drenched in aftershave. He quickly stood up and shook my hand; his palm pudgy, his fingers unusually thick. Next, he leaned in towards Oli like he was gonna kiss her hello, but at the last second he seemed to change his mind and gave her a quick little nod instead, his round glasses jolting. *Had I just witnessed the origin of Oli's own awkwardness? Mashallah!*

Once we were seated, we went straight for the menus. Cameron ordered a vegetarian pizza for himself (he was the first person I had ever met who did not consider pizza share-food); Oli ordered a vegetarian risotto; and I ordered a chicken parmigiana with a side of mashed potatoes and a green salad. While waiting for our food to arrive, I came right out with the one detail about him that I thought I knew for sure: 'Oli says you're against us getting married.'

Cameron looked at me perplexed, his bulbous cheeks drooping as he shook his head. 'It's not my decision either way,' he replied firmly, punctuating each word, but he said it to his daughter instead of me, as though he were annoyed at her for giving me this impression. Then, to me, he explained, 'Oli's mother and I were together for forty years, we never wedded, either one of us could have left whenever we wanted, but we chose to stay.'

I did not need to be an atheist or an infidel to agree with him. Little over a year ago I had made a legally binding commitment to spend the rest of my life with a girl from The Tribe, only to end up here. I was no longer searching for my wife; I was searching for my soul – your other half.

A pause lingered between all three of us until Cameron sighed at me, the hairs on his thick moustache fluttering, and added, 'I just don't want Olive to be the one making all the sacrifices here.'

I interpreted this to be the polite version of what Oli's uncle had said to her on Christmas Day – that ultimately, our union would result in me indoctrinating her into Islam and forcing her to live as an Arab. And just like her uncle's words, Cameron's did not offend me, they bored me. I was no different from the platypus: he wakes up on a rock, has a stretch and dips into the river. There he encounters two goldfish who are gliding past. He says, 'G'day fellas, how's the water this morning?' And the fish look to each other baffled. 'What the hell's water?' You see Kahlil, your mother wasn't swimming in my culture, I was swimming in hers; her family just couldn't see it.

'Shall we finish the conversation about who's making the greater sacrifices in Arabic?' I responded with an eye-roll. Your grandfather looked to Oli confused as a goldfish, wince intact.

The White girl palmed her forehead. 'Dad, do you really have to be so vanilla right now?' And I cracked-the-fuck-up. Khaleel, yaa aani, yaa habibi, yaa rouhi: take what you want from your Arabness. And do not feel entitled to your Whiteness. As both – you are neither.

'So, my father will give ya three cows and two goats in exchange for this chick right here,' I said to Cameron with a stern expression. He was about to reply, his small teeth chattering, when Oli quickly intercepted. 'Dad, it's just a joke, he made a joke.'

The waitress arrived with Cameron's pizza in one hand and my parmigiana and Oli's risotto in the other, in that skilful and graceful way that all waitresses know how to handle several dishes at once. This particular waitress was incredibly thin and tall, with terracotta skin and bright green eyes juxtaposed against the dim lighting of the RSL. She simultaneously placed all three plates down on our table and then, just as she turned and left, I noticed her throw Oli a greasy, her entire head joggling.

'I hate that bitch,' Oli whispered into my ear, picking up her knife and fork as if she were ready to shank someone.

'What?' I gasped.

In the background, I could hear the red-skinned, white-bearded, eyepatch-wearing Bogan screaming at the TV screen, 'Ah, come on, ya faggot, I could knock this guy out.' His comment reminded me of my boxing days, back when I was having my amateur fights at South Sydney Juniors in Maroubra. There was always some drunken deadbeat in the crowd watching the match, screaming that we couldn't fight for shit and that he could take us on.

'That skinny skank stole my boyfriend in high school – look at her now, a fucken waitress,' Oli gobbed at me, while her father quietly dissected his pizza with his utensils like a member of the royal family. It was here, on the bible belt of the western suburbs, that Oli finally revealed herself to me. She had her childhood swagger, and her childhood lingo, and her childhood enemies, and being very much at home, all her shame and awkwardness had disappeared. My loins throbbed at the thought of her – we were so different, and we were so the same.

Turning away from Oli, I set my sights on my chicken parmigiana, dug my fork into the thick top layer of glistening cheese and began cutting it in half. I sliced through tomato sauce, expecting to hit a thick piece of crumbed chicken, but instead found myself cutting into a thin layer of dark-red meat. 'Shit, that's ham,' Oli said, ogling my plate.

As common as it might have been out here in The Hills, a piece of pig meat on a chicken parmigiana for a Lebo who grew up in the halalified slums of Lakemba and Punchbowl and Bankstown was unheard of. *Fucken White people and their swine!* I thought to myself. They put it in everything – hamburgers, sandwiches, pizzas, salads, soups, fried rice, omelette waffles, butter rolls, casseroles, croissants. At times it even seemed as sacred to them as not eating it was sacred to us. A few years earlier, a segment had aired on *A Current Affair* called 'Why You're Being Forced to Eat Halal', which featured a clip of three Bogans going to Australia's first halal KFC in Punchbowl with their home video camera. They filmed their confrontation with the Brown staff behind the counter, in which they demanded bacon on their chicken burgers, screaming, 'This is *our* country,' and 'If you don't want to serve pork, you can go back to where you came from,' and 'We're gonna cover this whole building in pig's blood.'

As soon as Cameron noticed my facial expression – recoiling in disgust – he quickly reached out with his massive fingers and snatched my plate, tumbling his way towards the kitchen counter to return it. Oli grimaced at me, revealing a small dimple between her cheek and her eye. 'Sorry,' she said, 'he's trying.'

'I know,' I replied. 'You wait and see how Arabs try.' Her light-brown eyebrows jolted at me before she twisted her head, scanning until she caught the lanky skank who had nicked her boyfriend in high school. In that split second, I stuck my head down over Oli's dinner and licked a clump of Napolitana sauce from the edge of her plate. I couldn't resist – a thick red sauce made from real tomatoes with oil, garlic, a shitload of salt and a pissload of sugar was the middle ground between a hamburger and a kebab for a Leb. Oli turned back and looked down at her risotto, ready to dig her fork into the rice. Her eyebrows suddenly shot up as she spotted a clean white line the width and shape of my tongue gleaming through the Napolitana sauce across her plate. Her pupils dilated before me in excitement, her smile a mixture of joy and bewilderment and lust. 'Did you just lick that?'

———

Second. The street, deep within the hood of ethnic working-class suburbia, was filled with Lebs and Wogs and Sand Coons and every other kind of Arab you could imagine – the hot-headed gronk with bamboo-coloured skin and a long mullet and black sunglasses doing wheelies up and down the footpath on his dirt bike, and the overweight hijabi smoking hubbly-bubbly on the verandah with her three black-haired teenage daughters. As I drove Oli towards my parents' place, passing all my relatives' houses along the way, she became acutely aware of her Whiteness – 'Nobody wants me here, Bani.' Was it her dry freckled skin, which even after she'd lathered in moisturiser could never shine like an Arab's, her head of fine and cracked hair, her vivid eyes and light-brown eyebrows, that caught the attention of all the Wogs on the street as I helped her out of my car and walked her up my teenage-hood driveway? Maybe it was her preppy White-girl walk, arms and legs steady and restrained as if she were attempting to avoid a brawl, or maybe it was the way she dressed, a faded green shirt and a long faded red skirt, both of which she'd bought from an op shop, and a pair of brown flip-flops. Or maybe it was something else entirely, her shoulders hunched tightly, her hands hiding beneath her cardigan sleeves, her faint breath, that made it so obvious that she was different, that she did not belong.

Still guarding the stairwell to my parents' house were the two stone lions my father had installed when we first arrived in Lakemba. I had given them at least ten thousand greetings since 1997, but this time was unique; this time a White girl was greeting them with me. As soon as we stepped between those two proud unflinching big cats, I was reminded of a text message I had received in 2005. It came from a Leb who passed it on to a dozen Lebs who passed it on to a hundred Lebs who passed it on to a thousand Lebs: *Lions of Lebanon: Rise. Today 5000 Aussie scum attacked our brothers and sisters at Cronulla. Tomorrow we strike back. Allah is with you.* I felt my blood clotting throughout my entire body as I walked the White girl up my parents' short staircase – I was afraid, afraid that my parents and my siblings would not be able to see Oli as I saw her, a freckle; all they would see was a Cracker, waving the Union Jack.

Just before I could ring the doorbell, my dad unlocked the door and appeared in front of Oli and me, as though he had been peering through the peephole, impatiently waiting for us to arrive. He was dressed uncharacteristically 'Muslim' – in a white prayer cap and white thobe – and he'd grown his goatee into a full-blown extremist beard. It occurred to me that he was nervous too, overcompensating for the fact that me bringing a White girl home made him feel less Arab. His expression was neutral at first, taking in a deep long breath as he stared straight at the both of us. *Jeez – what the hell was I thinking bringing an Aussie to this house?* Then suddenly, as Dad exhaled, he gave Oli a whole-hearted smile, the wrinkles in his tired copper face compressing. 'Peace be upon you, Miss Olive,' he said. 'We don't hate anybody, except the Lebanese.' Then he gave her a wink, and added, 'Ahlan wa sahlan – Hello and welcome.'

Oli remained silent, but immediately after my father tipped his hand down the corridor, inviting the White girl inside, her shoulders dropped and her hands emerged from her sleeves. She had realised at the exact same time as I did that your jido never meant her any harm.

'Why are you being so nice?' I whispered at Dad while he walked Oli through our hallway. He replied in Arabic, 'Because we're Arabs, not Australians.' At first I was glad he had said this in our mother tongue, ashamed of what Oli might have thought if she understood him, but later, in the year you were born, I realised that my dad was right. Our prime minister at the time had won his election on a campaign promise to 'Stop the Boats', and it was evident that there was something shamelessly unwelcoming about Australians. This was in direct opposition to the hadiths I had been taught by Uncle Ehud about our Messenger when I was a small boy: It is said that the Prophet Muhammad's next-door neighbour hated him like the plague, and every day would leave his trash on Muhammad's front yard as an expression of that hatred. Then, one day, Muhammad's neighbour found the Prophet knocking on his door. When he opened, Muhammad said, 'Peace be upon you, brother, I am here to offer my help, for I fear you are unwell.' The neighbour replied, 'I am indeed unwell, how is it that you know?' And the Prophet explained, 'Because you did not leave your garbage on my yard today.'

We stepped past my parents' bedroom, and my father told Oli, 'I keep my four wives in there.' And then we stepped past my old bedroom, which had been empty since I left, and Dad said to Oli, 'Bani took everything with him except his poster of Pamela Anderson.' We stepped past the bathroom, and my father told Oli, 'We have a special tap in that toilet that washes your bum, but don't use it, the water's cold.' And then we stepped past the third and final bedroom along the corridor, which my sister Yocheved shared with our tayta until her final seconds. The door to the bedroom was open, and inside was my grandmother's wooden bed – the very bed she had died in thirteen years earlier. Every time I caught a glimpse of that bed, sitting in there like the stump of a colossal tree, I saw my grandmother beneath the sheets, her enormous body moving up and down as she breathed epic breaths in her sleep. My dad pointed inside the room, and said to Oli, 'That's my mother's spot, she was like you.' Oli slurped

316

her lips and cheeks into her mouth as her head jerked back, the comparison catching her completely off guard: *In what way could she possibly be like this ancient Brown woman who had sprung from the middle of the Arabian desert?* But I knew exactly what Dad meant. Your great-grandfather, Kahlil, had chosen a woman that his father and his godfather swore would condemn him to hell for all eternity, but Bani Adam did not flinch when he said back to them, 'So be it.'

Once inside our living room, my mother scuttled straight up to Oli and pulled the towering White girl towards her mouth. Mum gave her six kisses, from cheek to cheek to cheek to cheek to cheek to cheek. Every individual kiss Oli received was a surprise, and she had to keep bobbing down for each of them, mumbling, 'Oh one more,' and 'Oh one more,' until it was over. Then Mum said, 'I'll be back in one second,' and before Oli could say another word, this compact, frenetic Arab woman zipped down the corridor.

Fortunately and unfortunately, the living room was filled with plenty of other Arabs to keep the White girl enthralled: my brother Bilal, who was wearing a singlet and parading his biceps; his wife, Mandy, whose corn-fed palms rested on the base of her pregnant belly; my sister Yocheved, who gifted Oli with a picture of me as a baby with a cigarette in my mouth; her new husband, Ayaan, who was unpretentiously dressed in his work overalls and too shy to look Oli in the eyes when he greeted her; my sister Lulu, who embraced Oli with a casual hug, their skin clashing like fire in a field of snow; my second-youngest sister, Abira, who was only interested in finding out if Oli preferred *The Lord of the Rings* to *Harry Potter* (which Oli did); and my youngest sister,

Amani, who at age six did not yet understand that there was any real difference between Oli and the rest of us, and said, 'I've memorised twelve surahs from the Qur'an, how many do you know?'

Oli sat on the large floral couch beside me, nervously twiddling my baby photo between her fingers – nervous because she was always nervous anyway; and nervous because she knew that before her had come Fatima and before Fatima had come Sahara and before Sahara had come the words: 'Remember, it's a sin to marry a White girl.' I watched Oli carefully as she stared at the bathroom door at the edge of the corridor, once again appreciating her modesty, which in here was like a morsel of salt amid a mountain of sand.

My brother gave her a smug grin and pointed at the putty in the centre of the bathroom door. 'Are you wondering why that's been patched up? I punched a hole through it with my fist,' he bragged, flexing his arms. 'It was either that or Bani's head.' Straight over the top of Bilal, my brother-in-law, with his eyes to the floor, asked, 'Olivia, where do you live?'

Oli didn't correct the fact that Ayaan got her name wrong, answering his question with her eyes also on the floor. 'Ummm, Glebe.'

'Yeah, my family used to live there too,' Ayaan went on, 'but we moved out here because the people in your area pretend to be poor even though they're actually rich.'

Finally my sister said out loud, 'Oli, do you want ahwe?' And before Oli could even understand what she meant, let alone respond, Yocheved stood up and shot towards the kitchen to make her a coffee.

I felt the blood flowing freely throughout my body as I saw a way forward for the White girl in the House of Adam – just nod along and let us be.

Oli's hands started to look clammy as she massaged the old photograph of me between her right thumb and four fingers. I tried to understand why my sister gave her that photograph: perhaps Yocheved was warning the White girl of what she was getting herself into; what it meant to be with an Arab. I wondered what Oli thought of three-year-old Bani Adam whose aunt had stuck a cigarette in his mouth. Maybe she found it as funny as the rest of my family, who had run around the house in Alexandria looking for a camera to preserve the moment, or maybe she was mortified by the idea of these people one day taking photographs of you. Rest assured, Kahlil, there were other photographs in that living room too, mounted along the picture rail, which could give your mother a portrait of who we were. On the wall in front of us was a framed cloth embroidered with gold Arabic text, displaying the Muslim declaration of faith: 'There is no god but God; and Muhammad is the messenger of God.' On the wall to the left was a silver painting of the double-tipped sword of the Imam Ali, the first caliph of Shi'a Islam, which said in Arabic, 'There is no hero like Ali; and there is no sword like Zulfiqar.' To the right was a portrait of Hafez al-Assad, the Muslim Alawite former president of Syria, kissing his mother's hand. Oli may only have heard of him as a murderous dictator, but to my family, who had spent their entire lives afraid to tell outsiders what kind of Muslim they were, he represented the only authority and safety Alawites had ever known in thirteen hundred and fifty years. And behind where Oli and I sat, there was a picture of my dad's father, the man I was named after, Bani Adam, who wore an ancient sandstone frown and flared jeans and a tight black shirt and had a thin white cigarette dangling from his slender lips. Maybe one day Oli would understand: to be a Muslim of Australia, a Shi'ite of Islam, an Alawite of Shi'ism, a Bani of Alawites, was to be a minority within a minority within a minority within the House of Adam.

All of a sudden, my mum came scampering back into the living room with a skinny straight-blonde-haired, fake-orange-tanned girl clenched in her arm. The girl sported bright blue eye shadow and had sparkling pink lips. She wore tight white pants that were virtually see-through, revealing the front of her thin red panties, and sharp black high heels that lifted her above everyone in my family. 'Oli,' my mum said, excitement oozing from the pores in her face. 'This is Kristy, she's Aussie like you.'

'Mum!' I gasped, scraping both my hands into my forehead. 'Do you have to be so ethnic right now?'

'She's married to the Muslim man next door,' my mother continued, ignoring me. Her focus remained on Oli, eyes wide open as she nodded at her son's new girlfriend with an ecstatic smile. Then she twisted to Kristy, letting go of the girl's bony arm and giving her a little push. 'Okay, return to your husband now.'

Later that night, as we drove back to her townhouse, Oli told me about her first serious partner, a middle-class suburban White boy named Trevor who was obsessed with Michael Jordan and Mike Tyson and Tupac Shakur but had never met an actual Black person. She said he had pasty blue skin, and dry red hair, and lots of pimples, and a Southern Cross tattoo, and he only ever wore a Holden Commodore bomber jacket and tight navy–green jeans that displayed half his arse whenever he bent over. 'I broke up with him because I thought I was too good for him,' Oli murmured, and then she wound down the window and let the icy wind of August smother her ceramic face. She turned to me, her lips trembling, and laughed, louder than I had ever heard her laugh before, and louder than I would ever hear her laugh again; a laugh that reverberated along the green traffic lights and neon bodybuilding signs and yellow arches of Canterbury Road. Oli had seen herself through the eyes of an Arab woman, and she was nothing but White trash.

I stayed up all night on Oli's sofa while she slept with her head across my thigh, staring at her red front door as the moonlight seeped past the thin spaces in her purple curtains, waiting. Any moment now, the Prophet Muhammad would come knocking.

FORTY-THREE

Rubbing her hands up and down her arms, scraping at her fine hairs, Oli sat under a set of heavy grey clouds as ants scurried all over her mum's headstone. 'When she went into the fire, I wanted to go in after her.' These words on Oli's lips reminded me of a saying my dad had recited after his own mother had passed away: *Ithaa maat al ab, andak rab; isssa maat'it al em, hef ou tem – If your father dies, you have a god, if your mother dies, dig yourself a grave and jump in.*

Oli watched the ants avoiding each other as she spoke, recalling one of her earliest memories of your grandmother standing outside the school gate to pick her up from kindergarten. A small girl had been walking along the zebra crossing and dropped her lollies. Without thinking, the girl ran back for them and was struck by a moving truck. From that moment on, your grandmother demanded that Oli hold hands with her wherever they went, right up until her last days, and whenever Oli complained about not having enough freedom, your grandmother replied in the same way: 'You didn't see someone's child get killed right in front you!'

We hiked through the cemetery, from the crematorium to the Catholic section, where we discovered a small wood of trees trimmed into the shapes of children. It felt like we were in Narnia, with one exception – a vending machine right there in the open. This was the first time I'd ever seen the back of a vending machine; one which somehow ran on electricity even though I could not find any cables or power points. I became obsessed with locating the source of the vendor's energy, snapping my neck from left to right and shouting, 'Where the hell is it, bro?'

At last, Oli lost her patience and clutched onto my arm, spinning me with her towards a grave half the size of a normal one. Before us was a plush bear, a handful of toy cars and an unwrapped lollipop. On the tombstone was written: *Tread carefully, here lies our world.*

'No …' Oli cried out, tightening her grip around my triceps. 'This grave makes me so afraid to have children.' Such is the despair of a parent, Kahlil. The second you were born, my death began; the blood of my soul had been released into this world, vulnerable and fragile and flaky as recycled paper, so in love that I was already grieving every moment to come; your tears when you were hungry and scared and knew nothing but your mother's milk; your look of betrayal when I held you still so the doctor could vaccinate you, unable to understand that your mother and I were trying to prolong your life; your bruise when you attempted to stand and fell face first into your bowl of oatmeal, and I screamed at your mum, 'He's a Leb – feed him Froot Loops from now on'; your cut when you collided with the corner of our dining room table; your welt when your baby cousin planted a toy bus in your face; your groaning when you ate too much carrot cake and threw up all over our white tiles; your screams when you had nightmares as I rocked you in our glider, but no language to explain to me what you saw; your kicking and squirming when I tried to wipe your bum and you fell asleep naked in my arms with your crap all over my flared jeans; and every road I ever walked you across, only to hear you complain by the age of five that I was holding your hand too tight.

'But look how much love a child creates from so little,' I replied to your mother, pulling her with me as I began walking. Olive's child – even for just a second with you, I would bring you into this world, each second with you is its own eternity, each second of your life is worth my entire life.

Eventually, we reached the Muslim section of the cemetery, Oli refusing to let go of me the entire way there, clamping onto my elbow and digging her head into my armpit. I tried to pull away, conscious of my body odour, but all it made her do was hold on firmer. The cemetery was empty that day, at least of the living, but trudging through the shrubs of unloved graves back towards my car, I spotted a lone figure in the distance: a man down on his knees before a huge concrete headstone, in the prayer position called julus. Oli and I halted. 'A ghost?' she asked. The man was bald and the skin across his face was stretched tight, his shoulders engulfing his neck. Hands mounted upon his kneecaps, his arms bulged, waxed biceps solid as the sculpture of David. I would have identified this man straightaway were it not for his tears – Koda, the cousin of my cousin, who I had only ever imagined as some kind of vicious creature, groaning, 'Baaba. Baaba. Yaa Baaba.' The night he attacked Zane, I had completely neglected this aspect of his life – his father had died when he was a teenager, and as the oldest son he was left responsible for his mother and his five younger brothers, a burden too heavy for any boy to bear. Oli and I found ourselves in the presence of this man's humanity. 'No ghost,' I told her. 'No animal. No monster. Just a Leb.'

———

We returned to the cemetery a week later, heading in the direction of the graves of the House of Adam. I took Oli to my father's mother's grave first. Her headstone was dated 1997. I told your mother about the morning of this woman's death, her lifeless body and face dragging me towards her. My tayta's Arab skin had turned blue, but not on the outside, which still had its golden complexion – it was like the blue was rising from the inside. And rising, too, were her eyeballs, which bulged beneath her sunken eyelids. Tayta's lips were folded into her mouth and she lay there as still as a fossil. Two dozen of her children, children-in-law and grandchildren mourned around her body that morning, but it was the sight of my father which shattered me – the first time I had ever seen him crying. When our eyes met, he shrugged his shoulders at me as if to say, 'Sorry, Bani, I am only human.' And I cried back at him, all of my strength disappearing with the shrugging of those arms, those arms of rock that I always thought were indestructible. Sorry, Kahlil, I am only human too.

I recited Al-Fatiha over your great-grandmother's grave, starting with 'Bismiallah al-rahmaan al-raheem' and ending with 'Ameen'. The whole time, Oli remained cemented to my arm, even as we walked another four hundred metres to my father's father's grave. His headstone was dated 1971. I told your mother that this was the man I was named after, a man I only knew from the photographs and stories my father had told me: Bani Adam was born in Lebanon as the son of Syrian immigrants – a child who could read the entire Qur'an in fluent Arabic by the time he was seven. 'I guess our literacy died with him,' I said to my dad, and he smiled down at me affectionately, knowing something I did not. 'Bani Adam was and Bani Adam will be.'

Standing over your great-grandfather's grave, I recited Al-Fatiha once again, starting with 'Bismiallah al-rahmaan al-raheem' and ending with 'Ameen'. Oli remained clinging onto me, even more tightly now, and she began to tremble as the clouds of last week filled every space in the sky, the light around us thickening.

'What's wrong?' I asked, and she replied, 'There was nothing after my mum died, and now there's you.' Upon hearing these words, I felt a great sense of despair stabbing into my ribcage – I had failed Sahara and failed Fatima and Allah knew I was destined to fail Oli. 'You should have seen my wedding,' I told her. 'My grandparents would have been so ashamed.'

At once, it began to rain, droplets of water falling on every part of the cemetery, on the Muslims and the Christians and the Jews and the Buddhists and the Hindus and the atheists and those who did not know what they were until they were what they were. The rain landed on the grave where Bani Adam was buried, on the spears of the cemetery gates, on the barren thorns. My soul swooned slowly as I heard the drops falling faintly through the universe and faintly falling, like the descent of my last end, upon all the living and the dead. Oli pulled her hands from my arm and her face from my armpit and she rested her palms upon my chest. 'Would your grandparents have been ashamed if it was our wedding?'

'No more than their own,' I said.

'Then marry me.'

FORTY-FOUR

To marry a White girl is to hate myself enough to love myself. By now, the literary journals and newspapers and magazines that had commissioned my writing began arriving in the mail. Oli would always be the first to read my work in print, and immediately after she was done, she would ask the annoying questions that readers liked to ask writers: 'Did your whole family *really* just stand in front of the cops and pretend the phone wasn't ringing?' and 'Did your dad *really* throw that box of mandarins up in the air straight after your brother threw it?' and 'Did your ex-wife *really* superglue her belly ring to her belly button?' and 'Did your godfather *really* threaten to tell people you were in a porno?' I sat her down, took her hand, looked deep into her eyes and gave her a kiss on the bump in her nose. 'Imagine me; I shall not exist if you do not imagine me ...' And one day, you will be asking if your mum *really* recited her vows to me in Arabic. This time there were no wedding rings, no Hummers and Mercedes convertibles, no photographers, no groom's suit and wedding dress, no groomsmen and groomsmen's suits, no bridesmaids and bridesmaids' dresses, no reception hall, no hundreds of Arab guests – aunts and uncles and cousins and cousins of cousins and cousins of cousins of cousins – no insincere speeches and cheesy love songs, no hysterical dancing and skimpy dresses and thousands of sweaty hugs and slobbering kisses, no drums, no pudgy MCs with thick Arabic accents, and no paperwork. Just Oli standing before me and Uncle Ehud standing in front of us and my mum and dad standing behind us in their living room – The One God and the Prophet Muhammad and the Imam Ali and the Syrian Dictator and Bani Adam watching us from the picture rails.

Uncle Ehud instructed Oli to repeat after him: 'Ashadu an la ilaha illa'llah wa ashad anna Muhammadan Rasululu'lla.'

Imagine your mother, Kahlil. The White girl gave me a cheeky smile as she attempted to repeat the sacred verse, absolutely no idea what she was saying and if she'd pronounced even one word correctly. She had tied her messy brown hair up with a thin black hair tie, a half-hearted attempt to look like a bride. I had never really appreciated her neck until then; until she exposed it to me as elegant and milky and naked and vulnerable. I felt a great longing to step into her and clasp both my hands around her collar and kiss her passionately, unable to control my disbelief that I had come so far. If this were only a dream, then I would take as much as I could from this dream and die before it was over – to die was to sleep, and to sleep was to dream, aye cuz, there was the rub, for in that sleep of death look what dreams had come when I shuffled off my mortal coil and earned the respect that makes calamity of so long life.

When Oli finished her 'Declaration of Faith', Uncle Ehud gave her one firm approving nod, his globular cheeks jostling. Then he instructed the White girl to repeat after him in Arabic: 'I offer you myself in marriage and in accordance with the instructions of the Holy Qur'an and the Holy Prophet, peace and blessing be upon him. I pledge, in honesty and with sincerity, to be for you a respectful and faithful wife.' Oli fumbled and mispronounced and winced and attempted to restrain another cheeky smile, her gaze never once breaking from mine, as she spoke in the language of my ancestors, and as I dreamed in the language of hers.

Next Uncle Ehud turned to me – his enormous shoulders panning the entire house with him as he moved – and instructed that I also repeat after him in Arabic: 'I pledge, in honesty and sincerity, to be for you a faithful and helpful husband.' My greatest sin unveiled itself on the cusp of my vow. I had already made that vow to Fatima two years earlier, and I broke it to be with a White girl. But this time, Kahlil, I was not attached to the mountain of sand, I was a single grain that the wind had collected in its breath; and what was your mother but a morsel of salt that had been flung from the ocean in my direction?

I felt a nudge between my shoulder blades as my mum said, 'Yulla, boosa, boosa,' which meant 'Come on, kiss her, kiss her.' Mum's elbow was intended to be encouraging and affectionate, but it made me wonder about all the parents in this same position who would have wanted to stick a knife in their child's back for the betrayal of marrying an outsider. A few years earlier I had read about a Yezidi girl from Northern Iraq who had been stoned to death by a lynch mob, including members of her own family, because she had attempted to run away with her Sunni boyfriend. How could we hate each other so much that we would rather slaughter our own children than allow them to be together? How could any sane person believe that this is what Allah wanted? Perhaps the Yezidi girl regretted her decision to love a Sunni in those final milliseconds before one of her attackers launched the fatal blow to the back of her head, or perhaps it was as simple for her as 'to be or not to be' – her only option was to love or to die.

My mother's nudge was followed by a quiet prayer from my father: 'Allah-y wa'afe'kun – May Allah bless you.' I could hear his breath on the back of my ears, faint and steady, as though he had been defeated. But this wasn't the first time I had seen Dad go through a radical transformation: until I was thirteen, he had disciplined my five siblings and me with his bare hands and his leather belts and his steel-capped boots. Then one day we all found ourselves in this same living room where I was now marrying a White girl, watching *Gandhi* on the television. The Mahatma said, 'An eye for an eye only ends up making the whole world blind,' and Yocheved suddenly turned at our dad. 'Baaba, why don't you just talk to us instead of hitting us?' I remember my father's harsh Semitic face going dark and vacant as he processed Yocheved's question. He turned his sharp jaw back towards the TV screen, refusing to say a single word, but he never raised a hand to us again. Whenever we did something wrong from that point on, he would shout and punch walls and throw boxes of mandarins instead.

I stepped in and wrapped my hands around Oli's neck, which was warm and sweaty, and I tilted her head down towards my mouth. In one motion, I kissed her forehead and crawled my fingers up the back of her head, pulling off her hair tie and slipping it onto my wrist. I would wear this cheap piece of elastic as a wedding bracelet, and in return, I would share with Oli this ancient mess that swept through my blood – of sand and sunfire.

'Tay'iee ma'iee,' I said, taking her hand. 'Come with me.' The next steps we took together lasted longer than every night I had spent on the bathroom floor staring up at a light bulb; yet they were no more than ten steps into my grandmother's old bed, springs squeaking and rusted joints screeching as we sat at the edge of the spongy mattress. The memory of Tayta's smell – garlic and olives and fabric softener and summer heat – filled the air as I recounted to Oli a story that my grandmother had shared with me before she died. Kan yamaa kan, a wandering Alawite encountered a golden-skinned Sunni who descended from the Bedouins of the desert. He walked her through a citrus farm and asked her to be the mother of his children. 'Our parents will kill us,' she said. The Alawite did not say anything in response. Instead he picked an orange off a branch that hung low from a tree and slowly peeled it for the Sunni with his bare hands. He fed it to her, tenderly placing one piece after another into her mouth and watching her suckle on it as the dry heat fused with their skin. And he knew – this was everything.

FORTY-FIVE

THE RUBBER WAS BROKEN before either of us was ready. 'Love is such a messy thing,' said Oli. 'Al-humdulilaah for the mess that brought us here,' I replied. In the six years that we had been together, I ran into Mrs Laila Haimi once more, this time at my honours graduation, which took place in the same year as her doctoral graduation. Standing outside the university auditorium in our black and gold regalia, like two desert sorcerers, she said, 'I read your piece in the paper the other day. Did you *really* smash your head through a wall for a White girl?' And I ran into my ex-wife twice more. The first time was fourteen months after we separated, while I was alone eating six pieces of fried chicken at the Bankstown food court. She was holding hands and walking with a tall solid import who wore a chequered blue shirt with his collar up and had a head full of spikey gelled hair. I couldn't help but notice how much he looked like her cousin Amir, mumbling to myself, 'Told ya, bro!' Fatima caught sight of me, grimaced, then quickly looked away. The second time was three years after we had separated, again while I was alone at the Bankstown food court, only by now I had given into Oli's concerns about my fast-food intake, and was eating a sushi roll made of brown rice, tuna and cucumber. Fatima was strutting along in high heels, tight jeans and a tight red top – thin arms and legs and busty butt and chest as always. In front of her, she was pushing a slick silver pram with a shiny black hood. Our eyes met momentarily, and she gave me a very subtle smile – all I needed from her to let me know that she was okay – and then she was gone. There was only one woman who had not yet been conjured up, that I never saw again, and as the years went by, I accepted that maybe I never would; maybe she had been a ghost after all.

Oli and I bought a small three-bedroom house in Lakemba, just a few streets away from the garage at the back of my father's shop, and even fewer streets away from my parents' house, so close that every day my mum walked over with plates of Lebanese food. Nobody in our family was ever as excited about my mum's cooking, which was just rice and halal meat stuffed in some kind of plant, as the White girl who grew up on Chicken & Corn Rolls with mayonnaise on top. Mum took great pleasure in fattening her up – 'Yulla eat, you gotta be strong to carry my grandchildren, Bani had the biggest head, don't you know!' As it turned out, Kahlil, your own head was proportionate to the rest of your minuscule body, unless we include the nose you inherited from the House of Adam, in which case your tayta's concerns were legit ...

Shortly after we moved into Lakemba's last two-bedroom cottage, Oli and I made the decision to leave the beds we each owned before we met out on the street for the annual council pick-up, and then went and bought a bed together. We forked

THE OTHER HALF OF YOU

out the same amount I had once spent on my ex-wife's wedding ring, choosing the largest king-size frame and mattress available. You see, we already knew it wouldn't just be our bed, it would also be *your* bed, the family bed, forever saturated in the smell of breastmilk and talcum powder and your innocent drops of sweat.

Every morning since then it was just Oli and me in that bed, every morning until this one messy morning that the rubber tore and you finally decided to join us. Oli kissed the tip of my nose, smiled at the sight of the damp condom in my fingers, and said, 'Mistakes happen all the time.' But I refused to believe this was an accident, certainly not while we were lying in your crib! I placed my forehead against Oli's brow, the fine hairs that formed her fringe tickling my top lip, and I sighed into her ear, 'All Arabs are someone's mistake, but the Arab we bring into this world will never be yours.'

Oli made love to me again a moment later, only this second time, there was nothing between us. Then I asked her to come with me, and we drove to Alexandria, the inner-west suburb where my family had originally settled when they arrived from Lebanon. I parked in front of the double-brick house caught between a heritage-listed townhouse on the left, which belonged to the White man who owned a dozen dogs and watched gay porn in his spare time; and the barber shop on the right, which belonged to the White horse-faced alcoholic hairdresser who regularly told us to fuck off back to Islamabad. 'My entire generation sprung from this house,' I told Oli. 'Until my grandmother sold it to some yuppies and used the money to buy each of her sons a cheap property in Lakemba.'

From there, Oli and I walked all the way up Copeland Street towards Erskineville train station, and up King Street in

Newtown, past the mural of Martin Luther King Jr's head beside the earth, with 'I Have A Dream' captioned beneath. The self-righteous White hipsters with their purple hair and red polyester jackets and bohemian trousers and Doc Martins ogled my flared jeans and black beret and black eyes, and the self-hating Brown hipsters with their septum piercings and fake-blonde hairdos and green contact lenses ogled the White girl on my arm.

We walked through Victoria Park, which was attached to the university where Oli had completed her master's degree, and across Parramatta Road, where tradie Lebs drove past in their utes to service the City of Sydney, and towards the Broadway Shopping Centre, where a lifetime ago my dad's sister had seen me with a girl who wore a cross, and The Tribe had declared: *We will never allow you to disgrace us with that whore.*

The clouds had splattered throughout the sky, restraining the sunlight, as your mother, holding my hand tightly, delicate fingers spread over each of my calluses, pulled me all the way down Bay Street, down towards the apartment where the tomato-faced girl once lived – but the building was gone. The apartments that were once filled with hordes of housing commission tenants had been demolished, and in their place were deep holes that looked like the gaping wounds of a brown titan. Chain-link fences had been erected around the site to keep people like me out, and glossy billboards hanging off the wires featured computer-generated images of swanky new apartments with black text underneath that read: *Luxury Homes Coming Soon.* I knew then that Sahara's fate had been the same as mine, the inner west no longer any place for a poor Brown kid who kept chicken bones in her pockets and under her bed.

Your mother loosened her fingers between my knuckles as I peered my left eye through one of the diamond spaces in the fence, searching for Sahara. I found nothing but dirt and rock and clay and the dust of red brick and the shit of a pigeon. Sliding her body against my back, Oli wrapped her frail arms around my chest and rested her small chin on my shoulder. 'She's living her life, Bani, so live yours.' The sunlight pushed its way through the clouds, collapsing into my flesh, and the White girl eased her forehead upon my temple, inhaling the sweat that ran from my brow, and all at once I became whole. Oli was here, and soon, very soon, you would be here too, tearing into this universe, and tumbling into her hands, breathing your first breaths, the echo of all that was and all that is and all that will be. H-h-h-h-h-h-h-h-h-h-h-h.

ACKNOWLEDGEMENTS

Sophie Mayfield, Vanessa Radnidge, Camha Pham, Claire de Medici, Robert Watkins, Rosina Di Marzo, Fiona Hazard, Jumana Bayeh, Sara Saleh, Sarah Ayoub, Divya Venkataraman, Shirley Le, Lina Kastoumis, Christa Moffitt, Graeme Jones.

And Winnie.

Michael Mohammed Ahmad is the founding director of Sweatshop Literacy Movement and editor of the critically acclaimed anthology *After Australia* (Affirm Press, 2020). Mohammed's debut novel, *The Tribe* (Giramondo, 2014), won the 2015 *Sydney Morning Herald* Best Young Novelists of the Year Award. His second novel, *The Lebs* (Hachette Australia, 2018), won the 2019 NSW Premier's Multicultural Literary Award and was shortlisted for the 2019 Miles Franklin Literary Award. Mohammed received his Doctorate of Creative Arts from Western Sydney University in 2017.